Neil Down

Mike Van Horn

Charley;
Hope this takes you back
to a time when space was a
mystery and our heroes met
the challenge.
Hope ya enjoy!
Mike Van Horn

Neil Down
A Shot at Immortality

Copyright © 2019 Mike Van Horn

Published in the United States of America

ISBN: 9781733929301

"Those that tossed whole stacks of computer punch cards out of windows weren't aware some of the stacks didn't come apart and they hit like a brick. There were dents in our cars and bumps on our heads."

————Neil Armstrong, after the August 13, 1969 ticker tape parade in New York City.

From "Neil Armstrong: A Life of Flight," by Jay Barbree

Wapakoneta Overview

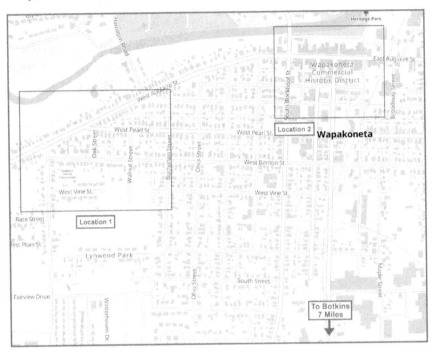

Location 1

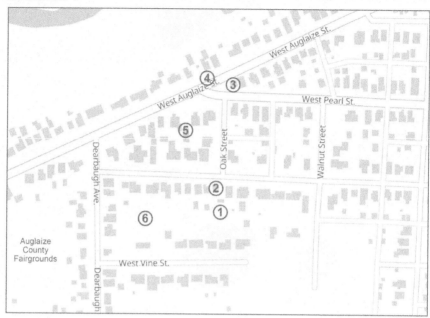

Legend

① Barn

② Malcom MacKenzie House

③ Max's Dairy Barn

④ Y-Shaped Intersection

⑤ Jacob Zint Observatory

⑥ "Short-Cut" Field

Location 2: Wapakoneta Commercial Historic District

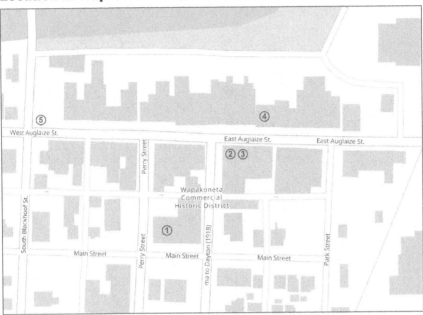

Legend

① Wapa Theater

② Bi-Rite Discount Store

③ Alpha Cafe

④ Rhine & Brading Drug

⑤ Jerry & Jane's Spot, 1966 Parade

PART ONE

WINDSHIELD TIME

CHAPTER ONE
Tuesday, March 7, 1967

Danny Hitchens stared at the flame.

It flickered from the top of a low mound less than twenty feet away. Danny stood on a hillside in Arlington, Virginia. Beyond the flame, down past the Potomac River, lay the city of Washington D.C. Danny raised his eyes every minute or so to take in the panorama in the distance. The Lincoln Memorial stood there, perhaps a mile away. Further away on the National Mall loomed the Washington Monument. The view was spectacular: especially for a teenager from a town of scarcely one thousand inhabitants.

Still, Danny's eyes were drawn back to the flame.

The Eternal Flame was surrounded by a simple, waist-high, white picket fence. It had been twenty by thirty feet when first erected after President John F. Kennedy's assassination barely three years earlier. After some modifications, the current fence was thirty by thirty.

The fallen president's grave was in the center, flanked by markers for his son Patrick, who died 39 hours after birth, and daughter Arabella, who was stillborn in 1956. Patrick's death occurred barely three months before his father's murder.

The Eternal Flame was hastily constructed after JFK's widow, Jacqueline, requested it two days after the assassination. A makeshift Hawaiian torch was situated below a wire dome. This was covered by dirt and evergreen boughs. It was fed by propane gas that ran through 300 feet of copper tubing. Over sixteen million visitors had witnessed the flame in person in the three-plus years of its existence.

Danny turned his head to the right. A three-foot high wrought iron fence just beyond the JFK site enclosed a much larger area. Workers busied themselves with construction equipment. Danny knew that a more permanent memorial site was being prepared. The crush of visitors demanded it. The Eternal Flame had been redesigned. Presumably the bodies would be re-interred and the flame transferred very soon. News reports indicated this would take place in the fall. To Danny, however, it looked like it could occur any day.

Danny's eyes moved back to the flame.

He had read Kennedy's book, *Profiles in Courage,* and was familiar with JFK's exploits on PT-109 during World War 2. What most often came to mind for Danny when conjuring a memory of the slain president, though, was his declaration that the United States would put a man on the moon before the end of the decade.

Danny was part of the junior class from tiny Botkins, Ohio. Forty-eight students and four chaperones faced the memorial. They stood solemnly, despite the voices and engine noise from the nearby construction site. Groups of strangers pressed in from their sides and rear.

A busload of students from Vermont stood just to the left of the group from Botkins. Some of the Ohioans and Vermonters, after a few minutes, glanced at each other: the natural curiosity of teenagers temporarily overcoming the situation. Their eyes quickly flicked down in embarrassment, either from being inappropriate in the moment, or from a collective shame stemming from the act that resulted in the memorial in front of them.

Virtually every person at the grave site flashed back to black and white television images from little more than three years earlier. The students remembered the anguish and anger expressed by their parents.

How could anyone do this? How could it be so easy? How could a man with a rifle be permitted to get close enough to pull it off? And, most perplexing, why the hell would anyone want to *be* that man with a rifle? An involuntary feeling of shame washed over Danny. He wondered how Texans must feel when visiting this site.

The Vermont kids began to move back to allow another group to take their place. Dave Mielke, one of the Botkins chaperones, decided they should move back as well.

Mielke was a large man in his early thirties. He wore wire-rimmed glasses and had straight brown hair that was just a bit too long for a teacher in a small Midwestern town, even in the sixties. "Doc," as he was known to his students, was an outsider. That is, he was not originally from Botkins, or even from any of the surrounding towns in Shelby or Auglaize counties. He grew up a couple hours north of Botkins and attended Bowling Green State University. After graduating, he was hired by superintendent Jim Degen to teach History, Government, and Social Studies.

Mielke, 31, was a track guy. He threw shot and discus at BGSU. He was quickly recruited to take over the Botkins Trojan track and cross country programs. Though he was technically sound in teaching the field events, Mielke was the first to admit that he knew little about, and had zero talent for, running. This would seem to be a major deficiency for a coach in these sports.

Mielke, though, threw himself into the job. He read everything he could find on running techniques, workouts, and equipment. He actively recruited athletes from other sports. He sold the baseball and basketball coaches––Botkins didn't offer football––on the idea that small schools had to share their participants and that running would improve endurance for all sports.

Mielke's teams achieved success despite the fact that Botkins High School did not have a track. They trained on streets near the school as well as country roads outside the village limits.

He also had a passion for history. His classes were part lesson, part story telling session. Not everyone was wired to receive Mielke's messages in class, but Danny sure was.

After leaving the Kennedy gravesite, the Botkins students and chaperones made their way up to the Custis-Lee Mansion, then to the Tomb of the Unknown Soldier. The teenagers walked respectfully along the cemetery path. The boys bunched together in twos and threes. They scanned to their right and left, imagining they might discover a famous name among the seemingly endless rows of markers. The girls clustered into small groups and spoke in subdued voices as they navigated the walkway. They fastened top buttons and crossed their arms as they walked. The forty-degree temperature was colder than many of them had expected. Wasn't Virginia a southern state?

Arrangements had been made to allow two from their group to take part in the wreath laying ceremony. Gary Poppe, an excellent student and the catcher on the baseball team, and Ann Becker, president of the National Honor Society, carried the wreath to the soldiers in front of the tomb.

Danny knew more about the soldiers than most in his group. They'd been given reading assignments about certain aspects of their trip for weeks in advance. Danny supplemented the reading with trips to the library to learn more. He knew the soldiers involved with the ceremonies at the tomb were members of the Old Guard: the U.S. Army's 3rd Infantry Division.

A black member of the Old Guard made an announcement that students from "Boskins, Ohio" had delivered this day's wreath. The ceremony was so solemn that not even the biggest smartasses in the class cracked a smile over the mispronunciation.

Danny focused on the black soldier. He, like the other members of the Old Guard, walked his twenty-one-step path in front of the tomb with almost machinelike precision. He wore black glasses and carried an M-14 rifle.

Danny knew about the rifle as well. His brother Eddie had carried one for a year or so. He had qualified expert with one at Fort Dix. Eddie now carried the M-16, "the Black Rifle," but he sang the praises of the 14. According to Eddie, the M-14 was durable, accurate, and its 7.62 NATO bullet packed a much bigger punch than the 5.56 round of the M-16.

When the ceremony concluded, the Botkins class of 1968 moved away from the Tomb of the Unknown, heading west.

From early March through May each year, Arlington National Cemetery plays host to high school groups from virtually every state east of the Mississippi. Typically referred to as class trips, the excursions consist of visits to the cemetery, the White House, and many of the Washington D.C. monuments and museums.

And long bus trips.

Up until a few years earlier, Botkins High School sent their senior classes on this trip. An unfortunate underage drinking incident, one that involved a student jumping from his fifth story hotel window to an adjoining roof, resulted in the change. The school administrators wanted to make sure they had an entire year remaining in which to punish an offender. Hence, the "Junior Class Trip."

The troop was approaching Section 3. Danny and his best friend, Reed Thompson, were near the front of the procession. Birds chirped and a hint of spring was in the air. Danny imagined he could detect the aroma of cherry blossoms from the Tidal Basin beyond the Potomac.

Danny, 17, had straight, dark brown hair that spilled over his ears. He stood six foot one and had a build that some might consider athletic. His buddy Reed, or "Reedo," was the same age, an inch shorter, and had a similar build and hairstyle. If not for Reed's blonde hair, the two could be mistaken for brothers.

"Looks like we're going to visit the astronauts next," Reed said, looking at the map he'd picked up at the Visitors Center.

Danny nodded without comment. The sheer number of gravestones was overwhelming. He'd expected this, of course, but was in awe as he strode through a cemetery that was several times larger than his hometown. Danny noted that most of the monuments and gravestones back by the Custis-Lee Mansion, the area that saw the first burials during the Civil War, were of varying shapes and sizes. Once he and his classmates moved further away from the mansion, the standard white military markers became more prevalent.

The chaperones at the head of the column came to a stop in front of two rectangular patches of bare earth. The students formed a semi-circle behind them, bunching together for warmth.

Danny peered between two heads to see the names etched on markers that must have been recently put in place.

Virgil "Gus" Grissom and Roger Chaffee had perished barely five weeks earlier, on January 27. They, along with Ed White, were trapped when a flash fire swept through their command module during a rehearsal. Their mission was designated as Apollo One. White was interred at West Point, his alma mater.

Danny was enamored with Grissom, who hailed from Mitchell, Indiana, another small town. Grissom had a haircut that boys in Botkins called a flattop. Danny had the same hairstyle from age 5 to age 12. By Danny's seventh birthday, he was engaged in an ongoing contest of wills with his parents about it. Danny would strategically bring up the subject when his dad wasn't home. "So and so's parents let him grow his hair out." His mother allowed debate: his dad was unbending. The monthly visits to Ed Counts' barbershop became more and more contentious.

As Danny's friends gained their follicle freedom, they derided him for still being under the control of "Injun' Ed and his electric tomahawk." The fact that Ed Counts was at least as WASPish as Ward Cleaver of 'Leave It To Beaver' fame had no impact on his nickname.

Finally, Chris Gerber, the son of Clyde Gerber, was permitted to grow out his hair. Clyde was the owner of Botkins Lumber Company, and employed Danny's father, Jerry. When he learned this, Danny again submitted a bill requesting a new hairstyle. This time the legislation passed both the House (mom) and Senate (dad).

What had begun as a gripe, percolated for years, and at times escalated into a verbal rock fight, had ended without fanfare. Danny would get his long hair.

Grissom didn't need long hair to be cool. He had been, after all, an astronaut. He'd also flown over a hundred combat missions in Korea.

The bus carrying the students from Botkins had driven down Pennsylvania Avenue before arriving at Arlington. A few protesters were visible near the White House. Danny, whose brother was in Vietnam, looked at them with disdain. He couldn't see the basic difference between the conflicts in Korea and Vietnam. Both were north-south chunks of land divided in the middle. Both had communist bad guys on one side that were attempting to conquer the other. The bad guys were even in the north in both circumstances.

What the hell was the difference?

The Korean War vets were not called baby killers. Danny hadn't heard of anyone spitting on them in airports. The only negative Danny had heard associated with them was their war ended in a tie. Danny knew some of these men back in Botkins. Stories floated that some of them, who had also served in World War 2, were not happy with being called back to serve in Korea a few years later.

But they went.

The group began to move toward another section. Reed noticed that Danny, the biggest history buff he knew, seemed subdued. They had passed several fresh graves as they moved through the cemetery. Many of these were combat deaths from Vietnam. Reed assumed the sight of them had sobered his buddy.

"Eddie is smart, he'll be okay," Reed offered.

Danny, distracted, answered "What?"

"Eddie. He's tough, he's gonna be okay," Reed assured, with more conviction than he felt.

Eddie Hitchens was three years older than Danny. He was a sharp kid: A's and B's in school. At six feet two, he was a good, not great, athlete and participated in several sports. Eddie had joined the Army after kicking around the idea of attending college. Eddie's unit, the 173rd Airborne Brigade, was often mentioned in news reports on the fighting. Danny suspected his brother was in the thick of it, but that wasn't the reason for his preoccupation.

Danny was worried about his mom.

Jane Hitchens was in the hospital back in Ohio. Danny's parents didn't tell Danny about the scheduled "procedure" until two days before the class trip. The implication was that Jane would undergo routine tests related to an operation she underwent a few years earlier. Danny searched his memory to see if there was any aspect of his mom's recent behavior that should have thrown up a red flag. Nothing seemed out of place.

Danny offered to stay home to be with his mom, but she encouraged—no, insisted—that he make the trip.

The Ohio kids began to make their way toward the parking area. When they reached a point a couple hundred feet from a line of idling buses, diesel fumes swept over them. This all-encompassing aroma had become the perfume of the trip. Danny had read somewhere that smells triggered memories much more than words. If that was true, he suspected he'd remember this trip as long as diesel engines existed.

Danny stood in the parking lot with the rest of the class. The chaperones were gathered in a small circle beside the bus, conferring with the driver. Thoughts floated through his head as his eyes settled on the bus.

What the hell was diesel, anyway?

Sure, Danny knew it was a type of fuel. But was it made from an entirely different base element than gasoline? What about kerosene? These seemed like simple concepts. Things he should know.

Did these liquids act and react like, say, blood? Danny knew that if the wrong blood type was given to a patient there could be disastrous repercussions. He assumed similar catastrophic results would occur if the wrong fuel was put into an engine.

Danny was a town kid.

Country kids knew all about these things. They knew about animals, machines, crops, hunting and fishing. They drove tractors at an early age and had all driven cars well before ever setting foot in a driver's ed car.

City kids, like those here in D.C., went to large integrated schools with exposure to the arts. They had a certain savviness.

It seemed to Danny that both country and city kids expected town kids to have the abilities of the other group: while in actuality they had neither.

The chaperones wrapped up their conversation and walked toward the students. In addition to Dave Mielke, the team included Sue Giltrow, Mark Rawson, and Sherry Fark. In a school the size of Botkins, the faculty was so small that they taught several classes over each of the four high school grades. Students quickly became familiar with their teachers.

Sue Giltrow, "Miss Giltrow" in school, was the high school guidance counselor. Most of the discussion of Giltrow among the students centered around her sexuality. Why was she still a Miss? The students had no basis for this. Giltrow lived in a neighboring town and may have had a steady boyfriend, but this was how the herd thought.

In Botkins, homosexuality was a mystery. The condition itself was to be avoided, of course. It was, Danny suspected, treated much like leprosy in the Middle Ages. No one wanted it and no one knew what caused it. Those with the condition were to be avoided, lest the affliction make the leap from body to body. In the case of homosexuality, though, there were no festering sores to alert observers of its presence.

Danny had read that some experts estimated that 5-10% of the population is homosexual. If anything near that number was correct, Danny had certainly spent time in close contact with them and came out no worse for the wear. For that reason, he didn't get as charged up as his high school brethren over the subject. He did, however, go along with the jokes when the subject came up.

If Miss Giltrow was "gay," the term now coming into vogue, she seemed normal enough to Danny. At 32, she had been at Botkins High School for seven years, about the same time as Dave Mielke. She was normal height, normal size, had curly brown hair, and a smart smile. The smile was 90% eyes, 10% mouth.

Her position as guidance counselor meant that she would have one-on-one contact with every student, particularly in their junior and senior years. She encouraged every student to take the ACT test, this being the preferred college aptitude test of institutions in Ohio. Even the kids that had no intention of attending college were prodded by Giltrow to take the test.

"You never know what will happen" was her standard refrain. It was also written on a poster she kept on her office wall.

Danny thought Miss Giltrow believed some of her students would do so well on the ACT that a college would offer scholarship money and pull a bright kid from nowhere into a new world. Wasn't this what colleges did?

Privately, Danny believed that even if students did well on the test, many of them wouldn't even be able to come up with money for the application.

For kids from Botkins, college was a collection of old stone buildings, football games, and, recently, protests. Danny's class numbered 56. His best guess was that no more than 15 would attend a university. All but one or two of these would be the first member of their family to do so. Even if many of the classes the student took were considered "college prep," there was no family history that helped steer a student through the maze of college preparation.

Miss Giltrow was trying to change this.

At her urging, Danny had taken the test several weeks prior to the trip along with many of his classmates. They were still awaiting the results.

In Danny's opinion, half the students coming out of Botkins were smart enough to do well in college. He'd met a few college students in the last year or two and some of them didn't seem all that intellectual. Hell, all of the teachers at BHS had *graduated* from college and some of them were downright dumbasses.

Miss Giltrow, though, was not one of them.

Danny hoped that the low percentage of college bound students didn't discourage her.

Mr. Mark Rawson was also on the trip. Rawson taught Math, and he bugged Danny. It was not just because Danny was challenged by any math above freshman level classes. Well, not just that. It was the fact that Mr. Rawson was seemingly incapable of getting through a 45-minute class without at least one grammatical error. In Danny's view, it was more like four or five.

Oh, sure, there were also the minor variety, like substituting "got" for "have," but the most glaring for Danny was Rawson's insistence on using "myself" incorrectly. He said things like "Ninety-nine people and myself are on train 'A' going 90 miles per hour....." He even started sentences with the word. "Myself and Mrs. Doering will be advisors for the prom this year." Danny thought, *My God!*

Danny *knew* these were incorrect. He would silently steam over the faux pas while glaring at the large red "C" on the tests that Rawson handed back to him in third period Algebra.

Rawson was 5'10", clean shaven, and wore wire-rimmed glasses. His glasses were more in line with grandpa spectacles, not the bug-eyed style currently in fashion. They were never straight.

Cheryl Fark, who taught English, rounded out the group and gave the girls on the trip the same ratio of supervision as the boys. Mrs. Fark taught in a structured, imaginative manner. Danny thought she was cheerful, positive, and encouraging. In her early thirties, Fark had dark hair that framed a round face that always seemed to be smiling.

Danny loved English. It was his second favorite subject, after History. He loved reading and applying the rules. In a way, it was like a game to him.

Fark once gave her creative writing class, of which Danny was a member, an assignment that was literally pulled out of a hat. She wrote the names of 25 emotions on slips of paper. This corresponded with the number of students in the class. Some words were positive, some negative. Each student drew a slip and had to produce a 500-word story on how that emotion pertained to him or her.

Danny had always secretly thought "shame" was the worst emotion. He, for whatever reason, felt shame more keenly than most. At one time or another he'd been ashamed of his clothes, his complexion, his haircut, even the family TV set.

Danny had drawn "hate" and was secretly pleased.

He did 500 words on grammatical errors.

When Danny learned that Doc Mielke, Miss Giltrow, and Mrs. Fark would be three of the chaperones, he knew it would be a great trip.

At the bus, the class was lined up for a count to make sure everyone was present. Forty-eight of the 56 members of the class had made the trip. This was considered a high percentage, maybe very high.

Two of the eight missing students were from dairy farming families. Dairy farmers, Danny had learned, seldom, if ever, took vacations. The cows had to be milked every day. Children, especially male children, were part of the team that performed this task. It had been apparent a long time ago that Bob Kohler and Rick Geyer would not be making the trip to D.C.

The other six were simply not able to scrape together $300, even with over a year to do so. Danny was not particularly friendly with Louise Schmerge, but it pained him to see the look in her face when announcements pertaining to the trip were made in home room classes at the beginning of the school day.

Danny clearly remembered one incident. in fact, he couldn't get it out of his head. It was the day they were asked to turn in their paperwork for the trip. Checks covering the $50 deposit fee were to be paper-clipped to the forms, then passed up the rows of desks and collected by a representative from the bus company. Louise was in the row to Danny's right, sitting three desks in front of him. He saw her turn to collect the forms coming up her row. There was a tear slowly tracking down her right cheek.

Out front of the assembled, the officious Mr. Rawson raised his clipboard and read from the itinerary. Danny noted that Rawson held the clipboard a bit too far in front of his face.

"We'll board the bus and head back to the hotel. Feel free to eat a snack on the way back. When we get there, you'll have an hour or so of free time to clean up, change clothes, or whatever." Rawson made an unsuccessful attempt to straighten his glasses and continued, "We'll then re-board the bus and drive back to town to view the monuments. After that we'll stop for a late meal then return to the hotel."

The tour bus company had a deal with a few Washington area restaurants. For a pre-arranged fee, each restaurant would provide a meal at a time chosen in advance. The bus would pull up and its occupants would pile out, each of them carrying a small book of perforated coupons given to them at the beginning of the trip. The student would tear the proper coupon out of the book, present it to the server, take a seat, and a plate would be sat in front of them. The restaurants generally shunted these group meals into off-peak time slots to optimize traffic.

Every student knew the schedule. They'd been handed the same itinerary weeks before the trip. Very little had changed. It was a running joke that Mr. Rawson had covered his copy with hand written notes and buried his head in it constantly. Gary Poppe had offered a five-dollar reward to anyone that could somehow draw a penis on Rawson's copy. Anytime a piece of 8.5 x 11-inch piece of paper blew past their group, dozens of pairs of eyes fixed on it, just in case.

Rawson continued, "Myself and Mr. Mielke will be in the hallways at the hotel making sure you stay in your rooms before you're asked to report to the lobby."

Danny winced at the incorrect usage of the pronoun. He opened his eyes and saw Mrs. Fark and Miss Giltrow off to the side. They were looking at Danny and smiling. In fact, Giltrow put a hand over her face to cover a laugh.

Rawson stopped talking for a minute and looked in her direction, then continued to drone on.

Danny kept his eyes on the female teachers for a few beats. One of the coolest things he could think of was to be liked by adults he respected. Liked in a non-creepy way, of course. Giltrow and Fark, he could tell, liked him.

Danny smiled back.

CHAPTER TWO

Mr. Rawson wrapped up and the class boarded the bus. It was a forty foot General Motors "New Look" bus built to hold 53 passengers. It was nearly at full capacity with its 48 students and four chaperones. When tour guides were aboard, they often stood, holding onto a support bar to keep from losing their balance.

Someone turned on a transistor radio and "Ain't Too Proud To Beg" by the Temptations flowed through the bus. A few of the boys tried to match David Ruffin on lead vocals, with predictable voice cracking results.

Most of the passengers grabbed the brown paper bags they'd brought from home. Candy bars, potato chips, and a few apples appeared. Danny reached in his bag for a Marathon candy bar. In a red paper wrapper, this was a chocolate-coated caramel creation about an inch wide and ten or so inches long. It was not solid, but had a laced appearance that must've been a nightmare to produce. The bar couldn't be bitten through completely. Your front and bottom teeth would come together and the caramel would somehow still stretch out from your mouth to the remainder of the bar you were pulling away from your face. The caramel would eventually snap—if the temperature was below, say, forty degrees—or elongate like taffy until it finally broke and adhered to your chin, neck, and chest. The whole while, bits of chocolate would dislodge from the expanding caramel, looking not unlike ice breaking up on a river when the temperature changes. The chocolate would drop onto your lap, homework, or pet dog as you chewed. The sweet concoction clung to your teeth with the consistency of tar.

They were wonderful. Danny couldn't fathom why some kids hated them.

Danny watched as Mr. Rawson did another head count, confirming the result he'd arrived at not five minutes earlier outside the bus. Rawson figuratively tapped each occupant with a right index finger. After 48 jabs, the bus was on its way to the hotel.

It was time again for the boys to immerse themselves in the Fart Game. The rules, largely unspoken but universally understood—by the boys, at least—were to produce the most rank, nausea producing gas release possible while, and this is the trick, keeping the odor and the revulsion it engendered, away from the girls.

No one wanted to be branded a "hog," which seemed to be the proper categorization for a person with substandard cleanliness or habits in small town America. One did not want to be seen as culpable by the girls, who sat in the front of the bus, but wanted one hundred percent credit from the guys.

Oh, and you had to name your fart.

Reed Thompson had once nearly brought tears to the eyes of the baseball team with his creation, "Hobo's Boot." Pat Jokisch got under the skin of his foil, Herm Barton, by repeatedly producing "Claudia's Perfume." Claudia was the first name of Herm's mom.

The thing was, guys thought a good fart was hilarious, especially one that came at a well-timed moment. Like during a speech by a coach. Or when your sister was talking. Sisters, as it happened, were not protected by the idiosyncrasies of the game like female classmates.

Some guys were better than others at the game, of course. In an all-male situation, the louder the fart, the better. In mixed company, the most admired practitioners were somehow able to extend the discharge for several seconds: lowering the volume to a level audible to the constellation of boys, while not being detected by the girls fifteen feet away.

Masterful.

Sadly, no one was able to muster one, or "dent the scoreboard," on the ride to the hotel. Not even Jokisch, who years earlier developed the ability to loudly break wind in mid-sentence, *in context* with the line he was delivering. This was stunningly funny to the guys.

Once, while imitating basketball coach Bill Elsass in the locker room after practice, Jokisch stood on a bench wearing nothing but a jock. Using the same mannerisms and voice inflection as the coach, he implored that "We need to get the rebound, turn and look for the outlet man, and get rid of the ball...*POOSH* the ball up the floor." When he said "poosh," he stamped his foot on the bench in precisely the same fashion as Elsass while at the same time releasing a fart that was high pitched, relatively short, but extremely loud.

The room exploded. Two or three players ended up on the floor.

Danny, like all the guys, admired Pat's ability. Not just the seeming "toot on command" control he exhibited. No, it was more the fact that Jokisch must've felt the gas coming on and quickly worked up a skit in his head that would play to the audience.

That kind of quick thinking was to be admired.

Their destination was Crystal City, Virginia, which was a neighborhood located south of Washington D.C. They were staying at a Holiday Inn. Danny kept his head on a swivel as the bus made its way east through the streets of suburban Washington. He caught a glimpse of the Pentagon after it was pointed out by the driver. Danny strained to see other landmarks out the left side windows. He could easily pick out the Washington Monument, of course. At 555 feet, it didn't require the eyesight of a fighter pilot. He could even make out the slight difference in shading about a third of the way up. The students had learned in Mr. Mielke's History class that construction of the monument had started in 1848, but a lack of funding stopped the project six years later. The Civil War began in 1861 and further strained finances. Work resumed in 1877 and was completed in 1884. The marble used to complete the project was from a different quarry than the original, leading to the difference in shading.

The monument was the tallest structure in the world for five years, at which time the Eiffel Tower was completed in Paris. It was still the world's largest obelisk.

In Mrs. Fark's Composition class they had been required to use the word "obelisk" in a story. The Washington Monument could not be mentioned. They had to use creativity to work in the noun in another fashion. Over a chunk of meatloaf in the school cafeteria that day, Reed wondered aloud if he would be banned from the trip if he used the word when describing his "unit" in a weird fantasy that involved worship by a lost tribe in Africa that he would discover.

Reed's creativity was perhaps a bit more than Mrs. Fark had bargained for. In the end, he went with a story about obelisk shaped piles of manure that mysteriously sprung up in and around Botkins, baffling police chief Vic Peters. Many members of the Composition class would remember the story for years. Most thought it semi-prescient when crop circles began to appear in England in the 1980s, with similar effect on law enforcement there.

Reed got a B- on the paper. He glumly noted that he should've gone with the wang story.

Vic Peters had been the town cop for eleven years. Botkins, a village of about 1,100, boasted a force of one full time officer and one part timer. Peters, the full timer, seemed to spend his days parked near the village limits watching for speeders and visiting the three gas stations in town, making small talk with employees and various hangers-on.

In his mid-forties, Peters was a thin man, a fraction over six feet tall. He seemed a bit unsure of himself and was universally perceived as nervous. These characteristics led to the inevitable comparison with Barney Fife of *The Andy Griffith Show* fame.

Barney was nervous, boastful, inefficient, and cocky: yet somehow still likeable. All of these traits were assigned to Peters by many people in Botkins. Peters knew it, and he hated it.

Another thing that Peters had working against him was, of course, his last name. A Barney Fife clone that gave you speeding tickets was bound to ruffle some feathers. One that did it while sporting a last name that was a synonym for "dicks" was...inelegant?

Peters tried to disassociate himself from the Barney comparison as much as possible. He grew a mustache, sported cowboy boots, and wore photochromic glasses that darkened in the sun. These efforts were marginally successful.

But that last name....

Danny reminded Reed to help look for District of Columbia Stadium. It would be off in the left distance. Being baseball fans, the boys had an informal checklist for the D.C. trip. High on the list was getting a glimpse of the Washington Senators' ballpark. The Senators were mediocre at best. A sportswriter had once said they were "First in war, first in peace, and last in the American League East." But their best player had attended Ohio State University.

Frank Howard stood 6'7" with bulging muscles. He, too, sported a flattop haircut. It was a flattop you could set your watch to: very precise. He had played basketball and baseball at Ohio State. Because he was a big-league player and former Buckeye, Howard was considered "mostly cool" by Danny and Reed. With longer hair, he could graduate to totally cool.

Howard, doubtless, was in Florida at spring training with the Senators. That didn't stop the boys from keeping an eye on pedestrians: looking for that flattop floating twelve inches above the masses like a banner being pulled by an airplane.

Arriving at the hotel, the travelers filed off the bus and through the lobby to the elevators. While waiting, Danny sought out Mr. Mielke and asked permission to make a phone call. Mielke, who knew that Danny's mom had health problems, quickly agreed and told him to use one of the pay phones around the corner from the elevators. Mielke said he would wait for Danny and ride up with him.

Danny walked down the hall to the three phones. None were being used, but he still selected the one furthest from the lobby. Danny grabbed the headset, dialed zero, and waited for the operator. When she answered, Danny asked to make a collect call. He gave his first name and home phone number with a 513 prefix. Danny had tried to call home the day before with no luck.

The bus had left Botkins at 5 am Monday. It made its way through Ohio to Pennsylvania, and eventually wound along Route 30 to Gettysburg. The trip took ten hours. There had been a restroom break and a stop for lunch. It had already been a long day, but most of the class was eager to experience the national park for a couple of hours. A licensed battlefield guide met them at the Visitors Center, and after another restroom break, jumped on the bus with them and directed the driver through a tour of the park. This proved to be the highlight so far, as they stopped often to explore parts of the battlefield and pose for pictures.

Danny had tried to phone home that night from the lobby of their Motor Lodge but hadn't gotten an answer.

He waited through three rings then heard his father pick up.

Operator: "Will you accept a collect call from Danny?"

Jerry Hitchens, after a long few seconds, answered, "Yes."

Danny wasted no time, "Hi Dad, how's Mom?"

There was another pause. Then, voice cracking, Jerry managed "Danny, I have some bad news...your mom passed away."

Danny gripped the phone. He opened his mouth but didn't, couldn't, speak.

Jerry continued, "She had the operation at St. Rita's. Partway through her heart stopped. They tried to revive her but couldn't."

Danny struggled to comprehend what he was hearing. *What the hell? This was supposed to be a routine procedure.*

Jerry took a deep breath, "They had to remove another section of her lung. Mom didn't want you to worry. She knew how much the trip meant to you and didn't want you to miss it. She was very clear about it."

Danny didn't know what to say. For a brief second he felt a flicker of rage. This was snuffed out by his dad's revelations. He vaguely realized he was crying and that Doc was standing a few feet away, eyebrows raised.

Danny couldn't remember what he said to his dad. After another minute of two he handed the phone to Mielke, leaned against the wall and let tears roll down his face. Mielke quietly finished the call. He hung up and turned to Danny.

"Wh-what should I do?" Danny managed.

CHAPTER THREE

The next morning, Wednesday, March 8, Danny found himself on another bus. He was on his way home. This was thanks in large part to Dave Mielke. With the help of the Holiday Inn manager, he had secured a couple spots on a Greyhound bus scheduled to leave the next day at 6 am. It took a different route back to Ohio, picking its way northwesterly through Pennsylvania, and eventually catching I-80, the Ohio Turnpike, and heading due west. The bus made several stops along the way to drop off and pick up passengers. In all, Danny and Mielke were looking at 12 hours on the Greyhound. This would get them to Toledo, where they would be picked up by Danny's dad.

Danny was red-eyed and exhausted when he boarded the bus. He had walked the four blocks to the bus stop in silence. Mielke also looked tired and Danny thought he saw red rims behind the teacher's glasses. The night before, Danny had walked through the hotel door and looked at his three roommates. Andy Craft and Gary Poppe were looking at the TV, watching Reed, on one knee, turn the channel dial. Craft had just asked "Is 'The Man From Uncle' on tonight?" when Danny walked in. Craft and Poppe didn't turn their heads, but Reed looked up and immediately knew from the look on Danny's face that something terrible had happened.

Danny gave him all the confirmation he needed with two words, "Mom died."

All four chaperones came to the room later that night. They asked the roommates to go down the hall and reviewed the travel arrangements with Danny for the following day. Sue Giltrow had called Danny's dad again and worked out the last leg of the trip. Danny packed his small suitcase, dropped into bed, and silently cried himself to sleep. He felt three sets of eyes looking his way in the darkness.

The first hour or so of the ride home was quiet. Most of the 15 passengers dozed or stared out the window, watching as the first rays of the sun brought the new day. Danny had a window seat, about halfway back on the right side of the bus. Mielke sat next to him on the aisle. As the bus pulled out of the city, it gave the pair a last, spectacular view of the Washington Monument.

Danny's eyes were drawn to the monument, but his thoughts were elsewhere. He was thinking of his mom. He was desolate, exhausted. Danny tried to shift his focus away from the painful thoughts. He let his mind float.

Danny thought back to their tour guide from the day before. That had been barely 12 hours ago, it was hard to believe.

The guide bounced up the steps of the bus, shook hands with the driver, looked at the students and touched the brim of his Smokey The Bear style hat. He introduced himself as William Fitzpatrick. At 5'6", 150 pounds, he had a smile that could only be described as contagious. Within seconds it had spread to everyone on the bus.

"Ahh, a busload of Buckeyes! We Yankees welcome the reinforcements" he exclaimed.

Fitzpatrick explained that he was originally from Rhode Island. Like many guides, Fitzpatrick liked to explain the three-day battle chronologically. This meant starting on the west side of the park. It also meant that the John Buford statue would be the first stop. Since it was located on busy Chambersburg Pike, the bus pulled over but the students were kept in their seats.

The monument to the Union General was a six-foot-high granite base topped with a statue of Buford gazing to the west, toward the Confederate positions. The base of the monument is surrounded by cannons, also mounted in granite. Fitzpatrick said that one of the cannons fired the first shot of the battle and was marked with a small bronze plate. He said he regretted not being able to take them to see the cannon up

23

close. Safety regulations did not permit guides to escort groups across the busy road.

Fitzpatrick explained that Buford, a cavalry general, held the ridgelines in this area of the battlefield on July 1, 1863. Despite being heavily outnumbered, Buford was able to hold on until Union infantry arrived. The infantry was commanded by General John Reynolds. Fitzpatrick then suggested that the group follow him to see the actual tree, still living, that Reynolds was standing beside when killed by a Rebel sniper. The tree was located a short distance away off a park road with much less automobile traffic. With that, the bus crawled a few hundred feet and stopped on one of the park roads. It emptied, the tree was surrounded, and General Buford was forgotten by many on the tour.

Not Danny.

As the Greyhound passed the Buford monument, he'd squinted at the cannons at its base and was sure he caught sight of the bronze plaque. Pretty cool.

He allowed himself a quick smile, and immediately felt guilty as thoughts of his mom swam into his head.

Jane Hitchens was born Jane Angela King on September 17, 1926, to Gene and Martha King. She grew up on a farm a couple miles south of Botkins. She was the oldest of 5 children. By all accounts, she had a pleasant childhood, tending to chickens, pigs, and 4 siblings. This despite the fact that the house had no indoor plumbing. Gene worked in town at the local grain elevator, Provico. Martha kept busy, trying to keep ahead of the appetites of Gene and the kids.

At age eight, things changed significantly when the family moved into town, having purchased a small two-bedroom, one story house on Walnut Street. The house was strategically located, roughly equidistant to the new Botkins Central School, a block to the east, and the Catholic "Ward School," two blocks to the west.

The Ward School was situated next to St. Lawrence Catholic Church. It was a K-6 school predominantly staffed by nuns. The King kids attended the school, as well as services at the church. When they reached seventh grade, they walked to the public Central School to complete their primary education.

Jane thrived at the new location. She maintained excellent grades. She was 5'7", had dark brown wavy hair, cut a few inches above the shoulders, and a smile that was described by more than one classmate as "mischievous." Proof of this could be seen in the inscriptions that friends wrote in Jane's copy of "The Trojan," the senior yearbook. She joined many of the clubs available to girls. She tried out, and was selected as, a cheerleader for the boys basketball team.

There was no football team at Botkins. In fact, none of the seven schools in the Shelby County League had football. The student bodies were small and infrastructure dedicated to sports were, by later standards, non-existent. The closest schools with football were Wapakoneta, seven miles to the north and located in a different county, and Sidney, 15 miles to the south. "Wapak" was the county seat of Auglaize County while Sidney performed the same function for Shelby County. While in high school, Jane and her friends would often travel to Wapak or Sidney to attend a Friday night football game. She met her future husband on one of these trips.

Jerry Hitchens was born on April Fool's Day, 1926. He grew up on the edge of Sidney. He had one sister. His mother, Donna, was a homemaker while his father, Charlie, worked at a local factory. Jerry, at age 18, was 5'11" 145 pounds, dark haired, and perpetually bored. Jerry had a bit of a rough childhood. Charlie battled alcoholism and he and Donna lived separately for parts of a decade. Jerry got in some trouble, usually for drag racing or skipping school, but hung on long enough to make it to his senior year. He was standing near the concession stand at Julia Lamb Stadium, the Sidney football facility, when he saw a group of unfamiliar kids get in line for popcorn and Cokes. He was immediately attracted to Jane.

They talked that night and went to a movie two weeks later. Jerry's car, a black 1933 Three-Window Ford Coupe, became a familiar sight on the streets of Botkins. Less than a year after their respective high school commencements, they were married at St. Lawrence. Jerry worked a series of blue collar jobs. He eventually settled at Botkins Lumber Company, where he began to work his way up the ranks.

Jane worked at Botkins Public Library, a small facility a couple blocks north of the school. They scraped together the down payment for a brick ranch style house on South Street. On April 26 1946, Edward James Hitchens was born. Daniel Eugene Hitchens came along on November 29, 1949.

Jerry worked longer days while Jane backed her hours down to part time, and the boys embarked on a childhood in small town America. Until they reached driving age, most of their lives revolved around the ten or twelve blocks that stretched from their house on South Street, to the library on Lynn Street, to the downtown section of Botkins a bit to the west. The schools were inside this circle, the baseball diamond, the Tastee Freez ice cream shop, Don Butch's general store, and for Danny, his buddy Reed's house.

Danny absentmindedly watched a Volkswagen Beetle, improbably painted with orange flames on the sides, flash past the bus. He realized they were slowing and was pulled back to the present moment. There was a rest stop ahead. He could use a bathroom break. The Greyhound had a small restroom in the rear but the amount of use it had withstood in the last few hours made it less than fragrant. Conditions inside the bus were beginning to mimic those normally only present after a few rounds of the fart game.

Doc waited for the forward seats to clear, got up, and preceded Danny out the door. It was a fair-sized building, 100 feet across by 80 feet deep, constructed of concrete block and painted in a color that might be described as "disappointment beige." Unfortunately, that seemed just about right for this trip. Danny said he needed to use the restroom. Mielke said he would buy some snacks in the vending area and asked what Danny would like.

"I can pay," Danny offered.

Mielke smiled, shaking his head, "It's on me."

Danny took a quick look and decided on a 7UP and some Seyferts potato chips. As he turned to the men's room, he remembered the chips were his mom's favorite, and he had to fight back tears.

Mielke fed a quarter into the drink machine, noticed Danny hesitate, wipe his eyes, walk a few steps, then stop completely. Danny seemed to be focused on a large free-standing ash tray in the corner. It was overflowing with butts. As they watched, a middle-aged woman walked to the corner, coughed, took a final drag on her cigarette, and push it into the overflow. Danny quickly stepped into the restroom.

Doc shook his head. He knew that Danny's mom had been a long-time smoker. Her death was no doubt hastened by the habit. He felt terrible for Danny. This was a sharp, friendly kid that didn't deserve the emotional beating he was taking. Mielke completed his purchases, duplicating Danny's selections for himself.

As they climbed onto the bus, Mielke decided to try to get Danny's mind off his mother's death. Danny took the window seat again. Mielke slid back in beside him.

"Hey Danny, what was your favorite part of the Gettysburg tour?"

Danny thought for a few seconds, took a swig of 7UP, and said "I don't know, I liked it all. I guess my favorite parts were Devil's Den, Little Round Top, and the Pickett's Charge area."

Mielke nodded, smiling. Danny saw that Mr. Mielke was beginning to get the same gleam in his eye that he had in History class when he was really rolling on a story. The bus began to move, as did the conversation.

They talked about the three areas Danny mentioned, and several others. Most of the Botkins kids had been amazed by Devils's Den, a collection of gigantic boulders on the southern part of the battlefield that had seen extensive combat. The students were surprised that they were allowed to climb on the rocks. After hours spent riding, they took full advantage. Seeing a few bruised knees and banged elbows, the chaperones realized they should put a stop to the liveliness before Gettysburg claimed more real casualties.

After a half hour or so, Mielke asked Danny, "Did you see the brass plate on the Buford Statue?"

Danny responded, "What? We weren't allowed near that monument."

Mielke smiled, "I saw you looking for it when our bus passed by."

Danny made out the "Welcome to Ohio" sign. They were getting closer to home but still had hours to go.

"Yeah, I think I did see the plate."

Mielke nodded, "Thought so. Can you keep a secret?"

"Uhhh, sure," Danny agreed, tentatively.

"The first year I went there as a chaperone, maybe six years ago, our bus did the exact same thing. It pulled off the road across from the Buford monument, the guide talked about it, and we moved on."

"Yeah?" Danny was interested.

Mielke continued, "About 11:30 that night I snuck out of our motel. It was a different motel, a little closer to that side of the battlefield, and walked about a mile out there to find the plate."

Danny laughed for the first time all day. "No way!!!"

"Yep. I started to jog out there but, well you know, I'm really not built to be a runner, so I just walked. It was really stupid." Mielke shook his head slowly, but kept a smile on his face. "There was still quite a bit of traffic. Some cars honked at me. It was really dark but I wanted to stick close to the road because I assumed I shouldn't be walking on the battlefield. I tripped a couple times."

Danny imagined the well-over 200-pound Mielke bumping along in the dark.

Doc continued, "I'll tell you what, I'm glad I did it. I'll remember reading that plate a lot longer than most of the books I've read about the battle."

Still smiling, Danny nodded.

"If you tell anyone, I'll kick your ass" Mielke concluded.

It was the first time Danny had ever heard a teacher swear. Well... if you didn't count incidents in the baseball dugout or during time-outs of basketball games.

Maybe stepping over the line just a bit, Danny asserted "I'm gonna tell Eddie when he gets back from Vietnam."

Mielke had really begun to feel a connection with this kid. The mention of the word "Vietnam" pierced the mood. He hesitated, regained his smile, and said to Danny, "Permission granted."

CHAPTER FOUR

At the same time, Jerry Hitchens sat behind the steering wheel of his 1964 Chevy Impala in his driveway. His right hand was pressed over his eyes. He had to get on the road in order to meet the bus carrying Danny and Mr. Mielke. It was nearly 4 pm and the bus should be in Toledo by 6. The last few days were a blur.

Sunday he had helped Danny pack for his Junior Trip. Early Monday morning he and Danny drove down South Street, picked up Reed Thompson, and continued on to the school. As they unloaded the boys' suitcases, Reed, usually a bit of a jokester, looked Jerry straight in the eye and said "Good luck tomorrow, we'll all be thinking about Mrs. H."

The comment wasn't meant to be sobering, but it had that effect. Reed pulled his suitcase out of the Impala's spacious trunk and walked to the gathering area, giving Jerry and Danny some privacy.

Danny grabbed the handle of his suitcase and lifted. He set it on the street and turned to his dad. Jerry had pulled out his wallet and was removing a ten-dollar bill. He handed it to Danny, put on a smile, and said, "buy something there that you can't get here."

Danny slowly reached for the ten. "You don't have to do that. I have some money."

Jerry insisted "Take it Danny, have fun and be safe. I know you're worried about Mom, but she'll be fine."

Danny heard the bus approach. A second later, Mr. Rawson, clipboard in hand, was spouting out instructions.

"You better get over there before he starts blowing a damn whistle" Jerry suggested.

Danny grinned and reached for the suitcase. He felt like hugging his dad, but the whole class was here, so he put his put his free hand on Jerry's shoulder, gave it a little wobble, and turned for the bus. Danny's grin instantly vanished. He thought his dad looked worried.

That had been less than 36 hours ago. Jerry drove from the school to the lumberyard. He usually started at 7, but he was up, would be off work the following day, and had plenty to do at the office.

About 4:30 that afternoon he called the Tastee Freez and asked if they could have two tenderloin sandwiches and a couple orders of fries ready by 5. Jim Kinninger said he'd take care of it himself and asked about Jane. It was the tenth or twelfth time that day Jerry had fielded this question. He'd distilled his answer down to "The doc says things should be fine, the operation's tomorrow."

The first few people that had asked, office receptionist Carol Roush and some early arriving customers, had gotten the long version. Jerry was tired of the long version.

At 5 pm, Jerry walked across Main Street to the Tastee Freez, and picked up the food. He walked back to his car and headed for home. He pulled into the driveway, saw that the garage door was up, and noticed Jane coming through the door that connected the garage to the house. She was struggling with a suitcase. Jerry jumped out of the Impala. "Let me get that."

Jane, breathing hard, said "I got it, I'm OK."

She didn't look OK. She was pale. Sallow. The green scarf covering her hair intensified the pallor of her face.

Jerry and Jane Hitchens owned exactly three suitcases. They were wedding gifts from Jane's parents. They were Samsonites with an olive green clamshell design, and, Jerry thought, were ugly as all get out. Eddie took the small sized case to boot camp a couple years earlier and it hadn't been seen since. Danny needed one for the Junior trip. Jane knew Danny would be embarrassed to lug something too large on a 5-day trip, so she asked him to take the medium case.

"I could really use the room in the big one" she said convincingly.

Danny quickly agreed, thinking he had dodged a bullet. The guys could be vicious. You didn't want to be the weak animal, cut from the herd.

Jane was told to pack a small bag. She was left with a suitcase large enough, she estimated, for a ten-day cruise. The expectation was that her hospital stay would be five to seven days. Her instructions were to bring an extra nightgown or two, a robe, slippers, change of clothes, and whatever toiletries she needed. Her piece of luggage was less than half full as she wrestled it into the garage. She wanted it ready to go in the morning.

Jerry grabbed the handle with one hand and steadied Jane with the other. She was breathing hard. Three years ago, when she was just 37, Jane had a lobectomy. The procedure involved making a long incision on the right side of the chest, and cutting out the lower lobe of the right lung. Dr. Brower, the surgeon, had explained that the right lung has three lobes while the left lung has two. His expectation for that first surgery was that Jane would have a rough 4-6 months, but she would eventually recover most of her "wind" and, if she quit smoking, had an excellent chance of a normal life.

Jerry was not sure Jane kept her part of the bargain. Since the operation in 1964, he never saw her smoke. Jerry, a longtime smoker himself, had quit cold turkey the day Jane was diagnosed. There were no longer ashtrays in the house. There was no evidence of cigarettes or matches. Still, he often detected a hint of his Right Guard underarm deodorant sprayed in rooms other than the bathroom, and he only used Right Guard in the bathroom.

They'd had a few arguments about it. Jerry knew first-hand how addictive it was. He had smoked Salems for years. Jane smoked Kools. Before the operation, Jerry would see the white and green packs in her purse. She never left them in the car or let them set out where the boys could get them. She was adamant that they were not to take up the habit, secretly believing that boys will be boys and they would bow to peer pressure somewhere along the line, at least taking a puff or two.

She needn't have worried on this count. Both boys hated smoking. They hated everything about it. They couldn't stand the smell, couldn't understand the allure, and couldn't believe the expense. Cigarettes were over 30 cents a pack and both parents bought them by the carton. Eddie and Danny spent virtually every trip of their childhoods sitting in a vehicle filled with a choking haze. They enjoyed sports and believed smoking would degrade their abilities. Hadn't the Surgeon General just stated that a year or so ago?

No, the boys would not be smokers.

Lifting the suitcase up onto the work bench, Jerry turned and helped Jane back into the house. She eased into a chair at the kitchen table and he sat across from her.

This operation was to be exploratory in nature. The medical detection equipment in use in 1967 had its limits. Jane had been experiencing pain in her chest for a couple months. She tried to ignore it. She was also experiencing more shortness of breath. This was impossible to hide. Jerry and the boys had been after her for weeks to see the doctor. She finally agreed after nearly collapsing after a square dance at a wedding reception in mid-February.

Dr. Brower strongly recommended the surgery, so here they were. Worst case scenario: another lobe would have to be removed. This would put greater restrictions on Jane but, if she heeded the instructions, she should still be able to function reasonably well.

"Wait here," Jerry said, "I have tenderloins in the car."

He retrieved the bags and was somewhat relieved to see that Jane seemed to be breathing easier when he returned. He grabbed plates from the cupboard and a couple Dr. Peppers from the refrigerator and they sat and ate.

The other female member of the family ambled into the kitchen. Suzy Wong was a pug, an improbable breed of dog.

33

She had the compressed facial features of a bulldog with none of the formidability. Maybe 20 pounds, light brown, and with a short tail that curled upward, Suzy entered the room with a look of expectation. Suzy smelled food.

Jerry reached down and scratched Suzy's forehead. He'd brought her home to the boys a year ago. Her look of expectation was... expected. She always wore a look of expectation. A customer at the lumberyard, Gerald Hemmert, had mentioned a new litter of puppies on his farm. "I gotta warn ya' though, it's a weird breed."

The boys had been lobbying for a dog, so Jerry thought "What the hell." He drove out after work that day and picked out the runt of the litter. Hemmert told him it was a female. Jerry looked into the disproportionately large eyes of the pup, noted her expression, and burst out laughing.

The name Suzy Wong swam into his head on the drive back to town. He had heard it in a movie or TV show. It seemed appropriately exotic. Jerry was the conquering hero to Eddie and Danny that night. Not so much to Jane. The care and feeding of Suzy was transferred to Jane after the requisite two weeks of attention from the boys. Eddie and Danny wanted to rename the pup, but Jerry insisted that Mr. Hemmert had christened her Suzy Wong, and Suzy Wong she would stay.

Jerry took a bite of his sandwich. The Tastee Freez tenderloins were so large that the oversized buns Jim Kinninger reserved for them could only cover the central two thirds of the meat. The tenderloin was fried, somehow attaining a thin crust. Roughly eight by six inches, each example was a slightly different shape: like a large, golden snowflake. Jerry broke off a piece from the edge of his sandwich and flipped it to Suzy.

Between chews, he asked "Who's taking care of Suzy tomorrow?"

Jane replied, "Caroline Craft is going to let her out every few hours." The Crafts lived across the street, a half dozen houses to the west of the Hitchens place.

They ate in silence for a few minutes before Jerry said "Danny should be in Gettysburg by now."

Jane instantly brightened and said "He's been looking forward to this trip for so long. I think he's read every history book we have at the library."

Then, her face darkening, "I know he's worried about Eddie, probably worried about me, and he doesn't know what he'll do after he graduates. I just hope..." She trailed off.

"He'll have the time of his life," Jerry said straight-faced. "He didn't have to take the big suitcase."

They both laughed.

They left for the hospital Tuesday morning at 5 am. Jerry steered for Interstate 75, the major north-south artery that was no more than a half mile from their house. Jane, however, asked Jerry to take County Road 25A. "Old 25' as it was sometimes known, ran parallel to I-75, and was roughly one mile to the west. Before the Interstate highway system, 25A was the main north-south pathway in western Ohio. Part of the historic Dixie Highway system connecting the southern states to the Midwest, Ohio's 25A ran from Cincinnati, down on the Ohio River, all the way to Toledo, up on the Michigan border. Along the way it bisected dozens of villages, towns, and cities including Botkins where it was referred to as Main Street within the village limits. It continued north for seven miles to Wapakoneta, then another 15 or so to Lima (pronounced 'Lie-muh'), where St. Rita's Medical Center was located.

The interstate was faster, but Jerry wasn't surprised. He knew that Jane loved Wapak. She was especially fond of the Wapa Theater downtown, with its large art deco neon sign out front. They started north, keeping the conversation light. Ten minutes later they approached the city limits. At the edge of town, they saw the green sign touting,

Wapakoneta

Home Of
Neil Armstrong
First Civilian
Astronaut

They both smiled. Jerry turned and said "Do you remember?"

"The parade" Jane said.

They both smiled again.

Neil Armstrong was command pilot of Gemini 8 on March 16, 1966. The goal of the mission for Armstrong and pilot David Scott was to conduct the first docking of two spacecraft in orbit. At first, all went well. Armstrong was able to steer the Gemini capsule to the Agena Target Vehicle and dock successfully. The connected spacecraft began to roll. The Gemini astronauts disconnected from the Agena, but the roll increased significantly. It was later determined that one of the thrusters had malfunctioned. The roll became dangerous, potentially fatal. Armstrong was able to shut down the system that was facilitating the roll and use the separate reentry thrusters to stop it. The decision was made to let the capsule reenter earlier than planned. Gemini 8 splashed down in the Pacific Ocean, about 500 miles south of Japan, rather than the Atlantic. It was picked up by secondary recovery forces.

Less than two months later, on May 13, 1966, Wapakoneta threw a parade for Armstrong. It was the biggest, most exciting event that anyone in the area could remember, and the Hitchens family was there.

CHAPTER FIVE

The memories washing over him, Jerry started the Impala. He noticed that the fuel gauge showed less than half a tank of gas. He decided to fill up before leaving town. He backed out of the driveway. Bob's Gulf sat on the edge of town near the I-75 ramp. Jerry had a Gulf credit card. He drove east on South Street for three blocks, made a left, drove another block, and turned into the station. As he checked for an open pump, he noticed a red Chevy Corvette peeking out from around the far side of the station.

"Aw shit." he said to himself. The Corvette belonged to Bob Bauman, the station's owner. Bauman was behind the cash register, handing change to a man that Jerry didn't recognize. Jerry eased toward the island, remembering to situate the car so that the pump reached the fuel door on the left side. Bauman finished the transaction and turned to see the grey Impala. He recognized the vehicle before he registered that Jerry was driving. Bauman quickly strode out the door.

"Hey, Jerry, how's Jane?" Bauman had a concerned and, Jerry supposed, optimistic look on his face. Most people in town knew that Jane was scheduled at St. Rita's today. Bauman's wife, Ruth, was one of Jane's best friends. She and Jane had coffee together every couple weeks and spoke on the telephone every few days. Jerry had hoped that Bob wouldn't be working this late in the afternoon. The station was open 24 hours every day and Bauman often worked the midnight shift. Outside of Jane's parents, Jerry hadn't yet talked to anyone in town about Jane's operation.

"Uh, Bob...we lost Jane today."

Bauman's smile froze, he stopped wiping his hands. "You don't mean it Jerry. Tell me you're kidding."

Jerry meant to say something, but he forgot what it was. He just stared at Bauman through eyes that had watered.

Bauman put his hand on Jerry's shoulder. He realized he'd left a small grease stain on Jerry's windbreaker.

"Oh damn, I'm so sorry Jerry. Aw shit, your jacket. Awwww......Jane?"

"There were complications and she didn't make it. I know she'd want me to tell Ruth, but Danny's coming back from the class trip on a bus and I have to pick him up in Toledo at 6. I just need to get some gas first."

"Sure Jerry, I got it." Bauman, relieved to be doing something to help, got the pump going, then ducked back into the station. Jerry pulled out his wallet and fished inside for the Gulf credit card. The card had a round, orange, icon with a horizontal white stripe through the center, emblazoned with the word "GULF." A sign that must've been 80 feet tall with the same logo at the top stood on the side of the building, near Bob's Corvette. At night, when the sign was illuminated, it's orange glow could be seen up and down the highway for miles.

Bauman came back out two minutes later with a couple bottles of Coke, and a handful of Hershey bars. He handed them through the window to Jerry.

"Sorry, I don't have any coffee on right now. Take these Cokes for the road. Get a couple of these candy bars to Danny."

Jerry lifted the credit card.

"No way Jerry." said Bauman, now removing the pump from the Impala and closing the fuel door. "You go get your boy. Let us know what we can do to help when you get back."

Jerry smiled. He waved, pulled away, and dabbed his eyes by pressing them against his shoulders, one at a time. He kept both hands on the wheel as he headed for the ramp. For the thousandth-time he thought *small town*. He didn't realize he'd put a small grease smudge near his left eye.

In the flow of northbound traffic, Jerry's mind inevitably drifted back to the previous day. They had arrived at the hospital a few minutes early. Jane was taken to a room on the fourth floor where she changed clothes. Dr. Brower came in and again reviewed that morning's procedure. A native

Alabaman, Brower pronounced the word with an emphasis on the second syllable.

Blood was drawn. Jane was asked to try to go to the bathroom one more time. The surgery prep went as planned. At 7:15, two orderlies came for her. Her bed was on wheels and she was rolled to the elevator. Jerry walked beside the bed, holding her hand. They reached the surgery floor, the doors opened, and Jerry bent over Jane and gave her a kiss. They'd been through this before. Jerry would be ushered into a waiting room until Jane was moved into recovery.

Jane, still gripping his hand, said "Take care of the boys, in case..."

Jerry shaken, could only croak "I'll be there when you wake up."

They wheeled her to surgery. It was the last time Jerry would see her alive.

At about 9 am, Jerry was summoned to an isolated room and given the news. Dr. Brower was near tears. Jerry was stunned. He vaguely remembered there were hours of discussions after that with various officials at the hospital. He signed several documents. He made phone calls. Someone asked if he had thought about "arrangements." He realized they were talking about a funeral. This gave him something to focus on. A couple members of the King family were buried in the Catholic cemetery on the north side of Botkins. Jane visited there from time to time. That would be what she wanted.

He thought of the Jacoby funeral home in Wapakoneta. There was no funeral home in Botkins. Jerry and Jane had attended visitations at Jacoby's. Jerry figured it would be fine. Someone at St. Rita's offered to place a call to Jacoby's. Jerry was told that, if it was convenient, Mr. Jacoby could meet with him that day. Seeing as how he had to drive past Wapak anyway, Jerry agreed.

Jerry walked into Jacoby's Funeral Home. John Jacoby stood in the lobby. He'd seen the car pull in through his office window. He stood, checked himself in the mirror and walked toward the lobby. When he was a young man, just starting in the profession, he made the mistake of opening the front door for a prospective "client" who had just lost a family member. Jacoby's father, John Sr., later impressed on his son that this act was "presumptuous... it simply isn't done." Nigh on 30 years later, Jacoby Jr. continued to follow his father's advice.

Jerry opened the door, spotted the mortician, and stepped to him to shake hands. Jacoby took his hand and said Mr. Hitchens, I'm John Jacoby, how can I be of service?"

Years later, Jerry wouldn't recall much of their conversation that day, until the last line Jacoby spoke, "Jerry, we'll take good care of your bride."

Jerry once again passed through Wapak on his way home from Jacoby's. He drove down Auglaize Street, the east-west street that passed through the business district. Turning south on Willipie, he saw the Wapa Theater sign and slowed.

A woman coming out of the post office across the street with a sheet of five cent National Grange postage stamps in her hand looked out at a slow-moving grey Chevy and wondered, *Is that man crying?*

After passing through Wapak, Jerry took 25A to Botkins and navigated to his house. He automatically responded to waves from two or three people as he drove through town. Not only did he have no idea who waved at him, he had no recollection of waving back. Everyone waved in Botkins. You did it without thinking. Jerry, in his state of mind, did not register any of these interactions.

Jerry came into the kitchen through the garage door. Suzy came to meet him with not just the tail, but her entire back end wagging. Jerry looked at her and burst into tears. This time he really broke down. He picked up Suzy, sat on a kitchen chair, and sobbed. Suzy licked at his tears. Jerry pushed her away a bit and looked at her. Suzy gazed back at him. This time her expectant look was completely appropriate. She had to be wondering what the hell was happening. Jerry smiled and continued to cry.

Jerry got up a few minutes later. He sighed. He walked through the kitchen into the living room and, out of habit, flipped on the TV. It was an RCA, a black and white. The boys had floated the idea of getting a color set—"The Crafts have one"—but the $1,000 price tag put that out of reach. They didn't complain much. Good boys. With the medical expenses that were coming, it might be a long time before Jerry could make a color television happen.

Jerry went back to the kitchen, opened a drawer under the sink, and removed a box of Gaines Burgers. It was past time to feed Suzy. Gaines Burgers were, well, Jerry didn't know exactly *what* they were. They were dog food, disc shaped, about the size and shape of a rice cake. They had the consistency of ground hamburger but were reddish brown. Suzy Wong loved them. Jerry unwrapped one, crumbled it (the instructions were very specific) and let it drop in the bowl.

Jerry was watching Suzy gobble her food when he heard Walter Cronkite mention Vietnam in the living room. Jerry went back, sat on the footstool, and watched a report that made him, if it was possible, even sadder than he'd felt all day.

Eddie. He had to get hold of Eddie.

And Danny.

Back in the kitchen he opened drawers until he found the Shelby County telephone book. An official at St. Rita's told Jerry that the Red Cross could facilitate getting an emergency leave for a serviceman. Botkins was in Shelby County. This meant that Jerry had to contact the office in Sidney. He had probably driven right past the Auglaize County office in Wapak a half hour earlier, but it would've done him no good to stop. Damn red tape.

Jerry opened the book to the yellow pages in the back. He realized the Red Cross office number was probably listed in the white pages in the front of the book. *Probably too late to get anyone but at least I can look up the number for tomorrow.* He was jotting the number on a piece of scrap paper when the phone rang.

It was a heavy black plastic rotary dial unit. And it was loud. He was two feet from it when it rang and it momentarily stunned him. Jerry waited through three rings then picked up, "Hello."

"This is a collect call from Danny, will you accept the charges?"

The tears came back.

As he drove toward Toledo late Tuesday afternoon, Jerry thought about Danny's call. The news had clearly shocked his son. Danny could barely speak: he'd turned the phone over to Dave Mielke.

Jerry talked with Mielke for a few minutes. He spoke to the other teachers later in the evening. He also spent time on the phone with three different Greyhound employees. By 11 pm, Danny's bus ride to Toledo was arranged. Jerry fell asleep, exhausted. He slept on the couch. He couldn't make himself use the bed.

Jerry spent most of the morning and afternoon Tuesday at the Red Cross in Sidney. He filled out several forms. He was told that he would have to provide a death certificate, or similar documentation, from the funeral home. Apparently there had been occasions where a deployed soldier was able to make it home after a friend or family member in the states fraudulently filled out the request for leave. The Red Cross, the entity between the service member and the family, was in a tough spot. Any request for this type of emergency leave now required proof positive of a death in the family and that the deceased was an immediate family member.

Jerry then rushed home and tended to Suzy. Checking the time, he decided he had time to make a couple phone calls. He called Jane's brother Jim, giving him what little news he could. Jerry asked Jim to keep the rest of the family informed, explaining that he had to get on the road. He was about to hang up when he heard a click come over the earpiece. Jerry asked, "Jim, you still there?"

"Yeah Jerry, what was that?"

"Havaners," Jerry responded. Never mind. Go ahead and make your calls Jim, I gotta go." Jerry slipped on his windbreaker and headed for the Impala.

The Havaners were neighbors across the street. They shared a party line with the Hitchens family. Each family had a separate phone number, but the phone lines shared a single circuit. Whenever a phone was in use at either house, a person at the other house could listen in by simply picking up a handset. Party lines were less expensive than private lines by about a dollar a month.

There was party line etiquette. If you went to make a call and heard the line in use, it was polite to slowly set the handset back in its cradle. This was typically repeated every few minutes. The current user, the thinking went, would get the hint and wrap up their call, allowing the other party liner access to an open circuit. It didn't always work that way. Sometimes the current user would become annoyed with frequent line checks, and would decide to extend their call just to be, as Jane would say, "spiteful."

Sometimes the party-liner waiting for the circuit to clear would slam their phone down while the other user was engaged in a call. This was the equivalent of a speeding driver coming up behind a car moving too slowly for his taste and accelerating right up to the rear bumper in an attempt to get it to move over. The pushy approach that some people used when they coveted an open line was almost always met with obstinacy.

One bold technique for seizing control of the line was to simply pick up and listen to the neighbors' private conversation. No covering of the mouthpiece to hide your presence. No response when the current user complained. Maybe even breathing hard into it to let them know you were there.

These were the dynamics of a two-party line.

There were also four-party lines. Jerry was thankful that he didn't have to contend with one of these.

The Havaners had three teenaged girls, all ravenous for phone time. Very seldom was a call made on Jerry's phone that wasn't interrupted by someone across the street. Now nearing Toledo, Jerry realized the Havaners must not have been listening closely to his phone calls since Jane had died. If they had, everyone in town would have heard the details by now, and Bob Bauman at the Gulf station was genuinely surprised to hear the news.

Danny was not surprised to see the Impala waiting in the parking lot when his bus pulled into the Greyhound station. He couldn't remember the last time his dad was late for anything. He and Doc grabbed their bags and shuffled off. They made their way toward Jerry. Danny walked to his dad and, just a bit hesitantly, put his arms around him for a quick hug. Jerry squeezed back. Mielke hung back a respectful distance. Danny pulled back and took a better look at his father.

Jerry had red, puffy eyes. He looked exhausted. He also had a grease stain under one eye and more grease on his left shoulder.

"Rough day, huh Dad?" Danny said through wet eyes.

Doc insisted on driving home. "I'm rested Mr. Hitchens, please."

Jerry relented and took the front passenger seat while Danny slid in back. As they started south, Jerry related details of his efforts to bring Eddie home on leave. Jane had been gone barely a day and Jerry was already growing weary of talking about it.

Feeling like an intruder, and sensing Jerry would welcome a change of subject, Doc offered, "We had a great time at Gettysburg."

Jerry picked up on it and asked for details. Danny talked for a few minutes about interesting features of the battlefield. Doc, trying to keep the conversation on this track said "Tell your dad about our guide."

"Oh yeah. He was cool Dad." Danny suddenly remembered a question and answer session that Fitzpatrick had with the group. Danny related that the guide had fielded four or five questions about the battle and about the town of Gettysburg when Gary Poppe asked "How did you get to be a battlefield guide?"

Fitzpatrick, who appeared to be in his early 60s, revealed that he'd lived in Hartford, Connecticut most of his life. He and his wife had raised two children. Both kids had married and moved out of state. Fitzpatrick said he worked as a salesman for 35 years, selling janitorial supplies. He travelled throughout Connecticut and nearby Rhode Island. It was steady work, but had begun to wear on him over time. He missed his kids and was tired of the constant give and take with customers.

Fitzpatrick said that he walked into the National Guard Armory in Smithfield, Rhode Island on August 25, 1962. He was told to walk back into the shop to see the head of maintenance. Fitzpatrick walked through the shop door and found himself gazing at a Civil War cannon. Not just any cannon. This one had a cannon ball sticking out of its barrel. "What the bejeezus?" he'd remembered saying.

The maintenance man, Ernie, told him the cannon had been at the Battle of Gettysburg. It had been displayed inside the State Courthouse in Providence for decades until it was discovered that there were still two and a half pounds of volatile black gunpowder inside the barrel. Ernie and his guys were preparing to drill into the barrel and remove the powder.

Fitz returned home. The next day he drove to a library and researched the cannon. He discovered It was part of Rhode Island's Battery B, First Light Artillery. During the artillery duel that preceded Pickett's Charge, on the final day of the battle, a Confederate shell exploded near the front of the Rhode Island gun. Part of the shell dented the muzzle of the gun. Other pieces of the shell killed two members of the gun crew. When the surviving members of the crew tried to load the damaged gun, they found that the cannon ball wouldn't go down the barrel. They couldn't remove it either. As the gun cooled, the ball became more solidly lodged.

The cannon became a museum piece. A very dangerous one. The maintenance workers finally removed the powder by forcing water down a hole they drilled in the barrel. When the gunpowder dried out, it fizzled and sparked.

Fitz was enthralled. He'd always been interested in the Civil War, but this was special. At company meetings, he would hear his superiors constantly say the salesmen needed to have a passion for the job.

"They were trying to light a fire under our bottoms. In my case, it backfired," he explained.

He realized his passion was somewhere else. Fitzpatrick's wife had family in Carlisle, Pennsylvania. They talked about moving. A year later, after passing the difficult test to be a licensed guide, he was working at the park and driving between Carlisle and Gettysburg.

The class of 1968 listened intently. When Fitz finished his answer, several students smiled and nodded, as did three of the chaperones. Danny noticed that Mr. Rawson frowned and shook his head. *What a jackass,* Danny thought.

As Danny finished the story, his dad smiled for what seemed like the first time in a month. "A man that figured out what's important and went for it. You don't see that very often.

Sounds like you were having a great trip, sorry it ended the way it did." Jerry's smile was gone.

Now Danny changed the subject. "Any idea when Eddie might make it back?"

Jerry turned toward the back seat to face his son. "The Red Cross says we should know something in a day or two. What's it been, a year since he was home?"

Danny wasn't exactly sure but thought that was about right.

CHAPTER SIX

Eddie reported to Army Boot Camp at Fort Dix, New Jersey a few days after graduating from Botkins High School in May of 1965. His decision to enlist was not met with enthusiasm by his parents, especially by his mom. Vietnam was beginning to heat up.

The Gulf of Tonkin incident occurred on August 2, 1964. This was a confusing naval engagement involving the destroyer USS Maddox. Two days later, a similar incident took place involving the destroyer Turner Joy. There were no American casualties, but assessments that the North Vietnamese had attacked the ships led directly to Congress, on August 10, passing the Gulf of Tonkin Resolution. This gave President Lyndon Johnson authority to escalate the Vietnam conflict with conventional forces without a formal declaration of war. Up to that time there were fewer than 25,000 US military personnel in Vietnam, many of them special forces acting in an advisory role. After the resolution, there was a significant escalation.

Eddie was working at the lumberyard that summer. He'd already talked with the Army recruiter in nearby Piqua a couple of times. Mr. Gerber allowed speakers to be hung in the corners of the work floor. On most days, music could be heard in between the shrieking sound of table saws ripping through sheets of plywood. The week of the Tonkin incidents, Eddie asked for the radio to be tuned to a news channel. He hung on every word. This did not go over well with some of the men in the shop. Chief among them William "Don't Call Me Bill" Doyle. A ponderous, red-headed former Kentuckian.

Eddie rode home from work with his dad most days. He would flip on the car radio for the five-minute drive home. He made sure to be in front of the RCA television set promptly at six. He took in every word by CBS's Walter Cronkite on the subject and flipped to Chet Huntley and David Brinkley on NBC when other subjects filled the screen. Eddie nearly wore out the dial flipping between channels 2 and 7. It drove his parents crazy. Eventually the VHF dial loosened and occasionally came off when it was turned. When this happened, the user had to rotate the circular dial, lining it up precisely with the oblong shaped prong, now naked, and fit it back on with precision. When the Milton Bradley product "Operation" came out in 1965, an electronic game that prized dexterity and punished those without steady hands with an annoying buzzing sound, the feat of television dial repair was christened "TV Operation" by thousands of Americans.

Eddie also followed the conflict through newspapers. The Hitchens family had subscriptions to both the Sidney Daily News and the Wapakoneta Daily News. Danny was a paperboy for the latter. Every day, 52 Wapakoneta newspapers would be dropped off in front of the Hitchens garage. Danny would deliver one to each of his 49 customers. The three extra papers were to be used as replacements for damaged copies or to be sold outright to non-subscribers. Sales of the three extras almost never happened. Replacement of damaged copies did, nearly every day.

Danny, then 14 years old, idolized his brother. If Eddie was interested in something, Danny would be too. His first attempt to gain more knowledge of Vietnam was to examine the family's collection of World Book Encyclopedias. Nearly two years previous, Jane Hitchens had succumbed to the pitch of a traveling salesman. Randomly ringing doorbells in Botkins, this man struck gold with Jane. His hook: "Don't you want the best for your children Mrs. *Hutchings*? Don't you want to give them every opportunity to succeed?"

Jane had very little sales resistance. In her mind, it was rude to offer objections. She didn't even correct the man when he used the incorrect surname in his presentation.

Jane had selected the installment plan option. Every two months the Hitchens household would receive a package containing one part of a 19-volume set of the cream and forest green tomes. Jane hoped to hide the $9.99 bills from Jerry for

49

as long as possible. This plan fell apart about the time volume four, *D,* appeared. Jerry picked up the mail one day while Jane was visiting Ruth Bauman and the jig was up. He had assumed the boys had checked out *A, B,* and *C* from the library.

Danny's attempt to glean knowledge of Vietnam from World Book fizzled when he realized that volume 18, a compendium that featured *U* through *V,* had not yet been shipped to them. The Hitchens library by 1964 was devoid of information beyond volume 15, *Q* through *R.*

Danny then turned to the village library, which apparently had chosen the "Buy Entire Set" option, and was disappointed to find several pages that described the flowers and fauna of the country but had mostly confusing references to "Indochina." Vietnam remained a mystery to Danny, as it did to most Americans.

Eddie excelled at boot camp. He had always been a team player. He played baseball, basketball, and ran track at Botkins. He'd lay down a bunt, set a pick, or fill in to run a relay leg. The coaches loved him. This carried over at Fort Dix. He had a positive attitude and followed instructions to the letter.

This paid off, particularly on the rifle range. He qualified Expert with the M-14. This was the highest level possible. Eddie had very few bad habits when it came to shooting. The sum total of his experience with a rifle before joining the Army was plinking at targets in the woods with Danny's .22.

Danny bought the rifle when he was 14. He'd been delivering the Wapak paper for nearly a year and had saved $50. He made about $5 a week. He'd use some of the money for "necessities" like baseball cards and candy bars. He would usually have a dollar or two each week to contribute to savings. He would ride his bike to the bank and make a deposit, using his small paper bank book to register the transaction.

A couple months into his career as a paper boy, Danny spotted the rifle in the small sporting goods department at the Western Auto store in Sidney. He was tagging along with his mom on a shopping trip.

"Wow, that's cool," he said at a volume level designed to get Jane's attention.

She followed his eyes to the gun on the rack. Jane was well aware that Danny, like most boys she knew, was attracted to action, and guns seemed to be a part of this. In most of Danny's favorite TV shows and movies, guns played a role in the good guys righting a wrong. He didn't particularly like Westerns, "Too much girl drama," but would sit through an hour episode of *Gunsmoke* to see Marshal Matt Dillon deliver payback to the villain in the final scene, usually with his Colt .45.

Jane considered Danny's fascination with firearms normal. When he asked if he would be allowed to buy a rifle "with my own money if I can save enough from my paper route," Jane responded "We'll see."

That got her out of the Western Auto without a debate. Jane smiled at Danny, but was a bit disconcerted as they walked to the car.

Eddie hadn't been home to Botkins since August, 1965. He'd completed Boot Camp at Fort Dix and was granted a ten day leave before reporting to his assigned unit at Fort Campbell, Kentucky.

Eddie would be a rifleman in the 173rd Airborne Brigade. Another member of Eddie's Boot Camp, Tommy Christopher, was also assigned to Fort Campbell. Tommy was from Tennessee. Tommy's father drove to New Jersey, picked up both soldiers, and gave Eddie a ride back to Ohio.

The changes in Eddie were obvious. His body had seemed to harden. He had short hair. He called adults "Sir" or "Ma'am." Danny had always idolized Eddie, but this incarnation of his brother, "Army Eddie," took it to a new

51

level. Eddie spent the ten days eating his mom's stuffed peppers and fried chicken, catching up with friends, and hanging out with Danny. Jerry Hitchens arranged for Danny to have several days off from his summer job at the lumberyard while Eddie was home.

The Hitchens boys went up to Cole Field, the ballpark across from the high school, and played one-on-one baseball games. In the heat of August, they wore shorts with no shirts. Each brother would pick a big-league team. Depending on a players' real-life specifications, they would bat either right or left-handed. Danny, for example, would bat left-handed when mimicking Reds switch hitting second baseman Pete Rose while facing Cubs right handed ace Ferguson Jenkins, portrayed by Eddie. He would bat right-handed when Tony Perez, an actual righty, came to the plate. Balls in play would be assessed by both brothers and the result would be agreed upon.

"That's a double down the line for Ernie Banks, Glenn Beckert scores from first." There were frequent disagreements.

"That's a base hit up the middle for Pinson."

"No way!!! Kessinger gets to that ball and throws him out."

Disagreements were settled by the logic, or volume, of each brothers' argument. Several times during the week passers-by saw Eddie and Danny standing on the infield between home plate and the pitcher's mound, gesturing wildly and shouting at each other while covered in sweat. Curiously, the brothers had smiles on their faces.

Eddie drove Danny a couple miles north of town to shoot the .22 several times that week. They went to a large stand of trees known as the boy scout woods. No one seemed to know who owned this land. The local Boy Scouts would use it for their annual camp out. The rest of the year it served as an open area for shooting or hunting for anyone with the inclination.

Eddie, Danny soon discovered, was now a magician with the rifle. Their skills had been roughly equivalent before Eddie left for boot camp. Now, firing through open sights, Eddie never missed: at any distance. Eddie explained the shooting techniques he was taught at Fort Dix. He said that one of the instructors at the rifle range was fond of saying "I can teach any 18-year-old boy in America to hit at target at 300 yards if he'll just get the shit out of his ears and do what I tell him."

Danny thought this was hilarious, but saw the evidence of this wisdom when watching Eddie nail target after target. Danny tried to follow Eddie's instructions to the letter. He mimicked Eddie's shooting positions, breathing patterns, and slow trigger pulls. Danny began to hit shots at ranges he'd never before approached.

Danny repeatedly asked Eddie for information about the Army rifle range and qualification standards, Eddie explained that recruits had several weeks of instruction with the M-14 before qualification day. On that day, they would be asked to take 40 shots. The test consisted of 10 rounds slow fire standing at 100 yards, 10 rounds rapid fire sitting at 200 yards, 10 rounds rapid fire prone at 300 yards, and 10 rounds prone slow at 500 yards. The number of hits was totaled to arrive at a final score. Twenty-three to twenty-nine hits gained the shooter "Marksman" status. Thirty to 35 attained "Sharpshooter." Those hitting thirty-six to forty were designated "Expert."

Eddie had scored thirty-seven. Hearing this, Danny realized his mouth was hanging open. *Five hundred yards!,* he marveled.

"What's it like shooting a real rifle like the '14? How much does it kick?" Danny peppered his brother with questions.

Eddie patiently fielded every inquiry, then said "We should get you something bigger. A .308 is basically the same round we use in the '14. Those rifles are easy to find." He hesitated "Of course, mom would have a cow."

Danny realized his mind had wandered. His dad was turned to him from the front seat with a questioning look on his face. "I'm sorry Dad, what?"

"I just wondered if you want to stop for something to eat before we get home. Were almost to Lima."

Danny brightened a bit. "Can we go to the Red Barn?"

Danny saw his dad's eyes flick down a bit and realized why. The Red Barn restaurant sat directly behind St. Rita's Medical Center.

Danny recovered and asked "Wait, how about McDonalds? Its closer to the interstate and the food is just about the same."

Jerry smiled and said "Sure. That sound OK with you Mr. Mielke?"

Even adults in Botkins adhered to the rules of proper respect for teachers.

"Please call me Doc, Mr. Hitchens." Mielke urged.

"OK, then call me Jerry."

They pulled off the highway at exit 125. This was one of several exits at Lima, a city of about 50,000. They had a remaining drive of about a half hour to get to Botkins. They drove toward the glowing golden arches that seemed to bolt the restaurant to the ground like two giant yellow croquet wickets. Doc pulled into the drive-through and all three studied the menu board as they waited on a couple cars in front of them. All three realized they were famished. The Hershey bars that Jerry had accepted from Bob Bauman had been dispatched miles ago.

Compiling their requests in his head, Doc placed the order through the microphone on the board when prompted by the attendant. Danny grinned when he realized Doc had requested two hamburgers, two cheeseburgers, a large fry, and large Coke for himself. Jerry seemed to feel Danny's expression but avoided turning to look. He didn't think they could avoid laughing, even on this night.

Danny ordered two hamburgers. The bouquet of burgers and fries that filled the Impala as the bags were handed over was intoxicating. All three began to work on their meals. Danny fell in love with fast food the first time he tried it. At the age of eight, he'd ridden along to Lima with Andy Craft and his parents, Dave and Caroline. They went to Lima to visit the new American Mall to do some Christmas shopping. Dave suggested they try a new restaurant, the Red Barn. As they pulled into the parking lot, it became evident how the eatery got its name. The building literally looked like a red barn. One with glass covering most of the front of the structure.

The taste of hamburgers from the Red Barn and those from McDonalds were, to eight-year-old Danny, indistinguishable. The key, he believed, was the combination of ketchup and mustard along with just the right amount of onions. Combining the condiments was a stroke of genius. It had never occurred to him. Danny tried to duplicate this taste at home when his mom fried burgers but could never come close. There was something about the flavor of the ketchup, he thought, that completely changed the equation. Store-bought Heinz Ketchup or Hunts Catsup couldn't pull it off. Danny asked his mom to try every brand on the grocery shelf. He never unlocked the secret.

Young Danny saw the Red Barn and McDonalds as two equal entities with very comparable food. Seventeen-year-old Danny, now riding in the Impala on I-75, had seen several hundred TV commercials for McDonalds. He now understood that the differences between the independently owned, single location, Red Barn and the rapidly expanding juggernaut of McDonalds could be measured in light years.

Still, he thought, the food tasted about the same.

As they neared Wapakoneta, Danny reached for his second hamburger. At the same time, Doc pulled his fourth out of the bag. Danny told himself to never get in an eating contest with the History teacher. Conversation had dwindled as the threesome enjoyed their food. Jerry broke the silence when he said "Your mom asked me to drive through Wapak on our way to the hospital yesterday. I think she wanted to see the town one last time... just in case."

Danny stopped chewing as his dad continued. "She really wanted to see the Wapa Theater."

Danny was instantly flooded with memories of going to movies with his mom at the Wapa. Jane took the boys whenever spending money was available and it fit the family schedule. The Hitchens family attended movies at other theaters, but the Wapa was their favorite.

The Wapa Theater had one screen. It would show a movie for a week, beginning on Friday night. Unless the movie was so popular that it was held over for a second week, a rarity, another film would begin its run the following Friday. Eddie and Danny stayed up to date on upcoming movies by watching the coming attractions notices in the newspaper. If an action film was scheduled, the boys began lobbying early in the week to get it on the agenda. Jane was able to work in one movie like "Roustabout" with Elvis Presley (one of her favorite entertainers) for every three action flicks such as "The Guns of Navarone," "The Alamo," and "Battle of the Bulge."

Occasionally a compromise was reached. Usually it was a comedy like "The Absent Minded Professor." Abruptly, Danny realized that his mom enjoyed the movie experience not because of the actors or storylines. She loved going because she was spending time with her boys. Tears now trickled out of both of Danny's eyes.

"Doc, can you get off at Wapak and drive by the theater on the way home?"

Mielke was tired and anxious to get home but there was no way he was going to turn down Danny's request. He got off I-75 at exit 111, Bellefontaine Street. He guided the Impala west, passing a few restaurants and other small businesses. It was 9:30 on a weeknight and there was little activity.

Doc made a series of turns and the trio found themselves on Auglaize Street. The Wapa was on Willipie Street, which T'd into Auglaize a couple blocks ahead. As they cleared that intersection, Jerry, Danny, and Doc found their eyes drawn to the large L-shaped neon sign. It was red, yellow, blue, and spectacular. Danny looked at the marquee, "The Busy Body," starring Sid Caesar and Robert Ryan, was advertised.

"Mom probably would've loved it" he said softly. When the next teardrop rolled down his face, it curved around lips upturned in a smile.

It was now the last leg of a brutal trip. Seven miles to Botkins. They passed the Neil Armstrong sign on the south end of town and Jerry asked "Danny, you remember the parade last year, right? Your mom and I were laughing about it when we came through here Monday."

Danny managed a quick laugh.

"You sure weren't laughing about it that day."

The welcome home parade that Wapakoneta put on for Neil Armstrong in April of 1966 was, unquestionably, the most celebrated event in the history of West Central Ohio. Danny discovered the details of the event before anyone in Botkins due to his role as a carrier for the Wapakoneta Daily News. The papers were dropped at the houses of the three Botkins paperboys (there were no papergirls in town in 1966). In the summer, industrious carriers would knock out their deliveries in the morning and have the rest of the day for sandlot baseball or visits to the community swimming pool. If the delivery boy waited until later in the day, he had to deal with the summer heat as well as phone calls from impatient customers.

From September through May, however, it was understood by subscribers that their copy would not arrive until the paperboys were released from school.

Danny got up every school day during his freshman and sophomore years, opened the garage door, and retrieved the papers. There were two bundles waiting for him each morning. The bundles were secured by twine. Danny would cut the twine with a jackknife kept on a workbench in the back corner of the garage. He'd reach under the bench and pull out the canvas "WAPAKONETA DAILY NEWS" carrier bag that he tossed there at the end of each delivery run. The letters were three inches high, emblazoned on the bag in jet black. Danny would carefully count the papers, making sure he had a sufficient number. If shorted, he'd have to call the newspaper office to request more copies.

His dad was not happy when this happened. Wapak, just a short drive away, had a different area code than Botkins. Wapak was 419. Botkins was 513. It was a long-distance call to the newspaper home office. This call would be billed to the Hitchens household.

Danny woke up early on a Monday in late March, 1966. He put on his slippers and grabbed a jacket on his way through the door to the garage. He hit the automatic opener and felt a chilly wind flow in under the rising door. His newspapers were waiting. Danny quickly shuffled over and grabbed the stacks. He was about to duck back inside the garage with bundles in hand when he saw the headline on the front page "WELCOME CELEBRATION PLANNED FOR HOMETOWN SPACEMAN."

"Alright!!," Danny said out loud.

Like many in the region, Danny had hoped for a chance to actually lay eyes on Neil Armstrong. He had cut out an article from the March 14 edition of the Wapak paper, two days before the Gemini 8 launch, in which Wapakoneta Chamber of Commerce President Don Wittwer was quoted as saying "all of the other astronauts have been permitted to return to their home towns. We're working on the assumption that he is going to return to his home town. We'll be ready for him when and if he does come."

That article left some doubt in Danny's head that there would actually be a parade. Danny had clipped it out and thumbtacked it to a cork board in his room. Subsequent stories in the paper about the Gemini 8 mission and a possible homecoming parade were added to the March 14 clipping. Danny's bulletin board was now overflowing. Until viewing this morning's headline, however, he still had doubts that Neil would return to the area.

Danny dropped one bundle, stacked the second one on top of it, and eased down to his knees to read the details. The sun was beginning to rise but it wasn't yet fully light out. The article laid out the plans for the upcoming homecoming parade in great detail. Danny had been waiting for this. He wanted to make sure he had as much information as possible. He had every intention of attending the event even if, as he now read, it would take place on a school day.

The event would be on Wednesday, April 13 and...

"DANNY!"

When he looked back inside the garage, he saw his mom in the doorway to the kitchen. She wore a robe and was pulling it tight around her upper body. "You left the door open and its freezing in here. What are you doing out there?"

Danny responded "Reading about the Neil Armstrong parade, Mom. It's all here in the paper."

"Well close the garage door and come in. Let's see what the Wapak Daily has to say."

Jane made herself a cup of Maxwell House instant coffee. It was their freeze-dried version. Jane believed that, if pressed, not one person in Botkins could explain the freeze-dried process. But the coffee seemed fine to her.

Jane and Danny sat at the table and pored over the two copies of the paper he'd brought in. By 6:30 in the morning they had pretty much formulated the plan for parade day. The plan went through some minor revisions when Jerry got involved, but for the most part remained intact.

On April 13, however, almost nothing went as designed.

The plan was simple, really. It was based on information gleaned from the Wapak paper. Neil Armstrong and his family were to leave Houston, Texas early on the morning of the 13th. They would land at Allen County Airport, around 10 am. The airport was just south of Lima, about 15 miles north of Wapakoneta. After some brief fanfare, a motorcade would travel south on I-75, merge onto State Route 33 just past Wapakoneta, drive west for 3 miles, then leave the highway, turning back north for a quarter mile or so. They would arrive at the Auglaize County Fairgrounds on the west side of Wapakoneta.

There would be a press conference at the fairgrounds. The parade units would be assembled there, and at 11:30 am, a Wapakoneta police car and an Auglaize County Sheriff's unit would lead the first unit out of the fairgrounds gate, onto Auglaize Street, and turn right, toward town. There were impressive, historic homes on both sides of this wide roadway.

Auglaize Street ran northeast from the fairgrounds for a mile or so, roughly following the line of the Auglaize River, which flowed along 100 yards or so to the north. There were no roads between Auglaize Street and the river.

One mile northeast of the fairgrounds, both the river and Auglaize Street itself veered due east, maintaining a more or less parallel track. Blackhoof Street ran due north from this bend, crossing the river and leading travelers toward the new high school, a mile distant. A person standing back on Auglaize Street at the bend and looking east would see the heart of the Wapakoneta business district. Stores, banks, fraternal clubs, and bars jammed this stretch and extended four blocks east, where it crossed a railroad track.

Beyond the railroad track, the retail establishments tapered off. Auglaize Street would be swallowed by a hodge-podge of other streets on the east side of town. Interstate 75 and its requisite collection of travel related businesses was located here, perhaps a mile from the business district.

Between the fairgrounds and the eastward bend that took it through the heart of town, several other streets ran into Auglaize Street. These streets intersected with, or ended at, Auglaize Street. Some did so from the south, some from the east.

The key four block, historic downtown section of Auglaize Street had been preparing for the parade for at least a week. It would be strewn with banners and plastered with signs. As the Wapakoneta Daily News had reported, the parade would proceed up Auglaize Street from the fairgrounds for several blocks, swing right (east) on Pearl, then make a series of turns through city streets before reemerging on Auglaize Street near the railroad tracks. With a left turn that had it moving due west, the procession would then traverse the four most festooned blocks of the route.

This, no doubt, would be the section that produced the bulk of the media coverage. Reaching Blackhoof, the entire collection would turn north and meander through several blocks before arriving at the high school. A banquet honoring Armstrong would start sometime after 1 pm. This was to be followed by a reception that included films of the Gemini 8 Mission.

Danny thought they should leave the house that morning by 10 am. One of the articles in the paper said at least 15,000 people were expected to attend the parade. Another pegged the number at as many as 25,000. This would be more than double, and possibly four times, the number of people that resided in Wapakoneta.

Danny and his parents would stop down the street and pick up Reed Thompson. There was no question in Danny's mind that Reedo would want to go. They would take drinks, sandwiches, a camera, and rain jackets. The weather forecast called for intermittent showers and temperatures in the forties. Reedo and his brothers owned a set of walkie-talkies. These would also make the trip.

The early departure would get them to Wapakoneta two hours before the start of the parade. They would find a prime parking spot a few short blocks from the key stretch of Auglaize Street. The foursome would make their way to the business district, toting their supply of baloney sandwiches and Cokes. Once ensconced in the perfect viewing spot, Danny and Reed would take one of the walkie-talkies and walk a mile or so toward the fairgrounds to the southwest. They would stake out a second great spot. This would allow them an additional view of the astronaut. It would also allow them to give a running play by play to Jerry's parents, who were saving them spots on Auglaize Street, presumably enjoying a nice outdoor lunch.

Jerry and Jane could ask pertinent questions about the composition of the parade over the handsets, allowing them to adjust their position as necessary. Danny and Reed would return to Auglaize Street a few minutes before the key components of the parade units. They should have a few minutes to grab a sandwich and a Coke.

Jerry, Jane, Danny, and Reedo would be in position for some great photographs. They would then leisurely make their way to the car to beat the traffic out of town. The afternoon activities scheduled at the high school were ticketed events. They'd had no luck obtaining passes, but they would have a fantastic day.

CHAPTER SEVEN

"Son-of-a-BITCH!!!"

Jerry Hitchens was not happy. The last two hours had not gone well. He hated to be late. He made a point to be on time for everything, even for events that he didn't want to attend. Early mass on Christmas day? Jerry was on time. The annual invasive physical examination for the insurance company? He reported early. The Thursday night card club that Jane loved? Even that.

Jerry had taken a day off work to take Danny to the parade. He had worked at the Botkins Lumber Company for over twenty years. This had earned him the maximum number of annual vacation days possible, ten. He had taken a week off earlier in the year. Burning a day today lowered his remaining days for the rest of 1966 to four. Once it was decided they'd leave at 10 o'clock and get to Wapak by 10:30, well, they should stick to the plan. But it wasn't meant to be.

First, Jane was on the phone with her sister-in-law until almost 10:15. Carolyn King was married to Jane's brother Jim. Carolyn had called at 9:25. She claimed she'd been trying for a half hour but the line was busy. Apparently the Havaners had been using their phone. Jane was too polite to cut the call with Carolyn short. She patiently listened, occasionally nodding and murmuring "Is that right?" or "That's nice." Jerry stood in the open doorway to the garage. Danny was in the back seat of the car with the food and drink. The Impala's motor was running.

During the call, Jerry pointed to the car, pointed to the clock in the kitchen, and pointed to his watch. Jane nodded, and finally said to Carolyn, "Well, I guess I'll let you go." This was polite-person code for "I'm hanging up now."

Jerry helped Jane with her raincoat and asked "What was that all about?"

"She was asking where I thought we should get together for Christmas this year," Jane explained.

Jerry was incredulous. "Let's go!"

The temperature hovered around 40 degrees. The air felt damp. Clouds, roughly the color of an old sidewalk, obscured the sky. Jerry drove the two blocks west to the Thompsons's just a bit too fast.

They pulled in at the Thompson house 20 minutes late. The Thompsons lived in a single story, three-bedroom structure known as a California bungalow. It was painted seaweed green. There was a carport connected to the right side.

Ten-year-old Teddy Thompson, Reed's younger brother, stood watching the street from the partially open front door. He was wearing pajamas. When the car pulled into the drive, Teddy turned, shouted something, and pushed through the door. There was a small concrete front porch surrounding the front door. It was bordered by a brick wall, about three feet high and topped with smooth, weathered concrete.

Teddy hopped up on the porch wall and twisted his body to face the Hitchens family Impala. "Hi Danny!" he shouted. "Reed's comin', I yelled at him."

Teddy had mussed strawberry-blonde hair and a face full of freckles. His eyes looked a bit red and his nose was running. He had a twelve-inch-tall metal robot in one hand. He strode barefoot across the cold, moist porch, sat on the concrete ledge, and steadied the robot.

"Watch my Atomic Robot walk the ledge!" Teddy flipped a switch on the robot's back and it began to shuffle across the ledge, lights flashing.

The front door flew open and a slightly flustered Ginny Thompson rushed through. "Teddy! You march right back to bed this minute!"

Sensing it might be construed as impolite to remain in the car, Jerry and Jane got out and took a few steps toward Ginny.

Virginia Thompson was a blonde woman in her early forties. She had intelligent eyes and stood 5'6" when she wasn't bending over to pick up the toys, dirty clothing or sundry sporting goods strewn about the house by her three sons. She was raising her three boys on her own, having divorced from the boys' father, Jim, six years earlier.

"I had to take a day off today to take Teddy to the doctor." Ginny said. "I was afraid he had the mumps, but Dr. Bergman doesn't think so. Back to bed Mister." Ginny guided Teddy toward the door.

"Bye Danny, say hi to Neil for me!" Teddy shouted.

Danny, now leaning against the rear driver's side door, laughed and said "Will do Teddy!"

The Thompson's front door swung open again and Reed burst though. He was clutching two walkie-talkies to his chest with one arm and thrusting the other into the sleeve of a raincoat. Reed trotted to the passenger side and reached for the rear door handle. He shouted "Bye Mom" over his shoulder as he ducked inside. Danny slid in beside him.

"Sorry Danny, Mom must've moved the walkie-talkies after I went to bed last night. They weren't on the table where I left them. I had to look all over for them."

Jerry returned to his spot behind the steering wheel. Jane, however, stood chatting with Ginny.

Jerry closed his eyes and slowly rubbed his forehead.

Jane finally turned toward the car. She hesitated, turned back, and wiggled her fingers while smiling at the front picture window. All eyes turned to see the intended target of the wave. There stood Teddy, wiping his runny nose with a pajama sleeve. The Atomic Robot was now patrolling the window ledge.

Ginny went inside to shoo Teddy back to bed. Jane got back in the car. Jerry sighed and backed down the drive. It was now nearly 10:40.

Jerry thought he could make up some time on the way to Wapakoneta. This possibility quickly went down the tubes. Jerry caught a red light at one of the two stoplights in Botkins. As he waited for it to change he couldn't help but notice that

65

there was a steady stream of traffic approaching the light from his right. It was coming down State Street from the direction of the highway. All of the vehicles, he counted eight of them, turned north toward Wapak. When the light changed, Jerry followed. He realized there were dozens of cars and trucks ahead of him. Apparently, many parade-goers that lived to the south had decided to get off at Botkins and take 25A north, rather than risk running into worse traffic at the main Wapakoneta exit.

Jerry glanced at his watch and clenched his jaw.

A little over two miles from the Wapak city limits, traffic slowed. Jerry was more than cognizant of the fact that he hadn't reached 45 miles per hour since leaving Botkins. Already irritated, he realized that he would be rolling to a stop directly in front of a large rendering plant, which sat on the west side of 25A. On windy days, the peculiar odor generated by the plant could be detected for miles. On this day there was a breeze. The air was laden with moisture, and, this close to the plant, was absolutely saturated with the stench of putrefaction.

Adults in Botkins assured their kids that the plant was an important area employer and performed a necessary function, but none of Danny's buddies really knew what a rendering plant did. Theories included "They throw dead animals in a vat and melt them down" (Gary Poppe), "They pick up grease from restaurants and turn it into jello" (Chris Gerber), and "They take left-over carcasses from butcher shops. You know, heads and hoofs and shit that's left over after the meat's chopped off, and cook it down and make the capsule part of medicine that melts in your mouth. You know, like Contact cold medicine has." (Johnny Muhlenkamp).

Danny leaned toward the last theory. After all, Muhlenkamp was a farm boy. Wasn't he supposed to know this "shit?"

Because of Muhlenkamp's postulation, Danny generally stuck with Bayer Aspirin when he needed non-prescription medication.

"Geez, look at all the Gut Wagons." This from Reed.

Gut Wagons were the bright purple trucks that returned to the plant at the end of each work day, fairly bursting with heads and hoofs and shit. Drivers did not want to be caught behind a rendering truck on the roads, particularly on a hot day.

It looked like the entire fleet was parked inside of the fence surrounding the facility. "They must've given everyone the day off to go to the parade," Jane offered.

After another 10 minutes of stop and go progress, the Hitchens family Impala approached the city limits. A large billboard proclaimed:

Welcome Home
NEIL ARMSTRONG
WAPAKONETA AREA
CHAMBER OF COMMERCE

The billboard was blue with black lettering. The left side of the sign showed a celestial view of planet Earth with a rocket, presumably Gemini 8, speeding away from the planet.

At an intersection, a hundred feet or so beyond the billboard, two Ohio State troopers directed traffic. Jerry just had time to mutter "I don't like the looks of this," when the trooper on the left pointed at them and motioned for them to turn to the west. There would be no primo parking spot near the downtown area.

It was at this point that Jerry unloaded his "Son-of-a-BITCH!!!"

The line of traffic was crawling in the direction of the fairgrounds. Neil would be there, participating in the press conference. In a few short minutes the parade would begin.

The units would leave the fairgrounds via the north gate and angle right, up Auglaize Street toward the downtown area. The Impala was approaching the southeast corner of the fairground. The north gate was at least a half mile away.

"We gotta find a place to park Dad!" Danny pleaded.

"I know, dammit!" Jerry shot back.

"Jerry!" Jane hissed.

Reed tried to act like he hadn't noticed the tension. He and Danny swung their heads in all directions looking for a spot on the street.

There were dozens of people hurrying along the sidewalks. A few darted between vehicles, drawing bursts from car horns. Boys, girls, and some adults were cutting through yards.

Jerry came to a fairly wide cross street. Turning right, he spotted an opening about 75 feet ahead. He had to wedge his 4-door Chevrolet into the spot by parallel parking. Danny recalled how he'd struggled with this maneuver during drivers' education.

Jerry nailed it on his first try, perhaps the only thing that had gone right all day.

The group scrambled to assemble their gear. Jerry said "Mom and I will still take the food. We'll walk straight uptown. You boys run up to see the beginning of the parade. By the time you work your way uptown, we should have a spot. Take the walkie-talkie and remember where we're parked." Reed grabbed one of the walkie-talkies from the back seat.

Standing outside the car now, all four of them turned their bodies looking for a street sign. "Dearbaugh!" Reed shouted. "We're on Dearbaugh."

A marching band was playing up ahead of them. "Go-Go!" Jerry shouted. "We'll try to get a spot close to the Bi-Rite. Call on the walkie-talkie when you get close to us!"

Reed and Danny sprinted due north up Dearbaugh. Auglaize Street was a few hundred yards ahead. A slow-moving group of six or eight older folks were in front of them now, walking abreast down the middle of the street.

"This way" Danny shouted to Reed over the music. They cut around the right of the group, squeezing past a street sign. Vine Street ran off to the right. A block ahead they flashed past Benton Street. Then they were at Auglaize Street. Directly ahead of them was a float with a red, white and blue sign "Auglaize County WWI Veterans."

"Wow" said Danny, looking at Reed, eyes wide. About a dozen men waved from the float. Danny thought a couple of them didn't look that much older than his dad. How could that be? Others looked more aged and worn out. But all of them looked happy to be included in the festivities. Danny didn't know as much about The Great War as he felt he should. He made a mental note to bone up on it the next time he visited the Botkins library.

Several open convertibles were easing toward them from the left. To the right, they could see the backs of the color guard carrying their flags. In front of them, a very professional looking, and sounding, marching band was just approaching an odd Y-shaped intersection.

"That was the Air Force Marching Band from Dayton." offered a woman next to Danny. "They were fantastic!" Danny nodded to her and smiled.

Their position put them about a quarter mile from the fairgrounds gate. Looking to his left, Danny saw a line of a half dozen or so cars crawling in his direction. Newspaper stories stated that Neil and his family would be in the third car. Supposedly the order of march had the Armstrongs in that position so that they would reach the high school before most of the other participants. This would allow Neil and family to climb a reviewing stand to watch the rest of the marchers go by.

Danny had his doubts, thinking organizers might decide to put the astronaut at the end of the parade. When he saw two convertibles, one black and one white, emerge from the fairgrounds then arrange themselves side by side as they pointed down Auglaize Street, Danny knew that parade officials had stuck to the original plan.

Behind each car was a bright red trailer, perhaps twelve feet long and six feet wide. Each of them had open wooden rails on three sides.

The press trailers! They were jammed with men, most of whom wore dark rain coats and Dick Tracy-style hats. Danny saw cameras of several shapes and sizes. The rear of each trailer was open, allowing riders to step on and off at their convenience to position themselves for shots at different angles.

The attention of the press photographers was focused on the red convertible behind them. Sitting on top of the rear seat was a smiling Neil Armstrong. A man that had actually been to space was about to ride past Danny! He felt himself momentarily go motionless, then felt a slap on his back. He turned to see a smiling Reedo, who was saying something that Danny couldn't quite make out.

The Air Force band was marching away from them to the right. Another band, it looked like Wapak High School's, was now about to come through the fairground gate. One band was playing "The Star-Spangled Banner" while the other performed "Stars and Stripes Forever." The notes of both songs intermixed with shouts from the crowd to make it difficult to have a conversation. They both turned their attention back to the left to see Neil, who was now waving to happy spectators on both sides of the street.

At this point in the route, parade goers were bunched here and there, two or three deep for a stretch, a gap for a few feet, then a single file, before joining another deeper group. Danny knew it would be jammed downtown and thought this would be his best opportunity to get a good look at Armstrong.

Danny got Reed's attention and pointed to an open spot about thirty feet to their right. Reedo nodded and the pair hustled over. They wedged themselves in between two clusters, aware that viewers were quickly closing in around them. Glancing to his rear, Danny saw that there were still a few people coming up Dearbaugh, most now running, hoping to not miss out on a close-up view of the spaceman.

The press trailers eased past the boys. One trailer seemed to be filled with still photographers while the other contained movie cameramen and commentators holding microphones. Each of the latter were facing a movie camera, their backs to the Armstrong car, prattling away. It was difficult to tell how many media members were assigned to the trailers. Danny counted over fifteen. They continually hopped on and off, swarming around the Armstrong vehicle, trying to get just the right angle. Danny had read that dozens, perhaps hundreds, were expected to attend. Most were no doubt stationed throughout the parade route.

As the media vehicles passed, Danny and Reed had an unobstructed view of the approaching Armstrong car. It was a large bright red, 1963 Pontiac Bonneville convertible. Danny didn't know this. He didn't know his car models that well and, anyway, didn't concern himself with such a minor detail while focusing on the celebrity sitting atop the back seat.

The car was driven by a member of the VFW who was dressed in an olive colored uniform. He wore a narrow hat of the same color in the style, Eddie had old Danny, that was known as an "overseas cap." He appeared to be about 60 years old and wore glasses and an intermittent smile.

Janet Armstrong sat above the back seat, directly behind the driver. She wore a knee length, light blue overcoat to protect against the chill. She had on dark gloves and wore a white, oversized pillbox style hat that wrapped around her jet-black hair. Danny thought she was pretty and that she looked happy.

Next to Janet sat the Armstrong's oldest son, Ricky. Eight years old, Ricky wore dark blue pants, a blue and white checkered sport coat, and a dark tie. Danny noted with a smile that Ricky had not yet won the argument about having longer hair, as the astronaut's son was sporting a decidedly uncool crewcut. But, thought Danny, isn't that what you'd expect from the son of a fighter jock/test pilot/astronaut?

The youngest member of the Armstrong family, three-year-old Mark, was not present. Danny briefly wondered about this. All of the newspaper stories confirmed that the whole family would attend. Maybe the combination of travel and a cool weather was a bit much for the little guy. Danny wondered if Mark was with extended family members somewhere in Wapakoneta.

Neil sat on the passenger side, wearing a dark suit, striped tie, and a dark overcoat. He also had a crewcut. Danny knew that Armstrong had a spectacular history. The pilot's military career and years as a test pilot were well-chronicled in the Wapakoneta Daily News. Media attention had increased exponentially when Neil was selected to be a member of the Gemini program, America's second group of astronauts, joining the original Mercury Seven.

Six members of an Air Force Security detachment from Wright Patterson Air Force Base in Dayton walked along with the car. They wore dress blue uniforms, white military caps with black bills, and white gloves. They wore matching sunglasses. There were three on each side of the vehicle. The first man on either side was roughly even with the rear tire and had two men trailing him, equally spaced. The security men kept their eyes straight ahead, reminding Danny of the red-coated guards outside of Buckingham Palace.

As the convertible neared Danny and Reed's position, Neil was looking off to the left, waving with his left hand. His position on the passenger side of the vehicle put him no more than ten feet from them. He turned to the right as he drew even with the boys. He was now waving with his right hand and, Danny thought, was looking directly at them with a big smile on his face.

The car rolled northeasterly up Auglaize. The three Air Force Security men screening the right side now somewhat obstructed Danny's view. He noted banners hanging off the front and rear of the car that read:

U.S. FIRST CIVILIAN
ASTRONAUT
NEIL ARMSTRONG

Danny and Reed turned to each other.

"WOW!" Danny exclaimed.

Reed managed "No Way!"

Danny later realized that he and Reedo both had the exact raised eyebrow look on their faces. This happened with them on a regular basis. The looks this time were of genuine awe.

"Neil Armstrong just looked right at us a waved!" Reedo exclaimed. "At US!"

Danny nodded and smiled. He glanced over his shoulder at the next unit in the parade. Yet another red convertible cruised toward them. This one contained Neil's parents Steven and Viola. Mr. Armstrong wore a conservative dark suit, overcoat, and hat. Danny thought he looked like Ohio State football coach Woody Hayes. Mrs. Armstrong was dressed in a light colored coat, gloves, and hat. She waved with her right hand, while her left held a huge bouquet of scarlet flowers. Danny thought they were carnations and a quick thought flashed through his head, *Is that the state flower of Ohio?*

"We gotta go, man." This from Reedo.

Danny quickly nodded once. It was time to link up with his parents. He looked down the sidewalk leading toward the business district. It appeared that the boys could move fairly quickly in that direction, especially if they cut through front yards behind the line of people on the sidewalks and the edge of the street.

They began jogging parallel to the parade units. They easily caught up to Neil, Janet, and Ricky. The pace of the parade had already seemed to slow. Looking ahead, Danny could see why. Auglaize and Pearl Street formed a Y-shaped intersection

73

in front of him. Pearl, running due east, formed the right arm of the Y. Auglaize continued northeast, forming the left arm. An ice cream shop, Max's Dairy Barn, sat at the confluence of the two streets.

The Air Force Band was completing its turn onto Pearl. Despite the band's precision, the physics of the geography necessitated a deceleration. The odd shaped intersection meant there were homes on several sides. People seemed to gravitate to this junction, some spilling out onto the streets, further slowing the procession. Many held ice cream cones.

Danny chuckled, remembering something he read in the Wapak paper a couple days earlier. Wapak's Director of City Services and Safety was quoted, "keep back from the street and out of the path of the parade vehicles and units. There will be ample and equal opportunity to see the parade at any spot along its route."

Danny shouted to Reed over the noise. "Let's try to cross the street before the intersection. Maybe cut in front of the press cars, then head up Auglaize to Mom and Dad."

Reed nodded and moved ahead. He and Danny caught and passed the media trailers and the cars towing them. The boys looked for a break in the line of onlookers. Reed found a sliver between an older woman holding an umbrella and man wearing a white raincoat.

"Excuse me, excuse me," he said.

Both Reed and Danny rushed past them onto the street and hustled across, ten feet in front of the press units. No one seemed to notice. All eyes were turned toward the approaching vehicles.

The pair excused themselves a second time on the opposite side of the street, slipping between two young boys in horn rimmed glasses that could've been twins. They moved a few feet behind the onlookers and turned. They couldn't resist one more look at the Armstrongs as their vehicle angled onto Pearl Street.

Danny heard shouts of 'We love you Neil" and "Where's Mark?" from the crowd. His view now was of the driver's side of the vehicle. He could see Janet smiling and saying something to someone in the crowd. Neil was facing to the right and waving. Ricky's crewcut was barely visible above the crowd as it floated past.

Danny and Reed turned and started up Auglaize. They walked quickly but didn't run. "OK Reedo, gimme the walkie-talkie" Danny commanded.

Reed handed it over. It was a "Sears Trans Talk 600" model. It was black and silver with an antenna on top that telescoped out a couple feet.

Danny pulled out the antenna as they walked. There was a rotary dial on the left side. Danny turned the dial and felt it click on. He pushed the dial up. The boys heard static. The volume of the static increased until the dial could no longer turn. The unit was in receiving mode. By depressing a button on the right side and holding it, the user could transmit. When the button was released, the unit was again receiving.

Danny held the Trans Talk at head height between himself and Reedo, both boys listening for Danny's dad. Hearing only static, Danny depressed the button and said "Danny to Dad, Danny to Dad, over."

Nothing.

"Ask if he found a spot at the Bi-Rite," this from Reed.

"Danny to Dad, over."

Again, nothing. Danny heard a chopping sound from above and looked up through a few descending raindrops to see a helicopter several hundred feet above, circling over town. *Crazy!* He thought.

"Danny to Dad."

After several more tries, Danny left the walkie-talkie on in receiving mode, hoping to hear from his dad. He and Reed would soon reach the noisiest, most densely packed stretch of the parade. If they didn't hear from Jerry soon, they would have to try to locate him without the aid of technology.

CHAPTER EIGHT

After watching Danny and Reed run toward the parade from their parking spot on Dearbaugh, Jerry and Jane busied themselves, gathering the various items they'd brought from home. Jerry opened the trunk and reached for the cooler. It was a dark green, rectangular shaped, metal contrivance with white plastic handles attached to the ends. Jerry lifted it and realized that it was heavier than expected. He sat it on the street and flipped open the lid. He saw ice, lots of ice, and several of the red soda cans with large white diamonds encompassing the words "Coca-Cola" in script.

"How many cans of pop did you bring?" Jerry demanded.

"I brought 8 cans. Two for each of us," Jane answered as she grabbed the brown paper bag containing baloney sandwiches and looked for her umbrella.

"There must be 10 pounds of ice in here" Jerry brooded. The cooler was 18 by 12 inches. Jerry realized he couldn't carry the thing with one hand. It was too large to tuck under one arm like a football. If he grabbed one handle and let it hang down while walking, it would snap open and the contents would spill out.

Jerry suggested "Maybe we just leave it here since we're running late."

"No Jerry, the boys would be disappointed." Jane was unwavering.

Shaking his head, Jerry closed the trunk and locked the doors of the Impala. He flipped up the hood of his tan raincoat, not wanting to be caught bare-headed if it began to rain while he was lugging the cooler.

Jane carried the sandwiches, umbrella, and Reed's second walkie-talkie. They were a mile or more from the Bi-Rite, a discount store in the center of the commercial district. They started up Dearbaugh. Danny and Reed had disappeared into the crowd. Jerry could make out movement on the parade route but couldn't identify any units. Both he and Jane heard

76

"The Star-Spangled Banner" coming from that direction and it seemed to inspire them to move faster.

"Good band!" Jane exclaimed.

Jerry, a few steps ahead, reached the Vine Street intersection and stopped. He turned to Jane and, not quite barking, said "We need to find a short-cut downtown."

Vine ran off to the east and, it looked to Jerry, seemed to dead end ten or 12 houses ahead in that direction. To the north was Auglaize Street and the parade. About halfway between their position on Vine and Auglaize was another east west street, Benton.

Jane suggested, "What if we cut through yards between here and there?" She was looking at the houses on Vine.

"Yeah, good idea," Jerry agreed. "Let's go."

They hurried east on Vine, passing a couple of the residences. These seemed to be two or three bedroom structures on small lots. There were no people visible anywhere on the street. Apparently everyone was at the parade. Jerry made a hard-left turn between two houses. He was moving as fast as he could but the awkward configuration of the cooler gave him an uneven, lurching gait. Jane followed, thankful that she'd worn flats that morning instead of heels.

Emerging in the back yard of one of the houses, the pair saw that there was about 200 feet of relatively open ground between the rear of the Vine Street homes and the back sides of the Benton Street homes ahead. This area had the feel of former farmland that had been claimed for new housing.

Jerry slanted to the northeast and tried to pick up the pace. He fixed on a small structure that sat behind a Benton Street home about 100 yards ahead.

About halfway to the structure, with the cooler slapping against his right thigh on every other stride, he turned to check on Jane. Jerry was wearing a two-month-old pair of Red Wing boots that he'd bought at Alonzo Steinke's. Lonzo was a retired deputy sheriff that ran a small shoe store out of the garage behind his house on East State Street in Botkins. Lonzo stocked a half dozen sizes each of men's, women's, boy's, and girl's shoes. The Hitchens boys strenuously avoided Lonzo's. They thought the selections were too few and too dull. They were also slightly creeped out by the metallic slide rule-like apparatus that Lonzo used to properly size a stockinged foot.

As Jerry turned to his right, his left Red Wing caught a slightly raised stone and he went sprawling. He was somehow able to push the cooler away from his body far enough that he didn't land on it. The Cokes and ice went flying.

"Jerry!' Jane cried.

She sat the paper bag she was carrying on the grass and hurried to him.

"AWWWWWW MAN!" he blustered.

"Are you alright?"

Jerry pulled himself up. "I tore my pants." He pointed to his right knee, where an eight-inch split in the material revealed a muddy abrasion. The knee was just beginning to produce some blood. Beginning to fume, he repeated "I TORE MY PANTS!"

"Are you hurt?" Jane asked, bending over to look at the knee.

"Let's just go" he growled, reaching for the cooler.

Jane stifled a laugh as she gathered the Cokes and as much ice as she could find. The now weed and dirt covered cans were repacked. Jerry snatched up the cooler and resolutely made his way in the direction of the out-building. The hood of Jerry's raincoat had flopped off of his head during the fall. He realized that it was now lightly raining. He felt his hair start to mat down to his scalp.

Jane sat the sandwich sack back down for a second and opened her umbrella. She grabbed the bag and rushed forward, trying to catch up and extend the umbrella over Jerry's head. She finally caught up to him about twenty feet from the building. She held the umbrella over him as he shambled around the side of the structure.

The building, a single slope pole barn, appeared to be decades old. It was constructed of wood planking, now bowed in several places. Jerry thought it looked like a large lean-to. It had walls on three sides. The rear, or south, side was over ten feet high. The roof sloped upward toward the front side, which was nearly twenty feet high.

Jerry peeked around the northwest corner and motioned for Jane. Together they eased into the open front.

"It looks like the manger they put out in front of St. Lawrence at Christmas," Jane commented.

Jerry agreed, "Yeah, just a bigger version."

The open front of the structure had no doors. The dirt floor was covered with old straw. A wooden-rung ladder connected to the back wall led up to a loft. There was a chain wrapped around a support post in the center of the building. It ran out into the grass in front of the opening. The free end of the chain ended with a snap-link connector. It was a heavy chain and it looked to Jerry like it had been set up to restrain a large animal.

"It looks like it was used to shelter equipment back when there were farms in this area. Enough room here for an old tractor and a good-sized wagon" Jerry mused.

He set the cooler on the ground. He swept the hair out of his eyes and pulled his hood back on. It looked like the light rain had stopped. "We better get moving," he said.

Jane picked up the cooler. "Let me take this for a while."

Jerry relented, "Okay, I'll grab the rest of our stuff."

Jane stepped out of the building, carrying the green cooler. Jerry grabbed the umbrella, walkie-talkie, and brown sack. He took two steps, then felt the sack tear. He looked down to see four baloney sandwiches tumble to the ground. Jane had wrapped them in wax paper. The paper came loose as the sandwiches fell out. Circles of baloney, adhered to slices of Wonder Bread by mustard, landed in the straw. Separate bread slices clung to straw and mud.

"AWW DAMN!" Jerry howled.

Jane spun around, half expecting that Jerry had fallen again.

He held up the bag "The damn sack tore open!"

Jane was relieved. "The bottom must've gotten soaked when I set it down back in the field. Just leave the sandwiches, it's OK."

"Sunovabitch" Jerry groused. He hurried ahead to catch up to Jane, not realizing that with his second step, the new Red Wing boot on his right foot squished into a large pile of dog poop.

Danny and Reed hurried up Auglaize Street. The music from the bands faded a bit to their rear. They began to overtake people moving in the same direction. One's and two's here, groups of a half dozen there. They reached the point on Auglaize where the street bent right to run due east. The boys edged around the corner of a building and could now view the heart of historic downtown Wapakoneta.

It was spectacular. People, there had to be thousands of them, were jammed into the four-block stretch in front of Danny and Reed.

To Danny, it looked like spectators were at least five people deep on both sides of the street. Almost all storefronts were obscured by the crowd. Upper story windows were open in virtually every building with men, women, and kids leaning out. Banners were strung every few dozen feet, reaching from a building on the north side to another on the south.

Danny saw "LIONS WELCOMES YOU" in blue and gold and "VFW WELCOMES NEIL" in red and white. There were flags everywhere, the stars and stripes as well as the red white and blue state of Ohio forked pennant. The downtown buildings themselves contributed to the spectacle. The signage from the dozens of small businesses packed into these four blocks seemed to act as punctuation to the scene.

On the left, there was a neon "LIQUOR" sign extending horizontally from the second floor of a building. Windows were open on either side of the sign, filled with smiling grade schoolers. Beyond that, the "UHLMAN's DEPT. STORE" sign hung vertically from the top of a three-story building. To the right he saw the bright red placard above Miller's Five and Dime. A large American flag protruded from an open window above the first "L." Beyond that, the white letters of "SEARS" on a blue background and another neon advertisement, this one for "EAGLES 691 CLUB."

Danny thought the scene was almost too Norman Rockwell for Norman Rockwell.

Reedo broke in "Do you still want to try to get to the Bi-Rite?" Both he and Danny focused on the sign jutting out of a building on the right side of the street two blocks ahead. This one was white, with "BI-RITE" in red over "DISCOUNT STORE" In black. It would be extremely difficult to press their way up that sidewalk for two blocks.

"Let's try the walkie-talkie again. Maybe we can figure out where they are before we wade in there" Danny suggested.

"Danny to Dad." Static.

He tried again. More static. "Okay, that's not gonna work." Danny pushed the extended antenna all the way back into the Trans Talk unit and thumbed the dial until it clicked off. Looking at the densely packed sidewalk on the south side of the street, he took a deep breath and slowly expelled it, his cheeks inflated.

"Maaan" he muttered.

A thought came to Reed "Why don't we just walk right down the middle of the street until we get there and then duck in?"

Danny looked at Reedo as if his buddy had pulled two tickets to a World Series game out of his back pocket. "MAAAAN!," Danny said again, this time with excitement. "Let's go!"

CHAPTER NINE

Jerry and Jane were trying to make up for lost time. They cut between two houses that sat in front of the open shed, emerging on Benton Street. They could see Max's Dairy Barn up ahead. A short street, Oak, ran north, and connected Benton with Pearl. They turned right on Benton Street, moving east. Jerry grabbed one side of the cooler with his left hand while Jane grasped the other handle with her right. They stayed in synch for the most part and walked in the street. Benton was not part of the parade route and was virtually deserted.

The parade was moving parallel to them, one block to their left, on Pearl.

"We'll have to find a way to cross through the parade units to get downtown and meet the boys" Jerry noted.

Jane was looking up at street sign. "We're on Benton. The newspaper said Neil grew up on Benton."

Jerry ignored the comment. "We might as well get it out of the way now. We can turn at the next corner, try to find a gap in the units and sneak through to the other side."

They turned left at the corner. Music from several marching bands carried to them. The intersection with Pearl was a few hundred feet ahead. There was an unbroken line of onlookers stretching along the street. The sidewalks running off to both the left and right were packed. Mr. and Mrs. Hitchens, cooler still between them, shuffled up the street.

Forty-two-year-old Irene Drabik stood on the southwest corner of Pearl and Walnut Streets. She had driven down to Wapakoneta from her home in Monroe, Michigan. She got a couple hours sleep before waking to her alarm at 2 am. She got coffee going in her percolator while packing a few things in the car. When the coffee was ready, she poured it in one of her husband Stan's green thermos bottles and headed for the door.

Forty-five minutes later she pulled the Ford Fairlane into her sister's Toledo driveway. Betty Clarke rushed out, jumped in the passenger door and, her face glowing, said "Let's go see Neil."

The sisters drove south another 90 minutes or so before exiting at Wapakoneta on Bellefontaine Street. Irene turned left, away from the downtown area, before making a quick turn into a truck stop.

"The Hub" had a 24-hour diner. Irene and Betty had plenty of time to enjoy a leisurely breakfast before boarding a shuttle bus. The Hub was, well, the hub for a planned four-bus shuttle system put in place to transport out-of-towners to the downtown area. Irene had read about the bus system in the Toledo Blade.

Upon arriving downtown, Irene and Betty decided that the size of the growing crowd would make it difficult to employ their matching Kodak cameras. They had purchased them at a Toledo camera store the previous year for each other as Christmas gifts.

The sisters consulted The Blade (Irene made sure to pack it that morning) and decided to find a spot on the parade route that would afford a better view. They moved a couple blocks south, to Pearl Street.

Their planning paid off. Both sisters were within ten feet of Neil when his convertible eased past. Irene and Betty both snapped photos, furiously advanced the film with their thumbs, and snapped again and again.

They were giddy, convinced they had some great shots. They couldn't wait to get them developed and find out.

Irene's mind was racing. She turned their attention back to the parade. After Neil's parents Stephen and Viola passed, the Governor of Ohio came by inside an Ohio State Highway Patrol car. Irene *did* know her cars, her husband Stan worked at the Ford River Rouge Plant. The Governor was in Ohio State Patrol car number 260. It was a 1965 Plymouth Fury.

There was something wrong with this though, what was it? The sign on front...

"Oh, excuse me."

Irene was knocked off balance. She turned to see a disheveled man. He had damp, uncombed hair. His jacket was muddy and grass stained. His pants were torn. Was that blood on his leg? And he smelled like... dog poop?

Jerry had advanced in front of Jane to approach the line of viewers. He picked a small gap between two women wearing rain scarfs and was about to try to ease through when Jane's momentum pushed the cooler into him and he tottered into the woman on the left.

"Oh, excuse me" he said apologetically.

The woman, startled, turned to Jerry. She wore cat eye glasses. She assessed Jerry from head to toe, her face now assuming a severe look. She wrinkled her nose and frowned, recoiling a bit.

Jerry saw that a state cruiser had just passed. There was a fifty-foot gap between the cruiser and the next unit, which was a flat trailer bedecked with a large portrait of Armstrong, a ten-foot Titan rocket, and a red metal gantry the same height as the rocket. It was towed by a red Cadillac convertible.

Jerry stared at the float for a second, refocused, and turned to Jane. "Let's go." He led her across Pearl, the cooler bouncing along between them.

Irene turned to her sister, "Betty, was that bum trying to steal that lady's cooler?"

Danny and Reed started walking. They gravitated to the right side of the street, rather than walking right down the center, perhaps unconsciously thinking they would draw less attention to themselves. It didn't seem to matter. Most people on the sidewalks were occupied: talking to companions, fidgeting with cameras, straining to see if the head of the parade had yet appeared on the eastern edge of the stretch.

Danny took in the scene. Most people wore jackets or even winter coats. A high percentage of the men were turned out in hats. Women protected their hair-do's with scarfs and umbrellas. There was a breeze and the flags and banners flapped and swayed. He could hear a marching band off to the south, not yet very loud.

Many of the girls in the assemblage appeared to be smaller versions of the women, dressed in slightly more colorful coats with a scarf here, a pair of earmuffs there. The boys in the crowd exhibited more variety. Danny saw blue jeans, dress suits, high school letter jackets, and raincoats. He even saw some in tee shirts covered with clear plastic to guard against the rain. A good number of the figures hanging out of upper story windows were eight to ten-year-old boys in flannel shirts. Glancing up at a few of these, Danny realized there were also people on the rooftops of several buildings. They leaned on ledges, some holding cameras.

In the course of the two block walk down the street, Danny detected perfume, cologne, popcorn, and the unavoidable odor of cigarette smoke. He also picked up indications of cigar smoke. Curiously, he categorized cigar smoke as an aroma, while identifying cigarette smoke as a stench. He wasn't sure why.

The Bi-Rite Discount Store had its Grand Opening the previous week. It occupied the southeast corner of a T-shaped intersection formed by Auglaize Street and Willipie, which ran in from the south. Danny slowed his pace near the crosswalk and looked south. The marquee of the Wapa Theater glowed above the heads of the crowd. It was just a couple doors down, on the right. The businesses of Wapakoneta were closed for the parade, but the Wapa proudly glowed for the hometown astronaut.

Danny excused himself as he pressed through folks in front of the Bi-Rite. He looked for his mom and dad. He turned to Reed, "Anything?"

"Nope, think we should just stay here and wait for them?" Reed asked.

"I guess so," Danny answered. He looked a bit uneasy.

Reed, trying to lighten the situation, opined "Jerry is gonna be *PIISSSED!*" He verbally stretched the word, like it was a Marathon candy bar being pulled on a hot day.

Danny smiled and looked back at the store. It had a fairly narrow front, perhaps 30 feet, but was three or four times that distance in depth. The Bi-Rite sold a little bit of everything; candy, toiletries, toys, housewares, even clothing. A full-page newspaper ad in the window shouted;

Bi-Rite Discount Store
5 East Auglaize
Former Location Of Yocum's
GRAND OPENING
Friday, April 8
Now! A Genuine Discount Store In Wapakoneta
A Prize Each Week For The Next Three Weeks!
Grand Prize---A Sony Portable T.V.

Danny quickly scanned through some of the prices listed on the ad;

Right Guard Deodorant
Regular Price $1.00
Our Price 58c
Save 42c!
And,
Rise Shave Cream
With Free Tube Of Groom N' Clean
Regular Price 79c
Our Price 47c

Nothing in the ad interested him. He thought he saw a comic book display back by the cash register, though. This made the Bi-Rite worth checking out. He filed this away and turned to Reed, who was looking at the rooftops across the street.

"Remember when we got up there?" Danny asked, grinning.

The previous summer, Ginny Thompson had dropped off the boys at the Wapa for a 7:30 movie and told them she would be back to pick them up. When the movie let out, Ginny hadn't yet returned. Reed and Danny walked up and down the "main drag" of Wapak while they waited.

There was a shared parking lot to the rear of the businesses on the north side of Auglaize street. Behind the parking lot flowed the Auglaize river. Reed and Danny slipped down a narrow opening between two buildings. Their intent was to test their throwing arms by chucking rocks into the river. If they were lucky, a tree branch or two would flow past, giving them a target.

When they reached the rear of the building, Reed began to look for stones. He walked along the back wall of the building to his right, his head canted downward. There was very little lighting back here and he nearly banged his head on a black fire escape ladder.

"Danny" Reed hissed in an excited whisper. Danny turned to see a goofy grin on his friend's face. "This ladder is just begging to be climbed!"

So, they indulged the ladder.

They reached the top rung and stepped onto a second-floor roof. An adjoining building was three stories high but the roof was sloped. Reed and Danny could reach the ledge of this roof on the back side. At that point, the roof of the second building was just two and a half stories high. After pulling themselves over the ledge, they walked up the slope to the front of the second building.

They had a fantastic view of downtown Wapak. The theater marquee was blazing a couple blocks away. A line of people stood at the teller window, waiting to buy tickets to the late show.

"Let's see how far we can go," Danny suggested.

For the next ten minutes the pair traversed the rooftops of virtually every building on the north side of Auglaize Street. Only when Reed spotted his mom's yellow Volkswagen Beetle slowly cruise past the theater did he rasp "Let's get the hell outta here!"

Danny followed Reed's gaze to the top of the First National Bank building. There were a few people up there now and they all seemed to be turning to their left. A man pointed in that direction and said something to the others. Danny heard cheers coming from the line of spectators to his right, then the crash of symbols. The Air Force Band was making the turn back onto Auglaize Street! Danny would see the entire parade this time. He momentarily forgot about his AWOL mom and dad.

CHAPTER TEN

Danny's parents were finally approaching the city center. After crossing Pearl Street, they made a series of turns east and north. They would walk a block in one direction, turn, walk a block or two in the other direction, then turn again.

They reached Auglaize Street just before noon. They were two blocks west of the Bi-Rite. There were several hundred people between them and the discount store. Jerry knew there was no way they would be able to navigate through that crowd, particularly when toting the cooler.

At that moment, the sound of music, somewhat distant until now, came crashing toward them from four blocks east.

"The Air Force Band?" Jane queried.

"Yeah. Hey let me try to reach the boys real quick on the walkie-talkie, before it gets too loud."

They sat the cooler on the sidewalk. Spectators in front of them were stepping off the curb and turning toward the sound of the band. Jerry extended the antenna of the Trans Talk and turned the On-Off dial to its maximum volume.

Nothing.

No sound. Jerry put it against his ear and concentrated. He could detect no static. He thumbed the transmit button and in a loud voice called "Dad to Danny" several times. He flipped the dial off and on, then tried again.

"Dad to Danny."

Silence.

Realization appeared in his face as he slid open the small plastic door on the back side of the Sears unit.

The compartment was empty.

"You gotta be shitting me... no battery!?" he shouted to Jane.

Jerry regretted this immediately. Several people in front of him turned at his words. A large man in a grey fedora frowned. A small girl, perhaps five, tugged at the man's sleeve. She wrinkled her nose and said "The stinky man said a bad word!"

It was at this point that Jane became aware of the odor emanating from Jerry's Red Wings. They had been on the move for a mile or more and were separated by the cooler so she hadn't detected it.

"Let's go Jerry." Jane grabbed both handles of the cooler, walked to the left a few feet, then finding a seam in the onlookers, made her way across the street to the northwest edge of the downtown strip. Jerry, glad to be free of the judgmental kindergartner, followed with a sheepish look on his face.

Jane found an opening near a storefront and sat the cooler down. She climbed on top of it and was afforded a view over the top of the crowd, now at least six deep, that stood in front.

Jerry tried to see by standing on his toes but had limited success. He shot a quick, longing glance at the cooler. Jane saw this and advised "You'd better keep those boots off the cooler until we can clean them off."

Jerry sighed.

They were in front of a bar. A black and white neon sign, about eight feet long and five feet high extended out from the building several feet above, exclaiming:

CIGARS

COZY CORNER
CLUB

A line of Ohio State flags extended across the street from a light pole nearby. Jane saw a speaker hanging from the top of the pole. A public-address announcer from an unknown location boomed over the speakers "The head of the parade is just turning onto Auglaize Street!"

Jane's eyes stayed on the speaker for a few seconds. On December weekends each year in downtown Wapak, Christmas carols would play through the speaker. The light poles were wrapped with garland. If you were fortunate enough to be doing some shopping on a snowy day, it really put you in the Christmas spirit. Jane smiled and scanned both sides of the street, looking for the boys.

Back in front of the Bi-Rite, Danny and Reed heard the music grow louder. Sirens wailed from the Wapak Police and Auglaize County cruisers leading the parade. They saw a Marine Corps color guard next in line, preceding the Air Force Band. They realized they had missed the Marines earlier.

The Marines were impressive in their dress blues, white hats, and gloves. There were four of them. The Marines on the ends had shouldered rifles. Danny noted that they were M-14s, and thought of Eddie. The Marines in the center carried the United States and U.S. Marine Corps flags.

The band was playing "God Bless America." Danny noticed that several of the male spectators had removed their hats.

A couple boys of about fourteen pressed between Danny and Reed in an attempt to get to the front of the crowd. Danny noticed that they both had canvas Wapakoneta Daily News bags slung on their shoulders. The bags were exact copies of the one Danny had carried for two years.

"Hey, are you guys working?" Danny asked.

The boy on the left had blue eyes, was a bit chubby, and wore a red stocking hat. His running mate was thin, and had mussed red hair and freckles.

"We're done now," said Stocking Hat. "We sold out."

"Did you have extra papers to sell?" Danny asked, remembering the procedure he had followed.

"They printed a special paper a couple days ago. They made a buncha' extras to sell at the parade." This from Mussed Hair.

Danny looked at the enthusiastic mass around him. "I bet those things sold fast."

"Yeah, in about 15 minutes" said Stocking Hat. "Sold 50 of 'em, got some tips, too." He smiled and pushed through the crowd, Mussed Hair in tow.

Danny looked across the street at the First National Bank building. A clock, maybe three feet square, extended out from the bank. It was about 20 feet high and was affixed to the right side of the building where the bank shared a wall with Abbotts Shoe Store. Danny was curious to see if the parade was following the posted schedule he'd seen in the Wapak Daily News. The two faces of the clock were positioned to be viewed by someone to the east or west, up or down the street. The hands of the clock were not visible to Danny, directly across from it.

Danny remembered that there was a large, free-standing clock across the street and a couple hundred feet to the right. As he swung his eyes in that direction, he observed the Rhine & Brading Drug Store. Danny smiled, remembering that Neil Armstrong worked at this store when he was a boy. Supposedly Neil was paid 40 cents an hour to stock shelves and sweep the floor. Neil put the money to good use, saving it for flight lessons. Armstrong earned his pilot's license before obtaining a driver's license.

Danny knew one thing for sure about Rhine & Brading. The store offered the best selection of comic books in a three-county area. The last time Danny was in the store, a couple weeks earlier, he was turning the metal carousel that held the comics. He was searching for the latest issue of his favorite mag, "The Fantastic Four," when he noticed a group of people near the rear of the store.

The owner of the business, Charles Brading, had come out from behind the counter where he dispensed prescription medication. Brading was speaking and gesturing toward a wall as his audience closed around him. Danny drifted back. Everyone in the group appeared to be looking at something on the wall. As he approached, one member of the assemblage peeled away, creating a gap.

Danny edged forward and saw... graffiti?

One of the women shoppers, holding a shopping basket containing three jars of Dippity Do Setting Gel, declared "You should coat it with lacquer so it doesn't fade."

Danny examined the wall closely. He saw several signatures written in ink. One read "Neil Armstrong." Neil had apparently signed his name on the wall when he worked there.

Danny's eyes lingered on Rhine & Brading for a beat, then continued past it, searching for the second clock. There it stood, like a miniature Big Ben. The clock had four faces, each with a placard mounted beneath spelling out "PEOPLES NATIONAL BANK."

It was twelve feet tall. Danny always thought of the clock as iconic. He thought that was the right word. The hands at this moment were positioned to show that it was 12:05. The parade was almost exactly on its projected pace.

The Air Force Band flowed past, still playing "God Bless America." Their rendition would've made Irving Berlin proud.

The World War One vets followed. They were still in good cheer, beaming as they waved and pointed at people in the crowd they recognized.

Up next were the press wagons, then the Armstrongs. Danny would've guessed the order, even if he hadn't already known. Cheers reverberated off the buildings to his right. Confetti was being tossed from windows and rooftops. It looked like a mini version of a "Canyon of Heroes" parade in New York City.

To Danny, it seemed like the number of photographers had doubled in the last half hour. They swarmed around the Armstrong car. They're heads swiveled constantly, apparently looking for aspects of downtown Wapakoneta that would enhance a shot. Seeing something interesting, they would hasten to a spot that put the Armstrongs in the proper position, then snap away. With more than a dozen photographers doing this at once, they occasionally bumped into one another. It was comical.

The wagon closest to Danny and Reed was still occupied by several men equipped with movie cameras as well as two commentators holding microphones. Both commentators, unfamiliar to Danny, peered into lens of their respective cameraman. The excitement of the crowd seemed to energize the correspondents. They appeared to be more animated then they were back on Pearl Street.

Three other movie camera operators had staked claims to a spot in the cramped confines of the trailer. They were taking dead aim at the Armstrongs. The height of the wagon and the fact that they were standing gave the operators a slight downward angle to Neil and family, who were still sitting on top of the back seat of the vehicle. One of the cameramen balanced a large, black, 16mm Mitchell motion picture camera on his right shoulder. The reel-to-reel functionality of the device was made apparent by the two prominent Mickey Mouse Ear-shaped features on top.

Danny was glad that he and Reed had already had a close up look at the astronaut. The packed downtown area made it difficult to get a good view. Some bystanders jumped out front of the convertible, pausing just long enough to snap a picture, then coalesced back into the crowd.

Several young boys had seemingly inserted themselves into the procession at this point. They walked along on both sides of the car. They were all bareheaded with damp hair. One had a trash bag pulled over his upper body, his heads and arms poking out.

Danny remembered the term "station keeping." It was used to describe part of the Gemini 8 mission. Armstrong and Scott, while in orbit, had to locate and maneuver to the Agena target vehicle. Before attempting to dock, the two crafts would maintain a distance of 150 feet or so while travelling at thousands of miles an hour. These boys seemed to be station keeping on the Armstrong target vehicle. Add the Air Force security men trailing the vehicle and you had quite an assemblage.

Danny thought about a class in Mrs. Fark's English class earlier that year. Each student was to do a report on a word origin. Johnny Muhlenkamp had selected the phrase "Bell Cow." Johnny's composition explained that a bell is attached to the collar of the lead cow. The rest of the herd stays near the lead cow and the bell makes them easier to locate. Johnny had extolled the virtues of the Muhlenkamp lead cow, "Bootsie." Danny thought it was the most interesting thing that Johnny had ever written.

Back to the parade, Neil Armstrong was most assuredly playing the role of the bell cow. The hometown boy still looked delighted to be there. He waved and turned from side to side. It seemed with every swing of his head a look of recognition would appear on his face and he would smile or point at an individual spectator.

Janet was smiling brightly, looking often from the crowd and back to Neil. Danny thought for a second that she seemed a bit confounded by the outpouring. He remembered that she was not from Wapakoneta. She and Neil had met while attending Purdue University. Danny guessed that Janet had underestimated the enthusiasm that Wapakoneta had for its hometown boy.

Ricky's eyes wandered all over the street, looking at people on rooftops and at banners overhead. He turned to the right and looked at two boys in blue jackets. Each boy stood on the ledge of separate windows, 51 inches above the sidewalk. The windows flanked the main entrance to the First National Bank. This afforded them a great view. They both waved at the Armstrongs. Ricky smiled and waved back.

Neil's parents floated by. An Ohio State cruiser appeared next. Reedo nudged Danny and pointed to a large white sign on front of the cruiser. In stenciled letters, the words "GOVERNOR JAMES RHOADS" were written. Both boys instantly realized that Governor Rhodes' last name was misspelled.

Knowing that grammar and spelling errors bugged his buddy Danny, Reed offered, "Myself and you could've done a better job than that."

Both boys snickered as the governor passed, waving out the front passenger side of the vehicle.

Danny became aware of several other Botkins kids standing a few feet to his right. A couple girls in the group noticed them and walked over.

"More fun than school, huh?" asked Chris Koenig. Chris was a member of their sophomore class. She was pretty, about 5'4", with dark hair and hazel-colored eyes. Chris earned straight A's in school, and was a member of the track team.

"No doubt" Danny managed. Danny had a thing for Chris, but was too shy to act on it.

Next to Chris was her friend Sandy Monnin, another classmate. Sandy was an inch or two taller than Chris. She had blonde shoulder length hair and blue-green eyes. Sandy played varsity basketball for the Trojans, having started on the varsity team as a sophomore, which was a bit of a rarity.

Both Chris and Sandy wore the girl's version of the Botkins letter jacket.

"Hi guys," Sandy ventured, enjoying the parade?"

Reed nodded. "We got to see Neil twice." He explained how they had arrived late with Danny's parents, had split up, and how they'd been within a few feet of the astronaut back on Pearl.

"Cool" the girls said in unison.

"If you see my mom and dad, let us know" Danny remarked. "How did you guys get here?"

The girls were girls, of course, but Danny sometimes found himself saying "you guys" to a mixed group of males and females. This time he had actually referred to a group that included no guys, as guys. He started to blush.

Chris ignored the error in etiquette. "We rode with my brother. We parked out at The Hub and came into town on a shuttle bus. We can get back on the bus at the end of the parade and meet him at the car."

They all turned their attention to the Wapak High School marching band, which was strutting past while playing "For He's A Jolly Good Fellow." The band members sported bright red jackets, black pants with a red vertical stripe, and had poofy, white plumes extending vertically from the top of their red and black caps. They were led down Auglaize by a line of majorettes, all twirling batons. Danny could just make out over the public-address system "The Wapakoneta Redskins Marching Band!"

The band was followed by a small group in uniform, the Civil Air Cadets. The Cadets preceded a much larger group, this one composed of Boy Scouts. There were at least a hundred of them. A half dozen of the taller boys were at the head of this unit, carrying American flags on staffs. Danny remembered that Neil was an enthusiastic member of the scouts.

A number of floats rolled past. Most had rocket or spacecraft themes. One float consisted of a blue papier mache globe, about six feet in diameter. Projecting out of the top, and angling forward, was a six-foot-long white rocket, also papier mache.

Well, it was supposed to be a rocket. It looked to Danny like an erect penis, straining toward an unseen moon. He turned his head slightly and found Reed's eyes. They both snorted short laughs. Danny, embarrassed, risked a look at the girls. Chris and Sandy both stared ahead, apparently oblivious to their levity. It looked to Danny, though, that both had a trace of a smile on their lips.

CHAPTER ELEVEN

Danny's parents finally got a look at Neil. From her vantage point on the cooler, Jane had an unobstructed view of the Armstrong family as the principal unit in the parade approached obliquely from the left.

Neil looked a bit smaller than Jane expected. But he seemed to exude a star quality. There was just something about him. Ohio's John Glenn had become the first American to orbit the Earth in 1962, when he circled the globe as part of the Mercury program in his capsule named Friendship 7. Now Ohio had produced another spaceman, one who had survived a very dangerous situation. One, also, who was from right here in their own backyard!

Later in the parade, as military related units passed, Jane's thoughts would turn to Eddie, somewhere in Vietnam. But for now, she was just thrilled to see the Armstrongs.

Janet looked radiant, if a bit tired. Ricky, Jane thought, looked a little ornery. Absent-mindedly, Jane wondered aloud "I wonder what happened to Mark?"

"Whassat?" Jerry asked from shoulder level.

"Their youngest son, Mark, isn't with them" Jane remarked.

"Hunh. Hope he's not sick. Crappy weather here today. They're probably not used to this weather, living down in Houston."

Neil's parents passed. Jane had met Viola Armstrong once at a church flea market in Wapak a few years back. She recalled the astronaut's mother being polite and pleasant.

The Governor of Ohio came past in a state trooper Plymouth chase car. Jerry tilted his head to Jane and asked "Is there something wrong with that sign?"

Jerry was a Republican. He had voted for James Rhodes every time the name appeared on a ballot. Jane, unbeknownst to Jerry, had always voted for Rhodes' Democratic opponents.

Containing a smile, Jane canted her head toward Jerry and answered "His name is spelled wrong."

98

The governor looked out the passenger window and waved to bystanders on Jane's side of the street. To Jane, James Rhodes looked very similar to Texas Governor John Connally, who survived being shot by Lee Harvey Oswald two and a half years earlier while riding with President John F. Kennedy.

JFK, of course, did not survive that day. Jane had been a Kennedy supporter. Jerry had even voted for him, though not for his politics but "because of what he did in the Navy in World War Two."

Jane also admired John Kennedy's widow Jackie for her sense of elegance before the assassination, and her dignity after. Jackie was sitting next to her husband in an open convertible on November 22, 1962 when he was killed. Photos and videos captured Jackie for posterity, wearing a pink Chanel suit and pillbox hat.

Jane froze for a beat. The lead units of the parade had turned north on Blackhoof Street to her right to head toward the high school. She looked over her right shoulder at another admired man, riding in an open car with his wife, who wore a pillbox hat.

Jane felt a chill. An ugly thought began to intrude on her brain. She pushed it away. She turned back to her left and looked at the many open windows and the rooftops sprinkled with viewers.

She nearly shuddered.

Jane told herself that she couldn't be the only person at the parade today whose mind had wandered down this ugly path. Another band approached. Jane refocused her mind on the celebration and continued to look for Danny and Reed.

The boys were less than 100 yards away, unintentionally blending in with the crowd near the Bi-Rite. They stood with Chris and Sandy, behind several layers of people. The foursome shifted from one foot to the other searching for an opening through which to see the parade.

Reed knew how Danny looked at Chris. He decided *What the heck, it's a special day.* He edged toward Sandy and said "Hey Danny, whaddaya say we give the girls a boost so they can see?"

Reed bent down next to Sandy, wrapped his arms around her waist, and lifted her up. Sandy laughed and, looking over the people in front, exclaimed "There's a hearse in the parade!"

Danny was mortified when Reedo committed him to picking up Chris. He realized that he really didn't have a choice at this point. He looked at her and she smiled. Danny uttered "OK here goes."

He bent down and latched on to Chris. As they rose, Chris reached across Danny's back and gripped his left shoulder. Danny thought she smelled wonderful.

Reedo looked at Danny and winked.

They stayed that way for several minutes. There had, indeed, been a hearse in the parade. The long red Limousine floated past. An eight-foot-long sign was affixed to the roof, looking like an oversized dorsal fin. It read:

WELCOME HOME NEIL!
HONORARY CHAIRMAN AUGLAIZE COUNTY
CANCER FUND DRIVE

Reedo turned to Danny. "Not very subtle, huh Danny?"

Local politicians flowed past. Bands from Cridersville, Minster, and St. Marys proceeded by. The Class of 1947 entry followed. This was Neil's graduation class at Wapak's old Blume High School. Several members of the class were in attendance. They were piled into three convertibles coasting along in line. The cars were red, white, and blue; a Plymouth, a Dodge, and a Chevrolet. The first car carried a placard reading; "HELLO NEIL & JAN, CLASS OF 1947."

The second car had a sign with an enlargement of Armstrong's high school graduation photograph. The trail car exhibited a blown-up image of the astronaut in his Gemini gear.

Danny's arms were beginning to ache, but there was no way that he was going to set Chris down before Reedo lowered Sandy. Thankfully, his buddy succumbed first. Once Sandy was back on her feet, Danny felt justified in lowering Chris. Danny let his hand linger on Chris's back for a second more than necessary.

Addressing both boys, but looking only at Danny, Chris said "Thanks guys, that was fun."

Reed was an outgoing guy that everyone liked. He was the rare adolescent male that talked to girls and boys with equal self-assurance. He didn't have a girlfriend. Assessing the situation, Reed thought *What the hell.* He looked at his three classmates and blurted "So whaddaya think about double-dating at the Junior Prom next year?"

Danny was stunned. Reedo had a goofy grin on his face. Chris and Sandy just looked at each other with widened eyes. Eventually one of the girls, Danny later thought it was Sandy, said "Sure that sounds like it would be a blast!"

Just like that, Danny had a date for the prom, though it wasn't until the following April. Sure, Danny was thinking about asking Chris, but he hadn't put the finishing touches on his plan. He had formulated an idea that included bike rides past the Koenig house to try to determine if Chris was home. He also planned to reconnoiter the Havaner house. He would only make a phone call to Chris when there was no chance of surveillance. Danny figured it would take at least three phone calls and lots of small talk in the hallways at school to work up to popping the question.

Reedo had just bulldozed that plan. What a guy! He truly was Mr. Fantastic.

"Okay, cool. You're good with that, right Hitch?"

"Sure... absolutely." Danny managed, smiling at Chris.

As more units rolled by, Sandy quizzed the boys "So, what are you going to write about in History class?"

Mr. Mielke had assigned the class to do a paper related to astronauts, the space program, or some aspect of the Armstrong homecoming parade.

Reed ventured, "I think I'll do mine on the psychological damage that can be done to an impressionable young mind when you see a giant, uh, male THING wheeled down the middle of a parade route."

Danny nearly snorted. All four of them laughed.

Reed continued, "I think it's cool that he's giving us five bonus points on our grade if we go to the parade." They agreed.

After giving the class the parameters of the assignment, Mielke mentioned that the parade was a special event. In his opinion, it was historic. It was an opportunity to see one of only a handful of men who have gone to space. He said he had tried to arrange a school-authorized field trip to the event but couldn't get it worked out.

Mielke said "I can't tell you it's OK to skip school to go to the parade, but let's just say I think it's worth five points on this assignment if you do."

Danny had pretty much decided on the subject of his report. He'd read a small article in the Wapak paper about the ship that had picked up Armstrong and fellow astronaut David Scott after Gemini 8 splashed down.

The ship was the USS Leonard F. Mason, a destroyer. The Mason was one of many ships stationed at various locations around the globe for the purpose of recovering the spacecraft. Gemini 8 was supposed to orbit the Earth 55 times before re-entering the planet's atmosphere and splashing down in the Atlantic Ocean.

After Armstrong regained control of the spinning craft, NASA implemented a recovery plan that would have Gemini 8 re-enter on its seventh orbit. It was to come down in the Mason's area of responsibility.

The Mason pulled off the rescue. That was interesting to Danny. But what made it really compelling to him was the fact that the ship was named after a US Marine Medal of Honor recipient from Cridersville, Ohio. Cridersville was a small town located about ten miles north of Wapak. What were the chances of that?

PFC Leonard Mason was killed on Guam in World War Two. His mother, Mollie Mason, still lived in Cridersville. She was supposed to be riding in the parade today. Danny had been keeping an eye out for her. It shouldn't be long now. Danny sensed that the parade was beginning to run out of units.

As if on cue, a light blue, two-door, Ford Fairlane 500 convertible coasted down Auglaize Street. Danny heard the word "Mason" over the public-address system. A man and a woman sat in the back seat of the vehicle. Danny didn't know who the man was. He stared at the woman. She wore a blue wool coat with a matching hat. She wore glasses and had greying dark hair.

A sign on the car confirmed that this was, in fact, Mrs. Mason. To Danny, she looked both happy and bewildered. She took in the crowds on either side of the street, occasionally waving. Danny saw her look to the rooftops and open windows filled by onlookers. She seemed a bit overcome by the enormity of the situation.

Another band followed, this one from New Bremen High School. As they marched past, Chris turned to the guys and said "I think we're going to try to get on the first shuttle bus back to The Hub. We're going to start back."

Reedo nodded, "OK we'll figure out the details on the prom later. We have plenty of time."

Danny smiled at Chris as she and Sandy began to pick their way through the crowd, moving off to the right. The bus pick up point was in a car lot a few blocks away. Danny was still watching Chris when she looked back over her shoulder. She caught his eyes, smiled, and was gone. Danny felt a flutter in his chest.

Danny turned back to Reed. The look on his buddy's face could only be described as a "shit eating grin."

"So whaddaya think, big guy?" Reedo probed.

"Well, I think I'm glad to have a prom date, and I think we might want to start back to the car. If Dad has to wait for us he won't be happy. Especially since our whole plan for the day fell apart."

Reed grinned. "Okay, lead the way."

Danny looked left and right, then turned around and looked south down Willipie, past the Wapa Theater.

"Let's go this way. We can go past the theater, maybe past the courthouse, then turn right and work our way over to the car."

"Works for me."

Jerry spent most of the second half of the parade trying to see as many elements as possible while at the same time trying to stay back out of sniff range of the bystanders. He missed a couple of the units, but was largely successful in keeping the odor of dog poo away from people. He received a couple of disapproving looks from a woman to their right, but Jerry wasn't sure if it was because of what was on the bottom of his boot or if it was his general appearance.

Jerry's right knee was aching. He hadn't noticed it when he and Jane were moving, but since they'd become stationary it was flaring up. The pants were probably ruined. Jane may be able to repair them to the point that he could use them as bumming around pants, but that would be about it. His jacket was stained up and down both arms. He had taken it off to examine it when one of the bands passed. He discovered that there was a large black-green stain there as well. Apparently, he had rolled over at some point during the fall, either on the way down or the way up. So, he looked like a hobo from the rear, too. His hair, he knew, was a mess. It wasn't as damp as before, but the clouds seemed to be threatening again.

Jerry moved back up to Jane. She turned and looked down to him, smiling. She was having a grand time.

"It's the New Bremen band, then I think I see the clergy members" said Jane.

Jerry nodded. The Wapak paper had printed that local clergy members would be bringing up the rear of the parade.

"OK, when they pass, we can look for the boys for a few minutes. If we don't see them, we can head to the car. We can just follow Auglaize Street all the way back to the street we're parked on...."

Jerry hesitated.

"Dearbaugh" Jane assisted.

"Yeah, Dearbaugh."

Danny and Reed walked under the marquee at the Wapa. "THE TROUBLE WITH ANGELS" with Rosalind Russell and Hayley Mills was playing this week. There was a poster for the movie displayed in the frame to the left of the ticket window. It showed two nuns, one clutching a rifle.

They stopped, eyed the poster, then turned to each other. "No way" they said synchronously, and then laughed. Like best friends everywhere, they could read each other's facial expressions and even react to external cues in exactly the same way.

Danny supposed he shouldn't have been surprised that Reed sprung the prom question on the girls. Danny seldom talked to anyone, even his best friend, about girls. Reedo had probably guessed Danny liked Chris months ago.

They continued south for a few blocks, passing the large stone edifice of the Auglaize County Courthouse on the right. As the pair reached Benton Street it began to rain again.

"Let's turn here. Maybe we can find a short cut to the car when we get closer," Danny offered.

The rain came down a little steadier. Still light, but persistent. The boys were passing groups of people here and there. These appeared to be mostly Wapakoneta residents who, like Danny and Reed, did not have tickets to the banquet at the high school and were returning home after taking in the parade.

Danny overtook a couple in their fifties a few minutes after turning on Benton. The woman held a black umbrella over her head. The man held an unfolded newspaper over his head with both hands. Danny could read the large type near the man's right hand, "Wapakoneta Daily News, Souvenir Edition."

The man's left hand clutched the paper near a large advertisement that featured a photo of Neil Armstrong in his Gemini 8 flight suit. Neil wore a helmet and, it seemed to Danny, a quizzical look on his face. The front of the suit was dotted with apertures of one sort or another. Near Armstrong's lower abdomen a hose was attached to one of the apertures. The hose ran down and out of the picture. Before passing the man, Danny read the words at the bottom of the ad,

GAS IS DEPENDABLE
WEST OHIO GAS COMPANY

Danny tapped Reed's shoulder and pointed to the newspaper. They both burst out laughing. They continued to walk. On another day, the light rain would've been miserable. But they had seen a spaceman and they had prom dates.

Life was good.

After the clergymen passed, bringing up the rear of the parade, Jerry and Jane stepped out into the street. They watched as hundreds of people melted away from the downtown area. Some passed their position and turned north toward the school. Others faded between buildings on their way to buses, cars, or houses. They saw lawn chairs being carried and baby carriages being pushed. They did not see Danny or Reed.

"Well, let's just head to the car" sighed Jerry.

They hoisted the cooler between them once more. After a block or so, it began to lightly rain. Jerry said "No sense in both of us getting soaked. I'll carry the cooler. You go ahead and use your umbrella."

Jane did her best to shield Jerry from the rain as he made his way along Auglaize Street, but it was a losing battle. It was over a mile to the car and the rain, light as it was, trickled into his eyes and matted his pants to his legs. Jerry got into a rhythm. He let the cooler slap onto his left hip on every other stride and increased his pace. Jane scrambled to keep up.

Danny and Reed began to jog down the Benton Street sidewalk. As they approached one intersection, Danny looked diagonally to his left. He stopped and pointed to the rambling two story house on that corner.

"Check it out Reed. That's Neil Armstrong's old house."

Confused, Reed managed "What?"

I'm telling you, that's 601 Benton. That's the house he grew up in."

"How the heck do you know that?" Reed demanded.

"I read a lot," smiled Danny.

They jogged on. After a few more blocks, they stopped to get their bearings.

Reed offered, "Your car is that way," and pointed ahead and to the left. "We can go another few blocks to Dearbaugh and take a left, or cut between some houses and try to get there quicker."

"Follow me" said Danny. He moved to the left, slipping between two small houses that were only twenty or so feet apart. This was the type of movement they enjoyed. In Botkins, where they knew every nook and cranny; every fence, spigot and swing set, they could quickly move through town. They had often sneaked up on friendly rivals, pelting them with apples picked from a tree or with snowballs, depending on the season.

But this wasn't Botkins, so Danny had to be cautious. He led Reed a few strides past the houses, then stopped. Ahead of him was a two-story building with no front wall.

"Let's duck in out of the rain for a minute" Danny suggested.

Getting no argument from Reed, Danny led the way. The boys stepped under the roof of the structure. The roof tapered down from the front toward the back. There was a loft 10 or 12 feet above their heads.

Danny took off his jacket and shook it out. He used the dry shirtsleeves underneath to wipe his face and eyes. Reedo did the same and commented "Looks like the rain is stopping. We should be able to cut through this field back here and—"

Reed had been turning to gesture toward the southwest, where the Impala would be. He froze in mid-sentence.

Danny turned to behold the biggest dog he'd ever seen in his life. It had long white hair that seemed a bit matted with dirt and straw. It just took them in with a non-committal look on its face.

The dog began to stand now and Danny noticed the large chain that led from its neck to a post in the center of the building. The chain clinked as the dog rose.

Danny and Reed pivoted together and hurtled through the open front of the building, turned left, and sprinted though an open field for a couple hundred feet before stopping to catch their breath.

They looked back expectantly. The dog was sitting at the front corner of the building, just staring at them.

"Oh my god, that dog was huge!" Reed exclaimed.

What kind was it?" Danny asked.

"No idea, I've never seen a dog like that before." answered Reed.

Danny had a checkered past with dogs. While he loved Suzy Wong and got along with all of his friends' dogs, he'd run into some trouble with a few others when he had the paper route. He was always cautious around a strange dog.

Walking now and in sight of the car, Reed noted "I think they feed that dog people food, I saw some scraps of bread on the floor beside him."

Danny and Reed made it to the Impala ten minutes before Danny's parents. They threw stones at a telephone pole across the street for a while. It was a contest, of course. Reed was the first to record ten hits on the pole, nailing it while Danny was still stuck on eight. They ran out of good rocks and were leaning on the trunk of the car when they spotted Jerry and Jane shuffling toward them.

From one hundred feet away they could see that Jerry's pants were torn and bloody. He bounced the cooler off his hip as he made his way toward the car. Jerry's face was set in stone.

Danny and Reed stood next to each other, silently assessing the situation. Without turning his head, Reed angled his mouth toward Danny and muttered "Ohhh man!"

Danny, with facial control that a ventriloquist would envy, whispered "Not good!"

Danny trotted to his parents.

"Let me take that, Dad."

Danny was thankful that Reed was with them. He reasoned that it would keep his dad from blowing his top.

"What happened to you?" Danny asked, looking first at his dad, then his mom.

"Your dad fell. He's fine. Wasn't that wonderful?" she asked enthusiastically, referring to the parade, a big smile on her face.

"Where were you guys?" Jerry demanded.

"At the Bi-Rite. We were there the whole time" Danny sputtered. What—"

"Aww forget it" said Jerry.

He unlocked the car, then the trunk. "Put the cooler in there, Danny."

Jerry reached toward Jane. "Give me that walkie-talkie." Jane handed it over and Jerry flipped it on. He turned to Reed "No battery."

Jerry held it out toward Reed, his face hard to read. Reed accepted the device and stammered "I'm really sorry. I checked it before going to bed. It was fine."

Jerry sighed. "Aww forget it Reed. At least we have Cokes. Open up that cooler and give me one."

Reed complied. He was reaching back into the cooler for more cans to give to the others when he heard Jane say "No Jerry!"

Reed looked up as Jerry lifted the pull tab on his can. A jet of pressurized Coca-Cola shot into Jerry's face.

Jerry just stood there, shoulders slumped.

Jane said "The cans fell out of the cooler less than an hour ago." She busied herself, cleaning Jerry's face with cloth kept in the glove box.

The boys got in the back seat. Jerry growled "Let's just go home" and started the car.

Jane said again "It was a wonderful parade."

Danny thought he smelled dog poop. He turned to Reed to mention it. Before he could, Reed, walkie-talkie in hand, leaned over and softly asserted "Teddy's Atomic Robot wasn't working last night. He must've taken my battery."

Danny strangled a laugh.

Danny was smiling when the Impala came to a stop. They were in front of Doc Mielke's house. Danny came back to the present. Memories of the parade faded. Thoughts of his mom rushed in. Danny's smile vanished.

Doc, Jerry, and Danny all got out of the still running Impala.

"Again, I'm so sorry about Jane, Mr. Hitchens. If there's anything I can do..." Doc said softly.

"You've been a great help, Doc. I can't thank you enough," Jerry answered.

Jerry went to the driver's side. Danny was about to turn back to the passenger side when Doc approached. Doc squeezed Danny's shoulder and said "Hang in there, Danny. Take as much time off from school as you need... see you at track practice."

They both put on sad smiles. Doc turned to walk up his front steps. Danny turned to face life without his mom.

PART TWO

SMALLTOWN, USA

CHAPTER TWELVE

Danny and Jerry rode silently the few blocks home from Mielke's. It was dark now, adding to the sense of desolation that each of them felt. It was Wednesday. A school night. Well, for everyone but the juniors back in D.C.

There were still some people outside. Danny realized that the whole town must've heard about his mom by now. He suspected that the Hitchens car would be a source of morbid curiosity. In his mind's eye, he imagined an impertinent neighbor, perhaps one of the Havener girls, oogling the Impala as it passed by, hoping to get a look at his face so that they'd have the foundation for a "You shoulda' seen Danny Hitchens" story.

In reality, the only reaction he saw to their Impala was quite different.

Passing by the Craft house, Danny noticed that Dave Craft, or DW, as his son Andy called him, referring to his given name of David Wayne, was in the driveway loading something into the back of his pickup truck. Dave was a bricklayer. He eschewed the title of mason, saying it "sounded a bit puffed up for a small town boy layin' brick."

As Danny and Jerry approached the Craft house, Dave glanced up at the headlights. Danny saw recognition in Dave's face. He saw Dave lean one hand against his truck and slowly drop his head. It was a profoundly sad gesture. Far from voyeuristic, Dave couldn't bear to look at the widower driving or the motherless son in the passenger seat. Danny didn't know what to think about that. His felt his eyes swell again with tears.

A few blocks later, Jerry pulled into their driveway. He switched off the ignition and let out a long sigh. He turned to see his son dabbing at an eye with the heel of his hand.

"I'm really sorry, Danny" Jerry said softly.

They sat for a while, not saying anything.

"It was your mom's decision to let you go on the trip. I really don't think she would've done that if she thought... this would happen." Jerry's last few syllables trailed off.

Danny turned to his dad. This was the man that, usually reluctantly, implemented the discipline often required in a two-boy family. The breadwinner. The advisor, coach, mentor. Sometimes a source of embarrassment. Always steady.

Now he looked completely helpless.

"I know, dad. We better get in and check on Suzy."

They unloaded the car and went in through the garage to the door to the kitchen. Suzy Wong waited inside the door with her tail wagging and her customary expectant eyes. She backed away when Danny swung his suitcase through the doorway. When Danny sat it down and knelt to her, she stood on two paws and licked at his face. Danny couldn't hold back a small smile. He made two half fists and rubbed under Suzy's ears with the knuckles of his index and middle fingers. Suzy loved this.

Jerry was reading a note that he'd found on the table.

"It's from Caroline Craft. She left some sandwiches for us in the refrigerator. She said she let Suzy outside a couple hours ago." Jerry smiled sadly, thankful again that he lived in a town where no one locked their doors.

Danny gave Suzy one last scratch then stood and grabbed the suitcase. On a normal day, he supposed, his mom would have him take it down the hall to the laundry room and she'd start a load. He never really thought about it, but now he realized his basketball and baseball uniforms were always clean and neatly folded when he woke up the day after a game. Mom had her ways of doing things. Some he noticed, some he didn't. Danny wondered how many of Mom's ways were now gone with her, and he would never know what they were.

He teared up again as he walked down the hall.

Danny dropped the suitcase in the laundry room and walked across the hall to use the bathroom. When he finished, Danny walked back to the kitchen. His dad was sitting at the

116

kitchen table. He had the telephone book and their address book both opened in front of him. The address book was maintained by Jane and included handwritten addresses and telephone numbers of all of their out of town friends and family. This was information not included in the Shelby County phone book they were issued once a year.

Jane had added many of the numbers from the phone book to her address book as well. It was easier to look up Don Busch's store under the address book "B" tab or Koenig Hardware under the "K" tab than flipping through 80 or so pages in the phone book. Many numbers, of course, were known by heart. Jane didn't bother to write these in the book. The Thompson's number, for example, was not there.

"Do you need to call someone, Dad?"

Jerry looked at his watch. It was approaching 10 pm. Past time for most weekday calls. But, unfortunately, this day was different.

"I have to call Uncle Jim. He was contacting some of the relatives for me. Then I have to call the Red Cross. They have a 24-hour line and they told me to call at any time to see if they've been able to get word to Eddie. Can you take Suzy outside?"

Jerry reached over to the kitchen counter and fitted his hand over the cradled handset. His fingers curled around into the concave area at the rear of the unit. He squeezed his palm over the handset, pinning it in place, and lifted the entire apparatus. He swung it over to the table and lifted the handset to his ear. Jerry stuck his left index finger into the opening on the dial at "6" and turned it clockwise until his finger touched a steel barrier on the right side. He retracted his finger and let the spring-loaded dial rotate back to its original position. Jerry then put his finger into the "9" hole to dial the second number.

Danny turned to look for Suzy. His dad must be calling Uncle Jim first. All Botkins numbers were in the "693" exchange. Suzy was at her water bowl in the corner. Danny pushed open the door that led back to the garage, making a clicking sound with his mouth. Suzy picked up on the cue and trotted through.

Instead of walking out the front of the garage, Danny reached for the door that opened to the back yard. Suzy dutifully made her way outside and began sniffing the ground. Watching from the doorway, Danny noticed that the tall wastebasket usually kept in the kitchen was setting just outside the back door.

Danny drew in a deep breath. When the wastebasket was full, his mom would sit it outside the back door. She didn't want anything in the house or the garage that could turn foul. One of Danny's chores was to regularly check the trash and to burn it when necessary.

Jane must've moved the full trash container outside before leaving for the hospital. She wanted everything to be in order.

Danny whispered "I'll get it Mom."

He began to sob. Danny walked to the garage workbench. He found the small box of wooden matches inside an old cigar box.

Danny picked up the waste can and turned toward the burn barrel in the back corner of the yard. Tears ran freely down his face in the darkness. As he passed the rear kitchen window, he could detect his dad's voice. Not words, just tone. It sounded weary, hopeless.

Danny reached the barrel. It was a rusted, steel, 55-gallon drum. His dad brought it from the lumberyard, where it had held lacquer that the business bought in bulk. Empty drums were in demand in virtually every small town in Ohio. The more of your trash you could burn yourself, the less you had to pay to be removed by the weekly garbage truck.

Danny dumped the trash into the barrel, which was already half full with compacted ash. He slid open the matchbox, removed one, and swiped it across the rusty exterior of the barrel. The match flickered.

Danny believed that fire triggered a process that weakened the metal wall of the barrel. Was it oxidation? He couldn't remember. Whatever, when it happened over a period of months, the steel turned brown, became coarse to the touch, and weakened. Danny could look at a burn barrel behind any house in Botkins and guesstimate how long it had been in use by seeing how brown it was. Eventually the sidewall would become so thin that pieces of it would fall off and daylight would shine through.

Danny realized he was holding a cold match. He had stopped crying.

He pulled a second match from the box and drew it across the barrel. He found the corner of a paper bag and let the flame bite into it. The bag looked like the style used by the Tastee Freez. Danny remembered how excited he and Eddie would get as small boys when they saw these bags. It would be on Friday. Payday. His dad would leave work, walk a block to the small First National Bank branch office, and deposit his paycheck.

Jerry would then walk back toward the lumberyard parking lot, stopping first at the Tastee Freez to pick up soft serve ice cream. A quart of vanilla, a quart of chocolate, and a quart of twist, half vanilla and half chocolate. He would cross the street to his car, make the two-minute drive home, and walk in the door shouting "Guess who's here?"

Danny and Eddie would see the bags and shout "The Ice Cream Man!"

On the rare occasion that their mom wasn't home, Danny's dad would let them eat a scoop before supper.

The flame had caught hold now. Danny gazed at it, mesmerized. He felt something above his right ankle. He looked down and saw Suzy. She was sitting, observing him. Those eyes. He bent down and lifted her. They stood together, lost in the fire. The flames reflected in their eyes.

Danny's mind wandered. He thought again of his mom at the Armstrong parade. The look on her face when they met afterward at the car.

"Wasn't that wonderful?" she had asked. She looked so happy. Danny smiled.

Of course, Dad was another story. Danny's smile broadened.

His dad's farcical day at the Armstrong parade led to behavior that was, for the most part, out of character for him. He had let loose a few cuss words in public that day. This was far from normal for his dad, thought Danny. He couldn't remember seeing it on any other occasion. Like all boys, Danny feared his dad's temper. All dads seemed to have them. Some displayed them more than others.

Danny was paddled by his dad just one time. He had skipped a stone off the street in front of Mrs. Englehaupt's house. Freakishly, the stone glanced off the curb and smacked into her ground level basement window.

A neighbor, Danny never found out which one, called his house and his mom and dad were waiting on him when he got home.

Danny remembered his father giving him one chance to explain what happened. Eight-year-old Danny denied knowledge of the incident, and punishment was swift.

Danny looked at Suzy and was about to rub under her ears when he felt her stiffen a bit. He watched as Suzy turned her head. Danny became aware of a raised voice. It was his dad. Danny turned and saw Jerry through the kitchen window. He was standing now, and gesturing.

Danny picked up the wastebasket and trotted back to the garage, still holding Suzy. He sat both of them down inside the garage and opened the door to the kitchen. His dad was shouting into the phone.

"GODDAMN GHOULS. That's what you are, a buncha' goddamned ghouls. You don't have the common decency to let me make a private call the day after my WIFE died? What kind of manners——"

Jerry saw Danny in the doorway. He realized he'd been screaming into the phone. His right hand seemed to choke the black handset. He forced air out of his lungs. Jerry smacked the handset back into the cradle.

"What was all that about?" Danny chanced.

"Aww, I was talking to your Uncle Jim about your mom and the Haveners were listening in. I asked them for some privacy and they knew I'd caught them so they hung up their phone, kinda hard, you know, like they do when they know they've been caught?" Jerry went on, "Anyway, ten seconds later I could tell they picked back up. They had a hand over the mouthpiece so I wouldn't hear them but I know they were there. It was just so... rude."

Jerry shook his head. "I just couldn't help it Danny."

That's alright Dad, it was none of their business." Danny could feel the anger in a part of his brain, trying to push its way into the space occupied by grief.

"The thing is, I'm not sure it was one of the girls. I had the feeling it was Gert. Trying to pick up some gossip that she'd spread all over town."

Danny thought of Gert Havener, a dowdy, easily offended woman. Danny had lived on the same street as her his whole life, but when he stopped to collect the weekly fee for the newspaper, she never called him by his first name. Not once in two years.

"Oh no," Jerry's head snapped to the phone. "Uncle Jim was still on the line. He heard me scream at them then I hung up on him."

Danny's anger was shunted into another corner of his brain now as he and his dad burst out laughing.

"Aw crap" Jerry said. I gotta call him back. I still need to call the Red Cross, too." He looked at Danny. "Why don't you try to get some sleep? We'll decide in the morning what to do next."

Danny nodded. He bent down and picked up Suzy, who was sitting near the refrigerator with her head cocked at them in confusion.

As Jerry started dialing a "6," Danny said "Thanks for coming to get me today Dad." Then, softly "I'm really sorry about Mom."

Jerry slowly lowered the phone. He came around the table and hugged his son. "I know Danny."

They clutched each other for a few seconds. When Suzy began to struggle between them, they released each other, both smiling at the pug.

"Okay Dad. Don't stay up too late." Danny carried Suzy to his room.

The morning sun reached through the window, angling down to Danny's face. As he stirred from a deep sleep, he had the momentary sensation of standing in a dark tunnel, watching a train rush toward him.

He half opened his eyes... sunny... is it summer? No, it's a school day.... a school day and the sun's up? WAS HE LATE FOR SCHOOL?

Danny quickly sat up and searched for the clock......8:22. Damn! He WAS late for school. This was bad, this... wait. He didn't need to go to school today. His class was in Washington D.C. He was here in Botkins, and his mom was gone.

Danny made his way down the hall. His dad forked a glob of scrambled eggs onto the floor, where Suzy Wong made short work of them.

"I made eggs and toast" Jerry said. He had showered and was wearing weekend clothes, not work clothes. Danny thought he still looked tired.

"Thanks." Danny reached for a plate on the kitchen counter. "How late did you stay up?"

"Oh, 1:30 or so, I guess" Jerry added "I was able to get through to someone at the Red Cross. They think we'll know something about Eddie later today or sometime tomorrow."

Danny brightened a bit at this." *Dang* he thought, *it'll be great to see Eddie.*

Jerry continued "I need to meet with Father Berg today about the service and burial."

Danny's eyes flicked to his dad's, then quickly away.

"It's a Catholic cemetery and I've been told he has to give his approval before you can be, uh, interred there. I figured there was no reason for you to go along. I wrote down a few things I could use your help with while I'm gone."

"Sure dad." Danny reached across the table for a small notepad his dad slid over. Danny glanced at the list.

Get mail.

Clean up Eddie's room.

Stop at Grandpa & Grandma's.

The list continued with a few other mundane assignments.

"Grandpa & Grandma's?"

"Uncle Jim says they're worried about you and want to make sure you're OK." Jerry hesitated. "To tell you the truth, Danny, I'm a little worried about them. I think it would do you both some good to visit for a while." Jerry paused, "As difficult as this is for us, losing their daughter has to be at least as bad. Come back and let me know if there's anything we can do for them."

Danny silently marveled that his dad would think of the well-being of his in-laws. He nodded and managed "Good idea."

"Why don't you get cleaned up? I'm heading for St. Lawrence. Come home after you finish your list and we'll figure out lunch."

Danny showered, went through his suitcase, and started a load of laundry. He walked down the hall to Eddie's room. For the most part, it looked exactly the way it did when his brother left after his visit following boot camp.

A bookshelf was crammed with books and magazines. The subjects ranged from cars to World War Two, to airplanes, to sports. On top of the bookshelf were two shoeboxes filled with baseball cards. Eddie's ball glove lay next to the cards. There had been a baseball in the glove up to a couple weeks ago. Danny had borrowed it to throw with Reed one cold, sunny Saturday. They thought they'd get a jump on the high school season with a little spring training. The ball was now in Danny's glove across the hall.

Eddie's bed was partially covered with items that belonged to the other three occupants of the house. The unused bed had become a catch-all area for items of all sorts. Danny supposed this was the area his dad wanted him to clear, so it was ready for Eddie whenever he made it back.

Pictures were thumbtacked to the wall, most featuring sports figures. A Cincinnati Reds pennant was tacked above the closet, next to an aerial photo of Crosley Field, the Reds' ballpark. Eddie had cleared the space on top of his dresser the summer before his senior year to make room for model rockets.

These were actual flying rockets. Eddie had seen an ad in one of Danny's comic books. He mailed 25 cents to Estes Industries in Penrose, Colorado. Two weeks later a catalog arrived. Danny remembered that Eddie spent hours looking through the catalog. The photos, Danny admitted, were almost hypnotic to a teenaged boy.

Eddie was working at the lumberyard that summer, ostensibly to save money for college, but he hadn't even applied anywhere. This despite the urgings of their mother. Danny was certain that Eddie already had his heart set on the Army, but was avoiding any discussion with their parents.

Eddie eventually used some of his college fund to purchase several rockets. They ranged in size from seven inches tall, the Astron Scout, to 25 inches high, the impressive Astron Farside. They were constructed primarily of cardboard, plastic, and wood, and came with colorful decals.

But the rockets were just the tip of the iceberg. They required a myriad of launch mechanisms, wire controls, igniters, and single use engines. Eventually Eddie had accumulated so much of this stuff that he cleared out an old fishing tackle box to hold and transport it. The engines were about the size and shape of a shotgun shell. They were filled with the solid fuel that powered the craft and came in different sizes and potencies.

Eddie had an audience of two at Cole Field, the Botkins baseball diamond, on the day of his inaugural launch of the Astron Scout. Danny and Reed had low expectations. They were riding their bikes up to Don Butch's to see if the proprietor had put out a new box of baseball cards—Danny was trying to collect every Red and still needed Tony Perez— when they decided to take a detour to watch.

Eddie was finishing the pre-launch preparation. He waved them over and they rode their bikes out onto the dirt skin of the infield. It was a hot, dry day and wind pushed the dust that their tires disturbed.

Eddie had set up the launcher several feet behind second base, near the edge of the dirt infield. He had calculated that the rocket, if it ignited, would travel as high as 100 feet, a charge in the engine would fire and pop the parachute out of the fuselage, and it would float to the ground somewhere on the infield.

Eddie finished connecting the remote Astro Launch Panel hand-held controller to the rocket itself via a long wire. While he did this, Danny and Reed decided to race each other around the bases on their bikes.

Reed laid down the challenge, "We start at home plate. When I say go, you take off to first base and go all the way around to home again." He paused for effect, "I will head to third and go in the opposite direction. First one to home is the winner."

Danny had smiled. Standing now in Eddie's room, remembering, he smiled again.

Reed and Danny rode to home plate. They backed their bikes into each other, the rear tires touching. There were no actual bases on the field. These were removed after every game and locked in the shed next to the first base dugout. The metal posts that held the bases, however, were plainly visible.

"Hey Eddie," Danny shouted, "be our starter."

Eddie, tightening a last connection, waved at them dismissively.

"C'mon Eddie, Reed'll cheat if you don't help."

Eddie finished with the rocket and stood. He removed his black Botkins baseball hat and wiped the sweat from his forehead.

"Yeah, help us out Eddie, I'm gonna kick his butt." Reed added.

"Okay, okay." His hat still in hand, Eddie instructed "You guys tell me when you're ready, I'll throw my hat in the air, when it hits the ground, you go."

The competitors smiled. They jostled a bit until both were satisfied.

"No cuts," Danny warned.

"No cuts," Reed agreed.

They hunched over their handlebars, left feet on the ground, right feet on raised pedals.

"Okay" they shouted in unison, their heads turned toward Eddie.

Eddie tossed the hat straight up in the air. It reached a height of 30 feet and began to float down. Reed and Danny, now coiled like springs, followed its descent with intense anticipation.

In retrospect, all three boys realized they should've paid more attention to the effect the wind had on the cap. It landed top down, just six inches behind the second base post. The wind had picked up and pushed it almost fifteen feet away from Eddie.

The instant the cap touched the ground, both boys were off. Danny rounded first base like a good baserunner who had just lined a ball to the outfield. He went wide into foul territory and cleanly passed a few inches beyond the post, his bike having cornered perfectly.

Reed tried to do something similar at third but realized too late that years of making left turns on foot at first base gave Danny a comfort factor that he, the counter clockwise biker, didn't have.

Reed had to slow when rounding third. As he accelerated toward second he glanced at Danny and realized he was losing already. He had to gain ground. Instantly Reed realized that he had to take a perfect path across second and first base, like the downhill slalom skiers he'd seen in the Olympics.

Accelerating, Reed moved his line left a bit, nearer shortstop. Danny was going to get to second before him. But if Reed took a better angle...

Too late, Eddie realized his hat was in the path of these two nimrods, looking like a squirrel on the track at the Indianapolis 500. "Hey WAIT!"

Danny knew he had the lead and pressed his advantage. He stole a glance at Reed then willed his eyes to acquire the second base post. He saw the hat, and despite his speed, may have had time to adjust, but was distracted by Eddie's shouting.

Danny plowed over Eddie's hat.

It flipped in the air after being run over by the front tire, made contact with the back tire, and tumbled back near the second base post, landing right side up.

Danny made several micro calculations in the space of a half second or so; that was Eddie's game hat from last baseball season, each player only gets one hat a year, that was Eddie shouting at him, and Eddie could beat the crap out of him.

Now off his game, sensing Reedo vectoring in at him, Danny swung wide toward deep shortstop, struggling to regain control of his wobbling handlebars.

As if in slow motion, Reed saw the hat compress under Danny's front tire. The cap's path would seem to take it out of the kill box. Reed's left foot was pistoning down with his final pedal stroke before passing the post. Then the improbable happened: the Botkins cap was clipped by Danny's rear tire, its trajectory bringing it into Reed's path.

Reed Thompson was a Pete Rose fan. The fiery young Reds second baseman was brash. Rose ran to first when he was walked. He hustled. He was often quoted as saying he watched every pitch all the way into the catcher's mitt, always followed the ball. That when his bat made contact with the ball, he could actually SEE bat meet ball.

As much as Reed liked Pete Rose, he always doubted a hitter trying to make solid contact with a ball moving 95 miles per hour could achieve this optical feat.

That was until he ran over Eddie's hat. Reed, moving at downhill slalom speed, clearly saw his tire tread crush the white block letter "B" on the crown of the hat. This crystalline image was imprinted on Reed's brain for years. He would have nightmares about it.

The hat was so thoroughly compressed by Reed's front tire it didn't move an iota. This, of course, positioned it for further disfigurement from the rear tire.

Reed didn't see this, but he didn't have to. Like Danny, he registered several things instantly; that was Eddie's game hat, you only get one hat a year, Eddie was screaming at him, Eddie could beat up he and Danny at the same time.

Reed wavered, but not as much as Danny. He concentrated on making a good turn at first. At this point he figured if he was about to face a vengeful upper classman he might as well win the damn race first.

Danny had similar thoughts as he cleared third. He glanced at his best friend. Seeing it was a dead heat, he redoubled his efforts.

Both boys were approximately twenty feet from the plate, moving at top speed, when they simultaneously realized that, damn, they were going to ram into each other.

Each of them instinctually jammed down backwards on their right pedal while jerking their handlebars left. Both boys went down, still on their bikes, their bare left legs sliding along on the Cole Field dirt.

Clouds of dust flew toward both dugouts, rose, and gently blew through the wire backstop.

"YOU IDIOTS!"

Eddie was furious. Danny and Reed were both under their bikes. They would later realize that they had matching world-class strawberries down their left legs.

Reed knew that Eddie was seldom mean to Danny. It was Reed's experience that on the rare occasions when Eddie might mess with his brother, he became reluctant to do so when he realized a friend was near. But he saw black rage in Eddie's eyes. Shooting a look at Danny, Reed saw real fear. He could think of only one thing to say.

"So Eddie, who won?"

Eddie, at an emotional peak, immediately switched from rage to hilarity. Danny and Reed joined in. All three of them displayed tears of laughter within seconds.

The first thing they did after regaining their composure, well, the first thing after checking to make sure no girls had seen the incident, was to look at the bike slide paths. To the surprise of all three they realized that neither bike had touched the plate.

"It's a tie, you dumbasses. No rematch."

Eddie tried to reshape his Botkins cap without much success.

"Maybe Mom can fix it" Danny ventured.

"Forget it, the rocket's ready. Come on." Eddie led them back behind second base. Reed and Danny walked their bikes, limping slightly. Eddie gathered the launch controller and backed 20 feet away from the rocket into short center. "Give me a countdown, guys."

Danny and Reed complied. "Ten, Nine, Eight." The pair were standing to the right of Eddie and slightly behind him. "Seven, Six, Five." Danny caught Reed's eyes. Virtually reading each other's minds for the thousandth time, they raised their eyebrows slightly and chose an affectation for their respective faces. This time they both chose "trepidation."

They both realized that if this rocket didn't fire, Eddie would be super pissed.

"Four, Three, Two, One, Lift Off!"

Eddie depressed the launch button. With a loud hiss and a flash, the little Astron Scout rose from a cloud of white smoke. It, well, rocketed through the air, reaching a height of 300 feet in less than five seconds, a thin white contrail visible in its wake. At its apogee, the Scout hung for a beat, then tipped over. The boys saw a small orange parachute burst from the rocket a split second before the "pop" of the ejection charge reached their ears.

The rocket slowly floated earthward.

All three boys stood frozen, their mouths hanging open.

"WHOAH!" Eddie was the first to shout. A few seconds of jubilation ensued. Danny and Reed forgot about their scraped-up legs. Eddie forgot about his battered hat. Then the wind began to push the rocket northeasterly.

"Uh-oh," Eddie muttered. The Scout was already over the Cole Field backstop and still well over 150 feet high. The boys began to run across the infield in the direction of the rocket.

Sycamore Street bordered Cole Field on the east. It ran parallel to the third base line. Botkins School was situated on the east side of Sycamore. The Astron Scout cleared the backstop and Sycamore with ease. It passed over the tallest part of the school, the band room, before disappearing from their line of sight.

The boys crossed Sycamore and raced around the northwest corner of the school. After a few strides Eddie, in the lead, came to a stop. There was no sign of the Scout. Reed looked up to the school on their right "Its gotta be up on the roof."

It was, of course. Rather than being pissed, Eddie was elated. A recovery mission was staged that night by the boys. Equipped with a ladder, dark clothing, and flashlights, the triumvirate was able to make their way on top of the 15-foot-high roof. They recovered the Scout as well as a collection of baseballs, tennis balls, and Frisbees.

Eddie's expertise with rockets increased over the next few months. In some ways, this mirrored the course of the actual American space program, which evolved from the Mercury program to Gemini, and its more demanding mission profiles.

By the time Eddie was launching the Astron Farside, he had acquired quite a following. Neighbor kids congregated to watch and to help track down the spent rockets. The Farside travelled three times higher than the scout. Falling from a height of nearly 1000 feet, the rocket could drift for several blocks. Eddie learned to angle the rocket launches into the wind.

Danny cleared the last item from the bed. His mind wandered to thoughts of his mom. He shook his head. The sooner Eddie made it home, the better.

CHAPTER THIRTEEN

Danny decided to ride up to the post office before visiting his grandparents. He coasted down the driveway on his bike before turning right. As he pedaled up South Street, he realized that he would pass Havener's house. Danny remembered how angry his dad was the previous night about the unwanted surveillance and realized his own temperature was beginning to rise.

The Havener's lived in an unexceptional one story home with white aluminum siding and green shutters. The house had a one car garage on the right side and a medium sized front yard. It sat on the opposite side of the street from the Hitchens place. As he passed, Danny saw Gert Havener standing in the picture window. She had a telephone to her ear. She made no attempt to hide the fact that she was watching him. He could see her lips moving.

I should flip her the bird, Danny thought as he passed by.

Danny rode past Reed's house. There was a football in the front yard and a pogo stick lying in the driveway. It was weird to be out on the street on a school day. No one was out.

Danny passed the lumberyard. He waited for a truck to pass, then cut across 25A in front of the Tastee Freez. He could see the small brick post office building beyond on the next street. Danny took a short cut down a narrow alley and pulled up just short of an outdoor mailbox.

Danny made his way into the building. There was one wall in front of him covered with brass mailboxes. Each one had a lock with a dial. The dials were surrounded by letters. Each box owner was assigned a different combination.

Botkins was too small to have mail delivery. Danny idly thought, not for the first time, how odd it was to live in a town where subscribers to a local newspaper expected their delivery to be on time yet had accepted that they would only get their mail if they made their way to the post office and picked it up.

Danny walked to box 103. It was low and toward the center of the wall. "One-Oh-Three, I-G-F," Danny thought. When his mom decided that Danny was old enough to go get the mail, she took him to the post office and let him work the combination, "I-G-F" over and over. His mom enjoyed catching up with other visitors to the post office that day. From then on, Danny repeated the mantra every time he passed the post office, "One-Oh-Three, I-G-F."

Danny's lips trembled. He wiped at his eyes and knelt to the box. He could see through the little window that the box was stuffed with mail. With everything that had happened this week, they hadn't retrieved it in several days.

Danny opened the box and pulled out the contents. It looked like mostly bills and a few advertisements. He walked outside and returned to his bike.

"Danny? Danny Wait!"

Danny looked up. Carol Roush, the office manager from Botkins Lumber Company, was walking quickly down the alley that Danny had used a few minutes earlier.

Carol was a thin woman in her forties. Her straight hair was cut short and had been prematurely grey, nearly white, for as long as Danny knew her.

"I thought I saw you ride past the shop. How are you Danny? I'm so sorry to hear about your mom."

Danny didn't know how to respond. It must have showed.

"I'm sorry," Carol shook her head. "I was out of line to chase you down like this. It's just that I'm, well, we're all really sorry about Jane and we're willing to do anything we can to help your dad and you boys."

Danny liked Mrs. Roush. His dad talked highly of her and she was nice to Danny when he worked at the lumber yard in the summer. She was a reader, too, and often asked Danny about books he was reading.

"Thanks Mrs. Roush."

She smiled, "Remember, you can call me Carol." Then, "Is Eddie going to be able to make it home?"

"I think so. Dad's working on it with the Red Cross."

"Oh, I hope that works out. Tell your dad we're thinking of all you boys. Mr. Gerber says he can stay away from work as long as he needs to."

"Thanks, I will." Danny climbed on his bike.

Carol fought an urge to give him a hug.

Danny tucked the mail under his left arm and pedaled toward the center of town. He stopped to wait on two cars passing through a green light. He saw Gene Peters' Botkins patrol car sitting in the parking lot of Steiner's Marathon station across the street.

The light turned and Danny eased across the crosswalk. There were two picture windows at Steiner's, one faced west, toward the pumps, one faced north. A half dozen chairs were arranged inside, allowing observers to view the main intersection in town.

Steiner's attracted a number of hangers-on every morning. They drank coffee, read newspapers, and watched hay wagons amble through town. Gene Peters was a frequent visitor.

When Danny started across the street, Danny saw Peters stand up and look his way. The police chief stepped to the picture window, his lips moving. Danny saw the heads and shoulders of the other occupants turn his way as well. The man next to Peters said something. Then everyone but Peters looked away from Danny.

Peters slowly tracked Danny's progress, eyes behind his photochromic glasses. Enough light came through the windows to keep his glasses dark.

It struck Danny that Peters probably thought he was skipping school. He liked to play truant officer, even though that was not part of a village police chief's responsibility. Someone in the station must've said "That's the Hitchens kid, his mom just died," or something to that effect.

Everyone else in the room had purposely looked away from Danny. Peters, the jackass, had stared him down. Danny filed that away.

Danny biked north a couple blocks to Walnut Street and visited his grandparents. Gene and Martha still lived in the small grey house where Danny's mom and her brothers and sisters were raised.

The house had a carport on its right side. His Grandma called it a breezeway. There was an outdoor glider-style seat positioned under the shade of the carport. Martha would sit in the shade on nice days and watch the children of Botkins walk home when school let out.

Danny couldn't remember ever coming here and not being greeted by a smile at the door by his grandma. He received another today, but it was such a sad smile Danny almost cried.

Danny spent 20 minutes with his grandparents. He could tell they were devastated but tried to put on a good front. Grandpa Gene was wearing his grey work uniform. He had retired from Provico, the grain and seed company near the railroad tracks, almost three years earlier. Old habits are hard to break.

Grandma Martha made him lemonade. They talked a bit about Danny's abbreviated trip, and a bit about Eddie. Gene sat in a recliner and was mostly silent. Danny sat with Martha on the couch, or davenport, as she called it.

Danny was glad he stopped but wasn't sure anything had been accomplished by him or his grandparents.

The Impala was in the driveway when Danny returned home. He went in through the garage and found his dad pulling a plate out of the refrigerator.

"Hey Danny, I forgot about the sandwiches from Caroline. You OK with that for lunch?"

They munched on roast beef sandwiches and talked about their mornings. Danny told his dad about talking to Carol Roush and Gene and Martha.

Jerry told Danny that things had been worked out with Father Berg. His dad didn't elaborate and Danny didn't press him. After lunch, Jerry said he had to meet with their insurance agent. He started to reach for his notepad. Danny got the impression his dad was trying to think of chores to keep him busy.

"I have laundry and some homework to do" Danny offered.

After his dad left, Danny worked on laundry for a bit. He tried to work on an English assignment that was due the following week but his mind wandered. It had been a depressing day and he felt he was going nowhere. He looked at the clock, 2:45. A thought came to him.

Danny went back to Eddie's room. He rummaged around the bottom of the closet and came out with the black low top converse sneakers Eddie had worn his senior year. Danny quickly dressed in shorts, tee-shirt, and sweats. He laced up the shoes, they were maybe a half size too large, and strode down the hall. Suzy looked up from where she was napping in a rectangle of sunshine on the kitchen floor.

"Suzy, I'm going to track practice" Danny declared, rushing by.

Suzy closed her eyes and settled her head back to the floor.

Doc Mielke was both surprised and delighted to see Danny Hitchens show up on his bicycle a few minutes after 3 pm that Thursday. He had hoped Danny would give it a shot. Sure, the track coach could always use another athlete on the team, but in this case the primary motivation was to get Danny interested in something that might help him get through a painful period in his life.

Doc had even spoken to Jim Sanders about Danny. Sanders was the Botkins baseball coach. He also taught Physical Education and was the Driver's Education instructor at the school. He was a trim man in his forties with short brown hair. A hint of Aqua Velva aftershave lotion greeted anyone within five feet of him.

Doc told Sanders "We might be sharing another athlete this spring."

Sanders had looked at Mielke warily, immediately wondering if he was about to lose half a baseball player to track or gain half an athlete from Doc's squad.

"Danny Hitchens, I'm trying to get him to come out. I'd like to keep him as busy as possible."

Sanders had nodded thoughtfully.

"Well, Danny will start for me at second base, he's solid. A lot like his brother. I'd hate to lose him, too, but I agree with your point."

Sanders was referring to the other baseball players he "lost" to track. Catcher Gary Poppe and first baseman Bob Klopfenstein were examples of multi-sport athletes that scrambled from ballgames to track meets. There were barely 200 students in the four upper grades at the school. As at all small schools, coaches knew they had to share participants. It had been much easier for Sanders, though, before Mielke arrived and generated interest in the track program.

The track team met in front of the school on Sycamore Street. Botkins had no track, so practices were conducted right there on the street for the sprinters. The distance runners utilized country roads. Sycamore, the street that Eddie's Astron Scout had floated over, ran north-south, separating the school on the east from Cole Field to the west.

The stretch from State Street (south) to Walnut (north) was a bit over 200 yards in length. Making do with the resources at his disposal, Mielke tailored imaginative workouts for his runners. He varied paces, distances, and recovery times, utilizing his ubiquitous stopwatch and clipboard. He tried to implement training techniques that he learned from talking to other area coaches and from magazine articles. He was currently fascinated with Oregon track coach Bill Bowerman.

Doc had obtained a copy of a publication called "Distance Running News" in which Bowerman laid out the workouts his runners executed. Doc tinkered with the repetitions and times, trying to make them realistic for high school kids while still being challenging. He threw out what didn't work and continued to use what did.

"Hey, Danny, it's great to see you! I'm really glad you came out!" Doc approached Danny and patted the side of his shoulder.

"I couldn't hang around the house by myself. Unless Dad needs me for something, I'll probably come back to school tomorrow." Danny glanced at a group 25 or so kids in sweats and shorts, both boys and girls. They sat in a loose circle on the grass in front of the home economics room of the school. All of them were stretching, several were looking at Danny.

"Stretching?" Danny asked.

"Oh yeah, it's one of the most important things we do. Come on Danny."

Doc walked over to the group. "You all know Danny Hitchens. I've twisted his arm to get him to come out and help us this spring. His brother Eddie was on the team a few years ago and he was one of the best leaders we've ever had. We're not sure what events Danny will do but there is no doubt he'll make our team stronger."

Danny blushed.

Doc had Danny workout with the group that spent the practice on Sycamore. They ran a series of 100 and 200 yard sprints. Danny finished in the middle of the pack in the boys group on most sprints. A smaller group of distance runners ran through the streets of Botkins on their way out of town.

After practice, Doc again thanked Danny for coming out and mentioned "I'm going to have you run with the distance group tomorrow."

Danny looked at him quizzically.

"Something about your stride makes me think that might be a fit for you."

At that same time, most of the class of 1968 was in Fairfax County, Virginia. Chris Koenig and Sandy Monnin sat in wooden chairs on the east side of Mount Vernon, George Washington's mansion outside of Alexandria. They gazed out at the Potomac River, which swept past below and just east of the mansion.

Reed Thompson stood in front of them, his back to the river.

"So, nobody knows anything for sure?" He asked.

Chris, Sandy, and several other classmates nearby shook their heads.

The guided tour of the mansion had ended five minutes earlier. Mr. Rawson had gathered the students and told them they had one hour to explore the grounds. They would meet at the bus at 5 pm. Several of Danny Hitchens' closest friends gravitated to the two-story porch, or "piazza," as the tour guide referred to it.

The group compared notes on information they'd been receiving from home in their limited phone calls. No one in Botkins seemed to know definitively if funeral plans were complete for Danny's mom.

"I actually tried calling Danny's house this morning from the hotel pay phone but didn't get an answer." Reed related.

"I just hope we don't miss the funeral" Chris opined. Chris had come to enjoy being around Danny's parents, especially his mom. She sensed how close Danny was to Jane and knew that he must be devastated right now. She barely had enough time to say goodbye to him and give him a hug before he left with Mr. Mielke.

"I would be surprised if Eddie can get home before we do" Reed ventured.

There was one more full day of scheduled activities the following day before traveling home Saturday.

Their eyes turned to the Potomac, where a sailboat drifted in the wind.

CHAPTER FOURTEEN

Danny decided to go back to school on Friday. His dad had to go to the funeral home in Wapak and Danny knew it would be a long, lonely day at home.

It was a cool, overcast morning. Danny walked the four blocks carrying a gym bag containing the gear he would need for track practice. He entered the building through a rear door. His locker, number 126, was in this hall. After stashing his gym bag and removing the notebook he took to each class, Danny made for his homeroom. He sensed several sets of eyes on him as he made his way.

It was an odd day. Some of the classes, on a normal day, were attended by a mix of juniors and seniors. The absence of the group in Washington D.C. made Danny feel like he didn't belong. In one class, Physics, Danny and Louise Schmerge were the only juniors in attendance. Louise, who hadn't been able to afford the class trip, looked at Danny with an expression comprised of pity and understanding. It must've been the same expression Danny had when he saw an embarrassed Louise tear up while passing the deposit checks for the Junior Trip up her row a few weeks ago.

Substitute teachers covered the classes normally taught by the three chaperones still away with the juniors. This resulted in 45 minute chunks that were little more than study halls. Danny's mind inevitably wandered to his mom during these periods.

He was glad to hear the final bell. He grabbed his gym bag from his locker and changed clothes in the locker room. Reporting to practice, he was informed by Doc that he would join the second group of distance runners.

"Okay Danny, after our stretching, all the distance kids will start at the same time. You'll run toward the pool," he said gesturing toward the community swimming pool at the corner of Sycamore and State Street, "take a left on State, and go out over the I-75 overpass. You continue to the next road. That is the mile mark. Group A will turn left and do the full, four-mile block, coming back into town on 25A from the north. Group B will turn around at the mile mark and come straight back. The goal is to get all group B runners into the other group as soon as they're ready."

Danny nodded. The longest distance he could remember running was a mile. Every varsity basketball player was required to run a six-minute mile to make the team. Danny remembered chugging along with a group that finished in about 5:50. It was harder than he'd thought it would be.

Doc gathered all the distance runners on Sycamore. He sat astride an ancient Schwinn bicycle.

"We'll start both stopwatches when I say 'go.' I'll take one with me on the bike. Coach Bensman will stay here with the other one."

He gestured to Mel Bensman, the assistant coach and industrial arts teacher, who stood nearby wearing a floppy hat and holding a clipboard.

"I'll ride with you, make sure the second group gets turned around, then stay with the others all the way around the block. Mr. Bensman will record your time." Mielke stressed, "This isn't a race, run at a comfortable pace. We expect you to improve gradually over the season."

Virgil Peoppelman piped up, "Hey Doc, you got plenty of air in those tires?"

The incongruous sight of a 250-plus pound man on a bicycle, carrying a stopwatch, was comical, Danny admitted.

Everyone laughed, including both coaches. Doc's practices, it seemed, were run in an easy-going manner than was geared to having fun.

Doc lined them up. "Ok, remember to stay on the left side of the road. Watch for cars. Ready... Go!"

Danny took a cue from the others at the beginning of the run, sticking with the pack. A few of the better runners began to pull away after a few blocks. Doc rode ahead with these runners. By the time they passed Bob's Gulf and reached the overpass, Danny was with a secondary group, holding his own.

Danny saw Mielke ride partway up the overpass incline, waver, and dismount. Doc pushed the bike up the rest of the way, encouraging his runners as they passed.

"Good, good. Use your arms going uphill, Danny!"

Danny complied and could feel a difference. He reached the top of the overpass and saw the traffic below on I-75 flowing north and south. The runners lengthened their strides down the other side and made for the turnaround. Doc coasted past them and pedaled to the corner. He stopped there in the middle of the road and palmed his stopwatch.

"Great job guys, go around me and head back."

Returning to town, Danny paired up with Shelly Maurer, who he knew was the best distance runner on the girls' team. They ran abreast most of the way, Danny twice moving behind her when trucks approached them heading for the interstate. Approaching Sycamore, Shelly picked up the pace. Danny stuck with her and, nearly exhausted, made the turn. They passed Mel Bensman 50 yards later. Shelly slowed to an easy walk. Danny put his hands on his knees and breathed heavily. He walked to the side of the street that faced the baseball field and flopped down in the grass.

"Breath... stretch and breathe" Bensman shouted.

Shelly came over to Danny and sat. She straightened her legs and reached for her toes. "Great job, Danny! You'll be up with the first group in no time."

Danny, sweating freely, looked at her and said "FOUR miles? I don't know if I can do two again."

Shelly smiled. "Stay with it."

They finished stretching and were doing a warm down jog when the first group finished, Virgil Poeppelman leading the way. Doc Mielke, looking nearly as fatigued as the runners, left his bike and went to confer with Mel Bensman. Doc walked over to Danny.

"Great job, Danny! Fourteen forty. Jeez-O-Pete, that's a great start!"

Danny smiled, remembering that Doc used terms like "Jeez-O-Pete." Then he asked "What, 14 minutes and 40 seconds?" That was much faster than Danny expected.

"Doc instructed, "Well see how you feel next week, but I think you can go right into the first group. I know you have baseball practice next week, just come to track practice whenever you can."

Danny felt a positive vibration for the first time in several days.

The Hitchens house began to fill up with food that day. Ruth Bauman brought a casserole. Carolyn Craft brought a cake. A half dozen others brought a selection of sandwiches, fried foods, and deserts.

The Red Cross reported that Eddie had been notified and was being flown to Hawaii. He would make multiple flights home from there and was expected to land in Dayton in two days, on Monday, March, 13.

Danny woke Saturday stiff and sore from the run. He'd decided to meet the bus when it returned from the class trip. He found the itinerary in his room and saw that the bus was expected at the school at 4 pm.

After lunch, Danny rode along with his dad to Don Butch's small general store on State Street. They now had plenty of food at the house, but Jerry wanted to pick up some essentials such as milk, bread, and eggs to have available when Eddie arrived.

Don Butch owned a small block building. It was barely 20 feet wide. The front window displayed items on wooden tables that slanted downward toward the glass. Upon entering through the front door, customers would see similar wooden displays against the right wall. These slanted down slightly from the wall toward the center of the room. They contained an extensive selection of candy bars and gum as well as baseball and, depending on the time of year, football cards.

Shelving covered most of the opposite wall. Essentials such as Wonder Bread, Campbell's Soup, and Dinty Moore Stew occupied this area. A large red Coca Cola cooler was wedged in beside the shelfs on the far corner.

Straight ahead was a meat and cheese display case. A cooler with a walk-in door was situated a few feet behind the case. In addition to large tubes of baloney and wedges of cheese, the freezer held ice cream treats and several boxes of frozen candy bars. If Don was in the cooler, he relied on a small bell at the top of the front door to alert him when a customer entered.

Don Butch's shop filled a niche that convenience stores would assume in later decades. It provided a source of essential items that a shopper could get quickly, without travelling greater distances. The relative high volume of treats for sale was another similarity.

Don Butch stood behind the meat case wearing a white butcher's apron. He was a cadaverous man of indeterminate age. Danny pegged him at somewhere between 75 and 200. He was operating the meat slicer that was situated on top of the display case. A woman stood in front of the case, her back to Danny.

As Jerry made his selections, Danny perused the wall of candy. He noted that wax packs of football cards were displayed, as well as half a box of last year's Topps baseball cards. Danny was waiting on the 1967 set to come out. He looked to the right, past the Necco Wafers, to the oversized box that held the Marathon bars. He removed one from the box and stepped to the counter next to the display case to pay.

Danny always felt a little self-conscious in the store. He knew that several kids in town took advantage of the proprietor by shoplifting. A few of them went out of their way to brag about their accomplishments. No one, it seemed, had more prowess in this endeavor than Rick Vannette, the older brother of Danny's classmate Mike.

144

Rick's go-to move was to approach the counter, get Don's attention, and ask for a frozen Snickers or 3 Musketeers bar. Don would dutifully saunter back into the walk-in cooler to retrieve it. Rick would then move quickly to his right and snag as many items as possible, filling his pockets. He put significant thought into his techniques, honing his craft. By the time he graduated from high school, Rick was employing a confederate, usually his friend Gil Horseman, to place the order with Don. This allowed Rick to remain "on station" in front of the candy display and eliminate the need to cover eight feet to and from.

Much of the ill-gotten gain was then moved at half price in the lunch room and study halls of Botkins High School.

Rick gave up his career of petty theft when he graduated. Danny wasn't sure if it was because the master thief realized it was exceedingly poor behavior to steal from a senior citizen trying to make a living, or if Rick had simply lost his sweet tooth. Danny never stole from Don, or anyone else.

Don accepted a dime from Danny, returned a nickel in change, then returned to waiting on his other customer.

Glancing to his right, Danny realized that the woman was Chris Koenig's, mother, Jan. Her attention was on the selections inside the display. Feeling Danny's eyes on her, Jan looked in his direction.

"Danny! Oh, it's good to see you. How are you?" She inquired, a pleased look on her face.

Jan Koenig was born in Australia. She met her husband, Emerson, when he was stationed there during World War Two. They were married after a brief courtship. When Emerson was deployed to the Pacific theater to fight the Japanese, Jan traveled to America. She first met her new in-laws the day they picked her up at the train station in Dayton. She and Emerson now had eleven children, Chris being the ninth.

Danny thought this had to be the number one love story in the history of Botkins. There were about 200 stories tied for second, all of them featuring childhood sweethearts growing up and walking down the aisle together.

Jan was slightly smaller than average. She had reddish-brown hair, somewhat darker than auburn. Perpetual smile lines framed her eyes. Her lilting Australian accent had travelled with her across the Pacific. Danny thought it, and Jan, were wonderful.

"Hi Mrs. Koenig, I'm OK." Danny responded.

Jan's face shifted a bit, from pleasure to concern.

"Oh Danny, I know this isn't the time or place, but we were so sorry to hear about Jane." Then, noticing Jerry approaching with an armful of groceries, Jan shifted her attention.

"Jerry, please let us know if there is anything we can do to help, anything."

Jerry, with just a hint of embarrassment, responded "I appreciate that Jan, people have been real helpful the last few days. If I think of anything, I'll let you know."

Jan turned to Don Butch, "Don, go ahead and check them out first. I have a bit more to do here and they probably need to be on their way."

"Uh, thanks Jan," Jerry managed. "Can you add a couple dozen of those eggs to this order, Don?"

Danny held the door for his dad on the way out. He was about to release it after Jerry passed when he sensed another person approaching the store on the sidewalk. Danny put pressure back on the door to hold it open. He recognized Elmer Marshall as the man reached the door.

Marshall was on the far side of middle age, in his late fifties. He had a block-shaped body topped by a short, wide head. Marshall's angular nose protruded under eyes that were perpetually narrowed. New acquaintances often missed the eyes, their attention focused instead on the poor complexion of his face. He seemed to possess just two expressions; suspicion and contempt.

It struck Danny that if you were to take a brand-new wheel of swiss cheese from Don Butch's meat display case, slice a couple inches from its side to expose the air bubbles within, then angle the remainder of the wheel just right, you could pretty well approximate the appearance of Marshall's head and face. Well, you would need to add some red threads to the cheese to make it just right.

Elmer Marshall took the Wapakoneta Daily News. He lived on the west side of town, across the street from the small welding shop that employed him. Danny delivered the paper to him for two years. Not only was Marshall notorious for avoiding payment, he didn't tip Danny once, not even the two Christmas periods this covered.

There was an understanding among newspaper delivery kids that the incumbent deliverer would hold onto his route long enough to avail himself of all the Christmas booty. Monetary tips, boxes of candy, and the occasional gift certificate awaited the carrier at this time of year. Every paperboy, and just a few aspiring paperboys, understood this. When a carrier made the decision to give up his route, be it because of a commitment to sports, girls, or a more demanding job, he ALWAYS hung onto the route through Christmas. It was not unusual to see a prospective paperboy following the current deliverer on a route during Christmas season. Ostensibly in training, the newbie was often loaded down with his trainer's loot.

Danny took over for Mark Dietz just after Christmas in 1963. He delivered through the next two holiday seasons, reaping the benefits. Elmer Marshall, however, had stiffed him both years.

Danny would have been fine with that if it wasn't for the weekly problems he had with collecting the subscription fees from the man. The weekly rate was 35 cents. This gave a substantial discount off of the 15-cent charge for a single paper from a vending machine. Carriers typically tried to collect on Fridays---paydays---when most customers had extra cash. Some customers paid a week at a time, accepting in return a small perforated receipt with that week's date printed on it from the carrier. Some customers paid a week or a month in advance. Others were difficult to catch at home and were sometimes in arrears. The carrier, who still had to turn in money to the dispatcher for these accounts, was often financially strained. Difficult decisions had to be made by a teenager; when to cut off a customer, how to do it without angering them, and when to get their parents involved.

Elmer Marshall was the Great White Whale. He lived alone and almost never answered his door when Danny knocked or rang the bell. He seemed to have a sixth sense that told him a paperboy was at his doorstep, rather than a friend or a neighbor. Of course, it could be that he had no friends, and his neighbors, Danny sensed, were in no hurry to share pleasantries with him.

Marshall only drove his car to bars at night and on the weekend, his choice of destination a significant factor in his facial complexion. He walked across the street to go to work. So, Danny knew with 99% certainty that if the 1961 cream-colored American Motors Rambler was parked in front of Marshall's sagging front porch, he was inside—not answering the door.

Marshall also owned a dog. It was a mean, patchy-faced mutt of about 60 pounds. His owner often let the dog roam around the neighborhood unchained. "Pick," Danny had heard this was the dog's name, seemed to have a real problem with paperboys. Danny dreaded coming around the corner of Gutman Street, fearing Pick would be there ready to charge him.

Danny once delivered to Marshall on a frigid winter day, was chased by Pick, and slipped on an ice-covered puddle. He banged the back of his head and his canvas bag went flying. Luckily, a neighbor who was waiting on his copy of the newspaper had seen the incident through a window and had come to Danny's assistance.

Elmer Marshall walked through Don Butch's door without acknowledging Danny, who was still holding it open. Danny turned to Jerry, and saw his dad slowly shaking his head.

CHAPTER FIFTEEN

Danny drove the Impala to the school at 3:45 on Saturday afternoon. His dad said he had some phone calls to make and wouldn't need the car. Several parents, mostly mothers, were there as well, waiting to pick up their son or daughter. Danny endured several well-intentioned but uncomfortable conversations while waiting for the charter bus.

The GM New Look ground its way onto Sycamore Street at 4:10. It's appearance allowed Danny to extricate himself from a conversation with Mike Vannette's mother, Judy. Known in town for her devoutness, Judy attended services at St. Lawrence two to three times each week. Danny surmised that Mrs. Vannette was either unaware of, or asking forgiveness for, her oldest son Rick's larcenous ways in Don Butch's store over the years.

The bus came to a halt in a haze of diesel fumes that seemed to make its air brakes sneeze. Danny saw movement inside the bus and realized that Mr. Rawson was administering a final clipboard-assisted sermon to the captive audience. The driver, the same pear-shaped man that drove the initial leg from Botkins to Gettysburg, exited the bus and busied himself with the opening of the side mounted luggage compartments.

Mr. Rawson, Mrs. Fark, and Miss Giltrow were the first passengers to exit the bus. They were followed by exhausted but happy looking juniors. The students descended the steps clutching pillows, small bags, and in the case of Sandy Monnin, a large stuffed animal. It was a two-foot-tall Snoopy from the Charlie Brown comic strip. Reed Thompson won it for her at the Shelby County Fair the previous July by knocking milk bottles off a platform using a softball.

Sandy was followed off the bus by Reed and Chris Koenig. They followed the line of students to the open luggage compartments to wait for their suitcases to be off-loaded. As Danny waited, he felt a tug on his sleeve. Turning, he saw a smiling Jan Koenig.

"Danny, I'm sorry to ask, but would you be a dear and make sure that Chris gets home? I've just remembered an appointment." Jan couldn't quite hide a knowing smile.

"Uh, sure Mrs. Koenig." Danny sputtered.

"Please Danny, it's Jan. Tell Chris I won't be long, and thank you." Jan smiled again and turned toward the parking lot. Danny was pretty sure that her appointment was imaginary.

Danny turned back to the bus and saw several classmates coming his way. They were led over by his friends Andy Craft and Mike Vannette.

"Hey Danny," Craft began, uneasily "We're really sorry about your mom." Danny noted that a few in the group were staring at their shoes.

"Uh, thanks guys...." Danny began, then realized he couldn't think of anything more to say. The earnest look on Andy's face was making an impact on Danny. He began to well up.

Vannette, in what Danny later concluded was a small-town teen boy's sincere effort to assuage the hurt experienced by a friend, clumsily managed "Hang in there Danny, we really need you at second base this year."

To an outsider, it would've sounded preposterous. Danny, however, received the comment in exactly the spirit it was meant. It was Vannette's way of saying "you're one of us, maybe if you throw yourself into the team effort, it will somehow lessen your pain."

This was about as sensitive a comment a high school middle infielder could receive from an all-league pitcher. In public, anyway.

"Thanks Vanny."

Reed walked toward the group, carrying his suitcase and Sandy's. She held Snoopy and Reed's pillow. Danny saw Chris just behind them and hurried to help with her suitcase. He turned to Vannette. "See you at practice."

"Let me get that" Danny said.

Chris was smiling at Danny, but her eyes showed concern. She sat the suitcase down, stepped to him and gave him a quick hug. "It's good to see you. Everyone is so sorry about your mom."

"Yeah, uhh, I promised your mom I would give you a ride home." Danny felt that half the eyes in Botkins were on him at that moment. He was uncomfortable and wanted to get moving. He eyed Reed and Sandy. "Do you guys need a ride, too?"

Sandy and Chris lived within a couple blocks of each other. Reed suggested that Danny take him and Sandy to her house. Danny could then take Chris home, before swinging back to Monnin's house to pick up Reed for the drive back to South Street. It was unspoken that this would give the couples some time alone before everyone ended up back at their respective houses.

Danny drove to the Monnin's house and popped open the trunk. Reed helped Sandy inside, carrying her suitcase. Danny was thankful that neither of her parents came outside. He knew they would have questions about the situation with his mom.

"See you in a few" Danny called out to Reed. Danny steered the Impala to the Koenig house and parked on the street under a magnolia tree. The Koenig house was a pretty, 50-year-old home. It sat on the corner of Main and Lynn. Large windows faced both streets. Well-tended flower boxes underscored each window. Hydrangeas and rose bushes surrounded the base of the house. Though not the most expensive home in town, the Koenig house acted as a showplace for motorists entering or leaving Botkins on the north side.

Chris slid next to Danny and put her head on his shoulders. He drew her to him and held her for a full minute. Neither could think of anything to say that would improve on the moment. Chris looked up to him with watery eyes and kissed him. Danny felt his eyes fill as well. They sat in the Hitchens

152

family Impala that March afternoon holding each other, their tears intermingling.

Their relationship had not been what Danny expected. Sure, they had "made out" at every opportunity. But they had never progressed beyond what books and magazines referred to as heavy petting. When you got right down to it, Danny thought that only Chris's father Emerson would consider what they did heavy petting. Danny would've classified it as something on the lighter side.

Still, there was a definite attraction between he and Chris. He just *liked* her. He liked being around her, watching TV together, talking in the hallways at school. Chris was smart, funny, and perpetually cheerful. He missed her when they were apart.

After a few minutes, Danny cleared his throat, released Chris, and checked their surroundings. He felt self-conscious about sitting in broad daylight embracing a girl in her own driveway. His tears exacerbated this feeling. Danny could imagine Chris's younger brother Rex surveilling them.

They talked for a few minutes. Danny promised to keep Chris up to date on arrangements for his mom. They tentatively agreed that Danny would stop back that night after dinner to watch TV. Danny said he wanted to check with his dad first to make sure he wasn't needed at home.

When he left Koenig's' to retrieve Reed, Danny realized he hadn't asked Chris one question about the Washington D.C. trip that the class completed without him. For weeks, it had been a main topic of discussion between them. Now it was barely an afterthought.

Reed came strolling out of Monnins' house sporting his trademark shit-eating grin. Seeing Danny, Reed made an effort to make the grin dissolve. His buddy was hurting and it seemed fitting to assume a subdued mood around him.

"Well you seem to be happy to get Sandy back home." Danny smiled at his friend.

Reed immediately sensed that Danny was trying to be upbeat. "Let's just say that the chaperones took their jobs very seriously in D.C. There was very little opportunity for 'fraternization'" he reported with mock seriousness.

Reed was relieved to see that Danny was smiling. He'd worried about his friend the last several days.

Reed, his brothers, and his mom had moved to Botkins seven years ago from Anna, a burg even smaller than Botkins. Though it was a move of just five miles north up 25A, to fifth-grader Reed it seemed like he was thrust into a completely different world. His dad was out of the picture, he was unfamiliar with the town and his teacher at school, and he had no friends.

Reed was used to being without his dad. The divorce, never fully explained, had occurred a couple years before the move. The unfamiliarity with a town the size of Botkins was easily remedied by an hour or two on a bicycle. Reed was a good student, so it stood to reason that he would be a welcome addition to any teacher's class. Only the lack of friends seemed unsurmountable.

Reed had seen a few students join his class at Anna. It seemed that they were always the new kid, never quite blending in, always a bit of an outsider. In retrospect, Reed felt sorry for them. At the time, though, it felt natural to continue to function as a member of his clique.

Reed spent exactly three days in Botkins as an outsider. He was throwing a baseball with his little brother Teddy in their front yard on a Sunday afternoon. Their mom had driven older brother Brad to a Boy Scout meeting. Both Anna and Botkins kids were in the same troop, so Brad already knew some kids from his new town.

Teddy had just uncorked a wild throw, low and to his brother's right. Reed pivoted and backhanded the ball with apparent ease. He would only later admit that that it had been a lucky stab.

"Hey, nice pick!"

Reed and Teddy turned to the street to see a smiling Danny Hitchens straddling a bicycle. Soon Danny was wearing Teddy's undersized glove. Teddy grabbed a bat. Danny and Reed took turns pitching to Teddy and shagging balls. When Teddy tired of the game, the two older boys took turns mimicking the batting stances of big league players.

Danny and Reed finally got around to introductions. Reed ventured "So, do you live close by?"

"Yeah, I'm Danny Hitchens, I live down the street. You're the family from Anna, right?"

"Yeah, I'm Reed Thompson. My brother's name is Teddy. I have an older brother too."

Danny stopped swinging the bat and queried "Your name is Reed? You're kidding?"

Reed had always been self-conscious about his name. He'd been, of course, the only Reed in the Anna school system and he suspected the only one in the entire state of Ohio.

"It's really Reed "he said sheepishly, readying himself for this possible friendship to be blown out of the water because of his unusual name. A name, he'd learned from hard experience, that rhymed with "peed."

"That is so cool!" Danny exclaimed. Have you heard about the Fantastic Four? It's a new comic book. There are four people with different super powers and their leader is Reed Richards."

Danny continued excitedly "He's super smart and he can stretch like Plastic Man, which I guess is kind of a rip off now that I think about it. But Reed is great. They call him 'Mr. Fantastic.'" Danny continued "You gotta come check out my comics."

Reed's face lit up. "OK, I have to watch Teddy until Mom gets home. Wanna wait for her?"

When Ginny returned home, she was at first annoyed to see a bike on its side in the driveway. She quickly realized it didn't belong to her sons. Ginny allowed herself a knowing smile. One of her worries with the move may have been resolved.

Indeed, it had. Ginny entered the house to find her two sons on the floor with a strange boy. They were sorting through a box of baseball cards, apparently dividing the players by position. She noted the stacks of cards were arranged in the same configuration as players were on a baseball field.

"Hi Mom, this is Danny." Reed said over his shoulder.

Ginny saw a boy an inch or so taller than Reed with darker hair. The newcomer turned to her and stammered "I, oh, I think I left my bike in your way, sorry."

Ginny, delighted, said "Don't worry Danny, I moved it. Would you boys like a snack?"

And with that, both Virginia Reed and Jane Hitchens seemed to gain an extra son. Reed and Danny were inseparable. Reed referred to his new buddy as Danny, or "Hitch." Danny assigned him the sobriquet "Reedo," or on special occasions, "Mr. Fantastic."

Turning on to South Street, Danny asked "So how was the rest of the trip?"

"Well," Reed began, "the monuments were cool. We went to some museums. Pat Jokisch got in trouble for farting in Ford's Theater."

Danny snorted, "Really?"

"Yeah, the guide took us up to the box where Lincoln was shot. He mentioned that the acoustics were so good in the theater that you could hear a person talking in a normal voice from the other side of the theater. They gave us a few minutes to walk around and Jock said he'd go over to the far wall and start talking to himself, you know, to see if we could hear it."

Danny turned into the Thompson driveway, grinning expectantly. "Yeah?"

Well, I'm standing on the other side with Vannette and Craft , under the box where Booth shot Lincoln. Jokisch waves to us from the other side, we're trying to listen. Jock says, in a normal voice 'John Wilkes Booth can't act worth a...' and then he rips this massive fart... you know, he turns his lower body towards us like he does and just lets it loose."

Reed chuckled while describing the incident. "Well, we're losing it. We can't control our laughter. The chaperones were kinda stunned, except for Rawson. He was pissed. First he looks at us, losing our minds. Then he turns to the other side of the theater and sees Jock trying to walk up the aisle and get away. Rawson moves over and blocks the aisle. He grabs Jock and takes him outside. He was really pissed. It sounds like Jokisch is gonna have a crapload of detention the next few weeks, but it was worth it."

Now sitting in the Hitchens family car in his driveway, Reed summarized, "It was probably the second loudest noise in the history of Ford's Theater."

Danny, laughing, said "Aww, that's GREAT! I wish I hadn't missed it."

Then, seeming to remember why he wasn't present, lost his smile.

Reed picked up on this immediately and continued with his review of the trip.

"We saw the FBI building and the Capitol Building. They took a class picture in front of the Capitol. They lined us up and used this old-fashioned camera that was on a tripod. It rotated from one side of our group to the other, I guess it slowly exposed the film."

"Yeah?" Danny followed.

"Well, before the picture, the photographer asked for a volunteer. Gary Poppe raised his hand. They put him on one end of our group, started the picture on that end, and when the camera moved toward the middle, told Poppe to run behind the group and stand at the other end of the line. The guy said Poppe'd be on both sides of the picture when its developed."

"Hunh" Danny grunted thoughtfully.

157

"And we went to the White House," Reed continued. We were delayed getting in. There was a protest."

Knowing his friend's respect for the military, especially since Eddie was deployed, Reed added "There were a buncha hippie types there with signs against the president, you know 'Lyndon's a Liar.' But they were also criticizing the military. You woulda hated it."

Danny paused before saying "Eddie will be home Monday."

CHAPTER SIXTEEN

Eddie's plane, a Trans World Airlines DC-9, touched down at James M. Cox-Dayton Municipal Airport at 1:45 pm on a sunny, 50-degree day. It was Monday, March 13. Jerry rode alone on the drive to Dayton, actually Vandalia, a smaller suburban city a few miles north of Dayton.

Jerry waited inside the concourse. As he watched the big two engine jet taxi toward him, his mind wandered. Danny had wanted to come along to the airport but Jerry thought it would be best if he went to school. The funeral was set for Wednesday and Jerry didn't want his son falling any further behind in his classes. When Jerry pointed out that today was the first day of outdoor baseball practice, Danny agreed. He would rush home to see his brother as soon as practice ended.

Jerry had intentionally kept some details of the funeral from Danny. In their meeting, Father Berg had urged Jerry to schedule the funeral within two to three days: a week at the outside, adhering to church tradition. Jerry was adamant that there would be no funeral until Eddie made it home. The priest had made it clear that the St. Lawrence Catholic Cemetery was reserved for members of "his" congregation. Berg, continuing, had emphasized "for members in good standing."

Both Hitchens boys had been baptized at St. Lawrence. This took place, Jerry remembered, through a combination of Jane's urgings and a real or imagined expectation from the entire Botkins community. The boys had catechism classes during their elementary grades at the Ward School next to St. Lawrence. Both Eddie and Danny had their First Communion's at St. Lawrence as well as taking part in confession.

But the family's attendance at mass became sporadic once Eddie moved to the public school for seventh grade. Guiltily, Jerry remembered how Jane had urged him and the boys to continue regular attendance. Jerry always seemed to be too busy. Eddie played off this: "Why do I have to go if Dad isn't going?"

Once Danny reached the seventh grade, their appearances for services had pretty much been relegated to Christmas and Easter. Jerry now regretted his role in this progression. Jane, he believed, had been silently disappointed by this.

Father Berg agreed to allow Jane's burial in the cemetery because "she was a Catholic at heart and is listed as a member of the congregation." By extension, her husband would have a place reserved beside her. But there was a strong implication that more participation was expected of Jerry and his sons.

Jerry sighed.

Jerry watched the silver and white plane come to a stop. The newly installed jet bridge, an artificial walkway that connected the airplane to the concourse, snaked toward the door behind the cockpit. A horizontal red stripe ran the length of the DC-9. A small "TWA" logo was painted behind the passenger door. A much larger version of the logo was prominently displayed on the tail.

People soon began to exit the jetway. Standing a few feet from the opening, Jerry saw the travelers emerge and search for friends or family members. After twenty or so passengers had appeared, Jerry saw his oldest son stride onto the concourse.

He was something, Jerry thought.

Wearing his U.S. Army Class A, Enlisted, green service uniform, Eddie cut quite a figure. There were two rows of ribbons on his left breast. The Private First Class single chevron insignias were evident on both shoulders. Above the left chevron was the 173rd Airborne Brigade patch, a white wing over a red bayonet on a field of light blue. Eddie cradled his green service hat, or "cover," with black bill, in one hand. He held a gym bag in the other.

Jerry felt his eyes water at the sight. His son looked like a hero in a World War Two movie!

160

Their eyes met and Eddie crossed the few feet separating them in seconds. He dropped his bag and embraced his dad. Several passengers stopped to view the scene.

Eddie gripped his father at arms-length "How are you Dad?"

Jerry dabbed at his eyes and smiled. He vaguely registered movement to his periphery and the odor of tobacco smoke. "I'm a lot better now. It's great to see you Eddie. How long will you be home? The Red Cross couldn't say for sure."

"My CO gave me twenty days" Eddie answered. I'll have a good two weeks home, even with all the flights."

Jerry nodded. Looking closer at his son, Jerry detected a harder edge, something that wasn't there when Eddie came home after boot camp. Jerry was sure that months in a combat zone would do that to anyone.

"Do you have other luggage?" he asked.

Danny responded, "Yes sir, a duffel bag."

Jerry smiled at the use of the word "sir." The boys had never called him that growing up. When Eddie returned from boot camp, however, it was ingrained in him.

"Well let's go to baggage claim, then." Jerry led the way.

Approaching the car, Jerry asked his son if he wanted to drive.

"Absolutely, it's been a long time" Eddie answered. He was now wearing his hat and still carrying his small bag. His father had insisted on carrying the larger duffel.

Pulling out of the parking lot Eddie mentioned "I'd like to get my uniform cleaned before the funeral. I didn't think my suit would still fit. I wanted to wear something nice to the service and my Class A was the best I had. I've had it on all the way from Da Nang, though, and it's pretty beat up and stinky."

Jerry chuckled, "I thought I detected some BO... and maybe the smell of an ashtray."

Eddie reddened slightly, "Yeah, there were lots of smokers on the flight. And the other three." He was referring to his flights from Vietnam to Hawaii, Hawaii to San Francisco, and San Francisco to Chicago. "The flights over the ocean were the worst. I think the guy beside me from Hawaii to California smoked a whole pack."

"I'll call Caroline Craft when we get home" Jerry suggested. She's asked several times if there is anything she can do to help. Dave was in the Navy. I'm sure they'd be happy to take care of your uniform."

As Eddie eased the car onto northbound I-75, Jerry continued. "Really, pretty much everyone in town has gone out of their way to try to help. There's just not much anyone can do." He trailed off. Then he added "If you're hungry, though, you're heading to the right place."

"I'm starving." Eddie admitted.

Jerry, as concisely as he could, filled his son in on the details of Jane's passing. Eddie insisted his dad skip nothing. "I'm a big boy now" he said with a sad smile.

When Jerry finished, Eddie asked "So how is Danny doing?"

Jerry didn't want to burden Eddie with too much. His son had come halfway around the world to bury his mother, and would be returning to fight a war in a couple weeks.

"Well, I'm kind of worried about him," he began. "Danny's always been close to your mom, but after you left for the Army, they seemed to get even closer."

Eddie nodded, his eyes on the road.

"He's been seeing the Koenig girl, Chris, for a while now and I think she's good for him." Jerry considered and said "Good girl."

Eddie smiled, thinking of the squirt he used to wrestle with now having a girlfriend.

Jerry continued, "Get this, Coach Mielke's got him going out for track."

The edges of Eddie's lips curled into a grin. "You're kidding!?" Then "Oh, he's gonna love that... actually both of them will love that."

"And baseball games start soon" Jerry added. "They have practice outside today."

Eddie glanced at his watch, frowned, and asked "What time is it here? I've lost track."

"Two-thirty." His dad answered.

Eddie, smiling, said "Whaddaya say we stop by baseball practice on the way home, Dad?"

Jerry thought this was a great idea, and said so.

The pair rode in silence for a few miles before Jerry inquired "So how is it going over there?"

Eddie had been thinking about how to answer this question for days. He didn't want to give his dad anything more to worry about, but thought he owed him a straight answer.

"Well, the people we're fighting are good at what they do," he began. "They try to avoid a straight-up fight and come at us when they have a chance to do damage." He paused before adding, "We've lost some guys."

After a few seconds Eddie continued, "But the Herd is damn good at what we do. We're well led. We have good officers. Lieutenant Checque is in charge of our platoon and he really cares about the men. And our company commander, Captain Kaufman, is top notch."

The Herd was the nickname for the 173rd Airborne Brigade. Legend had it that Colonel Richard Boland of the 1st Battalion, 503rd Infantry Regiment bought a copy of the Frankie Laine song "Rawhide" in 1963 and played it over the loudspeakers during formations at their base camp on Okinawa. The lyrics included references to cattle drives in the old west. The 173rd, being paratroopers, ran. A lot. The distinctive dust clouds visible over their formation when running on dirt roads led others to refer to them as the Herd.

The 173rd was a unique unit. It was formed to act independently and deploy rapidly. They were the only separate brigade that was assigned its own tank company. They were, in effect, a quick reaction force. With punch. Some senior officers referred to it as a "fire brigade." In May 1965, the 173rd became the first major combat unit to deploy to Vietnam.

Eddie went on, "We have the best NCO's in the Army. Our platoon sergeant, Sergeant Venable, is the best soldier I know. He's tough, smart, and he has two Bronze Stars... with 'V'." He emphasized the last words.

Jerry, confused, asked "With what?"

"Sergeant Venable's Bronze Stars were awarded with 'V', for valor." Eddie explained. In the military, you can receive a Bronze Star for meritorious service, for doing something well that has nothing to do with combat. If you are awarded a Bronze with 'V', it's for something heroic in battle.

Jerry had no idea. "It sounds like a regular Bronze Star should have a totally different name than the version Sergeant Venable has."

Eddie nodded, "Yeah, most people have no idea. Anyway, the 173rd is loaded with good soldiers." Eddie paused. "And we can *SHOOT!*"

Jerry assessed his son as they neared Botkins, thinking *He's still my boy...but he's a man now.*

Danny was standing at his second base position, trying to flag down any ball hit his way during batting practice. He watched as Coach Sanders pumped strike after strike to the hitters. Andy Craft was in the box now, lacing line drives to left field. Left handed hitting catcher Gary Poppe waited on deck. Danny should get lots of action when Poppe took his turn.

Classes had been fairly normal that day, now that the missing chaperones were back at school. Coach Sanders monitored Danny's eighth period study hall that was held in the cafeteria. A few minutes into the period, when the students had settled in to their studying, or in some cases their naps, Sanders had motioned for Danny to come see him at the head table.

Sanders, his customary toothpick jutting out of the corner of his mouth, gestured for Danny to take a seat. In a hoarse whisper that was several decibels louder than necessary, the coach began "I'm really sorry about your mom, Danny."

Danny, absentmindedly noting a whisp of Aqua Velva, winced. He could feel all the eyes in the cafeteria on his back.

Sanders appeared not to notice, whisper-shouting "Coach Mielke tells me you're going to double up with track this year?"

Reddening, Danny answered much more softly. "Yeah Coach, but baseball will be my main sport. I won't miss any baseball. I'll do track when I can work it in."

"That's fine Danny, I just wanted you to know I don't see it being a problem." Then, smiling and changing the subject, "We have some new wood this year, do you want to lug them out today?"

Danny brightened, "Absolutely."

The tradition at Botkins, as well as pretty much every high school and college in the country, was for freshmen to tend to and carry the equipment. As a freshman, Danny carried the bats from the small equipment room of BHS across Sycamore and down to the first base dugout before every practice. He did so again before the first game of his freshman year. The Trojans collected 12 hits that day in a win over the Fairlawn Jets and, baseball superstition being what it was, Danny was tasked with caring for the bats the rest of the season.

There was no junior varsity baseball in the Shelby County League. The schools were so small that the teams were lucky to get 15 players to participate. freshmen made the team, but typically didn't play much. Consequently, taking care of the bats became one of Danny's main functions that spring.

The following season Danny, on a lark, again carried the bats to the first practice and opening game. Botkins pounded out 15 hits against Jackson Center's Tigers. Danny let the Freshmen handle the bats after that but, it seemed, a tradition had been born.

Andy Craft took his last swing, scorching a liner down the third base line. As Gary Poppe positioned himself in the

165

batter's box, Danny backed up a step and sank into his defensive stance. His legs were still sore from his two-mile run the previous week. Danny pounded the pocket of his glove with his right fist. There were only two left handed hitters on the team. The balls hit his way by Poppe in BP would constitute a large proportion of the preparation Danny would receive before games began.

Before spring games, that is. Because no school in the Shelby County League had football, the fall sports offerings were almost non-existent. The league was granted permission by the Ohio High School Athletic Association to play baseball in the fall as well as the spring. Each of the league schools played every other school once in the fall. The six games counted in the standings. Thanks in large part to number one starting pitcher Mike Vannette, the Trojans were already 6-0 and sitting in first place before a pitch was thrown in the spring.

Poppe's first swing resulted in a lazy fly ball to center. It looked like he was using the new 33-inch Carl Yastrzemski Louisville Slugger. Danny began to track the ball, smiling at the thought of the pre-practice ceremony.

Danny had carried the canvas bat bag across the street. The bats rattled inside as the bag bounced lightly on his back with each stride. When he stopped in front of the dugout, Mike Vannette asked the team to gather round.

Vannette, using his right thumb as an ersatz microphone, intoned "Ladies and gentlemen, boys and girls, I direct your attention to our good luck charm, he's worked with lumber, he carries the lumber, I give you... Mr. Danny Hitchens!"

Through laughter and a smattering of applause, Danny took a bow, then held the bag with both hands, the bats horizontal. Danny uttered four words as he tossed the bag into the center of the circle, "Let's win the league!"

The bats hit with the peculiar sound only a full bat bag can make. It was a combination of ten bowling pins being struck down and an axe thudding into a tree. His teammates scrambled for the bag, anxious to see what new sticks Coach Sanders had acquired for them this year.

The new Yastrzemski looked interesting to Danny. He was also intrigued by a 33-inch Roberto Clemente and a 34-inch Brooks Robinson. All of these were Louisville Sluggers. There was also a 35-inch Hank Aaron model from the Adirondack bat company in Dolgeville, New York. Danny admitted this bat looked cool, but at 35 inches, it was too big for him.

The new bats joined the leftovers from last year that included a Frank Robinson, a Mickey Mantle, a Harmon Killebrew, and two bats that had been in the bag for years. These were 33 inch Jackie Robinson and Nellie Fox models. Both were thick handled, ancient, and apparently unbreakable.

Danny tracked Poppe's fly into the glove of Reedo in center. While a batted ball was in the air, Coach Sanders paused between pitches. He didn't want a second ball to be put in play while fielders' eyes were on the previous one. Danny began to turn back to the hitter when he saw a grey Impala cruise up Sycamore Street. The ballfield was several feet below the level of the street, so the car was plainly visible as it pulled to the curb behind third base. Danny realized it was his dad's car. That meant...

"Danny!" several voices screamed at once. Danny heard a buzzing sound and caught the blur of a dirt and grass stained baseball streaking past his head. All of their batting practice balls were beat up. This one also had a torn seam. A flap of leather covering stood out. When Poppe had taken his second cut of spring practice, he'd laced the ball in Danny's direction. Danny later realized that the spinning baseball sounded like what he imagined shrapnel from a Civil War cannon shell sounded like.

Jim Sanders saw the ball narrowly miss his second baseman's head. He screamed Danny's name along with several team members. Perplexed, Sanders followed Danny's eyes and saw a soldier emerge from a car above third base. Eddie Hitchens had been one of his favorite players.

Smiling, Sanders called "Everybody in!"

Coach Sanders gestured for Eddie to come down to the field. Danny rushed to give his brother a hug as he entire team surrounded them.

When Danny released him, Eddie quipped, "Jeeze, you lunkhead, Poppe nearly tore your head off."

This drew a laugh from the entire team.

The 45-year-old Sanders, who had served in the National Guard, gave an impromptu speech.

"It's under tough circumstances, but I hope everybody welcomes Eddie home. We're really proud of you."

Then taking a closer look at Eddie's uniform, Sanders continued. "Guys, I want you to look at that device above his ribbons." he pointed to Eddies chest, indicating a metallic badge about three inches long. It was a silver musket in a blue rectangle, surrounded by a silver oak wreath.

"Guys, that's the CIB, the Combat Infantryman Badge."

Sanders, now looking Eddie straight in the eye said, "Nothing on a soldier's uniform is more respected by another soldier. It means you've seen combat. Old timers called it 'The Silver Rifle.'"

Sanders went on, "Eddie ought to be damn proud to wear that badge, and everyone here should feel the same way."

Danny beamed at his brother.

Eddie simply nodded at Coach Sanders, then said, "Well, I came to see if you guys are still playing this game right. How 'bout you get back out there and show me?"

As the smiling players turned toward their positions, Eddie added "Hey Gary, take it easy on Danny, huh?"

Practice continued with an uptick in effort.

Above third base Jerry Hitchens smiled through shining eyes.

Jerry and Eddie stayed for the rest of the practice. When it ended, Danny turned bat bag duties over to a freshman and hurried across the street to stash his gear and grab his homework. He was inside the Impala less than ten minutes after practice.

"Eddie's starving so we're heading straight home." Jerry said.

Danny grinned, "You won't believe how much food we have."

As Jerry pulled into the driveway, Suzy Wong waited inside with her wide, wondering eyes. The sound of the car meant many things; it meant food, it meant companionship, it meant a chance to play outdoors. Suzy wondered about, and expected, many things. She did not expect Eddie.

When the door from the garage opened and the dark figure filled the doorway, Suzy sat back and cocked her head, confused. Her ears heard the excited words "Suzy Wong!" come from the figure at the same time its scent reached her muzzle. Suzy whimpered and bounded toward Eddie. He lifted her, laughing. Suzy proceeded to paint his cheeks with pug saliva.

It was good to have Eddie home.

CHAPTER SEVENTEEN

Jane Hitchens' funeral took place that Wednesday, March 15. Jerry, Eddie, and Danny spent several hours in Wapakoneta Tuesday afternoon and evening. The viewing was held at Jacoby's Funeral Home. The boys both wore ill-fitting suits. Eddie seemed okay with his. Danny was self-conscious.

Danny had expected a large turnout but was still stunned at the number of people that showed up. The hours were 4 to 7 pm but there were people in line twenty minutes early and John Jacoby kept the viewing room open until nearly 8 to allow everyone in line to pay their respects to the family.

Danny navigated through the proceeding, feeling like he was in need of new batteries. He felt his reactions were sluggish and his words slow to form. He would see a person approaching in line, register that it was a friend or acquaintance, but the name wouldn't come to him until the person moved on. By that time, several more familiar unidentifiables would be approaching his place in the receiving line. Danny was present for dozens of hushed conversations, even participated in most, but could recall the specifics of none of them.

His unsettled state of mind, he was sure, had its genesis in the private viewing earlier in the afternoon. Danny approached his mom's casket with an odd blend of trepidation and awe. Part of him felt like a four-year-old being led to a doctor holding a syringe. Another part felt like a child to whom the secrets of the universe were about to be revealed.

"Was this person, my mom, was her soul already in heaven?"

Danny expected he would have a significant reaction. When he looked upon his mom, though, he felt an absence of emotion. He'd dealt with the loss for over a week. Seeing his mother in this casket, for some reason, didn't register as a more concrete manifestation of his loss.

Danny, sorting through it later, decided this was because even though he was looking at his mom, it didn't really *look* like his mom.

Jacoby, everyone agreed, had been thorough and taken great care in his work. Danny didn't disagree with this opinion. But his mom had been animated. Her face had bounced from one emotion to the next while talking on the phone. She had a pensive expression while doing a crossword or working on a report for the library. Danny almost never saw her lying still with her eyes closed.

Looking close, Danny saw the waxy hue to his mother's lips. He realized a spray of some sort must've been holding her hair in place. Still, following Eddie's lead, he bent to give her a kiss on the cheek. He turned with his brother, leaving their dad to be alone with the casket. Danny entered the hallway feeling slightly numb. Unconsciously rubbing his lips, he decided to push this most recent, and final, view of his mom from his memory.

He searched his memory for a better picture, and came up with the one of her laughing at the Neil Armstrong parade, "Wasn't that wonderful?!"

Danny later learned that at the same time as his mom's viewing, John F. Kennedy's body was being re-interred in Arlington National Cemetery. Robert Kennedy oversaw the process. JFK's body, in an unannounced event, was moved under cover of darkness from where it lie the previous week when Danny had visited, to the more permanent location a few yards away.

A new Eternal Flame was lit. The original was extinguished.

The day of the funeral dawned cool and cloudy. Jerry woke first and let Suzy outside. She'd lately become enamored with sniffing around the front yard. Jerry gave her 15 minutes to complete her inspection while he rattled around the kitchen, assembling odds and ends for breakfast.

Danny joined him when Suzy came back inside. Eddie, still jet-lagged, dragged himself into the kitchen when the aroma of coffee from the percolator made it to his room.

"Ahh, Maxwell House, good to the last drop" Eddie said in his best impression of a TV commercial voice-over.

Jerry smiled, pouring two cups. "I figured a PFC would drink coffee."

"Every chance I get." Eddie took a cup from his dad.

"Cream or sugar?" Jerry asked.

"Nah, I'm used to combat coffee: the blacker, the better." Eddie smiled. Then, turning to Danny, "How about you, big guy? You a coffee drinker yet?"

Danny wrinkled his nose, "Never tried the stuff. It just doesn't smell good to me."

"What if I told you the caffeine would take thirty seconds off your mile time? I heard you're gonna run for ole Doc Mielke this spring."

They talked about juggling track with baseball for a few minutes. Jerry found a bag of maple rolls that Ginny Reed had dropped off, and the trio spent 15 breezy minutes together at the kitchen table. Jerry supposed it was the first time this had happened in five years, maybe ten. Jane had nearly always been present for these sessions. Now it would be just the three of them.

The discussion turned to the funeral. Jerry opened a small notebook and reviewed the order of events as he understood them from Father Berg; "There'll be a greeting by Father, then a procession up the aisle with the coffin. He'll sprinkle holy water during the procession. After songs and prayers, Father Berg will hold communion. Then more prayers and the coffin is taken back down the aisle."

"Dad, who did you decide on for pallbearers?" Danny asked.

"Well, the three of us, of course. Uncle Jim and Uncle Bob," Jerry referred to Jane's two brothers, "and Grandpa King. I thought he might want to stay beside your grandma during the entire ceremony, but he said he wanted to do it."

Jerry looked at his sons, then dropped his eyes to his empty coffee cup, "He said he wanted to do it for his little girl."

Danny and Eddie exchanged glances: this was going to be a long day.

Eddie flipped a piece of maple roll to Suzy Wong.

It was a long day. The service started at 2 pm. The sun had peeked out by then. It was windy with the temperature near 45 degrees. Jerry and his sons assembled at St. Lawrence an hour early.

Jerry and Danny were attired in the same suits they'd worn the previous day. Eddie wore his uniform. Caroline Craft had returned it that morning. Eddie told her it looked better than it had the day he bought it.

The church was a high roofed, narrow structure. Its cornerstone was laid in 1893 on North Main Street. The front of the building was barely 50 feet wide with a single entrance. Heavy oak double doors were stained an odd mustard color. The weathered, slightly orange, brick exterior framed eleven spectacular stained glass windows. Tall and narrow, these were distributed on three sides of the structure; four on the south-facing left side, four on the right, one on either side of the front entrance, and a larger version several feet above the doors. A copper-roofed bell tower extended twenty feet or so above the peaked roof at the building's front, reaching to a height of 60 feet.

Father Jurgen Berg greeted the Hitchens family in the nave. He was a short, silver-haired man with piercing pale blue eyes. Danny thought he was in his mid-sixties. He shook hands with all three of them, his palms cold and slightly damp. The priest reviewed the procedures for the service, asked if there were any questions—there weren't—then turned to Danny.

"It will be good to be seeing more of you, Danny." Father Berg smiled, glanced at Jerry and held his eyes for a second, then turned and walked toward the alter.

Danny looked at his dad with a questioning expression. His dad seemed to press his lips together. Was that a frown?

Jerry whispered to Danny, "We'll talk later."

The service was a confusing amalgamation of incense, holy water, and Latin phrases. Danny found his eyes wander to the windows. They depicted the stations of the cross, Jesus in varying degrees of distress.

As he mechanically followed the lead of the more practiced members of the church, kneeling, sitting, or standing when appropriate, Danny contemplated religion. Christianity as a whole, not just Catholicism with its peculiar traditions, seemed to have one giant flaw, or disconnect.

God the Father sent his only son to Earth. Jesus endured pain and death, sacrificing for our sins. *For God so loved the world, that He gave His only begotten son.* But, Danny reasoned, *if* there is a God, He would know that life is eternal, He would know for sure that his son would live forever.

Danny thought "We don't know for sure. No matter how much someone might believe, they don't *know*." When our loved one dies, we're sad, devastated, because they may be gone forever.

Danny supposed this is where the word "faith" comes in.

But, if the man upstairs knows for sure Jesus will appear in heaven an instant after His death, is the sacrifice as big a deal as its made out to be?

Danny felt ashamed as these thoughts rolled through his head.

There were three handles on either side of the casket. Danny grasped the middle one on the left side. Eddie was in front of him, their father at front right. The casket was much heavier than Danny thought it would be. As they solemnly made their way to Mr. Jacoby's hearse, Danny felt dozens of sets of eyes were on him. Feeling penitent over his thoughts about religion, Danny focused on Eddie's uniform.

The uniform, somehow, had given the funeral service an enhanced level of dignity. For the rest of the day, Danny fixated on the uniform whenever he was about to be overwhelmed; when thoughts about his mom appeared in his mind, when the casket was lowered into the ground, and when he was later surrounded by well-meaning people at the meal that was prepared by members of the congregation.

Jerry and his sons finally slid into the Impala at 6:15. Jerry stuck the keys into the ignition and sighed. "What a day." He started the car and put it in gear.

Eddie, in the front seat, said "Hey Dad, I could use a drink. How about stopping at L&H's before we go home?"

The L&H Café was a bar on the north end of Botkins. It was owned and managed by Louie and Hazel Altstaetter, a couple in their sixties.

"Jeez Eddie, it wouldn't look good for us to go sit in a beer joint the same day we buried your mother" Jerry assessed.

"No Dad, just stop and let me go buy some beer to take home." Eddie explained.

Jerry was not much of a drinker: Jane had frowned upon it. He'd been a bit of a hellion as a teenager but had been a family man for the last couple decades. Still, Eddie was serving his country in Vietnam and had just lost his mother. If anyone had earned a beer, it was his son.

"OK, I'll stop and you can run in. Danny and I will wait in the car."

Eddie was gone for several minutes. He returned, grasping a heavy cardboard case of Blatz beer by its handles.

Danny opened the back door for his brother and snickered, "Wow Eddie, I guess you did need a beer."

"The bartender, Louie? He wouldn't let me pay," Eddie related. "I asked for a six-pack of Blatz to go. He took one look at my uniform and went into the back room. He came out with a case. He wouldn't take any money... said 'Sorry about your mom, soldier.'" Eddie imitated Louie Altstaetter's whiskey-soaked voice.

"I tried to pay him but he wouldn't take a dime."

Jerry smiled, "Well now I've heard everything: old Louie giving away a case of beer."

Arriving home, all three immediately went to their rooms to change clothes. Eddie walked back to the kitchen, patted Suzy Wong, and grabbed a Blatz. The bottle had a brown triangular logo with gold trim. "Blatz" was spelled out inside the triangle in white script. Eddie dug an opener out of a drawer and popped the top. The beer was lukewarm, but Eddie was used to that.

He was sliding longneck bottles into the refrigerator when Jerry and Danny appeared. Eddie turned to them, "Anybody for a beer?"

Danny looked at his dad. He'd had a few beers with buddies but never one with his brother, and certainly not with his dad.

Jerry eyed Danny and said "If you want one, go ahead... one ain't gonna kill you."

Eddie opened a second bottle and slid it across the table to his brother. Danny palmed it, uncertainly. Eddie reached into the case for a third beer, opened it as well, and placed it in front of an empty chair at the table.

Jerry, standing, glanced at it, and said, "Stay right there, boys, I'll be back in a minute." He went out the door to the garage.

Eddie took a long pull on his beer. He looked at Danny and asked "Have you thought at all about what to get Dad for his birthday?"

Danny started to take a sip from his bottle, then stopped "Aww man, with everything going on I forgot his birthday is on April Fool's Day."

Eddie got up and stepped to the window over the sink. "Looks like he's messing around out in the shed. I don't know what he's doing, but we have a few minutes."

Danny asked "Do you have an idea?"

"Tell me what you think of this," Eddie began. I talked to Aunt Mary Ellen today. When she married Roger, they had a friend take pictures."

Mary was Jane's younger sister. She'd married her childhood sweetheart, Roger Geyer, two years earlier.

"Mary Ellen said she has a nice picture of Mom and Dad at the wedding. She said they were all dressed up and Mom looked real pretty."

Danny nodded, "Yeah, I remember. I think you might've been at boot camp."

"Yeah, I guess." Eddie went on, "Anyway, I was thinking about trying to get that picture copied, maybe blown up and put in a nice frame."

Danny brightened, "Yeah, great idea! I think you might be able to get that done in Wapak at Rhine and Brading. Or maybe at a new store there across the street, Bi-Rite."

"I'll borrow the car tomorrow when Dad's at work. Mary Ellen will have the picture ready for me and I'll drive up to Wapak. I should know if they can do it by the time you get home after school and practice." Eddie raised his Blatz and tipped it toward his brother.

Danny, smiling, clinked bottles with him.

Jerry walked back into the kitchen a few minutes later. He had one hand behind his back and a grin on his face. The boys turned to him expectantly.

"Well fellas, if we're going to have a drink to honor your mom, I figure it should be something special."

Danny and Eddie, confused, glanced at each other.

Jerry, with a flourish, brought his hand from behind his back and held an object head high.

For a moment, it was absolutely quiet in the kitchen.

Then Danny burst out laughing, "Where the heck did you get THAT?"

Eddie nearly choked on his beer, "You're kidding, is that real?"

177

Jerry sat the object on the table.

It was a bottle of Jim Beam's Choice Kentucky Straight Bourbon Whiskey. But that wasn't all. It was also an exact replica of the bottle that Barbara Eden's character came out of in the television show *I DREAM OF JEANNIE.*

"Pardon my French, Dad," Eddie joked, "but where the hell did you get that?"

Jerry chuckled "Clyde Gerber gave a bottle of it to a few of us at work at Christmas a couple years ago. He said the director of the show was walking past a liquor store window and saw this bottle. It gave him the idea for a prop for the show. Your mom wasn't too fond of it so I hid it out in the shed. I hated to get rid of it."

Eddie got up. He opened a cabinet and pulled out three glasses. "I'm glad you kept it. It's perfect for a special occasion, and I think this sure qualifies."

The bottle was over a foot high. It was round on the bottom and tapered up to an ornate stopper at the top. Jerry broke the seal with his fingernail. He pulled off the stopper with a "thunk."

Danny quipped, "No smoke... no genie."

They all three laughed.

Jerry poured a few ounces in each glass. He looked at Eddie, then to Danny. "Just one glass for you Danny."

Danny nodded. A beer was more than he had expected: his first taste of hard liquor was well beyond that.

Jerry raised his glass; the boys followed his lead.

"To Mom."

CHAPTER EIGHTEEN

On Thursday, Eddie did go to Wapak.

He'd set the wind-up alarm clock in his room for 5:30 before turning in. He had a dream. In it, he was floating downward on a parachute. He could see the jungle below. Okay, he was in Vietnam. Strangely, he was wearing his Class A green uniform, but had an M-16 slung over his chest.

He looked to his right and saw that Danny, wearing baseball practice gear, was floating below a T-10 parachute. He had a baseball bat in his hands. Eddie looked to his left and saw his mom, also under a T-10. She was looking from Eddie, to Danny, and back again.

As they neared the jungle, Eddie began to hear gunfire. It grew louder, and Eddie realized his mom was shouting at him. He couldn't hear her over the cracks from AK-47s and barks from M-16's on full auto.

Eddie could see movement in concealed positions below but couldn't tell if it was from friendlies or the enemy. He began to perspire: he was reaching for the rifle on his chest. The gunfire filled his head now but somehow a voice cut through to him.

"Eddie."

He turned to his mom. Her lips were moving again. Now, though, she had a look of panic on her face. She seemed to be pointing at Danny. As Eddie's feet neared the ground he realized his mom's parachute was beginning to move upward. But that wasn't possible...

"Eddie."

Eddie woke up covered in sweat: his hands were clenched near his chest. Gunfire didn't fill his ears. Now it was the clanging of the alarm clock. He looked up to see his dad.

"You still want to ride to work with me to so you can have the car? You can sleep in and walk up and get it later. Or I can bring it home at lunch."

Eddie reached for the alarm and turned it off. "Uh, no, I'll go in with you. Sorry, weird dream."

"You a little fuzzy headed this morning? You had a few extra shots last night." Jerry smiled.

Eddie sat up and winced. His head did ache a bit.

"I guess so. I'm not used to that stuff. We get a little beer on the firebases but there aren't any genie bottles filled with bourbon."

Eddie rode to the lumberyard with his dad just before 6:30. Jerry wanted to get an early start because he knew work would be piled up on his desk. He told Eddie to keep the Impala all day. Chris Gerber allowed Jerry to use one of the business vehicles any time he needed.

"I'll drive one of the trucks home, or maybe the new car. Chris just bought a Ford station wagon." Jerry smiled, "He had 'Botkins Lumber Company' painted on the side. I haven't driven it yet."

"Sounds good, Dad. I'll give Danny a ride to school."

Eddie drove back home and started some coffee. He popped his head in Danny's room. "You up, Junior?"

Danny rolled over and squinted at him. "Did Dad go to work?"

"Yeah, I'm gonna take a quick shower then I'll drive you to school."

Danny rolled out of bed. He put on his school clothes and checked his gym bag to make sure he had practice gear for both baseball and track. He was hoping to get to parts of both practices.

He realized that his head didn't feel too bad. He was afraid that a full beer plus a bit of whiskey would leave him hung over all day.

Danny filled a bowl with Cheerios. He lifted the lid off the ceramic sugar container on the counter and added two spoonfuls to his bowl, watching the crystals sift down through the cereal. He added milk, sat at the table, and gave Suzy Wong a scratch on the head as he dug into his breakfast. By the time he finished, Eddie was out of the shower and in the kitchen, going through the cabinets, looking for a thermos.

Eddie dropped his brother off in front of school. He smirked as he watched Danny angle the rearview mirror and run his fingers through his hair.

"Gotta look good for Chris, huh?" Eddie chided.

Danny reddened, started to say something, then smiled. He turned to Eddie, "You just worry about getting that picture blown up." He reached for the door handle, then added "Don't forget, I want to pay for half."

Eddie responded, "Deal." Then, "Say hi to Doc Mielke for me."

Danny was out the door now but turned back "Oh yeah, I have a story about him: remind me to tell you later." And he was gone.

Eddie drove a couple miles west of town to Geyers'. Mary Ellen had the picture ready for him, but insisted he sit and talk for a few minutes. She poured two cups of coffee and added a squirt of milk to each without asking. "This is a dairy farm," she said, "the milk's fresh."

They talked about Jane, how Jerry and Danny were doing, and skirted around the war in Vietnam. Before he left, Eddie asked if he could get some more milk for his thermos of coffee in the car.

Mary Ellen smiled, "Bring it in, we have plenty."

Eddie took his time driving to Wapak. Most of the shops wouldn't be open until 9, so there was no hurry. He took 25A instead of I-75. When he passed the rendering plant, he rolled down the window and inhaled. Bad, but not nearly as bad as some of the smells in the air in Vietnam.

Eddie guided the Impala into Wapakoneta. He went straight into the heart of town. The sign for the Wapa Theater was just ahead. Eddie smiled. It really was a cool sign. The letters W-A-P-A running vertically above the marquee. It was adorned with American Indian imagery, a tribute to the Shawnee history of the area. "The Busy Body" starring Sid Caesar and Robert Ryan was playing this week. Eddie eased the car to the right, finding a parking space across from the theater, just past the post office. He poured the now mocha colored coffee into the red plastic thermos cup and ambled across the street, looking up at the sign. "Mom really loved this place," he thought.

Eddie thought it would be a good idea to take Danny to a movie before his leave was up. He walked under the sign and looked to his left, past the ticket window to the wall space which held the posters for coming attractions. It looked like "In Like Flint" with James Coburn was starting over the weekend. Secret agents, space rockets: it sounded like it was right up Danny's alley. Eddie's too, he thought.

Sipping coffee, Eddie walked north. He looked at a street sign and realized he was on Willipie. *I always thought that was a funny name,* he thought. He reached the intersection with Auglaize Street. Directly across Willipie to the east was an unfamiliar store. Eddie glanced up at the sign, "BI-RITE DISCOUNT STORE."

"Ah," Eddie thought, "that's the new place Danny mentioned."

Eddie could see a few people on the street. Some were entering businesses, but it appeared many shops were not yet open. He checked his watch; 8:55. Eddie decided to return to the car to retrieve the picture. He drained his coffee and re-crossed the street.

Eddie returned the cup to the top of the thermos. The picture was in an envelope. Mary Ellen had paper-clipped the negative to the photo. He removed the picture and examined it. The photo was black and white. His mom and dad smiled at the camera. His dad looked like he'd just had a haircut. He wore a dark suit: probably the same one that he wore to the funeral. His mom had on a light-colored dress. Her hair was curled. She held a single rose in her right hand. Her left arm was on Jerry's shoulder.

Eddie thought he might start crying right there on the sidewalk. He wiped his eyes with the back of his hand and started for the Bi-Rite. He was just about to try the door when he noticed several posters in the front window. He stopped to read a few. Most had prices of current or upcoming sales. One contained information on Friday night Bingo at a local church.

Eddie was turning away when another advertisement caught his eye, "Gun Show, This Weekend, Allen County Fairgrounds." That would be in Lima, 15 or so miles north of Wapak.

Eddie smiled.

Danny wanted to help pay for the photo enlargement. What he didn't know was that Eddie had over $400 in cash in his wallet. He'd had almost no opportunity to spend money the last few months: the Herd had been busy. He'd collected the cash from the paymaster before leaving Da Nang. He could afford to take care of the photo himself. He planned to pay for all but a dollar or two then collect the rest from Danny. He'd tell his brother they'd gone fifty-fifty.

Eddie remembered he'd missed Danny's birthday last year. He'd make up for it. Eddie decided he'd take his brother to the gun show this weekend. Danny loved to shoot. Eddie knew rifles and had plenty of money.

It turned out that the Bi-Rite was able to help with the enlargement. The sales clerk led Eddie to the photo counter and showed him some options. They could blow up the photo to several different sizes using the negative. If Eddie only had the photo itself, it would've been much more problematic.

Eddie decided to order the photo in an 11 by 14-inch size. The clerk said it would take a couple days. It might be ready as soon as Saturday. Eddie spent a few minutes checking out frames. He found a couple that might do but decided to check around town before buying one.

He spent some more time in the store. They seemed to carry a little bit of everything. Walking out, he thanked the clerk, "Appreciate your help, I might be back for a frame."

Eddie crossed Auglaize Street and walked into Rhine & Brading. He was looking for a couple items that he thought might be for sale there, but drew a blank.

He turned left after leaving Rhine and Brading and walked into several stores. At W.T. Grants, a store that carried mostly clothing, Eddie came across a box of waterproof socks in the sporting goods department. Wet feet were one of the most troublesome conditions a grunt put up with in Vietnam. Soldiers were exposed to the elements. They patrolled through rice paddies. Trench Foot, a condition most often associated with World War One, was a significant problem in the current conflict.

Eddie picked up two pairs. They weren't cheap, at 99 cents a pair, but he thought they were worth a try. He took a few steps toward the cash register, then reconsidered. Every man in his platoon had the same problem. Eddie did an about face and returned to sporting goods. He picked up the entire box and made his way up front. He sat the box on the counter near the register and reached for his wallet.

"Whoa," said the woman behind the counter. "Twenty-four pairs of socks: are you outfitting a football team?" She was plump, not fat, perhaps 35 years old, with a round face and hints of grey in her brown hair. Her eyes seemed to smile on their own.

Eddie laughed, "Not hardly... just taking care of my buddies."

The cashier glanced at Eddie's short hair and muscular build. "Are you in the military?"

Eddie, now feeling a bit self-conscious, admitted that he was. "Yes, ma'am, Army."

"Where are your buddies now?" Her eyes were still smiling but the rest of her face was now hard to read.

"Vietnam, ma'am. Our boots get soaked over there and I thought these might help."

The cashier looked past Eddie to see if other customers were approaching the register. Seeing none, she directed, "Wait here a second."

She hurried past him and disappeared down an aisle. Eddie considered leaving the socks and walking out, but decided that would be impolite. Besides, he was curious.

A few minutes later the woman returned, followed by a tall, thin-haired man in his forties. He wore a white short-sleeved shirt and peered at Eddie through black-framed glasses. He introduced himself as Don Remick.

Eddie shook the man's outstretched hand. "Eddie Hitchens, sir."

"Doris tells me you're in the Army and want to buy a box of socks for your buddies." Remick was looking Eddie up and down.

"Uh, yes sir, they looked interesting. I thought they might be pretty useful."

"Well, we have another box in the stockroom: do you think you could use 48 pairs?" Remick questioned.

Eddie considered. The number of soldiers in his platoon fluctuated. There was a good chance that 24 pairs wouldn't be enough for everyone. "Yes sir, I probably could." His eyes gravitated to his wallet. Eddie had plenty of money, and...

"Good!" Remick smiled. Doris, could you be a dear and go grab that other box? I'd like to talk to this young man for a minute or two."

Remick turned to Eddie, "What unit are you with?"

Eddie told him, and Remick's eyebrows went up. "Rifleman, huh? Paratrooper?"

"Yes sir."

"Well believe it or not, I was a submariner in the Pacific in '44 and '45."

Eddie knew that submarines, especially in World War Two, were cramped. Remick was at least 6'5". "Bet that was fun," Eddie quipped.

Remick laughed, "Why do you think my hair's so thin? Must've scraped my head 15 times a day on that boat."

They talked about military chow for a bit. Eddie's C-rations finished a distant second to the legendary meals served on subs. Doris returned with the second box and began to put both packages into a shopping bag. Eddie opened his wallet in anticipation of the sale being rung up.

Remick put his hand on Eddie's arm. "Un-Uhh, these are no charge."

Eddie didn't comprehend at first. "Sir?"

"Don't let it be said that the Navy never did anything for you grunts in the mud. Damn glad to meet you Eddie, good luck." He winked, "I have a customer on hold, gotta get back to the phone in my office." Remick turned and walked quickly back toward an unseen office.

"I figured he might do something like that," Doris said, handing the bag to Eddie. "He watches the news every night and sees the protests: it really upsets him. He says our servicemen are in a tough spot and they need support."

Criticism of the war seemed to be rising. Eddie and the deployed soldiers and Marines were, ironically, somewhat removed from the debate by the nature of their distance from the U.S. Enough news did arrive overseas to give them a good idea of the level of opposition. Some of the guys received backdated magazines. Many read comments about protests in mail from home. Most of Eddie's mail had been from his mom, and she concentrated on family news and town gossip. Eddie was just fine with that.

Eddie thanked the cashier and walked out the door. *Free beer and free socks,* he thought. "It's good to be home. He smiled. He had money in his pocket and time to kill. No one was issuing orders for him to follow and there were no VC to worry about. He began to feel exhilarated. Then thoughts of his mom swam into his head. Eddie involuntarily puffed air into his cheeks, and sighed.

Eddie spent another hour checking out the shops. He made his way back to the Bi-Rite, picked out a frame with gold trim, and paid for it. It cost $4.99 but he'd remove the price tag and tell Danny it was just a dollar. Eddie stepped back onto the sidewalk. The downtown area was busier now. Eddie realized he hadn't eaten breakfast and he was getting hungry. He looked down the street to his right at the free-standing Peoples National Bank clock and saw that it was 11:10. The red neon sign for the Alpha Café was just above his line of sight, next to the Bi-Rite. That would work.

Eddie entered the dimly lit bar. There were two farmers at a table eating sandwiches. Two other men sat at opposite ends of the long wood bar. Eddie took a stool between them and laid his shopping bags on the floor. The man on the left had a half-full draft in front of him. The man on the right has drinking coffee and eating a bowl of chili.

"Help you?" the bartender asked as he approached. He automatically wiped at the bar with a white towel as he neared Eddie.

"How about a draft and a bowl of that chili," Eddie gestured to his right with his thumb.

"Comin' up, Budweiser OK?"

Eddie said that it was and asked if he could get some extra onions.

"That's the only way to eat it." The bartender smiled.

Eddie saw a sign for the restroom and slipped off his stool. He had to get rid of that morning's coffee. Walking down the dim hall to the restroom he found one of the items he'd looked for at Rhine and Brading.

Inside the restroom he found the other.

Eddie pointed the Impala south and started back toward Botkins. The smoke from the Winston in his right hand curled near his eyes, causing him to squint. Ruefully, he remembered the day he started smoking.

Eddie had always hated cigarettes. Even before his mom got sick, both he and Danny tried to avoid smoky areas. Eddie once had to go to the teachers' lounge at the high school to get a movie projector for Mr. Elsass. Students were required to knock and wait for permission to enter. Every kid in town knew this was to allow the smoking occupants a minute or two to hide their cigarettes. When the door opened, a blue haze filled the room. The educators inside would stare back innocently. Eddie hated the teachers' lounge.

Eddie avoided smoking through boot camp, even though many of the recruits imbibed. He wasn't tempted during jump school. When he was assigned to the 173rd, Eddie still resisted. His platoon did PT daily before deployment. During breaks, Sgt. Venable and the other NCO's often growled, "Smoke 'em if you got 'em, do push-ups if you don't."

Eddie would do push-ups.

In Vietnam, Eddie was surprised to learn that cigarettes were included in their C-rations. A brown foil "Accessory Pack" came in each box. Eddie remembers opening his first one after an uneventful patrol in the rain. It was the "Pork Steak" version. He pulled out the canned entre, then the brown foil pack, and read;

CIGARETTES
MATCHES
CHEWING GUM
TOILET PAPER
COFFEE, INSTANT
SUGAR
SALT

Eddie opened the pack. He initially set the cigarettes aside. After eating, he went back through the unused items. The cigarettes were Winstons. The small red pack held four cigarettes. The front of the pack displayed the Winston logo. The rear had the company slogan, "Tastes Good Like A Cigarette Should," above a comically suggestive drawing of a smiling, lipstick adorned woman. She held a cigarette horizontally with one hand, pinching the end between her thumb and index finger. The same digits of her other hand were under the Winston, seemingly measuring it, like someone would measure a man's, well, unit. The phrase "It's What's Up Front That Counts" was printed next to the woman's face.

Eddie remembers thinking, "Okayyyy."

Eddie opened the pack. Many of his platoon mates had lit up. Eddie was sitting near a raised area of ground around some tree roots. Little rivulets of rainwater cut into the soil. Eddie removed a Winston, positioned it at the top of one of the roots, and let it float down the miniature stream like a canoe.

"What the fuck?!" Al Johnson, a black paratrooper from Norfolk, Virginia, practically dove over Eddie to rescue the cigarette.

"Goddamn it Hitchens, if you don't want your smokes, give 'em to somebody." He was apoplectic.

Eddie and Johnson got along well. It was at that moment that he realized the hold that smoking had over many of the men. It actually made him want to avoid the habit even more. That would all change.

Eddie's first firefight was a confusing, deafening, terrifying event. It lasted 20 minutes. Eddie fired three full magazines through his M-16 and never saw a target. He remembers shouting and wild eyes. Someone threw a grenade, adding to the cacophony. As the shooting subsided, Eddie heard screaming to his left. A member of Echo Platoon had been shot through the thigh. A medic was desperately trying to tighten a tourniquet above the wound as another trooper applied pressure to the thigh and two more held the injured man down. He was thrashing about, in terrific pain.

Eddie remembered the next hour in fragments; the blood pulsing through the fingers of the assisting trooper, the radioman calmly requesting help over his PRC-25 radio, the UH-1 Iroquois, or Huey, helicopter swooping down to evacuate the wounded man, trembling hands, and lit cigarettes.

Al Johnson extended a lighted Winston: Eddie reached for it and took his first puff.

Eddie drove with the front windows down. It was too cold for this, especially if you'd just flown in from steamy Indochina, but he didn't want the car to smell like smoke. He glanced at the rearview mirror and saw the pine-scented, tree-shaped deodorant dancing on its string. After discovering the cigarette machine in the hallway at the Alpha, Eddie remembered seeing the deodorant at the Bi-Rite. He doubled back to buy one after finishing his beer and chili.

While at the urinal, Eddie's wandering eyes happened upon another vending machine. This one offered cologne, aspirin, and, yes, condoms. This was the second item he'd been looking for at Rhine & Brading. After zipping up and washing his hands, Eddie returned to the bar and asked for $5 in quarters.

He'd bought 5 packs of Winstons in Da Nang before starting home. By the time he reached Dayton two days later, he was out of smokes. Eddie was pretty sure his dad didn't suspect: his story about the numerous smokers on the plane was true. His uniform had really needed Caroline Craft's magic touch.

But Eddie had gone a couple days now without a cigarette and it was beginning to drive him crazy.

Eddie drove past the rendering plant and smiled as he watched one of the purple trucks turn into the entrance. What did Danny and Reed call them? Gut wagons? Eddie flicked ashes out the window. He made a mental note to check the car for evidence of smoking when he got home. There was no way he wanted his brother to find out he was hooked. Well, not hooked. He would quit when his time in Vietnam had ended. But for now...

As for the condoms, you never knew. Sex was the last thing on his mind when he got the call about his mom. That hadn't changed through the travel and the funeral. After the service, though, he was approached by Judy Winner. Judy had graduated with Eddie. She'd had the same boyfriend the last three years of high school but they'd drifted apart after starting at different colleges. Judy went to Ball State University in Muncie, Indiana. Her soon-to-be-ex-boyfriend, Jeff Krites, went to Ohio State in Columbus.

Eddie had always had an eye for Judy. She had long brown hair, a shapely figure, and soft green eyes. She told him how sorry she was about his mom. When she said she was home on spring break, Eddie thought, *hmm.*

Eddie asked about Jeff. Judy told him they'd broken up, then smiled.

Eddie thought, *HMMM.*

CHAPTER NINETEEN

Jerry brought tenderloins home from Kinninger's Tastee Freez. Eddie devoured his. "Wow, we sure don't get those in C-Rations."

Danny reported that he hit a ball over the leftfield fence in batting practice that day then hustled over to track practice and ran two miles in 14:22.

"Impressive, you're probably one of the best hitters on the track team." Eddie chided.

They watched Batman on the RCA. The villain was the Black Widow, played by an older woman named Tallulah Bankhead, who the boys didn't know. Jerry said she'd been in lots of old movies.

"This show is pretty good in color" Danny said. Sometimes I go down to Reed's just to watch it on their TV. If I watch it here, I have to ask him the next day what color some of the costumes were. I didn't know the Riddler's costume was green until the next day at school." Danny laughed. "I thought it was grey."

They talked about villains. Eddie hadn't seen many of the shows but was familiar with the comic books. He had Danny describe the TV versions of some of the more well-known characters.

"Of course the best female villain is Cat Woman," Danny asserted. "Hey, I just remembered... the first episode she was on was the night of Neil Armstrong's Gemini mission."

Danny continued, "I was at Reedo's watching and the network kept breaking in to tell about the emergency. The capsule was spinning and went into an area with no reception and nobody knew if the astronauts would make it out alive."

Eddie, who had seen an episode with Julie Newmar in her skintight costume while training in Okinawa, deadpanned "I bet Reed was pretty concerned that night. You know, watching newsmen instead of Cat Woman's ass."

They all laughed. Eddie liked Reed and kidded with him a lot growing up. Eddie once asked Reed for a lick of his ice cream cone outside the Tastee Freez. Reed, of course, indulged his best friend's older brother. He handed over the soft serve vanilla confection, only to see Eddie bite off the entire bottom half of the cone and hand it back. Eddie laughed hysterically as he watched Reed frantically lick his melting, leaking cone on a 90-degree day. It became a thing with the two of them. Every time Eddie saw Reed with ice cream, he asked for a lick. Reedo, knowing what was in store, dutifully turned it over, and Eddie bit off the bottom.

Danny was usually with Reed when this occurred. All three of them would laugh, no, guffaw, at this. Danny called Eddie's move a reverse-decapitation.

Talk of the Cat Woman-Gemini 8 mission led to Danny's recounting of the Armstrong Homecoming parade. Eddie got a kick hearing of his dad's escapades that day. Jerry, smiling, claimed that Danny was embellishing the story.

When Jerry took a phone call, Eddie leaned toward his brother and gave him the details of the photo enlargement. "Don't make any plans for Saturday." Eddie advised. "We're gonna pick up the picture that day, and I have something else planned."

The boys were up at 7 am Saturday morning. Their dad had some work to finish in the office. Eddie drove to the lumberyard and dropped Jerry at the front door. "Have a good day guys, I'll drive one of the trucks home when I'm finished." Jerry smiled, pulled his work keys from his jacket pocket, and walked toward the door.

Eddie drove a couple hundred feet up Main, then ducked into Steiner's Marathon. He'd been driving the Impala and he wanted to chip in for gas.

"Which side is the gas on?" Eddie asked.

"Your side."

Eddie pulled next to the pumps on the side facing the building. When the front tires passed over the black hose that stretched from the station to the pumps, they could hear the resulting metallic "ding-ding" of the bell inside.

"Twenty-nine cents a gallon, good to see some things haven't changed much." Eddie mused.

Ron Steiner pushed through the glass door. He wiped his hands on an orange shop rag as he approached, then tucked the rag in a back pocket. He smiled at the boys.

"Eddie Hitchens, good to see you!" Then, remembering what brought Eddie home, "Uh, I'm really sorry about your mom. One of us had to keep the station open and I drew the short straw so I didn't make it to the service." The smile had disappeared from Ron's face.

"No problem, Ron." Eddie knew the station was family owned. Brothers Ron and Dave Steiner and their father "Shorty" were the only employees. "Can ya fill 'er up for us?"

"Sure can," Ron answered, most of his smile returning to his face. Ron was a balding 42-year-old. He was 5'8", bespectacled, and, by the nature of his job, friendly to everyone in town.

As Ron got the gas going, another car pulled in to the other side of the pumps. Over his shoulder Ron said "Be right with ya."

Eddie looked back at Ron and asked "Are you sure you don't need to take care of him first?"

Ron followed Eddie's pointing index finger and saw that the other car was the Botkins Police cruiser. Vic Peters was opening his door. "Oh, hi Vic, get to you in a minute."

Peters looked to Steiner, turned to eye the Hitchens boys, then back to Steiner. He said "I'll be inside." He didn't acknowledge the boys.

"Well, good to see Peters hasn't changed." Eddie said, looking at Ron.

Steiner, in a low conspiratorial tone, said "He and gasoline are a lot alike, some people like their smell but they give most people a headache."

The boys cracked up. Danny offered, "It sounds like you've used that line before."

Eddie noticed that Peters, who'd just walked through the door, had turned back to them at the sound of laughter. His darkened glasses were beginning to lighten now that he was inside. At the same time, Peters' face began to redden.

Eddie remembered a couple guys in his squad playing with a chameleon at their base in Vietnam. They moved the creature from a green jungle fatigue shirt to a red shirt that one of the men had purchased in Hawaii, and back again. It was fascinating to watch the chameleon change.

Not so much watching Peters.

"I remember him chasing you when you were younger." Steiner chuckled looking at Eddie.

Danny piped up, "WHAT?"

Ron crouched by the driver's side window, crossed his arms and leaned them against the car. He looked at Danny.

"Yeah, seems your big brother thought it would be funny to ride his bike over our air hose and make the bell inside ring. You were what, ten or eleven?" he glanced at Eddie.

"Yeah, sounds right." Eddie confirmed, grinning.

So, you can't see the pump area if you're working under a car in the back bay," Steiner gestured to the right side of the building. The boys, knowing the layout of virtually every business in Botkins, kept their eyes on Ron.

"You have to slide out from under the car, stand up, and walk a couple steps to see if a car needs gas." he explained. "I did this six or seven times one day in August. It was hot as hell, and I wanted to know who was messing with me."

Ron shot a glance inside the station then returned to the boys. "Well, Vic walks into the station that day and I mention it to him. He pulls out a notebook and asks if I want to file a complaint. I say no, it's just kinda pissin' me off, you know?"

195

Both boys were now grinning.

"So Vic takes it upon himself to do a stakeout. He backs his cruiser into that little drive across the street beside the Tastee Freez, you know, the one that leads back to the post office?"

The boys nodded, their eyes flicking across the street to the area Ron described.

"Well, Eddie here comes flying up Main Street on his bike from the direction of the lumberyard. He passes over the hose right where the cruiser is sitting now, rings the bell, and cuts across the sidewalk there." Ron's left thumb poked the air. "He turns right on State and he's gone."

"Vic sees the whole thing. I mean he's got a perfect view."

Danny mentally gave Steiner a pass on the incorrect substitution of "got" in place of "has." He was into the story.

"Vic fires up his lights and siren and comes tearing out of that drive. He flies around the corner there. I remember the Stegeman brothers had just walked in to talk to me about something and they ran to the window to see what the hell was going on."

The gas pump handle that was inserted in the Impala shut off but Ron didn't move. "You want to take it from there, Eddie?"

"Sure," Eddie agreed. "Well, I was almost to Mielke's house when I heard the siren. I figured it might have something to do with me, so I look back, see Peters screaming around the corner with his lights flashing, and I cut across State."

He turned to Eddie, "You know that old barn next to the swimming pool, the one that sits way out in left center on the baseball field?"

"Sure." Danny answered.

"I rode between the barn and the pool, the ground's beaten down there, I think from trucks pulling in there to load and unload whatever's kept in the barn."

"That's Phil Heucker's barn now, he keeps plumbing supplies in there." Ron added.

"Yeah, well I'm pedaling my ass off through there and I come out in the outfield. I keep going about halfway to second base and I hear what sounds like a crash. I stop and look back. Peters had turned into that crease too fast. His cruiser fishtailed and the back end hit the swimming pool fence."

"He was madder'n hell." Steiner added, grinning.

Eddie continued, "He gets out, runs to the back side of the barn and yells at me to stop." He looked at Danny, "I didn't think he knew who I was... anyway, ain't no way I'm stoppin' at this point. So, I pedal right to the middle of the field and stop."

"About where you used to launch the rockets?" Danny asked.

"Exactly." Eddie confirmed. "Peters is hopping mad, literally hopping mad. He's jumping up and down screaming at me. He has his hand on his holster and I can see he's red in the face."

Danny laughed, reveling in both the narrative, and his brothers' correct use of the word "literally."

"I decide to wait to see what he does, I mean, he can't catch me on foot, and he can't drive the cruiser out onto the field, right? Finally, he gets in the car and drives up State. He turns left on Sycamore. He'd turned off the siren but his lights were still on. He pulls in up behind third base and gets on his loudspeaker."

Eddie mimicked Peters' nasal voice, "You on the bike, come this way RIGHT NOW."

"This tells me he definitely doesn't know who I am, so I realize the only part of Cole Field with an outfield fence is the stretch from the left field corner to left center, you know, where I entered the outfield near the barn."

"Yeah." Danny had just hit a ball over this fence in BP. To hit a homerun anywhere else in the ballpark, you had to leg it out while the outfielders chased down your drive.

"I decide to fake him out. I ride toward right center, angling toward two houses that sit up there facing Main Street, you know?"

Danny nodded, Gary Poppe had pulled a ball to right center last year against Anna that rolled between the houses. Poppe had good speed and had an easy stand-up homer.

Eddie carried on, "Peters floors it up Sycamore. I figured he was going to go all the way around the block to catch me so as soon as he disappears behind the home plate backstop I turn around and pedal like hell back through the opening by the barn and take alleys all the way home. I was afraid he'd show up at the house but he never did."

Eddie finished, "I guess he never did figure out who it was."

Ron added, "Well I knew who it was, but I wasn't about to tell Vic. He came back here asking if I could identify you. I figured you'd learned your lesson and wouldn't do it again."

Steiner stood up and removed the gas handle, "He must've driven that cruiser all the way around the ballfield four or five times with his flashers on."

Chuckling, he added "That'll be $2.85 Eddie."

Eddie handed over three ones, "Keep the change Ron, tell Vic to shine his bullets."

All three were smiling as the Impala pulled out.

Eddie took I-75 this time. He got off at the Wapakoneta exit, hooked a right at the top of the ramp, and pulled into The Hub truck stop.

"Nothing like a truck driver breakfast." he told Danny.

They ate plates of pancakes and sausage links. Eddie had coffee while Danny stuck with milk. They pulled back onto the highway, heading toward Lima. Eddie fought a powerful urge for tobacco.

"So where are we going?" Danny asked as they left Wapakoneta behind.

A bit evasively, Eddie replied with a question of his own. "Are you still shooting that .22?"

"The Marlin? Sure. I take it out to the boy scout woods every week or so." Danny added, "I haven't been there for a couple weeks... you know, with everything that's been going on." He lowered his eyes as he finished the sentence.

Eddie, more upbeat, said "I hope you haven't forgotten what I taught you, because we're going to step it up a notch."

Danny looked confused. "Huh?"

Eddie's lips curled, "We're going to the gun show in Lima, gonna look for something bigger."

Danny brightened, "Cool!"

Fifteen minutes later they pulled into the Allen County Fairgrounds. The lot was over half full. Danny saw several men handling weapons in the lot near vehicles. Others were carrying rifles, pistols, or shotguns toward the entrance.

Danny and Eddie walked to the entrance. A sign near the door alerted them that there was a fifty-cent entry fee and that there were "Over 200 Tables" inside.

Eddie handed a dollar to one of the workers at the door and they were inside. The building was rectangular, roughly 250 feet long by 150 wide. It was wide open, with no interior walls. During the Fair, it was used to display items for judging. On this day tables lined the exterior wall. A second line of tables formed another rectangle on the interior of the floor. Danny believed there were easily 200 tables inside the building.

"Let's walk to the right, look at all the tables on the outside, then move in and check out the inner area." Eddie suggested.

Danny was amazed at the number and variety of weapons. He saw ancient double barreled shotguns, World War Two German Lugers, and elaborately decorated pistols in commemorative cases.

"So, what are we looking for?" He asked his brother.

"I'm thinking a .308. It's the closest civilian caliber to the 7.62 that an M-14 fires. It's a damn good round."

As they walked past a table covered with .22 target pistols Eddie explained, "The bullets are almost identical. I wouldn't recommend it, but you can actually fire a 7.62 round through a rifle chambered for .308, but not the other way around." Eddie continued, "The 7.62 brass cartridge is a little thicker than the .308. One of the reasons is that it has to withstand the demands of being fired from automatic weapons. The .308 generates more chamber pressure and—" He glanced at Danny and realized his brother's eyes were glazing over.

Eddie laughed, "Anyhoo, we're looking at .308s. Maybe something with a scope."

Danny heard "scope" and thought *COOL!*

Danny discovered that there was a wide variety when it came to .308's. They looked at bolt actions, semi-autos, and single shots. There were different barrel lengths and styles of stocks. He noticed that some of the guns had price tags, while many did not. Several times in the course of the day he heard men haggling over the price of a particular firearm. Danny was surprised to see that a significant number of the transactions were trades, rather than outright sales. A customer would walk in with his rifle or pistol, see something he liked better, and exchange it with the dealer, sometimes with a bit of cash or some accessory or other also being thrown in.

Danny saw that several tables held the same model .22 Marlin that he owned. He saw a couple Civil War era rifles. He stopped at a table that sold authentic Indian arrowheads. The man behind the table wore a leather hat with a large white feather attached. He said he personally found all of the arrowheads within 25 miles of Lima, most in freshly plowed farm fields. Danny paid fifty cents for one that was crafted out of a pinkish stone. It still had sharp edges.

"Cool." he said to the man.

They made the circuit of the outer tables in a little over an hour. Eddie asked to handle several rifles. He looked closely at chambers and barrels. He talked price with two of the vendors, but didn't actually make any offers.

They were about halfway around the inner rectangle when a table with two dozen long guns caught Eddie's eye. Danny saw his brother move in and examine several rifles with a design that was different than most they'd checked out so far.

A serious looking man in his forties was working the table. He was barrel-chested with thick forearms. His short, steel-grey hair seemed to be standing at attention. He finished speaking to a customer who apparently had just purchased a rifle sling. The men shook hands and Steel Hair turned toward Danny.

Eddie looked the man in the eye and asked "Is it OK if I handle these?"

Danny had gathered that gun shows had their own peculiar etiquette, and Eddie was following it to the letter.

"Absolutely, those are all Savage 99s. They're great rifles."

They were lever-action rifles. Unlike the iconic Winchester lever-action rifles often seen in cowboy movies, these rifles were hammerless.

Eddie selected one of the rifles and worked the lever. He checked the chamber, looked at the bluing on the barrel, and brought the weapon up to his shoulder. He laid the 99 back on the table and selected another. He did this with four different rifles.

The vendor remained silent through this process. He stood back, next to shelves filled with ammunition and accessories. Like most of the other vendors, he'd brought along a folding chair, but didn't seem to use it. When Eddie finished, the man stepped to him with his hand extended.

"John Potter." He said.

Eddie took his hand and introduced himself and his brother. Danny noticed that the sleeve on Potter's arm slid up during the handshake to reveal a tattoo. It was a red number "1" inside of a home plate shaped badge. Potter saw Danny staring at it but said nothing.

"What can I tell you about the 99?" Potter asked.

"Well, I know a guy that owns one." Eddie began. "He raves about it. Says its real accurate and dependable."

Potter nodded, "That's right. Here, let me show you something." He selected one of the rifles. He pointed at the bottom of the receiver and explained "The 99 has a five-shot magazine." He half-turned the rifle so the left side faced up.

"Look here." his index finger touched the receiver near a small opening. "This is a counter; a number will appear that shows you how many rounds you have left in the magazine. I'd demonstrate it but we're not allowed to load weapons at the show. Danny and Eddie leaned in closer.

"Cool." Danny observed.

"Savage made the 99 in several different calibers," Potter explained. "I have three different calibers here." Then, "I noticed that all four of the rifles you picked up were .308s."

"It's a good round, packs a punch" Eddie commented. "In the right weapon, its dam—it's darn accurate."

Potter smiled, "In the right weapon, it's damn accurate."

Eddie grinned at Potter. Looking back at the table, he asked, "What can you tell me about the different barrel lengths?"

Two of the four guns that Eddie had handled had the long barrels typical of most of the other rifles displayed at the show that day. The other two had shorter barrels.

Potter nodded, "Well, when old Arthur Savage came up with this design in the 1890s, he got it patented and put it into production in 1899, that's where the model number comes from. Savage started hearing from hunters, most of them in western states with lots of brush to move through, that they loved the rifle but wondered if it could be made with a shorter barrel and still be accurate. Savage started to make it in different lengths."

Eddie reached for one of the 99s with a shorter barrel, hesitated, and looked at Potter while raising his eyebrows. Potter nodded, and Eddie picked up the rifle.

"This is, what, about a 20-inch barrel?" Eddie asked.

Potter turned to Danny, winked, and said, "Your brother has a good eye."

Danny smiled back and glanced again at the tattoo peeking out from under the man's sleeve.

"How much accuracy do you lose with the shorter barrel?" Eddie inquired.

"Not as much as you might think. There are all kinds of reports of game being brought down at 400 yards or more with that barrel. Course that's from shooters using a scope." Potter informed.

"Speaking of a scope, what do you have back there that might be a good fit for one of these 99s with a short barrel?" Eddie asked.

Potter smiled. He turned and fussed his way through items on the shelf. Danny looked at his brother and smiled when Eddie winked at him. Two winks in five minutes, Danny thought. He tried to remember the last time that had happened to him.

Potter turned back and set three boxes on his table; a Redfield 4x, a Weaver K4 4x, and a Weaver K6 6x. Potter explained, mainly for Danny's benefit—he could tell that Eddie was well-versed in firearms—that the number referred to magnification.

"In other words, a 4x, or 'four-power' scope makes your target look four times closer than it really is."

Danny mentally slapped himself for noting that Potter's last sentence ended with a preposition. He asked "So the 6x is better?"

Eddie jumped in, "Not necessarily better, it brings the target closer to your eye, but it can make it more difficult to acquire the target in the first place."

Danny let the confusion show on his face.

"Your brother's right." Potter added. "Let's say you need to make a shot at 100 yards quickly. You're hunting deer and see one at that distance with your naked eye and need to get a shot off before the deer spooks, or," Potter shot a glance at Eddie, then returned to Danny, "you're taking fire from an enemy soldier and need to find him and put him down fast."

Danny followed him, nodding.

Potter went on, "So you bring the rifle up and look through the scope. With a 4x, everything looks like its twenty-five yards away instead of 100. You're looking through a tube, though, and the actual area you see is limited. You might have to move the rifle back and forth quite a bit before you find the target. By then it could be too late. With a 6x, the field of view is even smaller."

Danny nodded slowly, but still looked a bit perplexed.

Eddie jumped in, "Think of it like this: you're standing on the goal line of a football field with a 4x scope. I put a target at the other goal line. I tell you to shoot the target as fast as you can. You can plainly see the target through your open eyes but when you raise the scope, now you're seeing maybe a ten-yard wide-section of the far goal line. You have to move the rifle around until the target swims into view."

Potter smiled, "That's a great way to explain it." He turned again to Danny. "With a 6x scope, you're seeing maybe a five-yard width of the other goal line, so you have to search even more. The good news is, the more you shoot through a scope, the better you get at it."

Danny smiled, "Got it."

So, what do you have on these scopes?" Eddie asked.

Sensing the discussion had moved to the money stage, Potter's tone became more business-like.

"These are all brand new. The 4x scopes, with mount, are both $60." The 6x would be another ten dollars."

"Mind if we look through the 6x?" Eddie asked.

"Be my guest." Potter opened the box and handed the scope to him.

Eddie sighted through it for a few seconds, said "Dual-X, huh?" and handed it to his brother.

Danny lifted it to his right eye. At first it was a bit disorientating as objects seemed to rush toward his eye.

"Try to pick up that vent up on the far side of the building," Potter suggested.

Danny found the vent near the roof about 200 feet away, lifted the scope, and manipulated it a bit until he had it in view. He clearly saw the individual slats of the vent. He noted that the crosshairs were bold lines from the edge of the field of view but were very thin in the center of the scope where they intersected. Danny correctly guessed that this was what "Dual-X" meant.

Danny thought this was cool as hell. It reminded him of a scene from his all-time favorite show, *JONNY QUEST*. The animated show revolved around the adventures of a boy, Jonny, his mysterious friend Hadji, and Jonny's father, Dr. Benton Quest. The elder quest was a genius who explored out-of-the-way parts of the planet. These three were accompanied by Race Bannon, who was, pound-for-pound, the most badass character on television. Race was their bodyguard and he took down many a bad guy over the course of the series.

Danny thought of one episode where Race shot a balaclava-wearing bad guy off the top of a camouflaged missile blockhouse in the middle of a jungle swamp. Race was using a long-range tranquilizer gun with a scope. The TV viewer saw Race's target on screen through the scope.

"Cool," Danny said again.

Eddie nodded and returned to the rifles. "And these?"

Danny noticed that a few other patrons, apparently sensing a negotiation in progress, had eased up behind them. His mom would've called them "Looky-loos."

Potter put each of his hands on the stock of a Savage Model 99 with 20-inch barrel. "This one," he patted with his left hand, "is brand new and costs one fifty." He shifted attention to his right hand, "This one is used, but is in damn fine shape. It was made in '62. I've shot it myself. I could let it go at... one ten."

Danny's head was swimming. Was Eddie really going to plop down that kind of money for a scoped rifle? He was only home for another ten days or so and certainly couldn't take it with him.

Danny looked from his brother to Potter, and again found his eyes wandering to the tattoo.

Potter noticed. This time he remarked, "You seem to be interested in my tat."

Danny blushed, then asked, "That's the Big Red One insignia, isn't it?"

Potter seemed pleased, "It sure is, First Army Division. That's a good eye, son. How'd you know about that?"

Eddie sniffed, "He reads a lot."

"World War Two?" Danny asked.

"Yep," Potter nodded. "Came ashore on Omaha Beach three weeks after D-Day and slogged all the way across Europe until we wrapped things up."

Potter turned to Eddie, "I'll bet you're in the service too."

"Yes sir, 173rd Airborne Brigade." Eddie nodded.

Potter was impressed. "You boys've been busy. How is it you're in Lima today instead of Da Nang?"

Eddie sobered a bit. He said, a bit softer, "I'm home for our mom's funeral."

Potter's eyes widened for a second, then narrowed.

"I came here today to buy Junior here," Eddie gestured to his brother, "an overdue birthday present."

Danny was stunned, "WHAT?"

Eddie continued, "Fact is, I have some selfish reasons too."

Potter asked 'Yeah?"

"Yeah, we use the M-16, it's a good weapon, but the barrel length can be a problem out in the bush. It has that tall, inverted 'V' front sight that can get caught up in brush when you have to snap-fire, and we have to do that quite a bit on patrols." Danny expounded, "I'd like to play around with a shorter barrel to see what it can do."

Potter nodded.

Danny regained his composure and blurted "You can't spend that much money on me!"

The spectators behind them now numbered seven. They followed the scene with renewed interest.

Eddie went on, "My buddy that owns a 99 is in my squad. He's from Oklahoma...big hunter back home. Says he wishes we still used a bullet that packs a punch like the 7.62."

"Sounds like some of the guys I served with, bigger is better." Potter smiled at Eddie.

It occurred to Danny later that Eddie and Potter were now two Army riflemen talking guns, not a seller and a buyer.

"And another thing," Eddie continued, "we worked with a couple snipers. I spent a lot of time talking to them. I'm interested in going to sniper school. They were using 8x scopes, but they're reaching out to pretty long distances. I don't have a place to shoot near home at those distances but I figure I can find a place at about 400 yards. Using a 6x scope at that distance will let me... what's the word?" Eddie paused and thought, "replicate those kinds of shots."

Potter was impressed, *Sharp kid,* he thought.

Danny jumped back in, "It's too much money!" and continued to make his argument. As the brothers wrangled back and forth over this revelation, Potter rubbed his chin. He arrived at a conclusion.

"Tell you what, I'll sell you the used Model 99, and the K6 scope, with mount, for $150."

Eddie and Danny had been facing each other. They stopped bickering and turned toward Potter.

"And you're gonna need ammo, so I'll throw in this." He reached down to the floor and hefted up a green metal fifty caliber ammunition can.

"Holds 640 rounds of .308." Potter said, grinning.

Eddie, incredulous, asked "Are you serious?"

Potter nodded, "I won't take a penny more from you. Then, looking past the Hitchens boys at the looky-loos, "But don't any of the rest of you yardbirds expect a deal like this, it'll ruin my reputation."

The men at the periphery exchanged chuckles.

207

Eddie opened his wallet and fished out some bills. Danny glimpsed into the wallet and saw it was thick with cash. His jaw dropped.

Potter completed the transaction, lifted the Model 99, and handed it to Danny. "Happy birthday, son," he said.

Potter turned to Eddie to give him tips on mounting the scope. Danny heard the man tell Eddie he drives down from Michigan to work the show in Lima because he "always meets good people." Danny marveled at the rifle.

It was really, really, good to have Eddie home.

CHAPTER TWENTY

It was nearly 3 o'clock when the brothers reached their car. They loaded their purchase into the trunk.

"I'm hungry," Eddie announced. "Let's get something to eat."

"That was wayyy over and above the call of duty." Danny said, still shaking his head about the rifle.

Eddie paused at his open door.

"So, do you still think the Red Barn is better than McDonalds?"

They sat at the Red Barn chewing their way through burgers and fries. It was between lunch and dinner so they had the place pretty much to themselves.

Danny unwrapped his second hamburger and asked his brother "Do you think you'd ever get a tattoo?"

Eddie thought about it, then, between fries, said "I guess I wouldn't rule it out. Potter seemed to be pretty proud of his."

"Would you get the blue 173rd insignia, the one that's actually on your uniform?"

Eddie considered, "Well, we actually might be getting a new insignia."

Danny cocked his head. "Really?"

Eddie looked over his shoulder, then leaned in. "We're not supposed to talk about it, but back in February we did a combat jump. As far as I know, it's the only combat jump by any unit in the war."

Danny stopped chewing. "Seriously?"

"Yep, Operation Junction City. We surrounded the 9th Viet Cong Division and pushed them out of the area. Scuttlebutt is we're getting a new insignia, one with a parachute in the design."

Eddie looked out the front window as he said "I could see getting a tattoo of the new design."

He looked back at Danny, "If it's cool, of course."

They both laughed.

"I heard something about a jump on the news but didn't know it was you" Danny stated.

Eddie thought, *There's a lot going on over there that you don't know about.*

They drove to Wapak and found a parking spot on busy Auglaize Street. On the way there Danny noticed the pine tree deodorant hanging from the mirror and asked, "Is that new?"

Eddie told him he bought it to cover up the smell of the rendering plant, which had been particularly intense when he drove past it on Thursday. When he pulled the Impala into the parking space, Eddie glanced across the street at the Alpha and felt the craving for another cigarette.

They walked into the Bi-Rite and made their way to the photo counter. Eddie paid, then opened the large envelope while they were still in the store.

"Wow, that came out great!" Danny exclaimed as Eddie slid it out. "Dad's gonna love it."

Eddie smiled, turned to his brother, and said "You owe me two dollars."

They walked out and stepped to the corner. From their position, they could see east and west on Auglaize as well as south on Willipie. Eddie glanced south and saw that the colorful neon sign of the Wapa was lit. He turned to the east to see the People's National Bank clock. "Hey, there's a matinee at four."

Twenty minutes later, Eddie was eating popcorn with his younger brother. They were watching a James Bond-like spoof with a ridiculous plot that included astronauts: and they were doing it in the home town of a real astronaut.

It was good to be home.

On Sunday morning, the brothers, with Danny now driving the Impala, followed their dad to the lumberyard. Jerry unlocked the door and led the way into the shop area, flipping on lights as he walked.

"Take what you want from the scrap bin in the corner." Jerry said. Hit the lights when you leave. I left some papers in my office. Meet you out there."

Jerry's sons made a beeline for the scrap wood. They were looking for pieces they could use as targets for the new rifle. When Jerry saw it the night before, he had mixed feelings. Jane would've had conniptions, of course, but Danny was so excited it was hard not to be happy for him.

Besides, Jerry reasoned, if Danny was going to have a weapon that powerful, it was important that he have instruction from someone that knew what he was doing.

Eddie certainly fit the bill.

Danny and Eddie drove south on 25A to Lock Two Road. They turned right, drove a quarter mile to a railroad track, crept over it looking in both directions, then immediately turned left off the road and ducked into a dirt turnaround. A large stand of trees stood in front of them, the boy scout woods. There was a strip of ground about 100 feet wide between the woods and the railroad tracks.

Danny began to pull the gear out of the trunk. "Hold on," Eddie said, "just the wood."

They'd selected a half dozen pieces of plywood to use as targets. Eddie directed Danny to help him carry the four largest pieces of scrap wood up to the railroad track. Danny was confused, but complied.

They struggled a bit with the wood when walking over the slightly inclined slope of rocks that bordered the tracks. When they reached the space between the steel rails, they looked back at the car. They were several feet above the roof of the Impala. Danny looked at Eddie, still bewildered.

"The tracks run south parallel to our shooting area. I'm going to pace off 100 and 200 yards. We can walk down from the tracks into the open land between here and the woods and place targets at the correct distances. If we pace up here, we don't walk through brush and trees, which would throw off our distance."

Danny nodded, but asked "Aren't we still kind of just guessing on distance?"

Eddie shook his head "Not if I use a pace count. They teach you that in the Army. My stride is 30 inches. There are 3600 inches in one hundred yards. That's exactly 120 paces for each 100 yards."

Eddie looked at Danny with a stern look and in mock seriousness said, *"Exactly."*

They both laughed.

They set two targets at both 100 and 200 yards. They returned to the car and Danny removed the Savage and ammo while Eddie stepped off 25 yards and placed the two smaller targets. Eddie spent several minutes reviewing the features of the rifle with Danny. Eddie liked the design of the safety mechanism, which was situated on the lever.

"Smart. Very safe." Eddie loaded the magazine and handed the rifle to Danny. "You get to throw out the first pitch."

Danny smiled and took the Savage.

They fired nearly 100 rounds over the next hour and a half. They started at 25 yards to get a feel for the weapon, then moved out to the longer distances. Danny was initially blown away by the power of the weapon. With Eddie coaching him, he concentrated on technique. He realized that most of the nuts and bolts of shooting stayed the same when you went up in caliber from .22 to .308. It didn't hurt that he had Eddie as an instructor. His brother was patient and was able to get his points across with great clarity.

What had Eddie's boot camp instructor said? "I can teach any 18-year-old in America to hit a target at 300 yards if he'll just get the shit out of his ears and listen to me."

So could Eddie.

Danny brought along a pair of binoculars at Eddie's suggestion. When one Hitchens boy was shooting, the other was tracking the results downrange.

Danny was again mesmerized by Eddie's ability. As his brother fired, Danny called out the results: "hit... hit... hit... hit... hit." It was almost eerie. Danny had some hits at 100, and two at 200. But this? Wow.

"You had enough for the day?" Eddie asked after shooting his final magazine at 200 yards.

"Danny's ears were ringing and he was sure he was talking too loud, but he answered, "I could shoot some more."

"Nah, your first spring baseball game is Tuesday, Coach Sanders will be pissed if your shoulder is too sore to make the relay throw to first on a double play."

Danny laughed but rubbed his shoulder, "You're probably right." He started to pick up their brass, then heard Eddie sliding more .308s into the magazine.

"You gonna shoot more?"

"I want to walk out to the targets like I'm on patrol, walk through some scrub and trees, take some snap shots." Eddie continued "See how the short barrel feels."

Eddie took an additional five rounds. "I'll fire a mag at the 100 and another at the 200."

"Cool," Danny said he'd get the rest of the brass and put the ammo can in the trunk. He did this quickly so he could watch his brother take these last shots. He grabbed the last of the empty cartridges then scrambled back up onto the railroad tracks.

Danny reached the tracks in time to watch Eddie push through a stand of saplings and fire five quick rounds at the two 100-yard target from a distance of about 75 feet. He moved the barrel from one target to the other while working the lever. Eddie continued toward the 200 mark while reloading. He seemed to seek out the thickest bit of brush he could find and put five quick rounds on those targets as well.

Danny met Eddie at the 100 yard targets and helped him lug them in. They had to be careful: the plywood was splintered badly.

"Maybe bring gloves next time." Eddie thought out loud.

"Man, you looked like Chuck Connors in "The Rifleman" working that lever," Danny raved.

Eddie grinned, "Let's eat."

They drove to 25A and took a right instead of heading back to Botkins. A mile later they pulled into a gravel lot surrounding a low-lying single story building. This was Betty's Corner, a beer joint that served the drinking and eating needs of Botkins residents as well as those from nearby Anna. It had an exterior of grey stone and mortar.

The pair walked in and stood for a second to allow their eyes to adjust to the darker conditions. They passed a beat up pinball machine and took stools at the bar. Over more burgers, these with cheese, and fried onion rings, they talked through several subjects; shooting, the army as a possible career for Eddie, and maybe Danny, and their mom.

When those subjects slowed to a trickle, Eddie asked "So, what's the Doc Mielke story?"

Danny furrowed his brow and cocked his head, "huh?"

"When I dropped you off at school the other day you said to ask about a Mielke story."

Danny's face brightened, "Oh yeah!"

He related the story about the John Buford statue at Gettysburg, that Mielke confided he'd sneaked out of his hotel room a few years ago to find the cannon that fired the first shot at Gettysburg.

"Ha! My 'El-Tee', Lieutenant Checque, is a big Gettysburg guy. He's from PA. He talks about Buford, about choosing good ground for a fight. Says we can still learn from those old soldiers."

"Seriously?" Danny asked.

"I'll tell him that story when I get back over there," Eddie promised.

Roger Miller's "King of the Road" played on the jukebox.

CHAPTER TWENTY-ONE

On Tuesday, March 21, the Botkins baseball team played their first game of the spring. Danny, of course, carried the bat bag to the field. The opponent was the Fort Loramie Redskins. Loramie had posted a 4-2 record the previous fall and sat in third place in the Shelby County League. Botkins had beaten them 5-2. They'd also lost to Russia, who was in second place with a 5-1 record.

The Redskins' top pitcher, and hitter, was right hander Mike Delmer. A solid six-footer with a perpetual smile, Delmer was very tough to hit. His hard, sidearm delivery often had right handed hitters backing out of the box. Sometimes he dropped his arm angle down even lower than sidearm.

The previous season Reed Thompson had returned to the dugout after a particularly embarrassing at bat against Delmer and, in his best cowboy voice, said "This sumbitch throws from down Laredo way."

The Trojans would have their hands full.

Delmer and Mike Vannette dueled through three scoreless innings to begin the game. Delmer struck out six, Vannette five. In the top of the fourth, Loramie had runners on first and second with two outs and Delmer coming to the plate. Coach Sanders called time and made a trip to the mound. The entire Trojan infield joined him there.

"OK Mike, let's be careful with this guy" Sanders whisper-shouted the obvious. "He's a dead pull hitter so let's go with hard stuff away. He can't pull your fastball, especially if you keep it out there." Sanders continued, "If you're going to mix in a curveball, don't be afraid to bounce it up there. Gary will block it, and if it does happen to get past him, that puts runners on second and third and we just walk Delmer to pitch to the next guy. You struck him out last time."

The meeting broke up and the infielders returned to their positions. Delmer, smiling, stepped into the box.

Vannette started Delmer out with a good fastball on the outside corner for a called strike. The 0-1 pitch was another heater away, but belt high. Delmer swung through it. Danny at second and Andy Craft at shortstop took turns feinting toward second, attempting to keep the Redskin baserunner close. In the event of a single to the outfield, their efforts could keep the runner from getting a good enough jump to score.

Vannette bent at the waist to take the sign, his glove closed and resting on his left knee, the ball in his hand behind his waist. Vannette and his catcher Poppe were going with the second sign with a runner on second. Gary would put down several signs, the second being the type of pitch he was asking his pitcher to throw. The baserunner at second had a clear view of the catcher. If a catcher went with just one sign, the type of pitch would be easier to decipher by the runner who, theoretically, could somehow signal the hitter what's coming.

Vannette took the sign, came set, and delivered. It was a curveball. Instead of keeping it down in the zone, hoping for the hitter to chase it, Vannette left it up. Delmer turned on the pitch and ripped a line drive past Senior third baseman Gil Horseman. The ball bounded all the way to the fence in left that acted as a boundary between Cole Field and the swimming pool. The fence was of simple chain length construction. It absorbed the energy of the ball, which came to a stop immediately. There was no carom whatsoever back in the direction of the infield so left fielder Mark Egbert had to chase it down. Egbert's hurried throw sailed over the glove of the cutoff man, Craft.

Loramie plated two runs on the double, the baserunner at first coming all the way around to score.

"Damn, missed the cutoff man... and that was an OH-TWO pitch!" Eddie groaned. He was sitting in the parked Impala above third base. It was 63 degrees outside, certainly nice enough to take advantage of the sunshine by sitting in the bleachers, but Judy Winner was snuggled up next to him.

Eddie called her the previous evening and asked if she would be interested in going to the game and maybe get a sandwich afterward. Judy had quickly accepted. By the end of the first inning she had slid next to him.

All had gone well until Vannette hung the curve and Egbert missed the damn cutoff man.

"Let's go guys, get you heads out of your asses!" Eddie couldn't help himself.

Julie laughed and asked "I thought it was sailors who talked like that?"

Eddie smiled back, "Sailors and baseball fans... certainly not soldiers."

She showed him a doubtful smirk, then leaned her head on his shoulder.

Danny was happy to see Eddie up in the Impala watching the game. He was surprised to see Judy Winner with him, but after thinking about it for a second, was happy about that as well. Danny hoped his dad would make it to the game. Jerry never made it to the start of games because of his hours at work. Sometimes, for home games, he was able to catch the last inning or two.

Danny's mom never missed a game.

Vannette, upset with himself, threw three vicious fastballs past the next Loramie hitter to end the inning, but the damage had been done.

Though just a junior, Danny often took it upon himself to speak out to the team. In this way, he was much like his brother. Returning to the dugout after the two-run inning, Danny angrily spat "Let's go guys, let's get our heads out of our asses!"

These were nearly the exact words Eddie had uttered five minutes earlier.

Botkins got a run back in the bottom of the fourth thanks to a throwing error. The Trojans tied it in the sixth when Craft timed up a Delmer fastball and drove it off the fence in left. Reed Thompson stepped to the plate next. He waved at a fastball for strike one. The next pitch was another fastball. Reed was right on this one but fouled it straight back.

Baseball people—coaches, players, and knowledgeable fans—know that when a hitter fouls a fastball straight back, he is locked in on that pitch. Reed was oh for two in the game so far but had better swings at Delmer each time up.

Fort Loramie's catcher saw this and called for a breaking pitch. Delmer didn't hang it, as Vannette had earlier. He executed it perfectly, starting the pitch at Reed's hip. Delmer's nasty delivery, neither curveball nor slider, but "slurve," a combination of the two, broke across the plate and was on its way out of the strike zone when Reed swung.

It wasn't an artistic swing. Reed's butt was on its way toward the third base dugout when the end of his bat made just enough contact to flare a single to short right. Craft raced home with the tying run.

In the Impala, Eddie joined several of the other occupied parked cars and honked his horn.

Ohio high school games were scheduled for seven innings. This game reached the bottom of the seventh still tied 2-2. Danny was due up second in the inning. Both he and Gil Horseman were swinging bats near the on-deck circle as Delmer took his warmup pitches. Before trotting out to the third base coaches box, Coach Sanders paused to say a few words to Horseman. He then spoke to Danny for several seconds.

Eddie, still in the Impala, said "If Gil gets on, Danny's bunting."

Horseman worked the count full, fouled off two tough pitches, and was able to check his swing on a fastball down and in. The Trojans had the potential winning run on board.

Eddie saw his brother return to the dugout and exchange the bat he'd been swinging for another. As he strode to the plate, Sanders called time and gestured for Danny to approach him. Danny hustled partway down the third base line and conferred with his coach.

"Get it down, Danny." Eddie said under his breath.

Danny took a high fastball for ball one. The Loramie third baseman, anticipating a bunt, had been charging. Danny, though, had given no indication that he was bunting.

The next pitch split the plate for a strike. Danny, on instructions from Coach Sanders, was taking a strike. If Delmer struggled to throw strikes to him, the Trojans might gain a second base runner without having to give up an out by bunting.

Danny checked Coach Sanders before the next pitch, watching as signs were flashed. This was not a giveaway that he would be bunting. Like most well coached high school players, Danny looked at his coach before every pitch of every at bat.

Danny settled into the batter's box. As Delmer started his motion, Danny squared around.

Eddie, a bit louder now, implored, "Catch it Danny, catch it."

Danny dumped a beautiful bunt down the first base line. Delmer had no chance at it. The Loramie third baseman had again been charging but the first baseman, John Boeckman, was holding Horseman on the bag. Seeing his pitcher couldn't make the play, Boeckman charged frantically and bent for the ball near the baseline as Danny passed him going in the other direction.

The entire Loramie infield had expected any bunt to go to the third base side, so their second baseman was late covering the bag at first.

The 6'5" Boeckman was a tremendous basketball player. He would be all-state as a senior in 1968 and play four years of college ball for Wittenberg University. But he was not accustomed to making the baseball play he was now attempting. He fielded the ball and turned quickly toward second base. Seeing he had no shot at forcing Horseman, he half-turned his upper body back toward first. Boeckman made an off balanced throw to the moving second baseman.

Predictably, it didn't go well.

The ball sailed down the right field line into foul territory. The Redskin right fielder was also late reacting. By the time he retrieved the ball, Sanders, no longer whisper-shouting but now full-bore screaming, was waving Horseman home. He easily beat the throw, sliding unnecessarily as car horns sounded up and down Sycamore Street.

One of the honking horns belonged to a puke green 1966 Ford Country Squire station wagon that had just pulled in to the last available parking slot on Sycamore. The wagon had faux wood grain on its rear and sides. The words "Botkins Lumber Company" were written on either side.

The Trojans were 7-0.

After the handshake line, Vannette slapped Danny on the back. "Great job Hitch!"

"Thanks Vanny, way to throw. What'd you have 12 strikeouts, thirteen?"

Vannette kept track of such things, "Thirteen" he said quickly.

Then, "I don't know how Delmer does it." Ticking off his fingers, Vannette said of his hard luck counterpart, "Fourteen K's, 2 walks, 4 hits, one earned run, aaaaaannnd" Vannette said theatrically, "one loss."

He continued, "And the guy was smiling in the handshake line... I'd be losing my mind."

Danny glanced back to the Fort Loramie dugout and saw Delmer talking to a dejected Boeckman. A few seconds later, both Loramie players were laughing. Danny, always the hard-core baseball guy, thought *I guess Delmer knows there are things more important than baseball.*

Danny thought of his mom, wished desperately she was still here, then went to help the freshmen bag the equipment.

"Why did you say 'Catch it, Danny' before the bunt?" Judy asked Eddie. They were sitting in the small dining area at the Tastee Freez, waiting on their tenderloins.

"Well, good bunters try to almost catch the ball with their bat" Eddie explained. "You don't just stick the bat out there and try to block the ball. And you definitely don't stab at it, that's the worst technique, you try to deaden the ball. Here..." Eddie searched the room, got up from their booth, and retrieved a straw from a dispenser on the counter. He held it horizontally.

"OK, here's my bat, you're the pitcher, you throw the pitch."

Smiling, Judy stepped out of the booth and mimicked a pitcher taking a sign, coming set, and delivering a pitch.

Eddie demonstrated how a hitter would allow his bat to give a bit while contacting the baseball. At the same time, he thought of a phrase his squad-mate Al Johnson often used, *Possible wife material.* He smiled to himself.

CHAPTER TWENTY-TWO

Eddie spent time every day that week with Judy. When he wasn't with her and was by himself during the day, he worked at modifying Danny's .22 cleaning kit so it would work on the Savage. He made a mental note to scrounge for an M-14 cleaning kit when he returned to Vietnam. These should be available without too much trouble now that the Herd had switched to the M-16.

He also mounted the Weaver scope to the rifle. He discovered the process was like most things, if you had the right tools, the job was much easier. He made a trip to the lumberyard to borrow the vises and drill bits that he needed. He was pleased with the result.

Jerry drove the Ford wagon to and from work. Mr. Gerber told him to keep it as long as Eddie was home. Eddie took advantage of the availability of the Impala. When he wasn't with Judy, he cruised through town, often stopping to talk to a friend or acquaintance. When he felt the need for a cigarette, he would leave Botkins and drive backroads, always on the lookout for someone who might recognize him with his Winstons.

The baseball team played an away game on Thursday. It was at Jackson Center, 15 miles southeast of Botkins.

"You coming to the game today?" Danny had asked his brother that morning before leaving for school.

Eddie, on his third cup of coffee, nodded, "Yep, don't want to miss it. There's no baseball in South Vietnam."

Danny wasn't sure what to say to that but was let off the hook when, only half kidding, Eddie continued "You should be good for at least three hits against JC. I'll want to see that."

In recent years, the Jackson Center Tigers had finished at the bottom of the league standings in baseball. Opposing teams usually padded their statistics against them. The Tigers, though, turned the tables on the opposition when it came to hoops. Their basketball team had aspirations of a state championship.

Danny cracked, "The fact that Judy Winner lives right on the way to the game doesn't have anything to do with you coming?"

"Now that you mention it, I might just swing by her place on the way." Eddie said cheerfully, as if he'd just thought of it. He raised his cup in mock salute.

Danny snickered, "See you at the game."

The Trojans did indeed pad their numbers. They beat the Tigers 15-2. Gil Horseman tossed a complete game, Danny had two doubles, and Gary Poppe homered. Eight of the nine starters in the lineup had at least one hit. The game, however, would be remembered for something else entirely: it gave birth to the ear rodeo.

Herm Barton played right field for the Trojans. Herm had above-average arm strength, but his accuracy left much to be desired. His swing was undisciplined, which, ironically, matched his hairstyle exactly. Herm sported an unruly curly brown mop that reminded Danny of cumulus clouds. On any given day, it could be puffy, irregular, or voluminous.

Herm, like most of the Trojans, was known to disregard Coach Sanders' instructions when it came to chirping at umpires. Sanders forbade it, but Herm couldn't help himself. Ironically, Herm became an umpire in later life and brooked very little criticism from players or coaches. Danny liked Herm and often hung out at his house listening to Herm's collection of rock albums. .

Herm wore multiple pairs of sweatbands on the baseball field. He insisted on using a "hot dog trot" when traversing any part of the diamond, apparently more concerned with style than substance. Some teammates watched him on the field with raised eyebrows.

Barton could also bend over backwards to gain the approval of his classmates, and, in particular, his teammates. An example was Herm taking orders for candy during the school day then sneaking out to visit Don Butch's store. Herm would return with contraband packs of Wrigley's Spearmint Gum and Hershey Bars and distribute them like a soldier liberating France.

In the 5th inning at Jackson Center, Herm, swinging late, slapped a hard groundball toward the first baseman. It hit a rock, bounded over the head of the waiting fielder, and rolled down the right field line. Barton legged it out for a triple. He stood on the bag, asked for time out, then adjusted the two pairs of sweatbands he was sporting despite the fact that the air temperature was a brisk 44 degrees.

He received some good-natured ribbing and didn't take it well. Herm hit ninth in the order for good reason, but lashed back at some of his teammates as they boarded the bus. His comment to Pat Jokisch, who had finally finished serving detentions for the Ford's Theater farting incident, was the match that lit the fuse.

"My name will be in the paper tomorrow for hitting a triple, how'd you do today, fart-boy?" Herm barked at Jokisch.

He regretted it immediately. Jock was the lone Trojan in the lineup that didn't join the hit parade against the Tigers. You could almost see realization of what Herm had said crystallize in his eyes a second after the words were out.

Danny remembered thinking "uh-oh."

Jokisch was the son of a hog farmer. He'd worked on the farm all his life. He enjoyed having a few beers, pulling pranks (the more outrageous, the better) and, apparently, farting at National Historic sites. He was stocky, muscular, and had a temper.

During his sophomore year, Jokisch surreptitiously removed several doze chalkboard erasers from various classrooms. He stashed the soft, brick-shaped objects in his locker, virtually filling it. When word spread that teachers would be searching lockers, Jokisch transferred them to a burlap bag and, one dark night, climbed to the roof of the band room, navigated across a narrow ledge, and stuffed them behind the two-foot tall aluminum letters that spelled out "BOTKINS CENTRAL SCHOOL." They were never found.

Conditions for trouble were heightened by the fact that Coach Sanders drove separately to away games. He lived in Sidney. Botkins was the northernmost team in the Shelby County League. Consequently, Sanders' home was closer to every other school in the league. He had permission from the superintendent to drive his car to the games then leave for home afterward.

Herm chose a seat near the center of the bus. Jokisch passed him going up the aisle and sat in the seat directly behind Barton, who eyed him warily. Seconds later, Coach Sanders honked at the bus and pulled out of the parking lot, heading for home. Barton realized that the only authority figure remaining on the bus was 68-year-old, 110 pound Eula Greve, the bus driver.

Herm swallowed.

Two minutes into the drive home, Jokisch leaned toward Barton menacingly and asked, "So Ted Williams, you're gonna get your name in the paper? I guess you're pretty hot shit."

Barton pressed his back against the side wall of the bus, but rather than say something that might diffuse the situation, as his brain may've been considering, allowed his mouth to take command. "At least I didn't take an o-fer against the worst team in Ohio."

That did it. Jock's right hand darted out and grabbed Herm's right ear. Barton thrashed about and tried to pull at Jokisch's arm, but he had an iron grip between his thumb and index finger.

"Hey!" Jokisch exclaimed, "somebody time this, see if I can hold on for eight seconds like they do in bull riding."

The rest of the team was pulled toward the action, physically gravitating toward the conflict. Someone, Danny thought it was Poppe, started a count. Others joined in. When the count reached eight, Jock released the ear and held his hands in the air, a triumphant grin on his face. Eula Greve glanced into the mirror that allowed her to see the interior of the bus, then returned her attention to the road, apparently unconcerned.

The scene was repeated multiple times over the remainder of the season. After that first incident, Jokisch tended to target the Freshmen and Sophomores.

A few members of the team became the targets of, and challenge for, the school bus cowboys of BHS. The victims had hoped the incident would be forgotten after that first ride. They realized it wasn't going away on subsequent trips when teammates boarded the bus with implements such as stop watches, cowboy hats, and silver buckled belts.

Eddie spent a good portion of his second weekend home with Judy. She would return to Ball State Sunday and start classes on Monday. He made sure she had his mailing address, with its peculiar "APO" heading. Eddie knew that any letters from Judy that reached him in Vietnam would be pure gold.

Eddie spent both mornings that weekend at the boy scout woods with Danny. They fired a total of 210 rounds. They brought enough scrap wood this time to add targets at 300 and 400 yards. Eddie first zeroed the Savage at 200 yards. He was again impressed with the performance of the twenty-inch barrel.

He walked Danny through the process of adjusting the scope. By his second full magazine, Danny was registering hits at that distance on a piece of plywood two feet wide and 4 feet high. Danny tried to hide his excitement, but it was obvious to his brother.

They left the targets overnight this time. When the pair returned to shoot on Sunday, they brought along a couple old blankets from the hall closet. Eddie suggested they fire at the more distant targets from an elevated position up on the railroad tracks. They spread the blankets on a relatively level spot near the railbed.

"Let's keep an eye out for trains." Eddie warned. "It'd be damn embarrassing to get through Vietnam without a scratch then get squished by the twelve-fifteen."

They would be shooting from the prone position, lying on their stomachs. Danny had learned the finer points of this position when his brother returned from boot camp and took him shooting with his Marlin. The .308, and these distances, required attention to detail. Danny intended to watch his brother like a hawk.

Eddie adjusted the Weaver scope for a series of shots at 300 yards. He explained each step to his younger brother. The Weaver K6 had "coin-slot" turrets. The scope adjustments had to be made by inserting a coin or screwdriver into the slot and turning. Eddie was using a dime.

After zeroing the Savage at 300 yards, Eddie used his dime to tweak both the upper adjuster that controlled elevation, and the side adjuster that controlled windage. The rifle was no longer zeroed. Eddie handed the weapon to Danny.

"There you go, zero it."

Danny nodded and accepted the rifle. It took several magazines, but Danny eventually scored hits at 300 yards. Before they could concentrate their attention on the plywood at 400 yards, the pair heard a train whistle coming from Botkins to the north. They moved all of their gear into the brush and carefully step-slid down the slope to the Impala where they retrieved Cokes from the cooler they'd packed. They sipped from the cans and spotted the train engineer as the deafening B & O locomotive rolled past.

The Hitchens boys waved their Cokes at the man. He smiled back and gave them a two-fingered salute. The caboose was just passing their shooting position when they heard the locomotive whistle begin to announce its approach to the residents in Anna, a few miles to the south. Eddie and Danny finished their Cokes and scrambled back up the bed.

Danny quickly learned that small mistakes were amplified at 400 yards. His brother let him shoot first at this distance. Only three of his ten rounds were close to the target: there were no hits. The hot .308 bullets tore scars in the short brush. The plywood rested against a tree. One round impacted the trunk a few feet above the plywood and knocked bark off the tree. It was the closest Danny had come to nailing the target.

Eddie then reviewed the characteristics of bullet drop at this distance. He followed this with a more in depth lecture on windage. A slight southwest breeze was blowing. Eddie explained how it would push their bullets from right to left and that the shooter needed to compensate for this by adjusting the scope accordingly. Eddie stressed that the longer the shot, the more it will be affected by wind.

Danny watched through the binoculars as his brother walked rounds into the target. Eddie scored hit after hit. Danny breathed *"four... hundred... yards."*

Eddie scrambled the scope again and moved aside. Danny assumed the prone position, his toes pointing out. He concentrated on breathing, a slow trigger squeeze, and shooting when his lungs were empty. Danny fired 25 rounds at the 400-yard target. He scored 2 hits each on the next to last and the final five-round magazines.

He was thrilled.

Eddie drove home. It was sunny and 69 degrees. Eddie's left elbow rested on top of the door, hanging out.

Tell me something Danny, back in the Loramie game, in the seventh inning, you changed bats after you saw Horseman draw the walk." He added, "You know, right before you bunted."

Danny nodded "Yep."

Eddie glanced across the front seat at his brother as the Impala slowed to a stop at 25A. There was a beat up pickup truck facing them on the opposite side of the intersection.

Eddie flipped down his left turn signal and turned to his brother.

"So, do you use a different bat when you know you're going to bunt?"

Danny chided him, "I guess you WERE paying attention. You were up there with Judy. I'm surprised you even knew a game was going on."

"Seriously... you have a bunting bat?" Eddie asked again.

"Yeah, especially with a guy like Delmer throwing, his ball sinks and—"

Eddie interrupted, "What the hell is this guy doing?" He nodded at the pickup across the intersection.

The driver, an older man wearing a straw work hat, was motioning for Eddie to enter the intersection first and make his turn.

Danny asked "He was here first, right?"

"Yeah, by about thirty seconds." Checking for traffic left and right, Eddie pulled out and turned left. As he passed in front of the pickup, Eddie gave a courtesy wave. The farmer raised his chin, the Shelby County equivalent of an astronaut confirming receipt of a radio message by saying "Roger, Houston."

"I forgot that old people have a quota," Eddie sighed.

"They have a what?"

"A quota" Eddie replied. "It's a theory I have. Old folks come to a stop and even though it's their turn to go, they let other cars go first." Eddie explained further, "Some have a quota of one, some as many as three of four. It's really annoying because you don't know what their quota is so you don't really know when to pull out." Then he added "It's a pain in the ass... watch for it, you'll see I'm right."

Danny snickered.

Anyway, Eddie said, cruising toward Botkins, your bunting bat?"

"Yeah, I was swinging the new Clemente bat in the on-deck circle. I used it in BP a couple days earlier and I like its feel." Danny added, "It's the bat I hit the two doubles with at JC."

Eddie nodded.

"When Gil walked, I knew I'd be bunting so I grabbed the other bat. It has a little thinner barrel and I can control it better." Danny continued, "Delmer is tough, his ball was moving and I needed all the control I could get."

"Smart," Eddie said with appreciation, then "What model was the bunting bat?"

Danny's face lit up. "Let's see how good your memory is. I'll give you a hint, December the fifteenth, nineteen sixty-five."

Eddie's face showed confusion, "What?"

"Here's another hint." Eddie's smile widened, "Milt Pappas."

Eddie groaned, "Ohhhhhhh, Frank Robinson!"

On December 15, 1965, Cincinnati Reds Owner/General Manager Bill DeWitt traded the team's star 30-year-old outfielder Frank Robinson to the Baltimore Orioles for starting pitcher Milt Pappas, reliever Jack Baldschun, and outfielder Dick Simpson. DeWitt claimed that Robinson "was not a young 30." Later versions of the story changed his comment to say Robby was "an old 30." Whichever was accurate, the trade did not go the Reds' way.

Robinson, who won the National League MVP award in 1961, went on to immediately win the same award in the American League in 1966, hitting 49 homeruns and batting .316. Pappas was good, but not great. Baldschun and Simpson were minor contributors.

"What a stupid trade!" Eddie wailed. "My buddy Al Johnson is an Orioles fan and he razzes me all the time about that trade."

As they pulled into town, Danny alerted his brother, "Hey, there's Reedo at the Tastee Freez."

Reed was taking his first lick of a soft serve vanilla and chocolate twist ice cream cone, having just paid at the window.

"Ahhh," Eddie crowed, "I suddenly have a hankerin' for ice cream." He and Danny laughed.

Ten minutes later Reed sat in the back seat of the Impala. All three occupants licked ice cream cones. Reedo, trying to avoid an ice cream headache, did so much faster than his counterparts as vanilla and chocolate leaked from his reverse-decapitated cone.

CHAPTER TWENTY-THREE

Dave Mielke sought out Danny during lunch period the following day. He found him shooting baskets in the gym with several of his friends.

"Hey Danny, got a minute?" Doc asked from the hallway door.

Danny eyed Doc, said "Sure," and flipped the ball to Andy Craft. He trotted over to the doorway.

"What's up, D..., uh, Mr. Mielke?" Danny covered a smile with his hand.

Mielke grinned, "You almost gave me the Bugs Bunny line, didn't you?"

"I guess I did" Danny admitted, still smiling. "I didn't mean to, but..."

"Don't worry about it, I've heard it a thousand times." Doc waved a hand. Come over to my room."

Mielke led Danny across the hall to room 8. Doc taught American History, World History, and Political Science in this room. Danny followed him to the teacher's desk at the front of the classroom and watched him pull out the top drawer.

As he reached into the drawer, Doc inquired, "You know the bus company had a 'no refund' policy, right?"

"Yeah, I guess so," Eddie nodded slowly. "To tell you the truth, I really haven't thought about it." His voice trailed off as he added, "With everything going on..."

Mielke contemplated this and nodded. He withdrew an envelope from the drawer and, handing it to Danny, disclosed, "A few of us met with Mr. Degen. He agreed to call the company on your behalf. They agreed to reimburse you $100."

Danny stared at the envelope.

"Open it" Mielke urged.

Sure enough, it was a check for one hundred dollars, made out to Danny.

"Wow," Danny managed. "I don't know what to say, I thought we just lost the money."

"We felt there were special circumstances here and the bus company agreed."

Danny was speechless. "Thanks Doc." He finally managed.

"Can I make a suggestion of how to use some of that money?" Mielke ventured.

"Yeah, of course."

"I think it would be a good investment for you to get some good running shoes. You've been wearing Eddie's old pair." Doc continued, "They're worn and probably don't fit you very well."

When Danny nodded, Doc resumed, "Get a pair you can train with out on the road." He added, "Since our meets are on cinder tracks, you might think about getting a pair of spikes, too." He paused, "You *could* wear your road shoes on the track, but I think you're going to do well and you'll want every advantage you can get."

Danny smiled, "I like it, where would I get 'em? Lonzo's?"

Doc winced, "Lonzo doesn't, uh, have the selection..."

Danny cut him off, "Dumb question, where would you suggest?"

"There are a couple stores in Lima... Dayton, for sure, but that's pretty far away." Mielke thought for a second, then, "Maybe try Goff's Sport Shop in Sidney. You can probably get both pairs for $30 or so."

"I'll do it!" Danny said enthusiastically. "I'll put the rest in the bank."

"One more thing" Mielke added. "I'm putting you with the four-mile group tonight. I know you have a game tomorrow so you'll miss our practice. Our first dual meet is Wednesday at Anna and you'll be running the two-mile."

Danny's eyebrows rose just as the bell rang signaling the end of lunch period. "Thanks again, Doc. Gotta go." Danny hustled for his locker.

Doc watched him go, wishing he could do more.

Danny ran the four-mile block on Monday after school. He completed it in just under 32 minutes. Up until the previous month, he'd never run longer than a mile. He was upbeat, he knew he was getting stronger and faster.

After practice he rushed to the bank, deposited the check and kept forty dollars. He walked a block to the lumber yard to see if he could borrow the Impala to try to make it to Goff's before it closed. It hit him as soon as he walked in the door that he'd forgotten that his dad didn't have the car, Eddie did.

"What's wrong, Danny?" Carol Roush asked. "You look confused, everything OK?" She peered at him from her desk with a concerned look on her face.

"Oh, hi Mrs. Roush" Danny began.

"Carol," she corrected him with a smile.

"Uh, Carol." Danny returned her smile. "I'm a dummy, I came here to borrow Dad's car. I forgot that Eddie's been driving it during the day." He explained that he was hoping to get to Sidney before Goff's closed at six.

"Well, your dad is on the phone in his office: I just put a call through. Carol glanced at the clock. "I'm going to make a command decision."

Carol stood and walked to a board on the back wall that held dozens of keys on wooded pegs. She selected one and walked to Danny at the front counter.

"You just go ahead and take the new Ford wagon down to Sidney. Your dad drove it in today and Mr. Gerber planned on him having it all week. I'll make sure Jerry gets a ride home." Carol slid the keys across the counter.

"Really?" Danny exclaimed. "Wow, that's great." Then, "You're sure it's OK, Mrs. R..., uh Carol?"

She beamed, "Absolutely." Then, looking at the clock, "Better get going. The wagon is in the back lot: you can't miss it...it's baby food green with fake wood panel." she chuckled.

Danny laughed, "Oh, I've seen it!" He headed for the door, "Thanks Carol, you're the best. Make sure you tell Dad this was your idea."

Danny made it to Goff's in time to buy a pair of size 10.5 running shoes. They didn't have track spikes in stock in that size, but said they could order them and have them for him by Thursday. Danny paid a total $33.95 for both pairs and walked out with his new road shoes.

He walked to the Country Squire and smiled at Mrs. Roush's line, *baby food green.*

Eddie received information from the Red Cross that his flights back to Vietnam had been finalized. He would depart from Dayton on that Thursday, the 30th. That meant he would miss his dad's birthday by two days. They would have to celebrate early. He started thinking about a birthday cake. He also made an appointment to get his hair cut at Counts' Barber Shop on Wednesday. Eddie thought that no one this side of Fort Campbell was better suited to give you a "high and tight" than Injun' Ed.

It would be a busy week. On Tuesday, Eddie watched his brother and the rest of the Trojans beat the Anna Rockets 6-0. Mike Vannette threw the first four innings, giving up no hits and striking out 10. Eddie thought Vannette had a real chance to go somewhere: he threw HARD. Vannette was removed by Sanders at that point and replaced by Andy Craft, who completed the shutout. Botkins had a game Thursday night at Russia that would go a long way toward deciding the league championship. Sanders planned to start Vannette again in that game.

The game featured a play that would be remembered by some for several years. With two outs and the bases full, an Anna hitter lofted a high pop-fly to right-center. Jokisch, in center, lost the ball even though there wasn't a cloud in the sky and the sun was at his back. As the Anna runners wheeled around the bases, Herm Barton flashed over from right and made a diving catch. Herm's play saved at least two runs.

Jokisch approached Barton and raised his throwing hand. Barton slapped it.

Dusty Baker and Glenn Burke of the Los Angeles Dodgers were credited with performing the first ever high five on October 2, 1977. The Trojans knew otherwise.

Barton, upon being greeted in the dugout, said Jokisch had good reason for losing the ball. There had been a "high sky." Nobody seemed to know what that meant. They just knew that Herm had picked up a teammate that had given him trouble in the past. Jokisch appreciated it and went out of his way to side with Herm for the rest of their time in high school.

On Wednesday, Eddie drove to Anna and watched his brother run in his first track meet. Danny ran two miles in 12:29, finishing fourth. Eddie was impressed. The laid-back nature of track meets meant that Eddie could hang out with Doc Mielke and kid around with team members.

Danny, Eddie noted, spent virtually all of his down time at the meet with Chris Koenig. The girls' events were interspersed with those of the boys. Chris ran the 440 and 880.

It was good to spend time with Mielke. Eddie characterized their discussions as "shooting the shit." Doc, he was sure, would describe the conversation in more G-rated words. Mielke peppered him with questions about the war, which Eddie could've done without, but the track coach was effusive in his praise of Danny.

"Loads of potential...I think he's getting the running bug. Great teammate."

Eddie was waiting at BHS when the bus returned. Danny jumped in and said "Let's go to Reedo's; he's gonna help us bake a birthday cake for Dad.

Eddie snorted, "Perfect, this oughtta be good."

Danny had given Reed five dollars at school that day and asked his buddy to buy all the necessary ingredients.

"Get the Betty Crocker mix: Mom always used Betty Crocker... chocolate."

Ginny Thompson was overjoyed to have the Hitchens brothers in her house. The boys let Teddy lick the cake batter off the beaters when they were removed from the electric mixer. While the cake baked, Eddie played army in the back yard with Teddy while Danny and Reed cleaned up.

They were watching Batman in living color and eating fried baloney sandwiches when the timer on the counter dinged. They pulled out the cake and let it cool while watching the Dynamic Duo match wits with Mr. Freeze, played by Eli Wallach. The episode featured Batman and Robin repeating their "walk up the wall" gag using a bat rope. It ended with a cliffhanger: viewers were instructed to "Stay frozen to your furniture! Tomorrow! Same Bat-Time, Same Bat-Channel!"

Eddie thought, *I ought to be somewhere over the Pacific when Batman escapes.*

The cake was still warm when Danny and Eddie slathered on the icing. They topped it with 42 candles, thanked the Thompsons again, and headed for home. It was nearly 8:30 when they reached the house.

"Why don't we light the candles before walking in?" Danny suggested. Holding the cake, he turned to the work bench to look for matches.

"Good idea." Eddie agreed, and without thinking pulled his Zippo lighter from his pocket and flipped it on.

Danny turned back, confused, "Where'd you get that?"

Eddie scrambled for an answer, "Oh, I picked it up in Wapak last week. My buddy Al asked if I could bring one back for him, he's a big smoker. I figured I'd use it for Dad's candles so I threw it in my pocket this morning."

Danny nodded and stepped to Eddie, holding up the cake. "Good thinking."

Eddie began to light the candles, thinking *Real smooth, dumbass.*

PART THREE

THE DESCENT

CHAPTER TWENTY-FOUR

Looking back on it later, Danny supposed that the following day, Thursday, March 30, could be looked at as the first day of a long downward slide. It was the day his brother left for Vietnam.

Eddie's flight out of Dayton was to take off at 9:45 am. He had packed the night before, after enjoying birthday cake with Danny and their dad. Jerry got a kick out of the slightly cockeyed cake. "Tastes better than it looks."

He was brought to tears by the enlarged photo. "This is just perfect, guys" he said, dabbing at his cheeks. Both of his sons teared up as well.

Eddie had an idea for the following morning, "How about we all go to Mom's grave in the morning?" He continued, "We can pay our respects, then drop you off at school," he canted his head toward Danny, "before going to the airport." Jerry and Danny agreed that this sounded like a good idea.

They awoke Thursday and Jerry fried eggs, percolated coffee, and broke up a Gaines Burger for Suzy Wong. Danny loaded his brother's bags in the car while Eddie showered. They rendezvoused at the kitchen table.

"My hair's dry already." Eddie rubbed his head with one hand and held a piece of toast in the other. He was wearing civilian clothes for the return trip.

"You mean because it's so short?" Danny guessed.

"Yeah, I didn't realize it had gotten so long." Then, "But Injun Ed took care of that, he scalped me yesterday." Eddie looked a bit sheepish, then concluded, "Oh well, back to work for me... gotta look the part." He smiled at his brother.

Danny tried to smile. The corners of his lips danced upward a bit, but his eyes turned solemn.

Jerry glanced at the clock above the sink and said "Better get going. Let me pour the rest of the pot into the thermos for you Eddie."

241

Just before walking out, Eddie bent down and picked up Suzy. She looked at him with her expectant eyes. He stroked her head and said softly, "You be a good girl until I see you again."

Jane's grave was a fresh scar in the otherwise pristine cemetery. It was, Danny noted sadly, a heap of dirt clods waiting for gravity to work its magic. The freshly dug earth, coupled with the lack of a gravestone, Danny thought, made the plot the most forlorn spot in the world.

My mom's down there. It was impossible to fully comprehend.

Danny's thoughts went back a couple weeks to Arlington National Cemetery. The gravestones there, most of which noted the awards and honors achieved by the deceased lying below, contained shorthand that helped tell that person's story. Danny had been excited, almost giddy, walking from the marker of one hero to the next.

Here in St. Lawrence Catholic Cemetery, he was unnerved.

As if reading Danny's mind, Eddie asked "When will we get a marker for her, Dad?"

As Jerry answered, explaining that he would pick on out in the next few days, Danny eyed his brother. *That was eerie,* he thought. Then, *Well, what else would you ask about a grave with no marker?*

As Jerry and Eddie discussed ideas for a stone, Danny's eyes wandered to the sign at the entrance to the cemetery. It depicted a resurrected Christ. Once again Danny's thoughts on Christianity invaded his thoughts. *Christ is like a pinball. The Father has an unlimited number of free games. So he loses this ball? Big deal. He pulls the handle back and puts that same ball back into play. New life. That kind of death isn't a sacrifice.*

Danny looked back to his mom's grave and shivered. He felt sacrilegious, standing there in a Catholic cemetery, having these thoughts.

"You ready Danny?"

"Sure Eddie, let's go."

Jerry pulled up in front of the school. All three of them got out of the Impala. Eddie approached Danny.

"Beat Russia tonight, send me letters to let me know about baseball and track. And let me know if anything works out for college." he said smiling. Then, "Keep working with that rifle. When I get back we're going to have a contest."

Danny uncertainly, extended his hand. Eddie ignored it and pulled his brother in for a bear hug. Eddie whispered "Take care of Dad."

He then turned to Jerry, "Ready?"

"Ready" Jerry answered.

As the Impala pulled away Eddie turned to Danny and smiled through the rolled down window.

All Danny could think to say was "Shoot straight!"

"I always do!" his brother answered.

Jerry sat in the concourse with Eddie, making small talk. It was that awkward time when the mind conjures scenarios that demand expressive conversation, but a mental check valve of some kind keeps it from being manifested.

Eddie excused himself to use the restroom. When he'd finished, he emerged, looked toward his dad to make sure his attention was diverted, and moved quickly to the gift shop down the concourse. He bought all the Winstons they had, eight packs, and tucked them into his carry-on bag. He planned to repeat this process in Chicago, San Francisco, and Hawaii.

He wouldn't be returning to his platoon empty handed, he'd be bearing gifts; smokes and waterproof socks.

When his flight was called, the two men stood and looked at each other.

"Hang in there, Dad," Eddie managed. He was afraid that the loss of Jane might cause Jerry to give up on life. "Take care of Danny, he needs you."

Putting on a bold front despite feeling he would lose control, Jerry countered, "You just take care of *yourself.* Write when you can. Stay safe, Eddie."

They hugged for 30 seconds, then Eddie turned for the walkway. Halfway there he turned and said "Thanks for everything, Dad," and he was gone.

The following day, President Lyndon Baines Johnson stunned the nation with a speech broadcast from the Oval Office. He looked at the camera with a solemn expression and intoned; "I shall not seek, and I will not accept, the nomination of my party for another term as your president."

Vietnam had been the catalyst that consumed the occupant of 1600 Pennsylvania Avenue.

At 304 South Street in Botkins, Danny and Jerry felt themselves just as absorbed by the issue. Their thoughts were clouded by a foreboding that they tried constantly to push away.

CHAPTER TWENTY-FIVE

Botkins bus number 3 chugged south down I-75. After 12 miles, it would get off the highway at Sidney, then head west another 10, and finally three more miles south before arriving in Russia. The name of the village was pronounced "Roo-She." Unless the Trojans advanced deep into the tournament and got to play someplace exotic like Urbana or Tipp City, this would be the longest road trip of the season.

Danny's mood was somber. He already missed having Eddie around. He had to get his mind back on baseball. The Russia Raiders were an excellent team and their top pitcher, Mike Schieltz, represented a formidable challenge for the Trojans.

It struck Danny that it had to be highly unusual for a conference as small as the Shelby County League to have three pitchers as talented as Schieltz, Delmer, and Vannette. The fact that all three had the same first name made it even more unusual. Vannette was the only underclassman of the three so, Danny supposed, he might choose his teammate over the two seniors. Still...

To occupy his mind, Danny decided to compare the three right handers. Vannette, he believed, threw the hardest. But it was very close. If someone wanted to argue on behalf of one of the other two, Danny would certainly understand. There was no way to know for sure, really. Danny had read about radar guns but guessed there wasn't one within fifty miles of Botkins, maybe a hundred.

Vannette was 6'3", threw from a three-quarter arm slot and hated, just *hated,* to lose. Danny thought if he were to compare Vannette to a big-league pitcher it would be Bob Gibson. Gibby, the St. Louis Cardinals' ace, threw very hard, but was best known for being an intense competitor. It was speculated that Gibson would throw at his own grandmother if she dug in against him in the batter's box.

Delmer was stockier, about six feet tall. His arm slot was closer to Don Drysdale of the Dodgers. He was a slinger. His fastball moved like crazy. Yes, Danny thought, Drysdale was a good comparison.

Schieltz, the pitcher the Trojans faced today, had the best control of the three. Standing 6'2", everything he threw was at the knees, or lower, and on a corner. He was just... Danny struggled for the right word, splendid? Yeah, that sounded about right. Danny thought for a bit then decided that a good comparison for Schieltz would be Jim Bunning. The Phillies hurler, formerly a Detroit Tiger, threw hard and kept everything down.

Danny began to have second thoughts on the Schieltz-Bunning comparison—Bunning was a sidearmer like Drysdale, but Schieltz threw at a higher arm slot—when his thought process was interrupted.

"Get the hell away from me!" Freshman Frank Nuss was shouting. Three teammates, Pat Jokisch, Gil Horseman, and Gary Poppe, had moved to the seats in front of, behind, and across from Barton. They leered at Nuss like cartoon vultures.

Ladies and gentlemen," Jokisch announced, "welcome to the pre-game ear rodeo."

Several teammates howled. Nuss slinked into his seat. His eyes were wild. He was hurling threats, "If one of you bastards even *thinks* about screwing with me, I'll kick your ass!"

It was all bluster, and everyone knew it.

Jokisch feinted an attempt for Nuss's left ear from in front, Nuss flinched backwards, and Horseman grabbed hold of the right ear. The count toward eight began.

Danny glanced to Eula Greve, the driver, and could've sworn he saw the hint of a smile on her face as she glanced up at the big rear view mirror.

"You gonna get in on that, Hitch?" It was Reedo, who was occupying the seat behind Danny.

"Nah," Danny said. "Looks like that really pisses off those guys."

Reed, in the seat behind Danny, nodded. "Yeah, I'm surprised someone hasn't complained to Coach Sanders."

When Danny didn't respond, Reed asked in a soft voice, "Hey Hitch, you okay?"

Danny turned to his buddy, "Sure Reedo."

The Trojans lost to the Raiders, 2-1. Vannette and Schieltz hooked up in an epic pitchers' duel: Vannette struck out 12, Schieltz 11. Russia had 6 hits while Botkins managed just 5.

Vannette seemed to struggle with his command in the later innings. He walked just two but was behind the count on most hitters. Russia's Dave Francis had the big hit, a two-run single in the fifth. Danny wondered if the four innings against Anna earlier in the week had affected Vannette.

Botkins had the tying run on third in the form of Andy Craft with just one out in the sixth inning. Reed Thompson came to the plate. Reed had lined out and singled in his two previous at bats. He was one of the few Trojans that had given Schieltz problems. Reed peered down at Coach Sanders before entering the box. Danny noticed that several Raiders were also watching Sanders.

Oh no, Danny thought as Sanders went through the signs, ending by gripping his neck with his right hand.

The suicide squeeze is a play designed to bring home a runner from third by having the hitter give himself up with a bunt. The runner takes off for home the instant he sees the pitcher begin his motion. The hitter disguises the play by squaring around late. He then attempts to get his bat on the ball, regardless of the location of the pitch.

The pitch is in the dirt? You bunt it.

The pitch is two feet above the strike zone? You bunt it.

Thus, the term "suicide squeeze bunt."

If the hitter gets the bunt down it is virtually impossible to stop the runner from scoring due to his early start from third.

The problem with the Botkins suicide squeeze was that Sanders had used the same sign, hand squeezes neck, for the play for years. Every team in the SCL knew the sign at least as well as the Trojan players. It was the baseball equivalent of a teacher giving the exact same multiple choice test every year. Eventually someone passes a copy of the test down to the next class and everyone gets an A.

Just let Reedo hit, Danny thought. But it was too late. Just before Schieltz, pitching from the stretch, began his delivery, Danny heard Russia coach John Hefner whistle loudly from the Russia dugout. Schieltz began his motion and Craft dutifully bolted for home.

Danny seemed to see the play unfold in slow motion. The Russia catcher moved a full step to his right just as the ball left Schieltz's hand.

Pitch out.

Reedo saw that the pitch would sail past him several feet off the outside corner. He did everything possible to protect the runner, actually diving toward the ball with his bat. He wasn't quite able to reach it. Catcher Mark Richard caught the pitch at chest height. He lunged back across the plate, past Thompson, with his mitt extended. He beat Craft to the spot with several feet to spare.

A large crowd had gathered to watch the showdown between the league's two best teams. It was composed almost entirely of Raider fans: few parents attended road games. The cheers from the bleachers seemed to return things to normal speed for Danny.

God dammit, he thought.

The bus ride home was subdued. Botkins and Russia were now tied for first. Vannette, Danny noted, was seething. There was a buffer zone of empty seats surrounding him. The freshmen hunkered a few seats in front of Vannette, warily scanning for bus cowboys.

There would be no ear rodeo on the long ride back to Botkins.

The weather grew warmer and flowers bloomed as spring progressed. The flower boxes at the Koenig house came alive and, thanks to Jan's green thumb, took a turn toward spectacular. Danny commented on the flowers one Saturday as he dropped Chris off after a movie.

"Your mom is the Hank Aaron of gardeners." The comment was only partly facetious.

Chris chuckled, "I guess that's supposed to be a compliment?"

"Yeah, you kidding? Hammerin' Hank? That means she's the best."

"Speaking of flowers," Chris deftly switched gears, "my dress for the prom will be light blue."

Danny stared at her dumbly. "Yeah?"

"The corsage, genius, you'll want to order one that goes with blue." She continued, "It will be kind of strapless, so you should probably get a wrist corsage."

"Oh, yeah. That makes sense" Danny managed with a bemused expression.

He would have to confer with Reed about this whole prom thing.

In the first week of April, Danny stopped at the post office, and after twirling the I-G-F combination, was rewarded with his ACT test results. He waited until he arrived home to open them. The results, he thought, were mixed; natural sciences, 21, social studies, 29, math, 16, english, 26. The composite score was 23.

The relative scores didn't surprise him. Danny knew he'd done well on the social studies section, with its emphasis on history. Math, he'd known, was his weakest area, but 16 was downright embarrassing.

He made a mental note to stop in to talk to Miss Giltrow, the guidance counselor. She tried to stay on top of everything related to the future endeavors of the Botkins students. She specifically requested that every student who took the ACT visit her when the results arrived.

On the baseball diamond, the Trojans had reeled off several wins in a row, keeping pace with the Russia Raiders. Danny was hitting over .300 and had made just one error.

Returning from a win in a non-league game at Lima Perry, Danny and Reed sat with their backs to the wall of the bus, Danny's seatback between then.

"How's track going?" Reed asked.

Danny brightened, "Really well, my two-mile time is down to 11:45." He added, "The spiked shoes really help on those cinder tracks."

Reed moved in, "What?" A spirited ear rodeo was being contested a few seats away. That, coupled with the thrum of the bus, made it difficult to hear.

"My new shoes help," Danny raised his voice. "I'm only a few seconds behind Virgil in the races and we run the four-mile block together in practice."

"Wow," Reed was amazed that his friend had become a distance runner. Just last winter Reed had finished nearly 20 seconds ahead of Danny in the mile qualifying run for basketball.

"So, about the prom?" Danny queried. "It's right around the corner, the twenty-second."

"I've been thinking," Reed said. "How about this; you drive your dad's car, I help you clean it up the day before, and I take care of ordering the corsages. Mom knows someone that works at Dudley's in Wapak. She says they do a nice job."

Danny knew the Thompson car, a VW Beetle, would be small for four people in formal clothes. "Sounds like a plan," he agreed.

Danny got a pass from study hall to meet with Miss Giltrow. Her office was on the corner formed by the main hall and the hall occupied by the science classrooms. Unless she was in a meeting, her door was open. She enjoyed watching the comings and goings of the students, cheerfully kibitzing with them as they passed by.

Danny knocked on the door frame and poked his head around the corner. "Hey, Miss G."

Sue Giltrow looked up and registered that it was Danny. A sunny smile formed on her face.

"Well, well," she began, "if it isn't Mr. Hitchens!"

She always called him this: never just Danny. It mystified him that she used his surname. Miss G was quirky.

"Come in, have a seat." Giltrow gestured to a molded plastic chair near her desk. She eyed the envelope in Danny's hand. "You brought your results?"

Danny nodded. He removed the report from its envelope and handed it to the counselor. She examined the contents for several seconds before stating "Twenty-three is a good score, Danny. It should get you accepted at most of the schools in Ohio."

Danny nodded once but didn't comment.

Giltrow continued, "We knew the math section would be the most challenging for you. Some people are retaking the test to try to improve their score. If you did this, you would almost certainly raise your score in that section."

Danny simply nodded.

Sensing Danny's reticence, Giltrow asked "Has anything changed with your plans for after graduation? Are you still considering college?"

"Well, sure," Danny began hesitantly, "but I don't know how I'd pay for it." Then, avoiding her eyes, "I'm also thinking about the Army."

With some kids, Giltrow may have thought it appropriate to explain the risks of joining the Army during a time of ramped up deployments to Vietnam. She figured that Danny, who had a brother in the thick of it, had already weighed these factors.

She nodded, choosing her words, "Do you think it might be a good idea to leave your options open? A lot can happen in the next year. If you prepare yourself academically for college and still decide on the military, you're not out anything. But if you decide halfway through your senior year that you don't want to join the Army and haven't checked all the boxes academically, it could be very difficult to get into college." She added, "I don't have to tell you that colleges are being flooded with applicants looking for a draft deferment."

Danny looked up sharply. This had been a sore subject with him since Eddie enlisted. "Yeah," he nearly spat, "I know all about that. You can't pick up a newspaper or turn on the TV without hearing about the protests."

Danny had read just that morning that 100,000 people were expected to attend a march in New York's Central Park the following Saturday.

Giltrow had a flash of inspiration, "You know, if you join the Army with a college degree, you can be an officer."

She had Danny's attention. "Yeah?" he asked.

Giltrow could almost see the wheels turning in his head. She added, "The Army needs good officers now, they have to come from somewhere." Giltrow smiled.

Danny, remembering how his brother talked about Lt. Checque and Capt. Kaufman in the 173rd, smiled back.

Giltrow crowed, "It looks like we are in agreement, Mr. Hitchens." She leaned toward Danny, "I'll zero in on financial aid options while you," she handed the ACT results back to him, her index finger pointing to the numeral 16 in the math column, "plan on taking Mr. Rawson's Algebra II and Geometry classes next year."

Danny groaned.

CHAPTER TWENTY-SIX

Prom week was busy, packed with ballgames, track meets, homework, and preparation for the event itself. The junior class was responsible for decorating the gym for the big night. The doorways to the area were covered in black plastic and only members of that class were permitted inside.

The theme was "Under the Sea" and representations of sharks, octopi, and swordfish adorned the temporary walls set up inside. The prom committee had acquired small fishbowls for each table. They would contain live goldfish on Saturday night.

Reed showed up at the Hitchens house on Friday night. He'd picked up the corsages and brought the one that Chris would wear. Danny took a look at it, uttered "Nice," and put it in the refrigerator. "Let's clean the car."

Suzy Wong came outside with them. As the boys washed and vacuumed the car, Suzy tinkled on each and every shrub in front of the house. A bit later they pronounced the Impala "good to go."

They took Suzy inside and retreated to Danny's room where they played Strat-O-Matic Baseball, a dice baseball game based on player-specific probabilities. They were able to get in three games while listening to Jim McIntyre call the Reds game in Houston on WLW radio. The Reds, playing in "The Eighth Wonder of the World," the Astrodome, won 3-1 behind a 2-run, 2-out triple by Vada Pinson in the tenth inning.

Reedo yawned and pulled himself up from the floor. "Long day tomorrow Hitch, I better head for home." Then, "We got a lot done tonight."

"Yep." Danny agreed, "Forty-five minutes getting the car ready and three hours of Strat-O-Matic."

Reed deadpanned, "Too bad all that cleaning took time away from our games." Then, "See ya' tomorrow, it's gonna be a great day."

It didn't quite work out that way.

Jerry shook Danny awake the next morning. When Danny saw the look on his dad's face he knew something was wrong.

"I have some bad news, Danny," Jerry announced. "The car is in the shop, looks like it'll need a new transmission."

Danny blinked once then quickly sat up, "WHAT?!"

"I drove it up to Steiner's to fill it up for you. I only made it a block and it started vibrating and making a grinding sound. By the time I got to the station, the gear shift wouldn't work." Jerry concluded, "Ron says it's definitely the transmission. He'll be able to fix it, but he has to order parts."

"Aww MAN!" Danny moaned. "What am I gonna do about the prom?"

Jerry sighed, "Well, Clyde said you can take the Country Squire."

"AWW MAAN!" Danny collapsed back into bed.

That night Danny and Reed picked up Chris and Sandy in a 1966 Ford Country Squire station wagon with wood grain trim and "Botkins Lumber Company" written in script on both sides.

It was green. Baby food green.

It represented the most humiliating day in Danny Hitchens' life.

Reed knew this. He felt bad for his buddy, but he had to stifle a laugh all night.

The baseball team finished the season tied with Russia for the league lead. They were named co-champions. Mike Schieltz was named first team all-league as a pitcher. Mike Vannette earned second team honors. Fort Loramie's Mike Delmer, at the very least the third best player in the entire league, was left off the first and second team. Danny imagined that when Delmer read this in the newspaper, he'd still be smiling.

Craft, Poppe, and Reed Thompson made first team for Botkins. Danny was honorable mention. He was really happy for Reed, who had played three positions during the season and solidified the lineup when others were hurt.

The Trojans made it to the sectional finals but lost a tough 5-4 game to Versailles, a team from another league. Vannette threw a shutout three days earlier and Sanders opted not to pitch him again with little rest. Gil Horseman took the loss.

Coach Sander's decision may or may not have been influenced by the fact that Vannette was now being actively recruited by several colleges. Some of the college coaches saw him throw his tournament shutout. Sanders had another year with his number one pitcher and a loaded junior class. Why burn out his ace with college coaches paying attention?

Danny got his two-mile time down to 11:19. Doc Mielke informed him that there would be a 500 Mile Club over the summer. It would be a challenge, especially with Danny planning to work full time at the lumberyard, but Doc promised Danny that the mileage base would pay huge dividends next year. Cross country was a fall sport. That race distance was also two miles. Danny would be one of the top runners on that team as well as a potential standout in track in the spring.

Danny rode to the lumberyard with Jerry at 6:45 am on a warm June morning. The Impala hummed along with its new transmission. Danny couldn't help but think of the car as traitorous after the prom incident. It was the first day of his summer job. He was a bit nervous. Danny had worked part time on and off the last few years at his dad's place of business. He'd assembled and nailed together wooden pallets, swept up, and run various errands. Today, though, he would be working with bread-winning men on the shop floor. He'd be using dangerous equipment.

Danny's mild sense of trepidation was allayed by the fact that he'd be earning the new minimum wage of $1.40 an hour. The jump from $1.25 had taken effect in February, the first increase in over three years.

"After you clock in, I'm going to have you start with Ray Bolan on the finishing saw" Jerry explained. "Have you met Ray?"

Danny searched his memory, "A little shorter than me, kinda fuzzy black hair with glasses?"

"That's Ray."

"I've seen him running the saws but I don't think I've ever met him." Danny decided.

As he turned into the parking lot, Jerry turned to his son and said "You and Ray will get along well."

Danny thought his dad looked, well, amused?

Danny found the time card with his name typed at the top—Carol Roush had been her normal, efficient self—and slid it into the slot on top of the time clock. He was rewarded with a satisfying *clunk*.

"We're a few minutes early, Jerry observed, "why don't you go out to the finish saw and get it plugged in, Ray is going to train you on it. He will be here in," Jerry looked at the clock, "two minutes."

As Danny walked into the shop he thought "Ray must be pretty precise."

The Botkins Lumber Company had been in business for over 50 years. Though relatively small, with barely 50 full time employees, the business was considered a full-service operation. That is, it supplied bulk lumber for builders in the form of two by fours, plywood sheeting and the like, as well as high end hardwood in custom sizes used for trim and finish work.

Danny walked toward a line of equipment. The last piece in the line was known by the employees as the finish saw. It was a large table saw with a circular blade protruding vertically near its center. When the shop was turning out bulk building materials, the finish saw was outfitted with a heavy ripping blade and performed the same basic tasks as other saws on the floor. That is, ripping plywood sheets at the proper widths or cutting groupings of two by fours, one by twos, or four by fours, at designated lengths.

When the shop was running more valuable hardwoods, however, the ripping blade was switched out for a composite blade. This made the finish saw capable of cuts that weren't nearly as rough.

Danny plugged in the finish saw. He cast an eye to the larger table saw just beyond the finish saw—he thought it was called the rip saw—grabbed its electric cord, and reached for the wall outlet.

"Somebody tell you to plug in my rip saw?" a voice boomed from behind Danny.

Turning, Danny saw that the voice belonged to a large man in his forties. The man wore work pants, a plain white tee-shirt, and an indignant expression.

This must be William Doyle.

Danny had heard a few stories about Doyle from his dad. He'd heard many more from Eddie, who'd had a couple run-ins with Doyle before joining the Army. Danny couldn't remember the specifics, but he'd heard the term "Big Red Ape" enough times around the house to know that Doyle was on Eddie's shit list.

"That's my saw and my 'sponsibility," Doyle had a southern accent and a deep voice. Danny had seen a preview for a movie called "Cool Hand Luke" and thought William Doyle would fit perfectly in a prison work gang. Well, not perfectly. Doyle also happened to have an unfortunate hair style that, from the eyebrows north, made him look like Larry Fine of the Three Stooges. The longish red mop surrounded a hairline in full retreat. It stuck out on one side, making Doyle look like he existed in a perpetual windstorm.

"Uh sorry." Danny managed, "Just trying to help out."

Doyle grabbed the cord and pulled it roughly from Danny's hand.

"I see you've met William."

257

Danny turned to see a smiling, thirtyish man with horned rim glasses. "Ray Bolan," he extended his hand. "You must be Danny."

Ray and Danny worked side by side all morning. Ray showed him the intricacies of the saw and concisely explained each task that it performed. Ray was a cheerful, well-spoken man. He seemed to get along with every worker in the building. Danny thought all of these things, positive though they were, made Ray a bit of an oddball. The shop was a loud work environment. When the saws weren't screaming, the music pumping through mounted speakers filled the void. Men tended to hunker over their work stations and stay to themselves. Ray, on the other hand, seemed to be a genial, white collar guy thrust into this cacophony, yearning for a conversation to join.

Danny remembered that his dad had hinted he and Ray would hit it off. Try as he might, Danny couldn't find any common ground. Ray wasn't interested in sports, he'd been married for eight years, he didn't even live in Botkins. He drove to work each day from his house in Jackson Center.

At 11:30 Danny jumped into the Impala to ride home. Employees got 30 minutes for lunch and the Hitchens house being just a few blocks away, meant they could drive home, make a cold meat sandwich, grab a few handfuls of chips, and make it back with a few minutes to spare. Jerry liked to flip on the TV and watch news commentator Paul Harvey's video editorial that was broadcast each day.

"Dad, you said I'd get along well with Ray, right?" Danny asked.

Jerry nodded, "Yeah, so what did you two talk about?"

Danny was a bit perplexed, "Well not much really. He doesn't seem interested in baseball. I don't know what to ask him about his wife. Seems like a nice guy but we really don't have anything in common."

Jerry smirked, "Ask him what he reads."

Danny partially squeezed his eyes shut and cocked his head toward Jerry. "What he reads?"

"Just ask him what he reads."

It turned out that Ray Bolan was a comic book nut. A thirty-three-year old, married, comic book nut. He received no less than eight different titles in the mail each month. Danny was pleasantly surprised. No, shocked. He'd never met an adult that collected comics.

Ray preferred Marvel comics, knew the superpower of each hero, and was able to suspend logic when watching Captain America's shield bounce off multiple villains and unerringly return to him. Ray owned issues 25 and 26 of the Fantastic Four, which featured an epic battle with The Hulk, and could describe virtually every page. These things made Ray a favorite of Danny.

These, and the fact that Ray was protective of his new protégé. The cuts on hardwood operations were precise and sometimes required getting one's hands uncomfortably close to the blade. Ray showed Danny a few tricks to minimize the danger.

Ray also watched over him when it came to William Doyle. The brutish redhead tended to forego safety procedures. His work station fed into the finish saw station. Doyle's job was to rip a large board or sheet of wood into two smaller pieces. If the finish saw was clear, Doyle would feed one piece to that table while stacking the second piece on a skid nearby. He would keep a steady stream to Ray and Danny, but usually had extra wood on his skid.

Doyle would sometimes, either out of impatience or malevolence, push a board onto the table in front of him and intentionally contact the piece then undergoing the more intricate cut. This was very dangerous, as it could move the hands of the finish saw operator into the path of the blade. Doyle did it once while Bolan was overseeing Danny. Ray turned off the saw and shouted at the bigger man, threatening to go to the foreman.

The foreman, incidentally, was Danny's dad.

Doyle simply looked at Danny and muttered "Another suck-ass," apparently linking Danny to Eddie.

"What the heck is his problem!?" a shaken Danny asked Ray. He was unconsciously flexing the fingers on both hands.

Ray shot a glance at Doyle and considered, "William is kind of like a supervillain that's mad at the world, you know, always out for revenge?"

Ray made the long work days more enjoyable, William Doyle notwithstanding.

The summer of 1967 passed quickly. Danny worked full days Monday through Friday, and half days every Saturday. He set a two-pronged goal: run 500 miles and bank $500. He was able to accomplish both, barely. Danny would be hard pressed to say which was more satisfying.

Just as college seemed closer to him financially, it moved further from him ideologically. There were hippies in a place called Haight-Ashbury, riots in the cities, and drugs as close, he had heard, as Sidney. Danny had still never set foot on a college campus. If their portrayal on TV was accurate, he didn't think he ever would.

Still, he thought the Rolling Stones were cool.

CHAPTER TWENTY-SEVEN

On a Saturday night in August, Danny and several buddies from the baseball team converged on the Thompson house for an outdoor sleepover. Three or four tents were pitched in the back yard. Reed's younger brother Teddy hung out with the older boys until Ginny made him come inside around 11:00. Teddy lobbied strenuously that he should be able to stay, but his mother insisted.

Five minutes after Teddy left, the beer appeared. Lukewarm cans and bottles had been stashed in bedrolls and pillow cases. Danny noted that cans of Schlitz, Bud, and Pabst Blue Ribbon, all national brands, were present. He also saw cans of Hudepohl and bottles of Burger. These were regional brews produced in Cincinnati. Danny always associated them with Reds baseball.

The boys that were under 18 had slipped money to Herm Barton earlier in the week. Herm had already turned 18. He made multiple trips to Don Butch's and stashed the hodge-podge of six packs in the trunk of his mom's car. Herm told everyone to keep their fingers crossed that Claudia didn't have a flat tire that week.

By midnight pretty much everyone was drunk. For the more experienced boys, this state was reached after three beers. One can was enough to do it for the uninitiated.

Discussions ranged from one topic to another and were punctuated with laughter. This was usually followed by an insistent "SHHHHHH" from Reed, after which all eyes would turn to the house. Seeing no light switch on, the deliberations continued.

The group became immersed in the time-honored debate over brands of beer. This was pretty much a given since attendees of the sleepover were all males, all consuming alcohol, and all between the ages of 13 and 100. Pat Jokisch, a PBR man, argued so heatedly for his brand that it appeared he was ready to fight. Thankfully someone changed the subject.

"Jock is not a happy drunk" Reed whispered. Danny nodded.

By 1:30 they were running low on beer. Freshman-to-be Rex Koenig, Chris's younger brother, was in attendance. He'd consumed two cans of Budweiser, which equaled the total number he'd drank in his life up to that point. Rex was given permission to stay at Thompsons by his mother because Danny would be in attendance.

"What are we doing now?" Rex asked. He knew his freshman season of baseball would consist primarily of catching pitchers in the bullpen before games and carrying equipment. He would get on the field to receive warmup pitches if the starting catcher was still putting on his shin guards and mask, but otherwise would be firmly anchored to the dugout. Reed's sleepover gave Rex the opportunity to hang out with the upperclassman. It would be the highlight of his freshman season, and school hadn't even started.

The two beers had been enough to remove pretty much all inhibition from Rex. Danny realized that any suggestion, no matter how ill-conceived, might be agreed to by the freshman. Being an upperclassman, and being nominally responsible for Rex's attendance, Danny thought it would be a good time to take the party down a notch. Then he heard Reed's voice.

"Hey Hitch, what do you think?"

Danny looked at Reedo, who had an impish look on his face. Their eyebrows went up as if synchronized.

"Swimming Pool!"

Twenty minutes later the boards of both the high and low dives at the pool were bouncing on their supports as the 1967 SCL co-champs sprung from them. The distinctive "Thunk-Thunk-Thunk" sound echoing throughout the otherwise silent village. Pat Jokisch, off the high dive, and Rex Koenig, from the low board, timed cannonball dives that hit the water within a split second of each other. This, for some reason, struck their teammates as hilarious. Roars of laughter from the teenagers added to the commotion. Lights came on in the bedrooms of houses across the street. Dogs began barking all over town.

"Peters will be here in two minutes!" Andy Craft, doing his best Coach Sanders imitation, whisper-shouted, despite the fact that there was enough noise to be heard a mile away. The boys howled at the comment, buzzed on hops, barley, and adrenaline.

They climbed the fence at several points, threw on shirts as they ran, laughing, and disappeared down State Street as blue and red light from the roof of the Botkins cruiser approached the pool.

"Peters will be here in two minutes!" said in a whisper-shout, became an accepted non-sequitur response to any question asked of a baseball player that year.

Danny's first class of his senior year was Composition with Mrs. Fark. Danny had always liked her classes. This would be a good start to his day. Second period, however, meant Algebra II with Mr. Rawson. The day went downhill quickly. Danny struggled to grasp most of the concepts. He thought Rawson seemed to enjoy the fact that Danny was in a class made up primarily of sophomores and juniors.

Cross country was a blast. Danny enjoyed running the varied courses, each with their distinct challenges. The weather was cool and Danny was in great shape. He and Virgil Poeppelman were the top two Botkins runners every race. By mid-season Danny was consistently finishing in front of his teammate. Danny shed seconds off his two-mile time almost every race. He PR'd in the district meet with a time of 10:29 and fell just short of making it to the state meet.

Mielke was ecstatic. "I'm going to have you double up in the mile and two-mile in the spring!" he informed Danny.

The baseball team was again 6-0 when the fall season ended. Danny hit .400. Vannette won four of the games. Rex Koenig had an at-bat in a blowout win over Jackson Center.

He popped up to the catcher. Returning to the dugout, Rex deadpanned "I missed a homer by this much." He held his thumb and index finger a millimeter apart.

Danny decided to go out for basketball again that year. He blew away the other players in the mandatory mile run, clocking a time of 4:46. Coach Elsass' eyes bulged as he checked his stopwatch.

September 27, a Wednesday, would've been Jane Hitchens' forty second birthday. Jerry and Danny visited the cemetery in the morning before starting their days. It was a calm day and came in with a pretty sunrise. The birds chirped cheerfully. Danny noted that the grass was now completely covering the plot, though it was a bit thinner than the surrounding area. The ground was still slightly elevated, but other more recent graves drew the attention of the curious.

The headstone had been installed a week earlier: they had hoped to have it by Jane's birthday. Below her name, the words "Beloved Mother, Daughter, and Wife" were etched. Jerry had insisted they were in that order. Jerry laid flowers on the grave. He'd vowed to remain strong for Danny, not to cry in his presence. He didn't, but his face betrayed a look of profound sadness.

A week or so after cross country season ended. A letter arrived from Eddie. It contained several lines on light topics; how he and Al Johnson were the only two members of their squad that preferred Aretha's "Respect" over "Light My Fire" by the Doors, how he missed tenderloins from the Tastee Freez, and that he was receiving lots of mail from Judy Winner. "She went with me to watch Danny's baseball games so maybe it's true love, ha-ha."

Eddie concluded the letter by saying the Herd was "gonna head 'em up and move 'em out real soon."

Danny knew that Eddie wasn't scheduled to be back in the states until Christmas. He assumed the Rawhide reference was his brother's way of saying that he would be returning to combat very soon.

Something about the letter seemed different. A couple hours after reading it, Danny realized it was the handwriting: it was a bit less legible than Eddie's past letters. Almost... shakier.

The next night, Danny was watching a report on the first unmanned flight of the giant Saturn V rocket. The mission had been designated "Apollo 4," and was deemed a success. This was considered a major achievement in the process that, if successful, would put a man on the moon before the end of the decade. President Kennedy had announced that as a goal in a speech to Congress on May 25, 1961.

When the report on the rocket launch ended, the screen filled with images of soldiers in Vietnam.

Danny sat up.

The report talked about a build-up of American troops in an area called the Central Highlands. This was southwest, and inland, of the big U.S. base at Da Nang, which was on the coast of the South China Sea. Danny scrambled to the World Book Encyclopedia to look at a map.

Midway through the segment, the correspondent mentioned that the codename for the action was Operation MacArthur. He went on to say that it would be conducted by "the Army's 4th Infantry Division in conjunction with the Sky Soldiers of the 173rd Airborne Brigade."

Jerry was bagging trash in the kitchen. He was just about to take it out and set it behind the garage when he heard Danny shout "Dad, dad come in here!"

CHAPTER TWENTY-EIGHT

Ammo and cigarettes, Eddie thought.

He was at Fire Support Base 12 in Ben Het. The 173rd was securing the area to allow the base to be completed. They'd had violent contact with the enemy almost every day since airlifting in from AO Bolling on November 2. It was now November 5, and word came down that the Herd would lead a large-scale search and destroy mission in the morning. Eddie and his mates in C Company, 2nd Battalion, 503 Infantry Regiment, 173rd Airborne Brigade were loading out with the necessities for the coming days.

Ammo and cigarettes.

Al Johnson leaned in over Eddie's right shoulder and said "Don't forget... as many grenades as you can carry. Those NVA muthafucka's gonna be dug in on them damn hills."

They were waiting in line inside the sandbagged ammo dump. "Yeah, we'll be tossing the damn things like baseballs." Eddie smiled.

Eddie liked Al for many reasons, not the least of which was the man's willingness to offer advice to others: even the FNG's, or Fucking New Guys, that came into the 173rd as replacements. These men were typically shunned by combat vets. Not by Al. Eddie had seen his buddy mentor a newly arrived E-2 just a week earlier. The man had expressed a desire to be a radioman. Al had warned, "Charlie likes to shoot the radioman first... the radioman talks to the big guns and the flyboys... Charlie don't like radiomen." The FNG had blanched.

It wouldn't be Charlie they would tangle with here in the Central Highlands. Scuttlebutt was that several regiments of Peoples Army of North Vietnam regulars, PAVN, or NVA, were waiting for them. Sgt. Venable reported hearing from a buddy of his in Headquarters Company that an NVA sergeant named Vu Hong had defected a couple days ago and had alerted U.S. intelligence personnel that over 6,000 dug in, well equipped regulars were there, spoiling for a fight. The 173rd would damn sure give them one, Eddie thought.

Al poked him in the back as the line moved. "Just hope you throw your grenades better than that fuckin' Milt Pappas we stuck you with." His eyes lit up, "You dumbasses sent us Frankee Robinson." Al belly-laughed.

Eddie grinned back at Al, "No respect, Al. You got no R-E-S-P-E-C-T."

On the morning of Monday, November 6, helicopters lifted the 173rd from Fire Support Base 12 to Dak To. They joined elements of the 4th Infantry Division and were designated the Division Reaction Force. Hill 823 was the first objective. The number, 823, represented the hill's number of meters above sea level. This was in keeping with U.S. military custom.

Hill 823 was, it turned out, laced with enemy bunkers and tunnels. Multiple airstrikes, artillery fire missions, and helicopter gunship runs assisted the ground troops. Seventeen Americans were killed that day. This was just the beginning. The fighting in Dak To would last 18 days.

Eddie had never seen anything like it. The entire might of the U.S. arsenal was brought to bear on the NVA positions. Still, enemy fire was withering. Crew served automatic weapons, B-40 rockets, and recoilless rifles added punch to the AK-47-weilding enemy. It brought to mind the island fighting endured by U.S Marines in the Pacific theater during World War Two.

If anything, the fighting intensified after the first day. Massive B-52 Stratofortress bombers conducted missions in the area. There was continuous air support available for the entire 18-day period. Tactical aircraft of several types stood ready to drop needed ordinance. Helicopter pilots braved accurate automatic weapon fire to pull out wounded soldiers. At several points in the fight, helos were ordered away from the area due to the volume of enemy fire.

The NVA was so well concealed that Americans were often attacked from their rear: this after passing over terrain they had examined closely. Defoliants had been used on the hills before the assaults. Even flame throwers were employed to take away the enemy's advantage of concealment. Still, the Americans absorbed staggering casualties.

Eddie alternated from one extreme emotion to another; terror, rage, hopelessness, and even love. On the fifth day of the operation, PFC Ron Griggs, was shot through the hip and died screaming in agony. When the AK rounds ripped into Griggs, Eddie was less than ten feet away. Eddie saw movement down the slope to the left rear and sprayed the area with his M-16, all the while screaming for a medic. Others added their fire to Eddie's.

The platoon radioman called repeatedly for helicopter evacuation but was told the area was too hot. Griggs screamed for several minutes until the morphine administered by a medic took effect. The platoon found several blood trails in the area where the NVA was believed to have sprung the ambush, but no enemy bodies. Griggs died on the slope of Hill 823. His body would eventually be returned to Oklahoma where his family was anxiously scouring news reports.

Each time they looked at his Savage 99 on the gun rack in their den, they said a hopeful prayer.

By the second week of the operation, Danny was consumed by a need for information. He pulled a kitchen chair into the living room and anchored it in front of the TV so he could more easily reach the dial to change channels. At one point both the UHF dial, which was used to tune in the higher numbered channels, and the VHF dial were off their posts.

His dad would rush in from work and, concern etched on his face, ask "Anything new?"

Jerry had begun to take the clock radio from his bedroom in to work each day. In his office, he turned the volume to its maximum level. The news reports coming over the clock radio competed with the music coming from the shop and the scream of the saws. Jerry's attention to detail seemed to be slipping and he vaguely realized that Carol Roush had to repeat herself, sometimes more than once, before he comprehended what she was saying.

By Wednesday of the second week, frustrated with the stories in the smaller local papers, Danny decided to ride his bike up to the Tastee Freez before school to buy a Dayton Daily News from the vending machine near the front of the establishment. He was scanning an article quoting the overall commander of Operation MacArthur, Major General William Peers of the 4th Infantry Division, when he realized he'd be late for school.

"Oh shit."

Danny made it to school in record time, pedaling up Sycamore Street in front of the school. He was in plain view of students in several of the classrooms and saw a few pointing at him, their lips moving.

Danny rolled the newspaper tightly as he ran in the front door and trotted to Mrs. Fark's room. He stopped at the door and tucked the paper under his belt behind his back, flipping his shirttail over it. Danny sighed, turned the knob, and walked through.

Mrs. Fark was speaking to the class and writing on the chalkboard when Danny walked in. She eyed him as he made his way to his desk, but continued with her instructions.

"So, the idea is to write two versions of a story. The first paragraph is to be exactly the same in each story, with the exception of one word or short phrase." She continued, "This is intended to show the power of words. You write a 200-word composition. You then begin a second composition, making a single word substitution that will change the meaning of the first paragraph in a substantial way, then finish the second composition, telling an entirely different story."

Several members of the class looked confused: a couple blurted out questions. Mrs. Fark's classroom environment was relatively loose. She encouraged discussion. Danny, in fact, was banking on her easy-going nature to keep from being reported as tardy. Botkins was a K through 12 building. A fifth-grade student was selected each morning to go from room to room collecting tardy slips. If you made it to class before the fifth grader visited, "cool" teachers often didn't report you. Mrs. Fark was a cool teacher.

In response to the questions, Mrs. Fark ruminated. After a few seconds, she brightened and stepped back to the chalkboard. She wrote a lower-case letter "a" on the board, left a space, then wrote "part."

"See if this helps." She began. "Danny Hitchens is a part of this class." She said underlining the "a," then drawing a second line under "part."

That is an example of the first line of a story. From there, the writer could describe Danny's wit, charm, or good looks."

Danny heard Gary Poppe snort from the back of the class. This drew laughter.

"Now I do this." Fark turned to the board. She erased the "a," moved it a space to the right so it was next to the "p," and pressed on. I change the sentence to "Danny is apart from this class." She turned to Danny and smiling, said "You could take the story from there and describe all the things Danny was out doing when he should've been in class."

Danny's classmates chuckled and eyed him. Danny managed a quick smile before Fark moved on. When the bell rang at the end of first period, Mrs. Fark asked Danny to come to her desk. She'd registered his less than engaged reaction and thought she'd embarrassed him. Danny loved puns and wordplay and her example earlier in the class was the type of thing he usually enjoyed.

"Sorry about that Danny, I didn't mean to put you on the spot."

"What... oh, no, I wasn't upset about that at all. It was actually pretty clever," he said with a distracted smile. He reached back for the newspaper. "I was looking for information about the big battle in Vietnam and lost track of time... I'm pretty sure Eddie's in the middle of it."

Sue Fark's heart sank.

After several more days, Hill 823 finally fell. It was on to Hill 882 for Eddie. Here, the "Battle on the Slopes" continued. During a lull, Eddie drew in the smoke from a Winston. He held it with a shaking, dirt-caked hand, wondering what number this was. Had he smoked 100 cigarettes on these hills? He couldn't guess. He'd used dozens of M-16 magazines. More than once he was down to his last mag with no resupply in sight and enemy fire coming from several directions.

Eddie's thoughts drifted back to the boy scout woods in Botkins. He'd watched his brother pull the trigger on the new rifle for the first time. Danny had been amazed at the power of the weapon. Now Eddie found himself surrounded by hundreds of men with weapons of similar power, all desperately employing them to bring death to their enemy. It was carnage.

Eddie, exhausted, began to doze. His mind couldn't fully rest. It replayed scenes from the fighting. Eddie saw flares floating in the night sky, followed by red tracer rounds from converted C-47 "Spooky" gunships, attempting to keep NVA night attacks from overrunning American positions on...was it Hill 724?

The tracers slowly dissipated and Eddie realized he was no longer on the ground, but was floating in the air. He was hanging from a T-10 parachute. With a sense of dread, Eddie turned to his left. He was not surprised to see his mother. Eddie swiveled his head to the right and saw Danny. Why the sense of dread? Eddie didn't know.

Eddie heard gunfire from the ground. He cast his eyes downward and saw green tracer rounds reaching up to them. He fought a sense of panic and turned toward his mom. She was there, smiling. Eddie turned to Danny: his brother wasn't where he should be. Eddie frantically contorted his body, searching the sky. He saw his brother descending into the danger. It was then that Eddie realized that he and his mother were both rising. The sound of battle grew.

"Hitch! Hitch!, they're comin' in! Hitch!"

It was Al Johnson. The gunfire was real.

Sgt. Venable screamed "Hitchens, base of fire, right flank. Gotta plug that gap... move!" Eddie scrambled to his right, the dream forgotten.

And so it went.

On Sunday, the 19th, Danny sat in front of the TV. He held Suzy Wong in the crook of his left arm and scratched behind her ears. He occasionally flipped channels, hoping to see an update from Vietnam. The Sunday edition of the Dayton Daily News was strewn about the room.

"Anything?"

Danny turned to see his dad set two plates of bacon and eggs on the table.

"No Dad, not on TV." Danny responded. "The paper has three or four stories," he paused, then, "They say over a hundred of our guys have been killed."

"My god." Jerry managed. He sat at the table and stared at the food. Jerry thought back to the previous night. He'd suggested to Danny that they attend Sunday mass at St. Lawrence. Since Jane died, Jerry and Danny had only made it to services three times. Jerry remembered the look they received from Father Berg on one of these occasions. The look didn't say "Welcome back": it seemed to convey "Where have you been?" Hearing the latest casualty news, Jerry was actually sorry he hadn't pressed his argument with more force.

But Danny was having none of it. He wanted to gather as much information as possible. That meant TV and newspapers, not songs and sermons. Jerry suspected that his son was growing more resistant to Father Berg. Jerry had tried to underemphasize the fact that the priest leveraged permission for Jane's burial in the Catholic cemetery in exchange for regular attendance at church. Danny, Jerry was coming to believe, was perceptive enough to strongly suspect the truth, and the boy didn't like it.

Jerry had acceded to Danny's Sunday plans. "Maybe we can make it to Thanksgiving mass Thursday before we go to Gene and Martha's to eat," he suggested.

Danny had answered, "Yeah, maybe."

That same Sunday, in Kon Tum Province, the Central Highlands, Eddie sat at the base of Hill 875, attending a mass that was hastily organized by the Brigade Chaplain, Father Charles Watters.

Second battalion of the 173rd would be assaulting up the north slope that morning. Intel believed the remnants of the NVA 66th Infantry Regiment defended the hill. Danny figured it couldn't hurt to attend the mass. A high percentage of the battalion joined him, even the non-Catholics. Watters had put out his customary Sunday announcement, "Church call, and no excuses!"

Father Watters was well liked and respected. Now 40, he'd joined the 173rd as a 38-year-old. He'd actually made the combat jump with the brigade earlier in the year during Operation Junction City. Watters had been in the middle of the fighting in the Dak To campaign, administering to the wounded.

"Our preacher a badass," Al whispered into Eddie's ear before communion.

"Shhhh," Danny admonished his buddy, but then turned to Al and nodded.

The plan was to assault straight up the hill. D Company would be on the left, C Company to the right, with A Company behind them in reserve. A trail running up the hill acted as a boundary between the two companies in front.

A Special Forces MIKE Force, consisting of U.S. Green Berets as well as indigenous Vietnamese allied personnel,

273

acted as a blocking force. If the NVA attempted to escape the assault, the Green Berets would cut them down.

The NVA had no intention of running. Instead of the depleted 66th Regiment, Hill 875 was occupied by 2,000 fresh troops of the 174th Infantry Regiment.

The lead American companies found themselves the target of blistering fire from multiple directions. Dozens of Sky Soldiers fell, dead or wounded. A Company, in the rear, was ambushed by well concealed NVA troops in overwhelming numbers. They were nearly cut off from D and C companies further up the hill. Incongruently, A Company had to retreat *up* the hill to link up with their fellow paratroopers.

Some of the most desperate, selfless acts of the war occurred that day. Eddie saw at least two medics shot and killed while rushing to help wounded men. The medics were easily distinguished and targeted by the enemy. Seeing one of the medics shot while shielding a wounded trooper with his body, Eddie boiled over with rage. He'd identified a fortified bunker where the shots came from. It was just 60 feet away but was nearly invisible.

"See that shell crater?" Eddie shouted at Al. Bullets hummed over the pair as they lay prone. Al followed Eddie's eyes and shouted back that he did.

"There's an opening between the crater and that downed tree to the left." Eddie pointed to the specific spot and Johnson nodded. "When I say the word, empty a mag on that spot... I'm gonna run toward the far edge of the crater then cut over and get a grenade in there."

Al looked at his buddy, glanced at the bunker, then turned back. He caught Eddie's eyes, hesitated, then simply nodded once. "Say the word."

Eddie adjusted his gear. He palmed an M26 fragmentation grenade in each hand, got to one knee, and assumed a stance similar to that used by a sprinter in the blocks.

"Now!" he shouted.

Al rose to a knee and began firing at the bunker. As the rounds tore into the opening, Eddie sprinted toward the bunker, angling obliquely to the right toward the bomb crater. As he neared the crater, Eddie realized Al had expended his entire magazine. Eddie saw the barrel of an AK 47 poke through the opening and dove toward the crater just as the NVA soldier began firing. The shots weren't accurate, though, and Eddie had now reached a spot that wasn't visible to the bunker's occupants.

Eddie lie on his right side. He pulled the pin on the grenade in his left hand with his right index finger and held down the spoon. As he readied himself to cross the final few feet, Eddie heard Al's M-16 again. He was putting a second mag of covering fire on the bunker.

"Good man." Eddie muttered, pulling himself up to a knee.

The second that Johnson's firing stopped, Eddie sprung from his position, took two strides, and stuffed the grenade through opening with his left hand. He instantly pulled the second pin from the M26 in his right hand and swung his right arm in a rearward arch, backhanding the grenade into the bunker.

Eddie heard shrill, panicked voices coming from the NVA soldiers below as he flung himself back toward the crater. There was an initial muffled explosion, followed by a larger, secondary blast that tore the entire top off the bunker. Eddie thought he heard screams in the second or two between explosions. He lay covered by parts of Hill 875. He couldn't hear; he couldn't move. Eddie thought of his mom. Was this what the parachute dream was about?

"Hitch!, HITCH!" Al was on top of him clearing away dirt and brush. Eddie began to regain feeling and realized he could sit up. He was OK!

"You crazy muthafucka!" Al was laughing... with tears in his eyes.

The Americans tried to get reinforcements to the pinned companies all day. Ammunition ran dangerously low. Helicopters made near-suicidal runs across the north face of the hill, slowing just long enough to kick pallets of ammunition to the ground. Father Watters braved enemy fire time and again to drag wounded paratroopers to safety.

Propeller-driven A-1 Skyraiders, F-100 Super Sabre jet fighter-bombers, and Army UH-1C helicopter gunships were indispensable. Troopers would mark their positions with smoke, call in "danger-close" fire and put their heads down as "Air" would make their gun, rocket, and bomb runs. They approached from the southwest so ordinance that flew long would impact higher on the hill.

Al Johnson was hit by a mortar fragment early in the afternoon. Eddie helped wedge his friend into a depression with cover. The fragment had entered under Al's right clavicle and left a hole the size of a quarter. There was no exit wound. Eddie knew that Al needed immediate attention but that was not possible. Johnson joined a growing number of Sky Soldiers suffering on the slopes. They had little or no water remaining and medical supplies were now nearly non-existent.

Al grabbed Eddies' arm and, through clenched teeth, said "Guess I won't be pitchin' for my Orioles anytime soon, huh Eddie?"

Eddie watched as one of the few living medics on 875 administered morphine to Johnson. As the medic removed the syringe, Johnson grabbed his magazines with his left hand and offered them to Eddie. "You gonna need these, brutha."

Eddie smiled and turned to leave, but Al squeezed his arm again. "Might not pitch for the Birds, but I bet I could still make that Reds' pitchin' staff... they awful."

Both men grinned and Eddie made his way back to the perimeter.

From his spot on the right flank, Eddie helped defend against several attempts by the NVA to overrun the American positions. During brief lulls in the assaults, Eddie concentrated on targets farther up the hill. The NVA sometimes exposed themselves immediately after U.S. bomb or gun runs. Eddie noticed this and, at least twice, dropped targets at 200-300 meters.

Late in the afternoon, an exhausted Sergeant Venable passed the word that a casualty collection area had been designated near Captain Kaufman's headquarters element.

"We need to get all wounded troopers that can't still fight back to that area." Venable pointed to the rear. "We don't have enough medics; I need some men to help with the move."

Eddie spent the next hour ducking enemy fire and moving the wounded. He insisted he be the man to move Al Johnson. Father Watters organized the effort and personally carried several of the wounded through exposed areas.

A few minutes before 1900 hours, or 7 pm, Eddie made his last trip to the casualty area. He wanted to see Al again before heading back up the hill. Eddie lit a Winston and gazed about the area. In the last instant of his life, Eddie thought he heard a roar from the northeast.

It was later determined that a Marine Corps F-4 Phantom flying out of Chu Lai Air Base had dropped a 500-pound bomb into the 173rd Brigade's perimeter. It had approached from the northeast, rather than the southwest. In the worst friendly fire incident of the war, 42 Americans were killed and 45 more wounded. Those killed included the on-scene commander, Captain Harold Kaufman (West Point Class of 1964), Father Charles Watters (who was posthumously awarded the Medal of Honor), and Danny Hitchens' big brother Eddie.

CHAPTER TWENTY-NINE

Jerry and Danny did attend Thanksgiving mass. They went with Gene and Martha. Afterward, they drove to the little house on Walnut Street and sat down to a traditional Thanksgiving feast with turkey and all the trimmings.

"I made pumpkin pie for you Danny," his grandmother said. "Homemade whipped cream too, it's in the fridge."

Danny helped himself to a generous wedge and plopped two large scoops of whipped cream on top.

"Do you mind if I turn on your TV?" He added, "The Lions are playing the Rams today and I like seeing Tiger Stadium, even if it's for football."

Gene smiled at his grandson, "Suit yourself."

Danny switched on the set and gave it a few seconds to warm up. Once the screen came on, he began searching through the channels. Danny was interested in Tiger Stadium, but that wasn't why he wanted to watch TV.

He'd been awake since 6:30 and was in front of the RCA, petting Suzy, when a report came across on the CBS Morning News about the fighting in Dak To. The commentator said that Hill 875 had finally fallen after four days of vicious fighting. He went on to say that helicopters, now able to safely land in the area, had delivered Thanksgiving dinners. These same choppers, he continued gravely, had departed Hill 875 laden with body bags.

Danny couldn't get that image out of his head. He sat through the service at St. Lawrence. He again automatically followed the customs of the church, kneeling or standing when prompted. The pews were full for the holiday mass so Danny and Jerry sat near the back with his grandparents. Danny suspected his dad wanted Father Berg to notice them so they could be credited for making an appearance.

There was no further news about Dak To. Danny put on the football game and watched it in the background while talking to his grandparents. Danny loved Gene and Martha, but he also really liked spending time with them. He knew you could have one feeling without the other. Some of his friends loved their grandparents, sure, but couldn't stand being with them.

Danny reminisced with Gene about the time several years previous when, while fishing at a gravel pit near Wapak, a large carp had taken the bait dangling from Danny's cane pole. Danny was throwing rocks on the bank, having laid his pole on the ground. He heard the bamboo skitter across the rocks and watched in fascination as it moved away from him, as if drawn into the water by a spectral being.

Grandpa King had solidified his near-superhero status to seven-year-old Danny by casting a hook with his rod and reel several feet beyond the floating pole, reeling it in until the wayward bamboo was snagged, then pulling it to the bank. When Danny grabbed the pole and pulled it in, the 15-inch carp was still attached.

Over the years, like any good fish story, some of the details were modified; Gene had snagged the pole on his first attempt, not his fifth, the bamboo target was 100 feet away from shore, not 40, and the fish was two feet long, not 15 inches. Danny thought the best thing about the story was that he and his grandpa were each fifty percent responsible for catching the carp. How many people had a story like that?

Danny spent several minutes trying to understand why his grandma insisted on calling the margarine on the table "oleo." He grasped her answer immediately: it was simply shortened from the original term "oleomargarine," but acted like he didn't understand. An exasperated Martha continued her explanation until she saw Danny's grin, then smiled back.

"More pie?" she asked.

The Rams beat the Lions 31-7. Roman Gabriel threw touchdown passes to Billy Truax and Jack Snow. Danny thought it was cool to see football players disappear into the baseball dugouts at halftime. He and Jerry helped clean up the kitchen. They thanked Gene and Martha and headed for home in the Impala.

A dark green unmarked military sedan sat parked down the street from the Hitchens house. Inside were an Army Captain and an Air Force chaplain, both currently stationed at Wright Patterson Air Force base near Dayton. Sitting in the back seat was Private Tom Christopher, Eddie's buddy who had visited Botkins after they'd completed boot camp. Tommy had been wounded in July. He was hit in the right leg by an AK round. The bullet glanced off his femur, cracking it. He'd been home in Tennessee for the holidays when the Casualty Assistance Office tracked him down and asked him to accompany the notification team to Botkins.

Tommy dreaded this duty, but he'd been honored to be asked. He knew he couldn't say no.

Three hundred seventy-six Americans had been killed in the fighting at Dak To, two hundred eight of them were his comrades in the 173rd. Tommy had a chance to do one last favor for one of them.

The occupants of the sedan watched as a grey Chevy pulled into the Hitchens driveway. When Jerry and Danny emerged and walked into the garage, Tommy drawled "Yep, that's them."

The captain started the car, turned to the chaplain, and sighed. Tommy reached for his crutch.

Gert Havener peered out her front window at the car as it pulled away from the curb; she glanced at her telephone.

"We regret to inform you..."

Jerry, at the front door, still had a smile on his face, looking at Tommy, when realization hit him. He physically collapsed, falling to his knees.

Danny had walked into the room holding Suzy. He knew instantly. He had no further memories of the next several minutes of the notification. It was not until twenty minutes later, when Eddie's buddy Tommy hobbled to the couch, reached down and pried the struggling Suzy Wong from Danny's hands, that his mind re-engaged.

Danny was overcome by shock and rage. He remembered the Captain asking to use their phone, and, when he'd finished with his call to Casualty Assistance to get further information, whispering to his comrades that "someone was listening in to my conversation."

Danny heard someone, Tommy, he thought, say that Eddie's will had originally specified that he wanted to be interred at Arlington National Cemetery. After returning overseas from Jane's funeral, however, Eddie had amended it to request burial in St. Lawrence beside his mother.

The Hitchens house was a center of activity for the next several days. Tommy was there constantly. Jerry insisted he sleep at their house but Tommy declined, hinting that it was against regulations. In fact, Tommy couldn't bring himself to sleep in his buddy's boyhood bedroom.

At some point Danny overheard his dad on the phone. He was pleading with someone.

"You have to understand, please, you have to allow it." Danny was in his bedroom. He took a few steps down the hall toward the kitchen. He heard his dad, now sobbing, continue, "They're bringing him home from Dover in two days... please!"

Danny clenched his teeth and burst into the kitchen. Jerry sat at the table, the phone to his ear. He gripped his forehead with his left hand.

Is that Berg?" Danny demanded.

Jerry looked up, a look of absolute despair on his face, and nodded dumbly.

"Gimme that!" Danny snatched the phone, pulled it to his face, and snarled "Berg? Let me tell you something... you either give permission for Eddie to be buried beside Mom or

I'll call the fucking Dayton Daily News and have them print a story saying 'Father Berg Denies Hero Burial!'"

After a few seconds of silence, Father Berg managed, "Danny?, Danny you can't talk——"

"BULLSHIT!" Danny screamed. The phone number for the editor is printed on the front page of the paper. I have a copy right here. You make this happen or so help me, my next call is to that number. You have 15 minutes before I make the call."

Danny slammed the phone down and walked back to his room.

Jerry, shocked, wondered at that moment if he'd lost two sons.

On Monday morning, without asking permission, Danny took the Impala. He drove 25 miles south down I-75 to Piqua. He marched into the Armed Services Recruiting Center, looked at the four desks; Army, Navy, Marine Corps, and Air Force, and strode to the Army sergeant's desk.

"I want to sign up....infantry." he demanded. Danny wanted revenge.

The sergeant had no idea of the kid's motivation but recognized that this would be the easiest processing of a recruit he'd ever had.

"Are you 18?" the sergeant asked.

Danny paused for a moment, then, as if struck by a revelation, answered "I will be in two days."

The recruiter sent him home with the paperwork. Danny could have his dad sign for him.

Might as well wait until after Wednesday, then I can sign, he thought. What could change in two days?

As it turned out, quite a bit.

Tommy Christopher sat down at the kitchen table with Jerry and Danny later that day. He explained to them that

Eddie's body would be available for burial on the 29th, Danny's birthday.

"The, uh, condition of the remains meant that, uh," Tommy groped for words, "preparation could be expedited." Then, "It will be a closed casket."

The family had not been given specific details of Eddie's death, just that it was violent and occurred in combat.

"I've been authorized to tell you that even though Eddie qualifies for a military headstone, you may want to wait before submitting a request. I'm told that he is being considered for military awards that are significant enough to be represented on the marker."

Jerry stared at Christopher blankly.

Danny asked, "You mean medals?"

Christopher replied, "Well, the purple heart for sure, of course." Tommy felt terrible mentioning this. He continued, "And there seems to be a good chance of an award for valor."

Neither Danny nor Jerry could think of a reply.

Tommy had noticed the Army enlistment application on a pile of papers on the table. He spoke to both Jerry and Danny, but kept his eyes on the latter.

"And this is not official, but it will sure as hell be coming out... it looks like Eddie may have been killed by a bomb from an American plane."

This time both Jerry and Danny looked at him, unable to comprehend.

Jerry tried to catch up to the meaning of Tommy's comment.

Danny registered it immediately, a part of his mind screamed *Who the hell am I supposed to take revenge against now?!*"

If Jane's funeral had been a blur, Eddie's passed so quickly for Danny that it barely existed. He later recalled Father Berg offering platitudes while Danny shot daggers at the priest through scornful eyes. He remembered the honor guard from

Wright-Patt, the jam-packed church, acting as a pall-bearer with his dad, Tommy Christopher, and three of Eddies' high school buddies, and the soul-jarring 21-gun salute.

Christopher refused to use his crutch during the service. His jaw set, Tommy held the coffin with an iron grip, limping through the service.

Danny noticed sweat running down the side of Christopher's head. Though he was devastated by the loss of his brother, Danny had to marvel at Tommy's tenacity.

Danny stayed at the cemetery long enough to say a few words to a devastated Judy Winner. He thought, *this should've been my sister-in-law*.

Danny cast a final look at the grave before sliding into the Impala. He noticed Tommy Christopher, in his Class A Green uniform, shaking hands with a burly man in an uncomfortable looking suit. When the man turned, Danny tried to place him, but couldn't focus. Ten minutes later it hit him: the man was John Potter, the World War Two rifleman that had sold them the Savage 99 at the Allen County gun show.

Potter had somehow heard that Eddie was killed and drove all the way from Michigan to pay his respects.

It was the following day before Jerry realized he'd forgotten to give Danny his birthday present. Jerry thought about the gift and wrestled with himself over whether it was appropriate. In the end, he decided it was a connection to Eddie.

"Happy birthday, Danny... sorry its's late."

Danny looked up from the couch, where he sat holding Suzy Wong.

"What? Oh, no problem Dad, thanks." Danny reached for the box.

Jerry offered it to him with both hands. "Watch out, its heavy."

Danny picked at the tape off one edge and peeled back the wrapping paper. Inside of a cardboard box, Danny found several smaller boxes of .308 bullets.

"I wanted to get you something you'd use," Jerry shrugged.

Danny let the hint of a smile appear on his face. "Thanks Dad, you did well."

CHAPTER THIRTY

It was apparent to friends, classmates, and teachers that Danny had changed. Doc Mielke believed that Danny would never be the same, but that he would eventually return to a semblance of his old self. As time passed, Doc allowed doubts to creep into his head.

Sue Giltrow waited until Danny had been back in school for over a week before tentatively approaching him in the hallway one day.

"Hey Danny, when you feel like talking about it, I have some financial aid information we should discuss." She delivered this with a hopeful tone.

Danny simply stared at her, snapped "forget it," and turned away.

The basketball coach, Bill Elsass, asked Danny to come to the coach's office on his first day back to school.

"You don't have to come to practice until you're ready, Danny. We know you're in shape and you know the offense—" Danny cut him off.

"I don't want to play anymore."

Elsass hesitated, then said "I understand it's a tough time..." But Elsass was talking to an empty chair: Danny was out the door.

Chris tried to be patient with Danny. She wanted to be there for him when he began to reconnect. It never happened. She had strong feelings for Danny, but he seemingly had no interest in keeping their relationship going. When the calendar changed to 1968, Chris reluctantly decided she needed to concentrate on her college plans. Her friend Sandy tried to cheer her by saying there was a good chance Chris and Danny would've grown apart anyway when one or both of them left for college. Chris understood this, but was still sad in the spring when her mom's blooms came back and the term "Hank Aaron of Flowers" came to her mind.

Reed Thompson stuck by his friend the longest. He stopped at Danny's regularly and even got him to play some Strat-O-Matic from time to time. In mid-January, Reed asked if Danny would come to the Trojan's basketball game that Friday—Danny had skipped every game—under the guise that he, Reedo, needed Danny to watch him shoot.

Reed had constructed an argument that he thought might work. "I'm in a shooting slump," he began. "Nobody knows my shot better than you." Reed pressed, "I need you to come watch and tell me what I'm doing wrong."

Reed was gratified to see his buddy show up at the game Friday with Fairlawn. Reed finished 4 for 6 from the field that night. Andy Craft scorched the nets for a school record 43 points, prompting a headline over the game story in the Sidney paper the next day that read "Craft is Crafty."

"Well," Reed asked after the game, "whaddaya think?"

"I think you should forget about shooting and just pass the ball to Craft every time down the floor," Danny delivered this with a trace of a smile. It made Reed's day.

Danny retreated to his room almost every day after school. He joined his dad for dinner at the kitchen table, maybe watched some television, then returned to his room, usually carrying Suzy.

The networks became dominated by reports of the Tet Offensive in Vietnam on the last day of January. Danny watched for a few minutes, reached for Suzy, and walked down the hall.

Coverage of Tet continued for weeks. Danny didn't watch any of it.

Spring arrived, and with it, baseball and track. On the diamond and the cinder, Danny was most like his old self, though with a new edge.

Danny now seemed to relish hard slides into the bases. He appeared to be looking for contact. A Russia Raider infielder,

Donnie Lundeen, was the victim of a slide by Danny that nearly led to an ejection. When Lundeen came to the plate for his next at bat, he asked catcher Gary Poppe "What's with Hitchens? Why is he being such an asshole?"

Poppe reminded Lundeen about Jane and Eddie. Lundeen stepped out of the box, peered out at Danny, and shook his head, muttering "Still..."

On the mound Vannette tracked Lundeen's eyes and watched him shake his head while glancing at Danny.

Vannette blew three fastballs past Lundeen, but not before first sending him sprawling with a purpose pitch that had been targeted at his chin.

Danny, to the great dismay of the underclassmen, became an enthusiastic participant in the ear rodeo. He approached the contest with a fervor. Younger players dreaded seeing Danny advance toward them on the bus and quickly learned not to hurl hollow threats at Danny. Herm didn't want to ratchet "fervor" up to "cruelty."

Reed Thompson watched Danny terrorize his teammates with a sense of disappointment. Even Pat Jokisch, seen by some as sadistic at times, conceded that "We have a new champion cowboy."

Vannette was untouchable on the mound that spring. He was a bit bigger across the chest than he'd been the previous season and was continuing to attract attention from colleges. On a couple occasions, major league scouts actually found their way to Botkins to assess him. The visit by one of these men led to a humorous story that even made Danny laugh.

Tony Lucadello was a major league scout: but not just any scout. He had been beating the bushes looking for talent since 1943. For the first 15 years, he was employed by the Chicago Cubs. Since 1957 he'd worked for the Philadelphia Phillies.

Lucadello signed dozens of players that would make it to the big leagues, including current Cubs ace Ferguson Jenkins.

Lucadello worked the entire Midwest. He lived in Fostoria, Ohio, an hour or two north of Botkins. Vannette's name came up several times at college games that Lucadello worked. Several of the college coaches had either seen, or heard, about the Botkins ace. Lucadello decided to check him out.

In early May, Lucadello called Botkins High School and asked for the baseball coach. The school secretary told him Coach Sanders was in class but took down Tony's number and put it in Sanders' mailbox. Later that day, Sanders retrieved it and assumed it was a joke.

"The Philadelphia Phillies called? Yeah, right."

Sanders returned the call and found that the Phillies, or one of their employees, had indeed called. Lucadello learned that Vannette would pitch the following Tuesday and said he planned to attend.

Word quickly spread that a bona fide major league scout would be at Cole Field. This was a first.

The big day arrived. Vannette was pumped up and ready to go after the Anna Rockets. His Trojan teammates planned on swinging from the heels in batting practice to impress the scout. Lucadello, though, did not see the game.

Botkins, being on busy I-75, occasionally attracted undesirable passers-by. Two weeks before Lucadellos's scheduled arrival, a traveler had pulled off the highway, cruised the town, and been spotted by sharp-eyed first grade teacher and playground monitor Wanda Beams. The man, Wanda realized, was "playing with himself" while watching the kids from his car. The weirdo got out of his car at one point and spread his trench coat, exposing himself to the first graders.

Wanda rounded up the kids, marched them into the building, and immediately went to the school office. A call was placed to the police department and Vic Peters sped to the school, siren wailing.

The suspect was gone, but Peters was on, well, peter patrol for the next few weeks. It was into this environment that Tony Lucadello appeared two weeks later.

Tony was known to arrive extremely early to games. This allowed him to watch the prospect interact with coaches and teammates and to see how the player prepared for a game. Lucadello was also known for something else: his trademark trench coat.

Lucadello arrived at Cole Field 10 minutes before school was out. He got out of his car, stretched, and eyed the field. Hearing kids on the playground, he turned in that direction, hands in pockets. He noticed a woman staring back at him with her hands on her hips. Tony thought it a bit strange when the woman bustled into the building.

Seven minutes later a police cruiser swung onto Sycamore Street with its lights and siren engaged. Lucadello froze. He was surprised when a thin police officer with a brush mustache and shaded glasses jumped out of the cruiser and drew his pistol.

"On the ground, creep!"

It took an hour, several phone calls, and a long discussion with Coach Sanders before Peters allowed Lucadello to leave. And leave he did, without watching the game.

Vannette was infuriated with Peters. Danny, along with the rest of the Trojans, thought it was hilarious.

The game became known for more than just the Lucadello incident.

Danny was on third base with no outs in the fourth inning. The game was scoreless. It looked like a big inning was possible when Herm Barton walked. Leadoff man Gary Poppe came to the plate and all eyes turned to Coach Sanders at third to see if he'd put on a play. Danny thought the steal sign was a possibility. He was incredulous when he saw Sanders bring his hand up toward his throat.

"Are you shitting me!?" Danny blurted from ten feet away. "That's why we lost to Russia last year!"

Time seemed to stop.

Sanders froze with his hand inches from his neck. His eyes widened. He was speechless.

In the third base dugout, Dick Ellsworth, the hawk-faced Anna coach, was aghast. A high school player had just embarrassed a coach in public, *with a curse word.*

Ellsworth was also disappointed. He knew the Botkins squeeze bunt sign and was about to signal for his third baseman to charge.

Poppe dug in and stroked the first pitch into right center, bringing home both runners. The Trojans went on to win easily, 8-0.

In the last inning with two outs, and a win over their rival in the bag, Andy Craft called timeout from his shortstop position and trotted toward the mound. He motioned for the rest of the infield and catcher Gary Poppe to join him. Sanders looked concerned in the dugout but Craft gestured for him to stay put.

When the last infielder reached Vannette, Craft began in a solemn voice, "Gentlemen, I have an announcement." He then dropped his voice into an urgent whisper-shout and intoned "Peters will be here in two minutes!"

Craft's teammates cracked up, even Vannette, whose major league chances had, ostensibly, ended a couple hours earlier when Peters rousted Lucadello.

As the players shook hands after the game, a couple of the Anna players smiled at Danny. He smiled back. Coach Sanders stayed back in the Botkins dugout, trying to decide what to do about the squeeze bunt incident. As he approached the end of the line of Anna players, Danny realized that Ellsworth was standing there, apparently waiting on him.

Ellsworth, red faced after the loss and the sleight he'd witnessed to a member of his coaching fraternity, spouted "That was disgraceful!" He firmly grabbed Danny's left arm and continued, "You have no cla—"

Before the word "class" had left Ellsworth's lips, Danny had grabbed Ellsworth's arm and twisted. Danny's eyes changed in an instant, from smiling to maniacal.

"Listen to me, you beak-nosed son-of-a-bitch, get your hand off me or I'll rip it off!" Spittle flew through Danny's clenched teeth.

The players from both teams turned to watch. Ellsworth, stunned, backed away. He regrouped, then sputtered, "You're lucky you're not 18." This was the age at which, it was believed by many, a teen-ager was no longer shielded from fighting adults by their status as a minor.

"I am eighteen, you candy-ass. Wanna take it behind the dugout?"

Ellsworth was shaken by the violence of Danny's reaction. Before he could say another word, Reed put his arms around Danny and pulled him away. The Rockets headed for their bus, stunned.

The decision was made to suspend Danny for a game. The suspension was punishment for his altercation with Ellsworth. The Anna coach was also suspended for a game—dozens of witnesses had seen him grab Danny—and it was determined the two would serve their suspension when Anna and Botkins played again late in the season. Everyone agreed it was best to keep the two apart.

Then there was the matter of Danny shouting at Coach Sanders while on third base. The next morning, a chastened Danny went to school early and knocked on Sanders' homeroom door. Danny was looking to lash out now whenever it made sense. He realized that the man that asked Eddie down onto the practice field so he could tell his team about the Combat Infantryman Badge did not deserve to be a target.

Danny apologized profusely.

Sanders accepted the apology and shook Danny's hand. As Danny turned to leave, Sanders popped a toothpick into his mouth, smiled, and said "Maybe I should change my squeeze bunt sign."

Danny laughed for the first time in weeks.

In Algebra II, Mr. Rawson made a remark that Danny considered condescending, "Mrs. Wenning and myself teach classes that are meant to be taken in order; Algebra, Algebra II, Geometry, then Calculus. So, you'll have Calculus next year... unless you're already a senior."

Rawson glanced at Danny as he made the comment.

"It's not Mrs. Wenning and myself!" Danny said sharply. "You have a college degree and can't speak English!" The comment produced a room full of uncomfortable underclassmen, three days of detention for Danny, and, he was sure, a final nine weeks' grade of D.

Danny dropped Geometry before the second nine weeks began, more or less ending any chance of getting into most colleges. In April, he withdrew $400 from the bank and used it to buy a vehicle. This reduced his college fund to $225. Without consciously recognizing it, Danny began to mentally refer to his college fund as a savings account.

He purchased a 1963 Ford Ranchero. It was considered a "utility cargo" vehicle. The front half looked like a car, the back half consisted of a pickup truck cargo bed. It was royal blue with black bucket seats. Mike Vannette's brother Rick sold it to him. Rick was now working at a factory in Wapak and had just bought a new Mustang.

For Danny, the best feature of the Ranchero wasn't the cargo bed. It was the fact that Vannette had installed an 8-track tape player. The same Saturday that he took possession of the vehicle, Danny drove to the Bi-Rite and bought a copy of Steppenwolf's debut album on 8-track. He would have *Born to be Wild,* ready to go whenever he liked. He could relate to the lyrics and hard-charging guitar riffs.

On Thursday, April 4, civil rights leader Martin Luther King was assassinated. Danny had lost much of his interest in current events after Eddie's death. This event seemed to pull him back. He scanned the papers the next day. Danny noted that the King assassination overshadowed the Apollo 6 mission, which took place on the same day. The Saturn V rocket engines had unexpectedly shut down. NASA was trying to determine the cause in time to keep the program on pace to put a man on the moon.

Danny continued to read about the assassination. Most of his interest focused on the loss of a famous person.

A part of his interest was on what type of rifle was used.

Danny broke the school record in the mile run late in the season. His time, 4:37, broke the ten-year-old record by 3 seconds. He finished fifth in a loaded regional. Danny missed making it to the state meet by one place, and three seconds.

The baseball team went undefeated in league play and won the district championship before losing to a team from Cincinnati. Mike Vannette accepted a partial scholarship offer to play baseball at the University of Toledo.

Reed Thompson also enrolled at Toledo, where he wouldn't play baseball, but would room with Vannette.

Danny skipped both the prom—Chris Koenig went with Andy Craft—and the graduation ceremony.

Danny punched the timeclock at the lumber yard on the Monday after graduation weekend. He had no mother, brother, or, seemingly, future.

CHAPTER THIRTY-ONE

Ray Bolan was a bright spot in Danny's days. They discussed superheroes at length. But Ray was often shuttled to other work stations. This left Danny with no one near him most days. Unless you counted William Doyle at the rip saw.

Danny didn't.

On June 5, Senator Robert F. Kennedy was assassinated while exiting through the kitchen of the Ambassador Hotel in Los Angeles after giving a speech. A Palestinian, Sirhan Sirhan, was the shooter. He claimed his motivation was Kennedy's support of Israel.

"Fuckin' nut," Danny murmured, watching Walter Cronkite report on the incident on television.

Reed continued to stop at the Hitchens house, though less frequently. Reed had a full-time job of his own that summer working for the village. He cut grass and painted curbs. It was tedious work but he was outside, which he liked, and it paid minimum wage. Reed needed all the money he could get to pay for college.

Reed continued to be concerned about Danny. He also grew troubled when observing Mr. Hitchens. Jerry had trouble following conversations. He seemed to be pulling away from reality a bit. Reed decided to mention these concerns to Danny.

One Sunday in July, Reed saw Danny tinkering under the hood of his Ford Ranchero. Reed pulled his mom's Volkswagen into the drive and got out.

"So, you're a car guy now, huh Danny?" Reed said cheerfully.

Danny peeked around the hood and smiled at his friend.

"Aww, I still don't know much about cars, but I know if you take off the top cover to the air filter and re-attach it upside down it makes your engine sound badass."

Reed bent to scratch Suzy Wong's head, stood, and said "That's more than I know, you should join an Indy pit crew." Suzy ambled down the drive to sniff the VW.

"How's your dad doing? Reed inquired.

Danny eyed him, "Pretty much the same as he's been since..." Danny hesitated, "November, why?"

Reed took a deep breath, "Well, I've just noticed he seems to be pretty... distracted. I was wondering—"

At that moment, a rusty pickup truck came rattling down South Street. It needed a new muffler so it drowned out the conversation. Reed and Danny both looked toward the truck as it picked up speed. Reed saw Suzy walk from the rear of the Volkswagen, toward the street.

"Suzy, No!'" Reed yelled.

Suzy stopped and turned toward the sound of Reed's voice. The pickup passed within a foot or two of the pug, still accelerating.

Danny ran toward his dog. He'd seen just a few seconds of the incident; his view being obstructed by the hood of the Ranchero. He swept Suzy up in his arms. "Are you OK, girl?"

Danny's concern then instantly changed to cold fury.

"Who the fuck was that?" he turned quickly to Reed.

"Uh, I think it was that Snider kid... Greg, I think his name is? That kid from Wapak that you see driving around the swimming pool in the summer. I think he has the hots for one of the lifeguards."

Danny stared after the pickup. "Greg Snider," he muttered. "Let's go inside, Suzy."

The discussion about Jerry Hitchens was forgotten.

Gerald Hemmert was a planner. Gerald had four children. Three were married with kids of their own. The fourth, and youngest, Tate, had graduated three years earlier and was working on the family farm. Tate still lived at home, but was saving to buy a place of his own.

Gerald had started savings accounts for each of his kids as soon as they received their social security numbers, a requirement of the bank. Gerald opened similar accounts for each of his grandchildren.

Gerald was always looking to the future.

When lightning felled a large walnut tree in the woods behind his farm, Gerald had an idea. Why not make heavy wood fireplace mantles for his kids with the wood? Walnut was prized by woodworkers and his kids all loved seeing the stockings hung from the mantle of the house that he and his wife Grace maintained. Might make good Christmas presents. Plus, there was a lumberyard right there in Botkins that could handle the work.

Hell, he thought, even Tate might get married someday. The boy was a bit of an oddball, but there's an Eve for every Adam, Gerald reasoned.

Using his chainsaw, Gerald worked on the tree until he had two sections of the trunk reduced to six foot lengths. He figured the boys at Botkins Lumber ought to be able to get two good sized mantles out of each section.

Gerald wrestled the sections into the bed of his truck and covered them with a tarp. It was Labor Day weekend and that meant he needed to hide them from the kids until the yard opened back up on Tuesday.

Gerald stopped and talked to Carol Roush in the Botkins Lumber office. She passed him on to Jerry Hitchens. Gerald explained what he wanted and Jerry, after asking a few questions, said they should be able to do the job that morning. Gerald noticed that Jerry seemed to turn one ear toward him when listening.

Gerald thought he should say something to Jerry about the loss of his wife and son, but didn't want to dredge up bad memories. The he remembered that Jerry had taken home a pug puppy from a litter on the Hemmert farm a few years ago.

"How's that pup doin'?... Suzy something, wasn't it?"

Jerry brightened and spent five minutes telling Gerald about the best dog in the world.

The trunks were offloaded in the rear of the building. They were debarked and trimmed. Gerald was permitted to follow his wood all the way through the building. He drank free coffee from a mug that Carol offered and chatted with the employees as things progressed.

Soon, the trunks had been reduced to two six foot planks about 40 inches wide and six inches thick. A forklift transported them to the front of the shop where they were off-loaded in front of a big red-headed man. The man easily lifted the first plank onto the saw's table and fiddled with the blade.

Gerald ducked into the office to refill his mug. There was a window in the rear of the office that allowed a view of the shop.

"Almost done, I see," Carol smiled. "William will rip the pieces in two, then Danny will finish the edges for you, lickety-split."

Danny had a headache that morning. He'd begun to drink a few beers on the weekends and had a few more than normal over the Labor Day weekend at the Turtle Soup festival in Freyburg, outside of Wapak. He'd been half-heartedly drowning his sorrow. All of his friends, including Reed, had left for college. When he'd clocked in Tuesday, William Doyle looked at his puffy eyes and smirked.

"Screw you, *BILL*," Danny muttered.

Doyle completed his adjustment of the blade height. He switched on the saw and bent over slightly, pushing the plank through the turning blade. Hemmert had stepped back into the shop. He was fond of the pleasant odor of sawdust and noticed that Doyle's ripping of the walnut had added a spicy-citrus element to the air.

When the cut was complete, Doyle slid one of the boards onto the finish table. Danny had already adjusted his table and was waiting for it. He wedged his body between the two table saws and began to slowly push the board into the blade in front. Danny was careful to apply just enough pressure forward: pushing too quickly would leave dark circular sawblade marks on the side of the board. He also needed to put pressure on the left side of the board to keep it braced against the guide on the right. This would ensure a level trim.

Danny eased the walnut board through the blade, his right hand was within inches of the spinning blade and he was about to reposition it when the entire board surged forward roughly. Danny's right hand was carried along with it. He jerked his hand back just as the blade nicked the side of his pinky.

Danny wheeled and saw that Doyle had a broom handle in his hand. He'd obviously used it to push the back end of the board toward the blade. There was a smirk on his face.

Danny snatched the handle out of Doyle's hand and charged toward the larger man. The smirk froze on Doyle's face. Danny brought the handle up, gripping it now with both hands like a lifter grips a weighted bar. Danny roughly pushed the bar under Doyle's chin, his momentum driving the big man against the back wall.

"You ASSHOLE!" Danny screamed. As with his altercation with Coach Ellsworth, Danny's teeth were clenched, his neck muscles taut. Danny shifted his feet to get more leverage and drove the handle against Doyle with even more force.

"You Fucking Asshole! What the fuck is your problem!?"

Doyle's eyes bulged like golf balls. He realized that he was in deep trouble. The handle was crushing his neck! Hitchens wanted to kill him! He had both hands on the handle now, too, but Danny had the leverage, and the boy was furious.

"Danny, Danny no! Let him up!"

The voice was Carol's. She had seen the incident through the office window. She pushed through the door, rushed past a frozen Gerald Hemmert, and pulled the back of Danny's work shirt with both hands.

Soon Jerry rushed in to help and, together, he and Carol were able to get Danny to release Doyle. Danny still had the broom handle in his hands. His eyes smoldered. He pointed at Doyle and snarled "If you EVER do that again I'll stick this handle up your ass and turn you into a scarecrow!" Danny flung the handle onto the floor and raised his bleeding hand in front of his face to assess the damage. His hands were quivering.

Thirty minutes later, Gerald Hemmert was 200 feet north, at Steiner's Marathon. Ron Steiner had filled up his truck with regular. Gerald got out of the truck and showed off the four walnut pieces in the truck bed.

"Beautiful!" Ron remarked. "They do that over there?" He tipped his head toward the lumber yard.

"Yep, helluva thing though." Hemmert started to tell the story about the Hitchens kid losing his mind. Partway through he decided he could stand another cup of free coffee and walked into the station with Ron.

Inside were Woody Stegeman and Vic Peters. Hemmert hadn't noticed the cruiser parked on the north side of the building.

Steiner walked to a shelf behind the cash register. He lifted the top off a percolator, looked inside, grimaced, replaced the lid, and poured the thick liquid into a Styrofoam cup. Steiner handed the cup to Hemmert and prodded, "You were saying?"

The farmer glanced at the Peters and Stegeman, shrugged, and started his story from the beginning.

Doyle was told to go to the break room. Carol looked at him and said sternly, "Let us know if you need to go to the hospital." She walked out and slammed the door.

Danny asked to stay and finish the mantles. Ray Bolan was brought up to run the rip saw. When the order was completed, Jerry suggested, "Why don't you come into my office?"

Jerry contemplated his son. "I don't have any magic words for you Danny." He sighed. "We just have to find a way to go on."

Danny was still focused on Doyle. "It was his fault!"

Jerry raised his hands, palms out. "I get it, I get it." Then, "Are you OK?"

Danny looked at his bandaged hand, "I'm fine." He was cooling off.

"Take a few minutes before going back to the shop. Ray will run the rip saw the rest of the day." He added "You guys can talk comics again."

Danny smiled, "Thanks Dad, I'm gonna walk over to Steiner's and get a candy bar."

Danny walked to Steiner's. Approaching the building, he could see Hemmert inside, gesturing, with his back to the door. Danny saw a man, Woody Stegeman, tilt his head toward the door. Hemmert turned, registered Danny, and froze. Danny entered the building and noticed Vic Peters was also present. The room went silent.

Danny assessed the scene, smiled, and asked "Do you have any Marathon's in this Marathon, Ron?"

Steiner was confused, "Huh?"

"Marathon candy bars... do you carry those here?"

"Uh, no," Ron said nervously. "Just Hershey's and Oh Henrys."

Danny selected an Oh Henry and plopped down a quarter. Waiting for his change, he tore open one end of the wrapper. Danny could feel Peters' eyes boring into him. He palmed his change, stared directly at Peters and asked "Workin' hard today, boys?"

The men just stared at him.

Danny took a bite of his candy bar and walked out the door. Hemmert, in a low tone, said "That boy ain't got no shame."

CHAPTER THIRTY-TWO

The year 1968 ground to October. Jerry watched coverage of Apollo 7, which lifted off on the 11th. Wally Schirra, Donn Eisele, and Walter Cunningham battled the common cold during the mission. Schirra, in particular. They orbited the Earth 163 times and worked out many of the problems that NASA had to solve. They even broadcast from space using a movie camera.

Danny paid it only passing interest.

By this time in the space program, pundits were beginning to speculate who would be on the first moon mission. Specifically, who would land and take the first steps on the surface. Danny noted that Neil Armstrong's name was one that came up often.

A couple weeks before the anniversary of Eddie's death, a representative of the Army called to say that Eddie had officially been awarded a posthumous Silver Star. This was the nation's third highest award for valor. Danny found it bittersweet. It was extremely gratifying, but Danny would trade a thousand Silver Stars to have his brother back.

Jerry thanked the representative and jotted down specifics about the marker that would eventually be shipped to them. After Jerry hung up, Danny asked "Do you think we should call Father Berg and let him know?" Danny's jaw was set.

Jerry eyed his son uncertainly.

Danny's 19th birthday, November 29, 1968, fell on a Friday. It was the one year anniversary of Eddie's burial. Danny had reflected several times over the last year that, for the rest of his life, thoughts of his brother's death would come to the forefront on this day. He wondered if it would ever get easier.

After work that day, Jerry picked up tenderloins at the Tastee Freez and met Danny at home.

"Any plans tonight?" He asked his son.

"I was thinking about visiting the cemetery," Danny responded. Then, "No partying, gotta work tomorrow morning."

Jerry nodded. Danny had become a loner since his friends scattered. "Maybe I'll tag along... if you don't mind." He handed over a bag containing a sandwich and fries.

"Sure, Dad."

They ate mostly in silence, making occasional small talk about work. Danny squirted French's mustard on his sandwich. Jerry dropped the occasional fry to Suzy. He threw out an idea.

"Maybe we ought to take that bottle of Jim Beam along... the Genie bottle? I think there's a little whiskey left."

"Sounds like a good idea, Dad," Danny acknowledged.

Jerry took a final bite of his sandwich and stood. "Gotcha a couple things, birthday boy."

Danny watched his dad move to one of the kitchen cabinets. He opened it and removed a cake box and a gift-wrapped present. Jerry fumbled putting 19 candles on the cake and pulled out drawers until he found a book of matches.

"I will not try to sing...don't want to ruin your day." Jerry said with a small smile.

Danny blew out the candles and they each had a piece. It was carrot cake, Danny's favorite.

"Your grandma made it," Jerry explained, unnecessarily. Martha made carrot cake for Danny three or four times a year.

"I was pretty sure you didn't bake it," Danny grinned.

"Now this," Jerry lifted the present from the table and held it out. It was roughly the size and shape of a record album, but thicker.

Danny accepted it and began to peel away the giftwrapping. "It's not a Simon and Garfunkel album, is it?" Danny asked in in mock disgust. He liked harder rock, and his dad knew this. Every time *Born to be Wild* came on the radio, Danny cranked up the volume.

Jerry chuckled, "Definitely not."

Danny removed the last of the paper and opened a flap on one end of the box. There appeared to be two items inside. He pinched the objects and began to slide them out. Danny saw that he was looking at the back of a frame. Had his dad enlarged other photos?

Danny removed the frames and flipped them over. The first was an official document of some kind. His eyes fixed on the heading. Danny was suddenly motionless. His eyes flashed to his dad. Jerry was smiling back at him.

"It came last week. I thought you might find a good place for it."

It was Eddie's Silver Star certificate.

The certificate had a gold star at the top, affixed to red, white, and blue ribbon. Eddie's name and rank were prominent. Danny saw the words "THE SILVER STAR" in the center of the document.

Danny's attention was drawn to the second framed document. He realized it was the citation: the actual description of the actions that resulted in Eddie's award.

It read:

The President of the United States of America, authorized by Act of Congress, July, 1918 (amended by an act of July 25, 1963) takes pleasure in presenting the Silver Star (Posthumously) to Private First Class Edward J. Hitchens, United States Army, for intrepidity and gallantry in action against a hostile force while serving in action with C Company, 2nd Battalion, 173rd Airborne Brigade in action on 19 November, 1967 in Kon Tum Province, the Republic of Vietnam. On that date, Private First Class Hitchens was acting as a fire team leader in an assault on Hill 875, an enemy stronghold fortified with bunkers, tunnels, and heavy weapons. Private Hitchens' company was ambushed by a numerically superior force of NVA regulars. Several members of Private Hitchens' platoon had been killed or wounded and were pinned down by grenade and automatic weapons fire from a bunker complex. Private Hitchens, fearlessly exposing himself, single handedly assaulted the bunkers, using only hand grenades. Private Hitchens subsequently provided accurate and effective rifle fire, engaging and eliminating enemy targets at ranges of up to 300 yards. Private Hitchens then personally carried several comrades to safety, moving them, under fire, to a casualty collection point. Private Hitchens was mortally wounded later in the battle for Hill 875. By his bold leadership, personal initiative, and total devotion to duty, Private First Class Hitchens reflected great credit upon himself and upheld the highest traditions of the United States Army.

It was signed by Stanley R. Resor, Secretary of the Army.

Danny read the citation three times. His brother was a hero. He'd known this, of course, but the documents in front of him offered final confirmation.

"Thanks Dad," Danny managed.

There was enough Jim Beam left for three shots; one for Danny, one for Jerry, and the final one for Eddie. Danny did the honors and poured the last shot of bourbon onto the still unmarked grave. The official marker would arrive soon, they thought, now that Eddie's Silver Star was finalized. The award would be noted on the marker.

After twenty minutes at the cemetery, Jerry asked his son how long he'd like to stay.

"Why don't you go ahead and drive home, Dad? I'd like to stay awhile. I'll walk or run home."

"Are you sure?" Jerry prodded. "Supposed to get down into the twenties tonight."

Danny assured his father he'd be fine. Jerry took one more long look at the grave, then headed for the Impala.

Fifteen minutes later, Danny walked through the door of the L & H Café. The bar was busy. Several people surrounded the pool table, watching a game in progress. In the back corner, a man and a woman were rolling softball sized wooded balls down a fifteen-foot long electronic bowling alley.

"Help you?" It was Louie.

"Case of Blatz to go?" Danny said it as a request, not a demand. "Oh, can I get an opener, too?"

Danny hadn't planned on drinking that night. Well, there was the shot of Jim Beam. But he didn't expect to be carrying 24 bottles of beer a quarter mile back to the cemetery. Danny told himself that the actions described on Eddie's citation deserved more than a single toast.

Danny sat the case in front of the grave and opened two bottles. He drank from one while pouring the other onto the plot.

An hour later, Jerry pulled back into St. Lawrence cemetery. He'd grown concerned when Danny hadn't returned. The temperature had, indeed, fallen to 29 degrees. Jerry saw a figure at the family plot. He pulled to within thirty feet and saw that Danny was curled up against Jane's headstone, shivering. Empty beer bottles were strewn about.

His son was sobbing.

On the 21st of December, Apollo 8 lifted off from Kennedy Space Center. During the six-day mission, astronauts Frank Borman, James Lovell, and William Anders became the first humans to leave low Earth orbit, reach the moon, orbit it (10 times), and return. They were also the first to photograph an Earthrise.

While orbiting the moon, the astronauts read the opening lines of the Book of Genesis on a live television broadcast. After returning to Earth, Borman, the mission commander, received a telegram from a stranger congratulating him and the crew. It read "Thank you Apollo 8. You saved 1968."

Not for Danny.

The success of the mission put the Apollo program on pace to reach its ultimate goal. By now, Wapak's Neil Armstrong had been selected to command Apollo 11. There was a possibility, depending on the success of the next two missions, that Apollo 11 could be the mission that featured the landing.

The local papers, especially the Wapakoneta Daily News, began to trumpet stories about Armstrong. Some, Danny recognized, were repeats of stories he'd read three years earlier around the Gemini 8 mission. One seemed to pop up often. It was the story of Jacob Zint, a Wapakoneta resident who had built an observatory on top of his garage. Zint claimed that a young Neil Armstrong would come to his house with neighborhood boys to gaze at the moon and stars. Danny wasn't sure he believed everything in this story.

Customers in the lumberyard would speculate on Armstrong's chances of commanding the moonshot and actually taking the historic first step. Danny was pulled into these conversations when a customer was in the shop area. Danny was also now spending parts of most days in the front office. Jerry was having trouble comprehending customer orders and Danny was one of a few line workers that came up to spell Jerry while he worked through projects and paperwork at his desk.

Armstrong was the talk of the town at Steiner's Marathon, Bob's Gulf, the Tastee Freez, and Don Butch's. And certainly, at Betty's Corner and the L & H Café. You couldn't buy a gallon of gas, a tenderloin sandwich, a pound of cheese, or a draft beer without hearing about the local astronaut.

Danny spent New Year's Eve at Betty's Corner. Reed Thompson was home from college and accompanied his buddy. Danny had several shots with beer chasers. Reed drank some beers but had just one shot.

Danny chided his friend, "I thought all you college boys were big drinkers," but later decided Reed's restraint had been for the best. Danny wasn't able to drive home; he'd handed his keys to Reedo.

They toasted at midnight: "To Eddie!"

An extra bartender had been hired due to the expected holiday crowds. He was a cheerful bearded man, in his mid-twenties. Hearing Eddie's name, he approached.

Are you talking about Eddie Hitchens?," he asked.

Danny's eyes narrowed, "Yeah, he was my brother."

The man extended his hand, "Tim Rogers. I went to school at Anna and played ball against Eddie. I just got out of the Air Force and came home."

Rogers continued, "Damn glad to meet you: sorry about your brother... next round's on me."

Rogers had made Danny's night.

Reed professed that he'd never again eat an ice cream cone without thinking about Danny's brother, then chuckled, "I gotta admit, I'm looking forward to finding out what the bottom of the cone tastes like."

Danny snickered and ordered another shot of Beam.

When Reed returned to Toledo, Danny's days became monotonous. The short days of winter meant that he drove the Ranchero to work in the dark, and drove it home as the sun was setting. His days were spent running pieces of wood through the same sawblade for hours on end.

William Doyle still ran the rip saw. He avoided speaking to Danny, doing so only when absolutely necessary to the job. He went weeks on end without looking Danny in the eye. Danny smiled with satisfaction whenever he thought about this. He thought back to Ray Bolan's description of Doyle, "He's mad at the world, always out for revenge." It was the only thing William Doyle had ever been right about.

Danny had completely stopped running. He couldn't remember the last time he'd visited the library. Aside from following baseball, shooting was the only one of his passions Danny kept up with. Danny still drove out to the boy scout woods most weekends to shoot the Savage. He usually stopped at Betty's Corner on the way home for a few drinks.

Danny drank every weekend. He'd also have a beer or two some work nights. Usually while sitting in front of the RCA with his dad. Danny noticed that Jerry liked the volume on the television louder than he thought necessary. His dad stared dully at the TV. He seemed to avoid conversations.

Most people assumed Jerry was depressed over the losses of his wife and son. Danny believed the same, but was beginning to wonder if there was something more.

One night in February, Danny made a suggestion, "Dad, do you think it might be a good idea to get your ears checked?"

Jerry looked at him blankly, then asked Danny to repeat himself. Danny would've laughed if he hadn't been concerned. Jerry promised he would make an appointment.

CHAPTER THIRTY-THREE

On Monday, March 3, 1969, astronauts James McDivitt, David Scott, and Randy Schweickart blasted off from Kennedy Space Center. Their mission, Apollo 9, did not leave Earth orbit. The lunar module was put through its paces: engines, navigation systems, and docking maneuvers were tested. As with previous Apollo missions, the lessons learned over the ten-day span contributed greatly to the success of the program.

Danny followed the mission on TV. He watched the six o'clock news after work, but not as closely as he had with previous missions. He worked until noon that Saturday. After work, he decided to walk across the street to the Tastee Freez to buy a Dayton Daily News from the vending machine. He could catch up on the mission. Maybe there would be some features from spring training on the Cincinnati Reds. Finding the machine empty, Danny decided to walk another block to Don Butch's. Don usually had a small stack of Dayton papers for sale in his store.

Danny walked in, hearing the bell on the door ring, looked to his left, and saw a single copy remaining. He picked it up and looked around the store. Don was apparently back in the cooler. There were no other customers. Knowing they were getting low at home on food supplies, Danny picked up a loaf of Wonder Bread and a couple cans of Dinty Moore's Beef Stew.

Don came out of the cooler and moved to the cash register. "Hey Don, just picking up a few things."

Even at this point in his life, Danny went out of his way to show Don he wasn't a shoplifter. Danny smiled, trying to estimate how many candy bars Rick Vannette could've pilfered in the previous 30 seconds. Danny saw a box of Marathon bars. Thinking he might stock up on them for the work week ahead, Danny set the newspaper, bread, and stew on a shelf to his right, on top of boxes of Kool Aid mix. He pulled out his wallet to see how much cash he'd brought.

As he counted, Danny heard the ding of the bell above the entrance. He sensed a shuffling movement, then heard a man's voice say "My usual, Don... pounda' sliced ham, pounda' bacon... love me some pigs."

Danny turned to his left to see Elmer Marshall, his old paper route nemesis. Feeling Danny's eyes, the man turned to look at him. As Marshall's upper body pivoted his way, Danny saw a Dayton Daily News tucked under his right arm. Danny spun back to his right. The bread and stew had been moved a few inches. The paper was gone.

Danny, infuriated, wheeled back toward Marshall. "Did you take my paper?"

Marshall smiled at him. "Didn't see your name on it."

Danny saw red. He advanced toward Marshall. "That's MY paper, hand it over!" he demanded.

Marshall, Danny later realized, had already been drinking. This, perhaps, gave him the audacity to lecture Danny.

"Boy, you got to respect your elders." Marshall turned to the cash register and laid the paper on the counter. "Put this on my tab, too, Don."

Butch looked uncertainly over Marshall's shoulder into Danny's eyes. He didn't like what he saw. "Elmer, maybe you ought to—"

Marshall cut him off. "You want me to take my business somewhere else? Put the damn paper on my tab!"

Don looked distressed.

"That's alright, Don. Let him have it." Danny said with a voice that could etch glass.

Marshall turned to Danny with a look of triumph. It disappeared when he saw the black eyes that stared back.

Danny's altercations with Dick Ellsworth and William Doyle had been immediate responses to provocations. There was no real consideration by Danny, just an instant absence of inhibition. A barrier had restrained Danny's darker emotions his entire life. There was a rage inside him now that could not be contained by this barrier.

For the first time, Danny began to scheme, to plot ways to employ the rage, not just react to it.

When Danny was a paperboy, he was particularly observant when it came to deadbeat customers. Movement behind a door? A shadow gliding across a window? These were signs that his quarry was home. When you're 14 years old and you collect baseball cards and comic books, having a customer that is six weeks in arrears becomes a significant strain on your finances.

Danny clearly remembered Elmer Marshall, on at least two occasions, parking his Rambler in front of his house and spying Danny on his way to collect. Marshall rushed to, and through, his front door.

He hadn't locked his car doors either time. Danny smiled as he recalled this.

Danny set his alarm on Sunday morning for 6 am. This had nothing to do with church. He knew that Marshall would've been drinking Saturday night. Danny wanted to test a theory. He threw on jeans and a sweatshirt, jumped in his Ranchero, and drove across town. When Danny reached Gutman Street, he pulled up beside Marshall's Rambler. He looked up and down the street for cars and checked neighborhood houses for activity. Seeing none, Danny simply opened his door, took one step, and tried the handle of the Rambler's driver's side front door.

As it swung open, Danny grinned and nodded.

Danny worked on details of his plan for the next few days. Old baseball bats and balls were stored in a couple 5-gallon buckets in the garage. Danny stacked these items in a corner and tossed the buckets in the bed of the Ranchero. He retrieved a spade from the shed and it joined the buckets. On Wednesday, Danny got up a half hour earlier than normal and repeated his door test at Marshall's. The result was the same, the door was unlocked. This time Pick, the dog that had attacked Danny years ago, sensed Danny and went crazy barking at him at the front window.

Danny sat for several seconds to see if Marshall would respond. When the man hadn't appeared after a full minute, Danny rose back out of the Ranchero, took a few strides toward the house and extended the middle finger on his right hand.

Danny mouthed *Fuck You* at Pick, smiled, and returned to his vehicle.

Barely a quarter of a mile south of Botkins stood the largest pig farm in Shelby County. It had been in the Blanton family for several generations. On hot summer nights, prevailing southwest winds blanketed the southern half of town with the pungent aroma of pig manure. Having lived on that side of Botkins his entire life, Danny had no problem thinking of a source that could provide enough shit to gain vengeance on the owner of an unlocked Rambler. Danny thought two full 5-gallon buckets would be just about the right amount.

Danny planned to carry out his mission on Friday night: this would set the stage for an unforgettable weekend for Marshall. On Thursday, he scouted Blanton's farm, looking for a spot that offered easy access to pig manure. Danny was cruising past the farm when he saw something that gave him a better idea.

After work on Friday, Danny drove to Don Butch's. He selected three bags of apples, then walked to the small medical section and plucked four family sized boxes of ex-lax from the shelf.

Don's eyes widened as Danny approached the register.

"All that?" he asked.

"Well, dad's been a little stopped up, and I figured I'd get some extra," Danny asserted.

Don shrugged and rung him up.

Danny had borrowed a carpenter gouge from work. As it turned out, it was perfect for removing just the right amount of flesh from an apple to allow for a section of the chocolate flavored laxative to fit snugly. Danny worked in the garage while Jerry watched TV. He tuned in CKLW radio out of Windsor, Ontario and cranked it up when *Born to be Wild* came on.

By 10 o'clock, Jerry was in bed. Danny rubbed Suzy on the head and jumped in the Ranchero. He made the short drive to the Blanton farm, making sure to switch off his headlights as he pulled off the main road. A dirt access road led directly to the pens.

Danny parked and quietly pushed his door shut after exiting. He slipped on a pair of heavy leather gloves and duck-walked to the pen. The two buckets full of loaded apples were on the passenger side of the Ranchero, but Danny had an "unprocessed" Red Delicious in each hand. He let himself in through the gate, nervous, as the pigs moved about and snorted loudly. Danny knelt, held out the apples, and waited. He had no idea if this would attract a pig.

As it turned out, it did. Barely three minutes had passed when a fine looking pink boar approached and sniffed at the apples. Danny didn't wait. He snatched the pig, one back leg in each hand, and struggled to the gate. He pushed through, leaned back against it so the catch engaged, and swung the now squealing porker into the bed of the Ranchero.

Danny wasn't sure if a pig could escape over the top of a tailgate, but he didn't think so. He jumped into the still running vehicle and backed down the lane. Danny was sweating. He figured the pig weighed in the neighborhood of forty pounds. The sweat, he reckoned, was 50 percent exertion-related, 50 percent adrenaline-related.

Danny drove slowly through town. He had no real plan if stopped by Vic Peters; *"Evenin' officer, I'm just cruising around town with my buddy Arnold Ziffel."*

Danny pulled next to Marshall's Rambler a few minutes before eleven. He tried the driver's door, finding it unlocked again. Danny quickly dumped both buckets into the car. The apples spilled across the front bench seat, several rolled onto the floor. Pieces of ex-lax were strewn here and there.

Danny sprung to the Ranchero's bed. He snagged one of the pig's back legs and wrestled it around until he could also grip the other. Danny lifted the squealing creature from the bed and took two quick steps toward the Rambler. Danny then stopped, allowing the pig to swing forward. The boar's momentum carried it into the car, where it landed perfectly onto the seat, just past the steering wheel. He slammed the door shut.

Danny's heart was pounding in his ears. He scrambled to the Ranchero. Turning toward the house, he realized Pick was barking enthusiastically and scratching at the front window. Marshall's lights, however, did not come on: he no doubt was sleeping off a big Friday night. From the lack of activity at the neighboring houses, it appeared no one was concerned enough about the noise coming from the surly man's residence to investigate.

Danny slowly pulled away. He again flipped off Pick, this time Danny's right hand was sheathed in a laxative stained leather glove.

Love me some pigs, Danny smirked, *take that, you asshole!*

John Jacoby called in April to report that Eddie's headstone had arrived at the funeral home in Wapak. Jacoby provided installation as part of his funeral fee. He said he'd have two men at the St. Lawrence cemetery on Monday to take care of it.

Danny decided he would swing out to the cemetery at lunch on Monday to see how the work was going. He parked the Ranchero about forty feet from Eddie and Jane's plots. Two men in their twenties were hunched over a wheelbarrow, mixing concrete. A few feet away lay the marble headstone as well as a rectangular base. The military marker apparently had arrived in two pieces and was to be assembled at the gravesite.

As Danny neared the pair, he caught a bit of their conversation.

"Helluva thing, sure as hell puts Wapak on the map." The thin blonde man on the left was saying. He was stirring the thick grey mixture as his partner added water periodically from a bucket.

"You kidding?" the man with the bucket responded. "We've been on the map since my Senior year, '66... that's the year Neil did that Gemini thing." The man was stockier than his coworker, with a head of thick black hair. "Puts the rest of these towns to shame. Why, I bet Neil..."

Dark Hair noticed Blonde Hair had stopped working the hoe and was looking to his right. Black Hair followed his partner's gaze in time to see Danny walk up.

"How's it going, guys?" Danny broke the ice.

They spoke for a few minutes. The men explained the installation process. They didn't ask why Danny was there and Danny didn't explain. Making conversation, Danny asked "Do many of these?"

Blonde answered, "Almost every day." He continued "Just did one last week that was kinda special."

"Yeah?," Danny asked, half-interested. He was staring at Eddie's marker, which was face down. He hadn't yet seen the finished product.

"Yeah," Blonde answered nodding. "Fella named Korspeter, he was Neil Armstrong's grandpa. His funeral was last week and Neil flew home for it. Got in and out of town without anybody knowing."

Danny showed some interest.

Black Hair chimed in, "We were supposed to do this one last week" he nodded toward Eddie's stone, "but Mr. Jacoby said it could wait... said to take care of Neil first."

The men didn't notice that they now had Danny's full attention: or that his eyes had narrowed.

Blonde: "Saw an article in today's Wapak paper about Neil coming home. It was in that little gossip column tucked in the middle of the paper somewhere."

Black: "Not as easy to find as the article on our boy on the front page, huh? What was the headline, 'Neil Probably First Man On The Moon'?"

Black: "We were just sayin' before you walked up, helluva thing havin' a local boy be the first man on the—"

Danny, heat in his voice, cut him off.

"Are you telling me my brother's marker sat in some shed somewhere so you could take care of Neil Armstrong's grandpa first? After we've waited for over a year?" Danny's voice was rising.

Blonde and Black were silent. Blonde offered "Uh, look buddy, we were just doing what John told us to do..."

"Shut the hell up!" Danny snapped. He brushed past them, bent to Eddie's stone, and lifted its 230 pounds in one swift motion. Danny turned it over and gently laid it back onto the grass.

His eyes were drawn to the wording;

EDWARD J
HITCHENS
US ARMY
MAY 26 1947
NOV 19, 1967
SILVER STAR
PURPLE HEART

Danny knelt and brushed dirt off the marker. When he stood he coldly eyed the two workers.

"That better be straight when I come back."

After work Danny drove home and walked to the front door. He bent and snatched the Wapak paper off the step. Danny looked briefly at the front page. The headline was indeed "Neil

Probably First Man On Moon." It was splashed above a picture of the smiling astronaut. A smaller headline read "announcement made today." Most of the front page was dedicated to the story.

Danny quickly flipped through the paper until he found a small article in the "Just In Passing" feature. Two paragraphs under the heading, "Neil in Town" confirmed that Armstrong had returned to the area the previous weekend for the funeral of Mr. William Korspeter, his grandfather.

Danny roughly folded the paper and walked into the garage, continuing through the next door to the kitchen. He tossed the paper onto the table and pushed past a waiting Suzy Wong. Reaching his bedroom, Danny marched to the far wall and began tearing away the yellowing newspaper clippings that covered his bulletin board.

CHAPTER THIRTY-FOUR

Danny lounged on the living room couch on the final Sunday of May. His head ached. He'd been out drinking the previous night at Betty's Corner. Being a Saturday, the bar had been crowded, but Danny wasn't there to meet people: he was there to drink. His head was telling him today that he'd had a few too many. He remembered talking to the bartender, Tim Rogers. Danny learned that Rogers had worked in Air Force security when he was overseas. He'd been stationed at Nakhon Phanom air base in Thailand near the North Vietnamese border, guarding special operations aircraft.

"Pretty cool," Danny had told Rogers.

"Pretty boring" Rogers had responded. Danny thought the bartender was downplaying his role in the war but before he could follow up and ask for details Rogers inquired "Another Blatz?"

Danny was paying the price now. His plan for the day was to pet Suzy, listen to the Reds on the radio, and try to follow the progress of Apollo 10. Not necessarily in that order.

Jim Merritt was pitching for the Reds today at Crosley against the Expos. Danny had grown to like the Reds new radio pairing of Jim McIntyre and Joe Nuxhall, a former Reds pitcher with folksy stories. The Reds seemed to have a nice group of young players. They were led by catcher Johnny Bench, who had homered yesterday.

"Stud," Danny muttered, whenever Bench's name came up in conversation.

The Apollo mission was a complete dress rehearsal for the moon landing scheduled for July. Astronauts Thomas Stafford, John Young, and Gene Cernan had blasted off on the 18th. Cernan and Stafford actually flew the lunar module to within 8.4 miles of the lunar surface before reuniting with the command module and beginning the return trip to Earth. They were due to splash down the following day.

Danny's attention to the Apollo program had waned after his brother's death.

No longer.

The phone rang just as the Reds' Lee May had homered for the second time in the game. As he got up to answer it, Danny was chuckling at Nuxhall, who could be heard in the background of McIntyre's call, yelling at the baseball. "Get, get... get oughta here!"

"Hello."

"Is this Mr. Hitchens?"

Jerry was shopping for groceries in Sidney. Thinking it was some sort of solicitor, Danny's first instinct was to hang up. Many of the calls from Army officials after Eddie's death had begun this way, however, so he hesitated.

"He's not here right now, can I take a message?"

The voice was cheerful, "Mr. Danny Hitchens?"

Something about the voice now seemed familiar, but Danny couldn't place it.

"This is Danny Hitchens."

"Of course it is! How are you doing, Danny, this is Sue Giltrow."

Danny was confused, "Miss Giltrow? What..."

"You can call me Sue now, Danny. You've been out of school for a year." Her tone was light, upbeat. Just the way Danny remembered her.

"Uh, OK. Why are you calling?"

"No small talk, huh? Ahh, you always liked to get to the point."

Danny reddened, "Sorry, I—"

"I'm kidding! She laughed. Then, "Don't worry Danny, I need to make this quick, anyway. I'm finishing final paperwork for this year's seniors. There is still a bit of administrative work required by some of the universities, things like that."

Danny heard a click on the line.

Distracted, he answered, "Yeah?"

"Yes, well, I came across your old file in my, uh, unfinished drawer."

Danny's face continued to color, but the source of the redness had shifted from embarrassment to shame. It was an emotion he hadn't felt since....

Giltrow continued, "And it made me remember seeing information in the small print of a new financial aid handbook I received from the federal government this year."

Danny tried to follow: his head ached.

"There is money set aside for surviving members of families that have lost loved ones in the war." Giltrow continued, "I still have all your pertinent information and have done some preliminary paperwork for you."

Danny was confused. Before he could reply, there were a series of clicks on the line.

Giltrow asked, "You still there, Danny?"

"Yeah, sorry. So, you sent in my information to this... program?"

"Yes, I just wanted to let you know in case you receive a response in the mail." Then, phrasing it as delicately as she could, "I thought it could give you... options... something to think about."

The clicks on the line became more insistent. Danny furrowed his brow, trying to concentrate on the subject of the call. The ache in his head was unrelenting.

Aware of the politics of party line, Giltrow decided to wrap it up. "Anyway, I just wanted to keep you up to speed. Hope you're doing well, Danny. Come and visit me sometime: corner office, remember?"

Another click on the line. This time background noise from a TV could be detected.

"I remember," Danny smiled for a brief moment. Then Giltrow was gone.

Danny could hear breathing coming through the party line. His mind flashed to the memory of his dad using the phone after the death of his mom: how the Havener's had listened in, prompting Jerry to scream *God damned ghouls!*. He recalled them eavesdropping on Eddie during his final trip home.

The rage boiled up from deep inside.

"You need this fucking phone, Gert? Well, fuck you!," he shouted into the phone. Danny's eyes fell upon the transistor radio in the living room. He tossed down the handset and retrieved the radio. Danny turned the volume dial all the way up. He picked up the handset.

"Hope you like the fucking Reds," he growled, before situating the mouthpiece an inch from the radio and walking to his bedroom.

Sixty minutes later, Danny was helping his dad put away groceries.

"So, did you have a nice talk with Gert?" Jerry asked conversationally. He'd seen the phone next to the blaring radio. Joe Nuxhall was talking to Lee May on "The Star of the Game" portion of the broadcast when Jerry returned from Sidney.

Still angry, Danny had clicked off the radio and put the phone to his ear. He heard the "ENK-ENK-ENK" tone that told him the Havener's had hung up their handset.

"She was really impolite this time." Danny proceeded to tell his dad specifics of the call, leaving out a few of his more... incendiary words.

Jerry asked him to repeat himself a couple times. Danny noticed both times it was when one of them was turned toward a kitchen cabinet or the refrigerator. It was as if his dad had to see Danny's lips moving to comprehend the speech.

"Dad, you really have to see an ear doctor." As Danny said this, he was reaching to put a five-pound bag of sugar in the cupboard. Danny's eyes noticed a small bottle of McCormick's red food coloring. He stared at it for a long beat, then smiled.

Danny experimented in the back yard. He'd filled the sprinkling can with water and added a liberal amount of the food coloring. He walked at different speeds and held the can at different heights. Every few seconds he stopped to view the trail of crimson in his wake. Suzy Wong followed along, looking up at Danny with eyes that wondered.

"Just working on something, Suzy" Danny said in explanation. "Gonna get even."

Danny removed the sprinkling head and poured a line of red water in the yard. He smiled at the results.

Danny looked at the Havener place every time he passed it the next few days. On his way home from work on Wednesday, Danny saw Jim Havener mowing the front yard.

Game On, he thought.

At 10:30 that night Danny went to the shed. He grabbed the sprinkling can, now without the head, and the steel 5-gallon container of gas. Danny filled the can with gas and lugged both containers into the garage.

Danny went inside, rattled around the bathroom a bit, and then walked down the hall to the living room.

"Night, Dad."

Jerry looked up from the TV, "Yeah, night Danny, I'm beat." Jerry flipped off the set and walked down the hall. Danny went into his room, changed into dark cloths and lay on the bed. He waited 30 minutes, smiling through most of them, then crept down the hall. He heard his dad's snoring.

Danny turned toward the garage.

The guitar intro from *Born to be Wild* played in his head.

It took a while for Danny's handiwork to become evident, but three days later, there it was: the outline of a forty-foot dick had appeared in Havener's yard. Danny drove past the house in his Ranchero and saw Gert in her driveway, hands on hips, taking in the...enormity of the situation. She looked aghast.

Danny slowed to get a better look. He'd decided to go with a limp penis, rather than an erect version. He'd gotten the curves just right. From the testicles on the east side of the yard to the head near the driveway on the west side, the results were perfect. Danny had even added a couple drips coming out of the tip of the massive wang with the last quart of gasoline.

Gert turned to look at the Ranchero. She was indignant, furious.

Danny held an imaginary handset to his ear, mouthed the words "Call Me," and cruised home, laughing.

Vic Peters showed up at the Hitchens house the following day. Jerry and Danny had just finished supper when the doorbell rang. Jerry opened the door.

"Vic? What's going on?

"Jerry," Peters nodded. "I need to talk to you and Danny," he shifted his eyes to Danny at the table. "Gert Havener has filed a complaint."

Peters proceeded to lay out the facts of the matter, finishing with "The thing is, we've had some other incidents in town lately. A few weeks ago, somebody stole a pig from Blanton's farm and put it in Elmer Marshall's Rambler."

One side of Danny's lip curled, barely discernable. He saw Peters' eyes begin to materialize behind the lightening glasses.

Peters continued, "The pig, uh, defecated all over the interior of the car. Elmer wants his insurance company to call it a total loss but they're fighting him on it." Peters concluded, "Elmer almost had a heart attack the next morning when he opened his car door and the dirty, scared pig jumped out. It ran right between his legs."

Both sides of Danny's lips were now curled.

"I heard all about it at the yard. It was the talk of the town for a week" Jerry said.

Peters looked at Danny, "You wouldn't know anything about these... incidents, would you Danny?"

"Nope, sounds like you have a real crime wave on your hands, Vic."

Danny had nearly called him "Barney."

CHAPTER THIRTY-FIVE

Danny drove his dad's Impala past the rendering plant on 25A. Jerry sat in the passenger seat. It was Sunday, the 8th of June. The sun heated the pungent air surrounding the rendering facility.

"Hold your nose," Danny advised.

They were on the way to the fairgrounds in Wapak. Nationally-known news commentator Paul Harvey was appearing there for Armed Forces Appreciation Day. The event was sponsored by the Wapakoneta Area Jaycees. Danny wasn't sure how they had convinced Harvey to attend, but suspected it had something to do with the fact that Neil Armstrong grew up there. One thing that Danny did know was that the minute his father had become aware of the event, he had decided to attend.

Jerry loved to listen to Paul Harvey.

Danny believed that Harvey was seventy five percent Regular Joe and twenty five percent blowhard. Danny had to admit that he liked it when Harvey came to the end of a report about someone who had done something offensive. Harvey would conclude with "He would want us to mention his name..." He'd then pause for a few seconds, then move on to the next subject.

He and Reedo used to take turns doing poor imitations of Harvey. Danny missed Reedo. His buddy was staying in Toledo all summer, painting dormitory rooms.

As they neared the fairgrounds, Danny glanced down a street—Dearbaugh, was it?—and remembered his dad's bad day at the Armstrong parade a few years ago. He again remembered the smile on his mom's face. Danny produced a smile of his own as he pulled into the fairground parking lot.

The event went well, Danny supposed. Harvey was well received and said all the right things to honor members of the military, but the crowd in the grandstand numbered barely 250 people. Danny thought back to the Armstrong event, with its thousands of parade-goers. He could only imagine the throngs that might appear if a similar event were scheduled in Wapak after a successful moon mission. Danny pondered this with a critical view, not realizing that several hundred people had lined the streets to welcome Harvey.

Harvey wrapped up with his now famous catch phrase, "Good Day." Danny and Jerry made their way to the car. Jerry had smiled through Harvey's entire speech. In the car, he turned to his son and asked him to repeat several lines that he hadn't comprehended. Danny, noting that they had been sitting just forty feet from a loudspeaker, said "That's it, either you call the ear doctor or I do it for you."

Stories now appeared on a daily basis on TV, radio, and newspapers about Armstrong and Apollo 11. Nowhere were they more prevalent than the Wapakoneta Daily News.

On June 16, Danny picked up the paper to read: "Moonshot awaits 'go' 30 Days til Neil's space voyage."

On the 25th, "Moon flag may fly forever!"

Two days later, "Neil dreamed of landing on moon someday." This article focused again on Armstrong's relationship with local genius-eccentric (as Danny had come to view him) Jacob Zint.

This was followed by "TV spotlight on Wapak for flight."

Danny watched Wapak's glorification with a critical eye.

Apollo 11 lifted off from Pad A, Launch Complex 39, John F. Kennedy Space Center at 8:32 am, July 16, 1969. Commander Neil Armstrong and his crew, consisting of Edwin "Buzz" Aldrin and Michael Collins, were bound for the moon, and if all went well, immortality. It being a Wednesday, Danny was at work. Every saw in the Botkins Lumber Company was silent as the employees listened to the live radio feed. Danny heard a few minutes of the broadcast, then went to take a leak.

The lunar module, "Eagle," began its descent from the Command Module, "Columbia," on Sunday afternoon. Armstrong piloted the vehicle downward with Buzz Aldrin at his side. Collins continued to orbit the moon, silently hoping and praying that all went well for his comrades and that they would return to Earth together.

Danny sat at the bar at Betty's Corner. Tim Rogers, now the full-time manager, had decided to open up for the day. The bar was usually closed on Sundays. He thought he might attract some business. Maybe some folks would enjoy the shared experience of history while tipping a few cold ones.

Besides, Tim had a little surprise planned. At 2 o'clock in the afternoon, Rogers approached a large blanket-covered object in the corner of the room and raised his voice.

"Can I have everyone's attention, please?" The thirty or so patrons quieted. Danny turned on his barstool, curious. Rogers continued, "I'd like to unveil a new addition to the bar." He tugged at the blankets, revealing a brand new Williams "Apollo" pinball machine. The contrivance had colorful artwork, depicting rockets and astronauts. Cries of appreciation went up from some of the barflies as they jockeyed to be the first paying contestants. Rogers returned to his spot behind the bar.

Danny cocked his head and eyed the man.

"You're shittin' me, right?" he questioned.

"What?" Rogers asked innocently.

Danny smiled, "You too, huh, Tim?"

Rogers gave him a knowing smile as a quarter was dropped into the slot of the Apollo. "Just tryin' to cash in."

"The Eagle has landed."

Neil Armstrong's first words from the moon echoed through the bar. The crowd, now numbering over forty, burst out in a cheer. Most of them, anyway.

Armstrong had found a landing spot just as Eagle was on the verge of running out of fuel. It was 4:17 pm. The actual moonwalk was not scheduled to happen until the following day. Danny had two more beers and drove home. His work day would start early on Monday and he'd had more beers than he could remember. He hit the sack a few minutes after 9.

Danny didn't hear Walter Cronkite's surprising report that the moonwalk would occur earlier than planned. Jerry was watching the RCA and hurried to Danny's room to wake his son. He heard heavy breathing from within, paused, and walked back to the living room.

When Wapakoneta's favorite son made contact with the surface of the moon with his booted left foot at 10:56 pm, Danny Hitchens was in his bed, snoring; something that would have been incomprehensible a couple years earlier.

The next morning, the Wapakoneta Daily News blared, "NEIL STEPS ON THE MOON" across the front page above a photo of his smiling parents, Stephen and Viola. Danny stared at the headlines in his underwear and thought, "Hunh."

Botkins Lumber was abuzz with Landing talk. Ray Bolan reported that he and his wife had driven to Wapak the previous day to see the sights. He just wanted to feel like he was part of history. They had hoped to see the current home of Armstrong's parents, situated, of course, on Armstrong Drive, but couldn't get close. The house was in a new development with narrow streets. The national TV networks had erected a temporary broadcast tower on the property that they were sharing. It was a zoo.

"The governor's pledging half a million dollars to build a museum about Neil in Wapak" Ray added, excitedly.

"I heard," Danny managed.

Danny spent a couple hours in the front office taking customer orders. While he was there, a contractor from Wapak, Jake Sitzman, came in and placed a large order for 2x4s and plywood.

"Starting a new house?" Danny asked, conversationally.

Sitzman replied, "Nope, just want to be ahead of the game. I figure Wapak'll be havin' a helluva big parade sometime soon and things'll need to be built."

Danny nodded, his mind working.

There was more than one "helluva big parade." Richard Nixon, president of the United States since January 20, flew to the aircraft carrier USS Hornet in order to greet the Apollo 11 crew after splashdown. The astronauts spent three weeks in quarantine while the world waited to greet them.

Crowds estimated at 6 million people got their chance on August 13 as the astronauts and their families were honored in twin parades in New York City and Chicago. A record amount of ticker tape was showered on them in New York's Canyon of Heroes. The Chicago Tribune prepared its headline for the following day; "3 MOON HEROES WIN CITY." The whirlwind day concluded with a State Dinner in Los Angeles that was attended by the president, vice president, 44 governors, and representatives from over 80 countries.

Tiny Wapakoneta waited its turn.

The first notice of a parade for Armstrong in Wapak appeared in the local paper on August 7. Above a story with few details ran the words "Set countdown for Neil's homecoming." And below that, "Armstrong returns here Sept. 6."

The following day, a Saturday, a much more detailed article filled in the gaps of the story. The bold header read, "WELCOME HOME NEIL." Below that, in narrower type, appeared, "100,000 visitors expected to join fun."

Danny was at the kitchen table contemplating Wapak's plans, thinking of possibilities, when a loud vehicle sped down South Street, approaching the Hitchens house. Danny barely registered the noise as he glanced back to the story about the planned parade.

Suddenly brakes squealed directly in front of the house. Danny heard an animal yelp: followed by the sound of the vehicle accelerating.

Panicked, Danny looked about for Suzy. He remembered that he let her out to the back yard earlier... but Suzy had been wandering into the front yard now for months.

"Suzy!" He shouted.

Danny rushed to the front door. He saw a rattletrap pickup truck disappear around the corner to his left. He frantically searched the yard: no Suzy. Danny examined the street. There she was. She lay there, unmoving. There was an uneven trail of blood leading from the curb directly in front of the house. The trail was thirty feet long and ran crookedly toward the center of the street.

Danny screamed again "SUZY!" He sprinted to his companion, hoping for a miracle.

It was even worse than he'd expected. Suzy was bleeding from several abrasions. The entire right side of her body was disfigured. Possibly worst of all, Suzy was whimpering. She looked at Danny with those expressive eyes. Danny saw fear. He also saw that she was begging for him to help her.

Tears ran down Danny's face as he cradled his pet and rushed her to his vehicle. He gently laid her on the passenger seat and ran around to the driver's side. Danny backed down the drive, put the car in gear, and floored the accelerator. There was a veterinarian, Doc Boyer, just past Betty's Corner on 25A. Danny hit 90 mph before approaching the bar. He began to brake, his right hand never leaving Suzy's body.

Danny suspected Suzy was gone as soon as he lifted her. He had to try, though, and rushed into the building.

"My dog was hit by a car!" he shouted.

"This way." The woman at the desk ordered without hesitation. She directed Danny into an empty exam room them knocked on the next door to alert Dr. Boyer. The vet spent several minutes with Suzy, but it was too late.

Danny waited near the desk while Doc Boyer prepped the body. Danny had said he wanted to take Suzy home for burial. He was, he thought later, in some form of shock. He stared at a poster on the wall showing different classes and breeds of dogs. He found the drawing of a pug in the "Toy" group. Suzy had better eyes than this dog, he thought. Danny's eyes wandered to the edge of the poster where he saw a large, white, majestic looking dog.

Danny leaned in: *Great Pyrenees*. It was in the "Working" group. Where had he seen...?

Doc Boyer entered with a small bundle in his hands. It was wrapped in white cloth.

Time for another burial.

Tears streamed down Danny's face as he slowly drove past Betty's Corner toward Botkins. In another mile, darkness had overtaken grief. Danny remembered the pickup truck.

That Snider kid, Reedo had said.

Mutherfucker!

Danny gently laid Suzy on the garage floor. He went inside and called Botkins Lumber. Jerry picked up. He was there by himself that afternoon, again catching up on work. Danny told his dad what happened and said he'd wait for him to come home before burying Suzy.

Danny entered the shed and grabbed a shovel from the corner. Turning to leave, he thought, *Maybe a marker for Suzy?* Danny stepped to a stack of wood that was piled on an old bucket. When he grabbed a suitable piece from the center and tried to wedge it free, the entire stack fell down. "Sunofabitch!" he fumed. As he reached for the wood, he realized the bucket had also overturned. Something had spilled out.

Danny looked closer: it was a sealed plastic bag containing several packs of Kool cigarettes and a lighter.

Mom's brand, Danny thought.

It came to him quickly. Mom had never stopped smoking. She simply walked out to the shed when she felt the need. He was astounded.

Another thought occurred to him almost immediately. Eddie's smoke-saturated uniform. The air freshener he'd bought for the Impala. The lighter he used on the birthday candles. Danny had memorized his brother's Silver Star citation. If environment could drive a soldier to take up smoking, wouldn't Eddie's qualify?

Danny thought of the losses he'd sustained over the last couple years, culminating with Suzy today.

"Screw it," he said, and reached for the Kools.

Greg Snider lived with his parents in a farmhouse south of Wapak. There was a junkyard on 25A a quarter mile before you reached the rendering plant, on the opposite side of the road. A country road, Pusheta, ran to the east, where it crossed over I-75 a mile away. The Snider farm was the first property past the junkyard. The farmhouse sat 100 feet or so from the road. It had a dirt U-shaped drive in front. A pickup was parked in the drive.

Danny killed his lights and drove past the house. He was sure he was holding his cigarette wrong. He took a final puff and tossed it into the ditch. He'd coughed all the way from Botkins. He was sickened by a combination of tar, nicotine, loss, and self-loathing. He passed the farmhouse and saw the old pickup.

Mutherfucker, he thought again.

Danny pulled into the next drive, did a K-turn, and drove slowly back past Snider's. When he reached the junkyard, Danny put the Ranchero in park. He circled to the bed and retrieved the Savage. Danny had filled the magazine with .308s after he and his dad buried Suzy. After sundown, he told Jerry that he needed to go for a drive to clear his head. His father looked beaten.

Danny jogged a few feet toward 25A. He needed to check traffic and had to peer around a mature cornfield on the right and the junkyard to the left to do so.

All clear.

Danny jogged back. He braced the 99 against his shoulder while leaning against the Ranchero's passenger side roof. There was enough light being cast from a utility pole near the house for Danny to pick up his target. For a second, he glassed a lit window on the second floor. A figure passed behind it. Snider?

Could be his mom or dad, Danny thought. He brought the scope back to the pickup, slowed his breathing, and squeezed.

Danny figured the range at 150 yards, an easy shot, especially for a target this size.

The crack of the rifle ripped through the night. Danny worked the lever quickly, remembering Eddie do the same as he walked through the brush of the boy scout woods a lifetime ago.

Bullet after bullet slammed into the truck's engine block. Danny couldn't remember how many times he'd fired. His heart racing, Danny glanced at the counter on the side of the rifle.

He had one round left. Danny put the Dual-X crosshairs onto the windshield, directly above the steering wheel, and squeezed. The glass spiderwebbed.

Danny tossed the 99 into the front seat and eased out onto 25A. A half mile south he turned on his headlights.

He popped in the Steppenwolf 8-track and clicked the selector button to program D, where he'd find *Born to be Wild.* It was hardly necessary. His head was already filled with the opening guitar lick.

CHAPTER THIRTY-SIX

Danny had formulated a plan. He was about 60% committed to it. Would he attempt it? In the movies, he would've been given some kind of a sign. He was poring over the newspaper after work a few days after the Snider shooting when the doorbell rang.

It was Vic Peters again.

This time Danny answered. Jerry had finally made an appointment with an ear, nose, and throat specialist in Sidney. He'd taken the last appointment of the day, 4:30, so he wouldn't miss much work. Danny didn't expect him home for some time.

"Danny," Vic nodded at him.

"Vic," Danny unconsciously mimicked Peters.

"Mind if I come in?"

Danny stepped aside, allowed the officer to enter. "Have a seat?" Danny asked.

Peters sat on the couch and cleared his throat.

"The Auglaize County Sheriff has put out a request for help. There's been a shooting in their area."

Peters' glasses were exactly halfway between dark and clear. They reminded Danny of a photo of John Lennon and Paul McCartney he'd seen in a magazine. The two Beatles were wearing red-lensed glasses. Cool people, Danny conjectured, could pull off the look. Vic, not so much.

"I know you do a lot of shooting. We're doing routine checks to see who might have a rifle that could've been used."

Danny probed, "Routine, huh? How many guns did Gert Havener have when you checked with her?"

"I didn't check—" Vic began, then caught himself. Exasperated, he charged ahead. "We're just checking with shooters. Do you have a rifle here?" Vic's face and glasses both exhibited the same levels of cloudiness.

"I do," Danny nodded.

"I'd like to see it," Vic said authoritatively.

Danny got up and walked to his room. He reached into the closet and grabbed his Marlin .22. It rested against the Savage. Danny walked back to the living room. Peters saw him enter the room carrying the weapon. He sneered at Danny triumphantly.

"There you go," Danny handed the Marlin to Vic.

As Peters examined the weapon, his face fell.

"A .22, huh?" Peters looked at Danny. "The weapon we're looking for fires large caliber bullets."

Here it comes, thought Danny. He'd decided that he'd hand over the Savage when Peters asked for it, he wouldn't lie. What bigger sign could he hope for than to have a cop walk into his house and ask for the rifle he would use?

Peters scratched his head and handed the Marlin back. "OK, I guess you check out. Sorry to bother you."

Peters showed himself to the door as Danny stood stupefied.

He didn't ask if I had any other guns? What an idiot!

Danny had his sign.

Danny wasn't sure if he would mention Vic's visit to his father. Jerry would certainly see the connection between the police chief's visit, the shooting, and the high caliber rifle that Danny hadn't presented.

Danny was still weighing the pros and cons of the problem when his dad returned a half hour later.

Jerry walked in through the garage, looked at Danny, and announced, "They're fitting me with hearing aids."

Thoughts of Peters' visit evaporated as Danny asked his father for all the details of his appointment.

Danny spent several days through the middle weeks of August shooting at the boy scout woods. He wasn't sure of the range required of him so he varied the distances, often using Eddie's pacing trick. He decided he'd have to scout the entire parade route to see if a shot was even feasible. He did not

337

intend to be caught, but how could this be accomplished with 100,000 witnesses?

The parade route was laid out in the Wapak paper. Units would start at the high school north of the Auglaize River and cross a bridge to the south side, where they would turn left on Auglaize Street and head east toward the business district. The route was more or less the same as the 1966 Gemini parade, but in reverse. The route wound east through the heart of town, south a few blocks, then took Pearl Street west, all the way back to its Y-shaped intersection with Auglaize Street. A left there took them to the fairgrounds.

Danny began to make scouting trips to Wapak. He saw that storefronts were being spruced up, banners were being hung, signs and billboards were being replaced. Danny was sure that Jake Sitzman was putting his extra lumber to good use.

Danny quickly realized that the downtown area would be out of the question. The many buildings were excellent shooter's perches, but they would be swarming with spectators. Danny thought back to 1966, then imagined ten times more people packed into the same area. He shook his head.

Next, Danny eyed the streets south of the Wapa Theater. The parade route snaked through some residential streets in this section, but the houses were densely packed and there were no clear fields of fire.

Danny drove out to the fairgrounds. The inner area where the grandstand was located was unworkable. Law enforcement could easily secure this area. He supposed a shot could be attempted from outside the fairgrounds toward the stage, but the range would be at least 500 yards and, besides, he would be shooting from an area that would be utilized for parking. How could he expect to avoid apprehension afterward?

Danny began to doubt that it could be done. He was driving home from work on the 25th of August thinking about the work day. Again, the talk was of the parade. Bob Hope would be the

Master of Ceremonies, and Johnny Carson's sidekick Ed McMahon would be there. Even Dr. Albert Sabin, inventor of the polio vaccine, would attend.

Danny passed a woman walking two curly-haired dogs down South Street. Standard poodles? Airedales? Danny began to think about revisiting the Kool's in the shed when his thoughts swam back to dogs. A memory popped into his head and he nearly slammed on the brakes.

The dog!

Danny thought back to that terrible day in Doc Boyer's office. He'd been staring at a poster showing dog breeds and saw the Great Pyrenees. He couldn't place it at the time, but it had just come to him. He had seen that kind of dog the day of the first Armstrong parade. It was at the open building near Dearbaugh Street. The building had a loft, it was in a secluded location set back from the parade route, and there was quick access from the structure to several parking spots.

Danny's heart quickened.

Danny needed a way to examine the target area and shooting perch up close. An idea came to him that night. He went to the shed and rooted through the nooks and crannies. No luck. Did they still have it? Where had they put it?

He went back to the garage and checked every shelf. Nothing. Frustrated, Danny let his eyes travel around the garage until they stopped at the rear corner.

Yes, it's under the work bench!

Danny got down on his knees and reached under the bench. He pulled out a couple partially used paint cans before finding his prize: his old Wapakoneta Daily News canvas delivery bag.

The following day, Danny borrowed an item from the lumberyard. Work orders were attached to clipboards in the office, then hung on nails in the shop area. There were always a few extras hanging there.

After work he drove to Wapak. He cut over to Dearbaugh and drove slowly north. Looking ahead to his right, he could see the rear of the structure. Danny continued past a few houses before turning right on Benton. He remembered that the barn—Danny had decided to think of it that way—sat several feet behind the line of houses on this street. Danny pulled to the curb and parked. He reached for his props and got out. Danny slung the canvas bag over his head. The strap curved around his left shoulder while the bag, stuffed with old newspapers, hung at his right hip. Danny picked up the clipboard and sauntered down the street.

He walked ahead until reaching a small white house on his right, the address read 801. The next house, grey in color, was no more than 20 feet ahead. Danny saw that this house was numbered 717. He took a few steps on the sidewalk until he was exactly halfway between the houses. Acting like he was reading something on the clipboard, he slowly tuned south to look between the houses.

There was the barn. It set back a hundred feet or so behind the houses. It had an open front. Danny could see the elevated loft, which appeared to be about 12 feet high, just as he had remembered it.

Danny then turned 180 degrees. He was standing on Benton. Directly to his front, a short street T'd in from the north. This was Oak. Danny saw that Oak ran just one block before connecting to Pearl Street.

Pearl was part of the parade route. Danny walked up Oak to Pearl. Arriving, he saw this was the area of the Y-shaped intersection he remembered from the 1966 parade. Just beyond Pearl, Auglaize Street angled in from the downtown area several blocks to the east. Max's Dairy Bar sat at the convergence of Pearl and Auglaize.

Danny remembered the 1966 parade slowing as it made the necessary diagonal turn in this area. The configuration of the streets combined with the attraction of ice cream to form a natural bottleneck.

The target vehicle would be travelling slowly through this area. Very slowly.

Danny turned to look back at the barn. It was visible: but you had to be looking for it to see it. Danny tried to estimate the distance. 200 yards? He would pace it.

Danny turned back north. If he took one step off the curb, he would be standing on Pearl. *Might as well be totally accurate,* he thought. He checked for traffic, then walked out into the center of Pearl: exactly where an open convertible would be idling in a couple weeks. Danny began to pace back toward the barn. He tried to look nonchalant, occasionally glancing at houses, then down at his clipboard.

As he reached "50," Danny glanced to his right and noticed, for the first time, a large brick house. There was an unattached garage behind it with an odd roofline. Danny paused, looked closer, and realized he was staring at what appeared to be the top of a silo sitting on the crest of the garage.

Has to be Jacob Zint's homemade observatory, Danny thought.

The base of the dome was covered in sheet metal while the curved roof was encased with a white material of some sort.

Danny stood transfixed, trying to imagine a young Armstrong inside the structure looking at the heavens. He then remembered that many people believed Zint had made up the story. Danny shook his head and continued pacing. When reached the sidewalk in front of 801 Benton, his count had reached 135.

Okay, Danny thought, *from here back to the barn is another, what, 50 paces, 70? It would help if I could find a way to walk back there without being noticed...*

"Help you, laddie?"

Danny was shaken away from his thoughts. He turned to see a grey-haired man standing on the porch of the white house, 801. Sitting next to him was a large, very large, white dog. *Great Pyrenees.*

"Uh, sorry, what?" Danny stammered.

The man smiled and said "You look like a man deep in thought, can I be of service?"

Danny noted that the man had an accent....British?

"Uh, no, I'm from the newspaper office, we're trying to map out new routes for our carriers."

Danny fell back to the cover story he'd concocted. "The streets in this area," he gestured toward Pearl, "are jumbled. It's hard to draw up fair boundaries for our delivery boys." Danny smiled, "You know, when it comes to Christmas tips."

"Ahh," the man's eyes twinkled, "say no more." Then, "I saw you eyeing Mr. Zint's place."

Danny blinked, "Sir?"

"The big brick place with the garage set back. That's Jacob Zint's place, the one that's been in all the papers. His observatory is on top of the garage. It's where—"

"Where Neil Armstrong supposedly came to look at the moon," Danny interjected.

The man chuckled, "Supposedly...sounds like you're familiar with our Mr. Zint."

The dog eyed Danny and produced a single bark. It was low and powerful.

The man addressed his pet "It's OK, Angus, he's not a criminal."

Then, to Danny, "Come meet Angus."

A short wrought iron fence bordered the porch. It separated Danny from the pair, but he thought it might not be much of an obstacle to a creature of this size.

The man held out his hand, "Malcolm MacKenzie."

Danny took the hand, "John Kay." It was the name of the lead singer for Steppenwolf.

"Let John pet you, Angus."

Danny reached through the fence and rubbed under the dog's ears. Danny imagined that Angus was eyeing him with suspicion. He shook away the thought.

"Ahh he likes that." Malcolm said. "He's very protective, it's in the breed."

"Great Pyrenees, right?" Danny offered.

"Yes! I'm impressed. Most people here have never seen one." Malcolm continued "I've had him for five or six years." McKenzie explained that he'd moved from Scotland to the U.S. several years ago. He'd worked as a chemist at several food production companies before retiring from Fisher's Cheese in Wapak.

"Brought Angus here with me from Wisconsin. He was just a pup."

"Not anymore." Danny laughed.

"He's a good boy, never leaves the yard if I let him out. I used to chain him in the old barn out back but never do any more."

This brought Danny's focus back to the job at hand. "Mr. MacKenzie, would it be okay if I walked through your back yard to that street back to the south, uhhh, Vine?"

"Suit yourself laddie," MacKenzie said cheerfully. "Watch your step, though. I'm afraid I haven't cleaned up after my pup in a few days. Say goodbye to Mr. Kay, Angus."

The dog's eyes fixed on Danny, unreadable.

Danny stepped back to the sidewalk, made a show of checking the clipboard, then stepped toward the barn; 136, 137...

Danny reached the barn at 191. He jotted the number down on the notepad attached to the clipboard. Danny peered at the open north side of the structure. It was just as he remembered. The roof was roughly 18 feet high on this side, it slanted downward, reaching the back wall at a height that he estimated at 12 feet. The building was close to 30 feet wide. The lower area housed mowing equipment, garden tools, and various fragments of small town America.

Danny was particularly interested in the loft. He glanced back at the MacKenzie house, then at neighboring homes. All clear. He stepped quickly to the wooden ladder at the right rear corner and scrambled up. He poked his head through the opening, saw nothing to block his path, and hoisted himself

343

up. There was a thick layer of straw on the loft surface. Danny had to duck at the rear of the loft but found he could stand as he neared the front. Still, he told himself, he should stay low.

Danny turned his attention to the view in front. He saw Oak Street stretch out in front of him, leading directly to Pearl. He imagined a line of spectators along Pearl with parade vehicles just beyond. From this perspective, 12 feet above the ground, Danny believed he would have just enough elevation to glass someone sitting on top of a rear car seat in the middle of the street.

After returning home Danny painted head-sized targets on several pieces of scrap plywood. He was careful to make sure they resemble something else; bullseyes, peace signs, baseballs. His favorite was a head-sized circle with two smaller circles inside, strategically dotted with two beady eyes and a smiling mouth. The addition of a curly tail and pointy ears made it look like a pig squinting back at him.

"Bet Elmer Marshall would like to take a shot at this fella" Danny thought.

Danny began to shoot in earnest at 191 paces. He'd purchased extra boxes of .308's in Sidney. He realized that the elevated railroad tracks at the boy scout woods were, if not precisely the same height as the barn loft, very close to it. Danny concentrated on his breathing and trigger pull while firing prone. This would be the position he'd utilize on September 6. He made a point to shoot on windy days, experimenting with the scope adjustments. He fired so many rounds that the targets at 191 paces actually began to look comically large through the Weaver K6.

On Wednesday, September 3, Danny lifted the Wapak paper from his doorstep and read "Wapak ready for visitors." He thought back to the target he'd riddled the night before. The grouping within the hastily painted peace sign was as tight as he'd ever produced. Danny would be ready too.

It was still a long shot, but it wasn't a longshot.

CHAPTER THIRTY-SEVEN

Danny spent his last few days concentrating on details. He'd decided he'd been lucky at Snider's. Firing from the passenger side of the Ranchero, all of his spent casings had been ejected into the bed of the vehicle. If he'd taken the shots from the other side, they would've landed on the street, with fingerprints imprinted on them.

Danny would wipe the five rounds in the magazine this time. More than once. He planned to carry the canvas newspaper bag. He'd fill it with copies of newspapers that he'd been saving. He remembered newspaper boys roaming the parade route in 1966 hawking souvenir editions. Danny could pose as one of these carriers to move freely through the few short streets he'd have to traverse.

Fortunately, the Savage had just a 20-inch barrel. The weapon wouldn't completely fit into the bag, but Danny would wrap the protruding barrel in newspaper and tuck it under his arm as he walked. He would hold the barrel against his body in the same manner that he held a thermometer under his arm when his mom checked his temperature years earlier.

He experimented with different ways to wrap the canvas bag around the Savage, searching for the best way to trap the ejected cartridges. In the end he decided, to his dismay, that he would have to leave the rifle in the shooting hide when he left. It would just be too dangerous to try to make his way to the car now that everyone would be looking for a weapon. What if he made it to the car but was stopped later? Danny couldn't count on Vic Peters being the man who stopped him. No, he'd have to leave the 99. If he left the rifle and removed the casings, they would be just as damning if he was stopped. He'd leave it all behind with as little trace evidence as possible. Who knew, they might not ever find it. He would bury it under the straw before leaving.

Danny brought sandpaper home from work. He spent two days sanding the rifle in the shed. He wore gloves, careful not

345

to touch any part of the weapon with his uncovered hands. He sanded not just the wood, but all the metal as well. It ruined the bluing, of course, but destroyed any fingerprints that weren't wiped.

Danny loaded the magazine with five pristine Winchester rounds. He careful wrapped the Savage in newspaper and wedged it into the papers inside the bag. He slung the assemblage over his shoulder and checked to make sure he could conceal the barrel completely with his arm.

Yep.

The bag would be leaving the barn with him after the shot. It seemed like it might help throw off suspicious eyes.

Danny tucked a few more items into the bag; a thermos filled with water, two baloney sandwiches, binoculars, and almost as an afterthought, the Kool cigarettes and lighter.

He was ready.

Danny walked back into the house the night of the 5th to see his dad on the phone. After hanging up, Jerry turned and said "Big day tomorrow."

Danny was momentarily taken aback. Did his dad suspect what he was planning? They had talked about the parade weeks ago and Danny said he wasn't interested in going. "Too crowded" he'd said. His dad, sensing the loss of interest Danny had with the space program the last couple years, didn't argue. "We'll find something else to do that day. The shop's closing for the parade so we'll have a day off."

That had been the end of the discussion, until now.

"Big day?" Danny asked, tentatively.

"Yep," his dad beamed. I'm getting my hearing aids tomorrow."

Danny let out his breath.

Danny went to bed early. He barely slept, finally dropping off near midnight. His alarm rang at 1:30. He slapped at it quickly to silence the clatter. His dad almost certainly wouldn't hear it, but why take a chance? He dressed quickly. It would be a warm day, with temperatures in the upper eighties. He chose a short sleeve shirt. He'd wear a sweatshirt over the top of this. He could remove the sweatshirt when it got too warm. He'd tuck it in the newspaper bag. He'd worn his watch to bed last night to make sure he wouldn't forget it in the morning.

Danny crept to the kitchen. He laid a note on the table. It explained to his dad that he'd decided to go fishing at one of the gravel pits near Wapak. It might help if he was seen driving north in the pre-dawn hours. Danny's note said he left at 5 am. He planned, however, to get out of town by 2. He didn't want a repeat of the mad scramble to get to the '66 parade.

Danny silently opened the door to the garage. The rifle and gear were in the shed. He retrieved them and walked around the house. He'd parked on the street the night before so he could pull away quicker. He checked to make sure his fishing gear was in the Ranchero's bed. He'd placed it there last night so he didn't have to fool with it this morning. It was there. It had laid in the open bed all night, but this was Botkins, after all: there was never much crime.

Danny eased the canvas bag into the front seat and turned the ignition.

He stopped at the Catholic cemetery on the way out of Botkins. He pulled into the narrow drive, parked, and walked to the familiar section. As he approached, Danny realized he couldn't bring himself to look at his mother's marker. A part of him knew what she would think about what he was going to do. He suppressed this thought and looked at Eddie's headstone.

Eddie's loss had pushed Danny to this point. Many things had subsequently influenced him. Everywhere he turned, it seemed, he saw a disrespect for his brother and what he stood for. The country had marginalized, even belittled, its Eddies while transferring its adoration, its veneration, somewhere else. Danny needed to lash out at this. He was in perfect position to do it.

The marble marker bearing Eddie's name was illuminated by the Ranchero's headlights. Danny had imagined that somehow his brother would reach out to him in this moment, urging him to "Shoot straight." It didn't happen.

Danny turned and walked to the car.

Every road into Wapak, it seemed, featured a billboard welcoming Armstrong back to town. Danny passed one as he entered the city limits on 25A. This one included the requisite "WELCOME HOME NEIL ARMSTRONG." Danny noted that it also included "THE SPRINGFIELD OUTDOOR ADV. CO." in letters just as big. Danny smiled.

He drove into town until he reached Pearl Street. Making sure to use his turn signal, he hung a left. Danny wanted to get a quick look at the target area before parking. As the Ranchero rounded through the turn, he caught a glimpse of the Wapa Theater two blocks to the north. Memories of his mom floated into his consciousness. Danny pushed them away.

There was nothing unexpected to see near the target area. Danny saw a few vehicles moving in and out of the fairgrounds to the west, but there was no activity yet where Pearl met Oak. The Ranchero made a left at Oak, heading directly for the hide. Remembering that Jacob Zint's place was just to his right, he slowed and eyed the garage. The homemade observatory was silhouetted against the sky. Could Armstrong have really been inspired there?

Danny drove on.

He made a right on Benton, then a left on Dearbaugh. He was now, for all intents and purposes, on his getaway route. He drove several hundred feet then pulled over to park under a large ash tree. It would be easy to find after the streets became congested. Danny checked his windows and mirrors for activity. Seeing none, he popped the door and tugged the canvas bag until it was close enough to duck his head through the strap. Danny stayed behind the open door so it blocked any unwanted eyes. Once the bag was in place and the rifle barrel tucked under his arm, Danny closed the door.

Danny looked northeast. He could just make out the barn in the starlight. It was roughly 200 yards away—about the same distance as the shot he'd be making—across a former farm field.

He set off in that direction. Halfway across, he remembered the story of his dad tripping while carrying the cooler. It must've happened almost exactly where he was treading. Danny continued to walk; remembering his dad's torn pants, the Coke that exploded in his face, and the walkie-talkie with no battery. Danny was smiling when the memory of his mother's happy face swam into his head.

"Wasn't that wonderful?" she'd asked happily.

Danny again pushed his mom away. He had arrived at the barn.

The closest artificial light was coming from a pole on Oak Street, nearly 200 feet away. There was virtually no chance that Danny would be seen entering the barn at this hour, but he still moved cautiously. He crept to the northwest corner, alert to any movement coming from the homes in front. Danny slowly inched his head around the corner and peeked into the barn. There was just enough light coming from the street to confirm that the lower level was uninhabited. If someone was in the loft, well, Danny had no way of knowing that until he went up himself.

He ducked around the edge of the building and, with his right hand feeling the interior wall, made his way back to the ladder. Danny did not have a flashlight. He'd purposely left theirs at home, afraid he be tempted to use it and reveal himself to a homeowner or, worse, part of the large contingent of law enforcement personnel that would be on hand.

He grabbed the ladder and pulled himself up. When he'd climbed the ladder two weeks earlier, he hadn't noticed any sound. The creaking produced by his weight now seemed ridiculously loud. Danny was reminded of the pops and groans of an ancient sailing vessel in a wind storm. He winced with each one.

Danny's head reached the opening. He eased his eyes above it, then another few inches to clear the layer of straw. His head swiveled slowly, like a submarine periscope in a World War Two movie.

The loft was empty.

Danny pushed the bag onto the floor and scrambled up. He crawled to the opposite rear corner of the loft. He planned to leave the bag and rifle in that corner on the off chance that Malcolm MacKenzie, or someone else, climbed the ladder. The Savage would stay disguised until Danny needed it. To Danny, it didn't look like this upper level of the barn saw much activity. He couldn't be sure, though, so didn't want the rifle in plain sight. If discovered, he would apologize for being there. He needed an early start for his newspaper duties, he'd say, and remembered the loft just last night, too late for permission.

If he was detected, he would consider it a sign that he should scrap the entire undertaking. Danny certainly didn't want to harm any innocents.

Danny removed the thermos, binoculars, and one of the sandwiches. He crawled toward the opening, stopping five feet from the edge. He chose a spot just to the right of center. He angled his watch face until he could make out the hands. It was 3:23 am. He was in place in his hide. The parade began at 1:30 pm.

He gathered handfuls of straw until he'd formed a small mound. The straw would make a fine pillow.

The dream, as many are, was a kaleidoscope of impressions: a vignette here, a memory there. Danny was looking up. He saw his fishing pole floating across the water, grandpa Gene's line snaking out to rescue it. This scene was replaced by one of Reedo reaching out and slapping a single to right against a smiling Mike Delmer. Danny followed the flight of the ball and wasn't at all surprised when it transformed itself into a model rocket... he heard Eddie's voice off to the left and looked that way, expecting to see a launcher in his hand. Instead, his brother hung from a parachute, one that seemed to be rising away from Danny. He felt his hand brush against something with a point. Part of his brain suggested "straw," but when Danny looked down he saw the edge of a spinning sawblade and felt a distant rage...he turned to see a smirking Doyle and, behind him, the red-lined face of Elmer Marshall... they were daring him to come after them. Danny's heart raced. He ached to punish them. He shifted his body, then heard... Suzy? She was above him. Danny lifted his head and saw Suzy Wong. She was in his mother's arms...both of them rising away from him...he didn't know if he could catch them. Danny heard the bark again...but, it was lower, more powerful than Suzy's bark. Danny opened his eyes and turned his head to the open side of the barn.

He saw Angus standing outside the back door. The dog was looking skyward. He barked again. Danny followed the dog's gaze.

He saw the Goodyear blimp.

Danny wasn't sure what was weirder, the dream, or waking up in a barn loft with the iconic craft overhead. The Goodyear blimp was known for being at the Rose Bowl or the World Series: certainly not above Wapakoneta, Ohio.

He glanced at his watch and was surprised to see it was 10:20: he'd slept nearly seven hours. A niggling thought told him he'd had a descriptive dream but when he tried to access

351

the abstract part of his memory, all he could see was that damn blimp.

He realized he was sweating. He estimated it was already 80 degrees. His body odor combined with the aromas of straw and old wood. The musky blend was punctuated by the faint hint of gasoline emanating from unseen equipment in the lower level. Danny pulled off his sweatshirt. He took a long pull of water from the thermos and opened the sandwich that lay next to him. The warm baloney wasn't ideal breakfast food, but he was famished. As he chewed, he surveyed the scene in front of him.

Angus was resting on a bare spot that Danny hadn't noticed before. It was between MacKenzie's house and the house next door at 717 Benton. It looked like Angus enjoyed laying there where could watch activity in front of the house. The dog would have an eyeful today.

Danny saw that Angus was in the shade right now. When the sun rose just a bit higher, the area between the houses would be bathed in sunlight. He suspected that, unless MacKenzie called Angus back into the house, the dog would move back to the shade of the barn. A defensive, 150-pound dog would be waiting at the bottom of the ladder after being startled by the crack of a rifle.

Danny thought of his second baloney sandwich and decided to save it. He may need to bribe the Great Pyrenees.

The next hour was spent prepping his perch. He quietly pushed straw into a two-foot high pile several feet back from the edge of the loft. He didn't want the barrel of the 99 to stick out from the silhouette of the barn. He retrieved the binoculars and, now sitting Indian style with his elbows braced on his knees, swept the area to the north.

Lawn chairs occupied almost every square foot of the Y-shaped intersection. Several dozen people, many with cameras around their necks, laughed and talked excitedly. Max's Dairy Barn was already doing a thriving business. Danny saw several cones and at least one banana split. There was a buzz in the crowd.

Danny had an almost overwhelming urge to creep to the edge of the loft so he could look to the right and left. There were already significantly more people on the streets than the 1966 parade had at its peak. This was historic and he wanted to take it in, but he stayed disciplined.

He glanced at his watch again: 12:20. Better get the Savage ready.

Danny slipped on the gloves he'd brought home from work. He unwrapped the rifle, laid it down, and stowed the paper, thermos, and plastic wrap from his sandwich in the canvas bag. The bag went near the ladder opening, positioned for an escape. The binoculars hung from his neck on a strap. He kept the second sandwich near the straw mound. If he needed it to get past Angus, he didn't want to be fishing through the newspaper bag for it.

Danny assumed the prone position, resting the rifle on the straw mound. He heard helicopters, and music in the distance. It was 1:40. A charge of electricity surged through his body. He closed his eyes and tried to slow his breathing.

Danny had scoured news stories about the celebration for weeks. He had to assume that Armstrong would be at the front of the parade, as he was in 1966. Once the parade passed in front of him on Pearl, moving right to left, it was to continue on to the fairgrounds. Regardless of its position in the parade, Danny was confident that the Armstrong vehicle would be moving so slowly through the odd street configuration that there would be ample time to recognize the target. And to shoot.

Danny saw articles in the Wapak paper beginning in mid-August that revealed specifics on the parade. A headline on August 13 trumpeted "125 units set for parade." The following day another front-page story was headed by "Parade route to be altered." He gleaned from these articles that there would be two luncheons in Wapak this day. One at the Chalet Inn near I-75 and a second at the high school. Both were scheduled to begin at 11 am. Armstrong would attend both, then report to the parade assembly area by 1:20. The parade would kick off ten minutes later.

A subsequent article in the Lima paper (Danny was buying every paper he could get his hands on) revealed that the parade would have nine sections; one for each letter in "Armstrong." The "A" section would be headed by Bob Hope. Governor Rhoads would come next, followed by the press vehicles.

Then, the target.

It was well past 2 pm now. The parade had definitely started. There were estimates that it would take the head of the parade nearly two hours to reach the fairgrounds. By Danny's calculation, the target vehicle would fill his scope somewhere around 3:15 to 3:30.

He remembered the packed downtown area during the Gemini homecoming and imagined what it would look like now. The hometown hero hadn't just survived a close call in space: he had walked on the moon! It was mind boggling! Danny began to imagine what it must've been like for Neil—he shook his head.

His target would soon be here. Had to get his mind right.

A thin layer of perspiration formed on Danny's face and upper body. He hadn't noticed the uptick in temperature until now. It had to be 85. He glanced up at the sky and noted there were few clouds. He concentrated on the trees and vegetation to gauge the wind. There appeared to be a light, steady, southwesterly breeze of less than five miles per hour. He figured maybe two inches of wind drift, left to right, over the 190-plus yard distance. He made the necessary adjustment on the scope. Having practiced for weeks shooting from the elevated railroad track, he'd already allowed for the bullet drop.

Danny realized that when he'd checked for wind, he hadn't noticed Angus. He peered down at the area between the houses and saw that the dog was not there. The shade had disappeared, and with it, the Great Pyrenees. *Too hot for the big fella.*

There seemed to be more movement at the intersection. People in line at the Dairy Barn were leaving their place to hurry toward the curb. For the tenth time, Danny checked the counter on the left side of the Savage—5—fully loaded. He removed the binoculars from his neck then tucked the Savage into his shoulder and brought the Weaver scope to his eye.

He glassed over the word "Dairy" on the distant building. He recalled that a full-sized likeness of Armstrong, carved completely out of butter, was on display at the Ohio State Fair in Columbus.

Danny smiled, realizing his mom would've liked that.

He blinked hard, holding his eyes shut, and purposefully summoned painful memories from the rage that lurked in his head. Memories of hearing about his mother's death over a pay phone, of soldiers at their front door, of gravediggers laughing, of Suzy sprawled in the middle of South Street.

Gotta get my mind right.

Danny heard a helicopter overhead. He opened his eyes and checked his watch. He was surprised to see the time had crept past 3:30.

Game time.

The slight breeze was completely negated by the enclosed nature of the loft. High humidity contributed to the now uncomfortable conditions of the hide. *Might reach 90,* Danny thought. A few late arriving observers scurried along Benton Street from the right and turned up Oak. Music from a marching band grew louder.

Danny saw the flags of the color guard appear in his field of view. The flagbearers moved steadily westward down the center of Pearl. He could see all of them from the chest up. He'd been concerned that his hide wasn't quite elevated enough to see over the line of people on the near side of the target area. He was now sure that he would have a clear shot.

Red and white pennants waved in the air. There were small American flags everywhere. Virtually every person along the route was on their feet. Kodaks and Super 8 movie cameras were aimed toward parade units approaching from the east.

Already the procession was slowing. The honor guard was angling slightly to the left as they reached Auglaize Street. The diagonal nature of the turn meant that the flag bearer closest to Danny kept his legs churning, but did it in place, without progressing, while his counterparts on the far side continued to wheel in a slight arc.

A car crept into view. Danny excitedly leaned into the scope. The driver of the car wore a round styrofoam hat with a red, white, and blue band. Danny couldn't make out the writing on the band but was sure it had something to do with the astronaut. He noted that several others in the crowd also wore one. Between bystanders, Danny was able to read the sign on the driver's side door; "BOB HOPE *Grand Marshal.*"

Danny edged the scope toward the backseat. The entertainer's wife, Dolores, sat behind the driver. She wore a light blue sun dress and, though smiling, looked very warm. Above her, sitting on the top of the rear passenger seat, was Bob Hope. He saw the familiar ski slope-shaped nose and infectious grin. He wore a white shirt with gold tie, apparently having removed his sport coat.

A part of Danny's brain recalled that Hope was also an Ohioan. A quick memory of Hope entertaining the troops in Vietnam, going above and beyond the call of duty, swam into his head before he was able to push it away.

Danny flicked off the safety on his Savage Model 99.

Danny imagined the entire parade yo-yoing almost to a halt behind Hope's convertible. He remembered reading that curves in the roads in the Dealey Plaza area of Dallas may have been a contributing factor in the shooting of John F. Kennedy less than seven years earlier. Danny's mind paused when the JFK thought popped into his head.

He blinked and focused his attention again through the scope. He realized that a convertible carrying Governor Rhoads was leaving the kill zone.
How the hell had that happened?

A doubt, a resistance, had been percolating inside of him.
A fury coalesced inside of Danny, black as obsidian. Danny had constructed a barrier around it that consisted of pain, resentment, and hopelessness. This barrier fed the fury within. The random thought of JFK poked through from the old Danny. It was one impression, but it was quickly followed by more.
John Kennedy, Martin Luther King, Robert Kennedy... Neil Armstrong?

Danny saw the cab of a truck edge into view. This was a much higher profile vehicle than the cars that had preceded it. As the rear of the truck came into view, he realized this was the press vehicle. This was the confirmation Danny had been waiting for that Armstrong was about to appear. His pulse quickened.
The truck had a flat bed and was packed with media members. Danny thought there were over twenty people, all men, all standing, jammed into the 16 foot by 8 foot space. There were half a dozen video cameras and at least as many still photographers. Virtually every man on the truck's bed wore a short sleeved shirt and tie. They looked miserable in the heat as they jockeyed for a clear view to the rear of the truck.

Red, white, and blue bunting lined the sides of the truck's bed coming up to waist height on the media members. Danny realized that this type of vehicle was known as a "Stakebed" truck. This was a term he'd heard while working at the lumberyard. Danny saw that bunting also covered the door of the driver's side of the cab. It no doubt covered the name of the business that had lent it for use in the parade.

As he stared through the reticle, Danny wondered which business had made the truck available. Could it have come from Fisher's Cheese?

At this, he recalled reading about a special run of "Moon Cheese" that Fishers was producing to honor Armstrong. He smiled, knowing his Mom would've loved this.

Seconds later Danny realized the truck had moved out of the kill zone. He'd lost several seconds when his Mom's face had popped into his head. He blinked sweat from his eyes, set his jaw, and refocused through the scope.

Wake up dammit, you're letting it slip away!

If Armstrong's convertible had been directly behind the press vehicle, as it had been in the 1966 parade, Danny would've missed his opportunity. On this day, there was another vehicle behind the press truck and in front of Armstrong. It was a 4-door sedan, a light tan 1969 Ford Custom 500. It had an insignia of some sort on the driver's door. Danny couldn't get a good look at it. From his vantage point, anything that low on a vehicle was blocked by spectators along the parade route. He realized that the rear doors of the Galaxy were open. It looked like law enforcement personnel were sitting in the back seat, leaning out to peer at the most famous man in the world, thirty feet behind them.

Danny was barely able to register these facts before the Galaxy eased into the Y-shaped intersection and made room for the principal element of the parade.

Several police motorcycles cruised into view. A cherry red 1969 Buick Electra 225 convertible floated into Danny's scope. The crowd went wild. It was the First Man On The Moon.... *speak of the devil.*

The Buick was barely moving. It was bracketed, as Armstrong's vehicle had been in 1966, by uniformed Air Force security personnel. There were eight of them: four on either side of the Buick. They were spaced every ten feet or so. Danny saw that one of the men was positioned astride the driver's door. The guard to his rear was parallel to the rear bumper. This left Danny a clear view of the occupants in the rear of the Electra.

Danny quickly brushed sweat from his brow then leaned back into the Weaver scope. Armstrong was sitting on top of the back seat on the driver's side of the vehicle: perfect position. He wore a dark blue suit. He was turned away from Danny, waving to the delirious crowd on his right near Max's Dairy Barn.

The names came to Danny again: JFK, MLK, RFK, *Neil?*

Armstrong leaned back slightly. Danny saw figures to the astronaut's right. A small boy in a light blue suit. Mark? The boy sat on the seat next to his father, his faced also turned to the right.

Next was Janet. She sat down in the back seat, not on top like the three other members of the family. She wore a suit. Its color was midway between her husbands' and Mark's. Twelve-year-old Rick sat atop the right side of the rear seat. His suit the same shade as his mother's.

All four continued to look to their right and wave.

Danny's heart pounded. This was the first living target he'd viewed through the scope. He tried to concentrate on slowing his heartbeat. *Lee Harvey Oswald, James Earl Ray, Sirhan Sirhan... Danny Hitchens?*

Danny shook his head.

The Fury said, *SHOOT!*

Inside his head, the old Danny screamed, *Lee Harvey Oswald was a fuckin' nut!*

The Electra crept forward. Danny again centered the Weaver Dual-X on Armstrong, who was now leaning back and turning in his direction. This repositioning meant that six-year-old Mark, also turning next to Neil, was fully visible. Danny focused on the boy's head. More specifically his hair. Mark had a crew cut. He hadn't yet won the haircut argument with his dad.

Or he still wanted to look like his dad.

"Damn," Danny said out loud, much louder than he intended. His word was immediately followed by a challenging bark from below. Distracted, Danny flicked a glance toward the corner of MacKenzie's yard and saw Angus sitting alert, glaring into the loft.

The Fury urged Danny to refocus on the task at hand, but the dog's eyes held Danny's. The Great Pyrenees stared up at eyes influenced by rage. Danny looked back, transfixed, at the expectant eyes of a pug.

The Fury made one last attempt at immortality, forcing *Born to be Wild* into his consciousness.

Danny couldn't remember the lyrics.

"What the f—what the hell am I doing?!!!" he said out loud.

He turned and flung the rifle into the corner near the canvas bag. It clattered off the wall and disappeared into the straw.

Danny turned to the parade. Neil Armstrong was now facing the south side of the street, he smiled at the crowd. He seemed to be acknowledging them as much as they were him. The First Man On The Moon floated out of Danny's view with one hand waving, a smile on his face.

EPILOGUE

Friday, August 31, 2012

The young man watched the planes as they drew closer. There were just two of them, propeller-driven and approaching from the east, maybe 1000 feet up. He squinted. it was nearing dusk and the moon hung in the still-blue sky. The planes flew abreast, separated by perhaps one hundred feet. From his vantage point, the planes appeared to pass on either side of the moon.

Should've had my phone ready, he lamented, *that would've made a sweet pic.*

He watched the planes grow small as they continued their westerly course, then turned his attention back to the east and peered again at the iconic structure. Wapakoneta's Armstrong Air & Space Museum lay before him. The defining feature of the building was a fifty-six-foot wide white dome. It seemed to loom out of the ground like a rising moon, which, he supposed, was the intent of the design.

"Did you see them bracket the moon, Kenny?"

The older black man looked at his grandson. "We were standing in the perfect spot." He continued, "If we'd been closer to the Bob Evans, we woulda missed it." The man gestured to the restaurant to the north.

Al Johnson, combat veteran, former member of the 173rd Airborne Brigade, and retired Virginia Beach postal employee, turned to the man on his right. "Whatcha think, D-Hitch?"

"Pretty appropriate, I'd say" Danny answered.

Al and his grandson, Kenny, were visiting Ohio for the fourth consecutive summer. The first year, 2009, the pair had made the 700-mile drive without knowing what to expect.

"How do you say the name of this place, Pop......Bokkins?" ten-year-old Kenny had asked.

"It's Botkins, Kenny. I've never been there, but I used to hear stories about the place almost every day." Al had explained patiently.

Al's son Eddie and daughter-in-law Lena were both school teachers. Their last week of the summer was hectic every year. When Al invited his grandson to tag along on a road trip to Ohio, the boy thought it might be fun. As they motored through sparsely populated West Virginia and stopped at small town gas stations, Kenny was having second thoughts.

Sensing this, Al had turned to Kenny and said, "Just remember, your daddy is named after a man from this place. The man that saved my life."

Kenny had heard the story many times. He was curious about their destination: but wondered if a final summer week with his friends back at the Beach would've been a better choice.

Something unforeseen happened to the black kid from the resort city when he arrived at the small Ohio village: he thoroughly enjoyed it. Kenny fished with cane poles at small farm ponds, he rode horses, and he learned to drive a tractor. He and his grandpa looked forward to visiting the Inn Between, formerly Betty's Corner, where Tim Rogers, now the owner, served up tenderloin sandwiches as big and tasty as those served decades ago at the Tastee Freez. Or so the locals said. If a summer blockbuster movie was out, they would drive to see it at the Wapa Theater, which was still in business, it's fabulous neon sign shining brightly at night.

Al and Kenny's visits before Labor Day each year coincided with the town's end of summer festival, the Botkins Carousel. The festival centered on and around Sycamore Street, which was blocked off and covered by large tents that housed food and drink stands. Cole Field was utilized for rides, tug-o-war contests, and, Kenny's favorite, Cow Pie Bingo. Event organizers marked off a large grid and numbered the squares. The area was fenced off, the squares sold for $10 apiece, and at the designated time a cow was led to the grid to do its business. The lucky holder of the ticket with the now-covered number would collect his winnings.

"Never saw anything like that at the Beach," Kenny had said, fascinated.

In 2009, Botkins announced it would rename Sycamore Street for Danny's brother. A new green street sign adorned with "Eddie Hitchens Way" was unveiled. Dave Mielke, then retired for ten years from his teaching and coaching positions, was honored to speak at the dedication. Al Johnson watched with pride. He remembered Eddie assaulting the bunker on Hill 875. He never forgot that Eddie had carried him to the casualty collection point after keeping him safe for most of a hellish day. When the bomb struck, both of Al's eardrums had burst, but he was just far enough away from the explosion to survive.

The Johnsons would begin their trip back to Virginia each Labor Day weekend after attending Sunday service at Botkins Church of Christ. It was only polite, seeing as how the pastor, Daniel Hitchens, had fed and housed them all week.

Daniel Hitchens had been pastor of the church for nearly twenty years. In was the culmination of a journey that could not have been foreseen, certainly not on that day back in September of 1969 when Danny had lie in wait in a humid loft, planning to shoot Neil Armstrong.

Standing on the expansive lawn in front of the Armstrong Museum in 2012, Danny scanned his surroundings. Hundreds of people faced a stage that had been assembled for this day. Many had carried in lawn chairs. The atmosphere was collegial, respectful. The purpose of the event was to honor Neil, who had passed away six days earlier. The modest two plane flyover had captured the spirit of the unassuming man perfectly.

A private memorial was being held that same day one hundred odd miles away in Cincinnati, but that was for family and invited guests. Neil had been so significant in the life of many people, and, for that matter the world, that many longed to honor him in some way.

Armstrong's family had released a statement. It read, "For those who may ask what they can do to honor Neil, we have a simple request. Honor his example of service, accomplishment and modesty, and the next time you walk outside on a clear night and see the Moon smiling down at you, think of Neil Armstrong and give him a wink."

Wapakoneta was one of many towns and cities that hastily organized a "Wink at the Moon" memorial celebration. It coincided with the Johnson's annual visit, so here they were.

Danny noted that the crowd was not unlike those that attended the parades of 1966 and 1969. Those events dwarfed this one in size, of course, but the spirit of the attendees here was comparable. Danny thought that many, like he, could say they had been at one or both parades. This was confirmed when several of Neil's high school classmates spoke from the stage, relating stories from those days.

As they spoke, Danny's thoughts drifted back.

September 6, 1969 was the day Danny Hitchens had intended to do the unimaginable. Instead, it put him on a path to the inconceivable.

After throwing the rifle away from his body—and out of his life—Danny crawled toward the ladder and made his way down. He had a memory of standing near the opening of the barn, looking into the eyes of Angus, whose gaze now seemed more challenging than wondering.

Danny remembered looking into his gloved right hand and seeing the remnants of a baloney sandwich. His hand had settled on it as he made his way to the ladder. It was now deformed; having been there as he'd grabbed rungs on the way down.

Danny tossed the sandwich toward the dog and immediately turned to make his way back to the Ranchero. He robotically trudged away from the barn, away from the Savage, the canvas bag, the Kool's, and the rest of his gear. Danny moved away from the still flowing parade, which was now 192 paces away, now 193...

Danny walked through the field, angling toward the ash tree he'd parked under hours ago. It felt like years. He'd walked for several hundred feet before realizing that tears ran down his face. Danny reached the car and pulled out onto Dearbaugh, heading home. He'd driven just 100 yards when he passed the phone pole that he and Reedo had hit with rocks after the Gemini 8 parade, when they were waiting for Danny's parents.

Danny rolled past the exact spot where his mom had exclaimed "Wasn't that wonderful?" while wearing the happiest smile he'd ever seen. In his mind's eye, he saw her again.

As tears dropped onto his lap and he fought to steady shaking hands, a part of Danny's consciousness began to realize he had, metaphorically at least, dodged a bullet.

Danny arrived home. He sat in the Ranchero for several minutes before entering the house.

His dad greeted him. "Do any good?"

Danny stared at his father.

He managed "I... what?"

Jerry smiled, "Fish, catch any fish?"

Absent mindedly Danny mumbled something about having the wrong bait: his mind was still focused on the parade.

"I heard that" Jerry said with a bigger smile.

Perplexed, Danny cocked his head and asked, "What?"

"I heard every word you said" Jerry responded, "and you didn't say it very loud." Then, "What do you think?" He turned his head and pointed to his left ear, then did the same to his right. Danny looked closer and saw the hearing aids.

"These things really work" Jerry said with some excitement.

Danny managed a smile.

Days later, Danny decided he should retrieve the Savage from the loft behind Benton Street. Nothing good could come from a loaded, high powered weapon left to the fates. Danny parked in front of 801 Benton the Sunday after the parade. He hoped Malcolm MacKenzie wasn't home. A quick climb up the ladder and two minutes in the loft should be all he needed. If Malcolm was home, Danny wasn't sure how he'd explain the need to enter the barn. He supposed he'd use the presence of the newspaper bag in the loft to formulate a cover story.

Danny detected the odor as soon as he'd parked. It was the smell of wet ash. He saw that the grass between 801 and 717 was worn and muddy. He got out of the Ranchero and stepped toward the gap between the houses.

The barn was gone. In its place stood a blackened mound.

"Helluva thing, hey laddie?"

Danny spun to his right. Malcolm MacKenzie stood on the porch. Angus sat by his side.

Startled, Danny managed "Sir?"

"The fire, helluva thing. Angus woke me two nights ago. I looked out and saw the flames and called the fire department, but there was nothing they could do...all that straw and old wood." MacKenzie shrugged.

"One of the neighbors saw kids running away from the barn just before the fire took off. The Chief thinks they were up in the loft smoking." He paused, then added, "I always hated smoking."

Danny, eyes slightly wide, nodded, "Me too."

"Say," Malcolm asked, "did you ever figure things out?"

"Sir?" Danny was confused.

"The paper routes, you're John Kay, the man with the clipboard, right?"

Danny shifted his gaze to Angus.

"I figured out some of it."

In October of 1969, a letter arrived in box 103 at the Botkins post office that would change Danny's life. It was from a government survivor's program, offering financial aid for higher education. Most of the money was in the form of a grant: it would not need to be paid back. The program was the one referred to by Sue Giltrow months earlier in a phone conversation.

Giltrow had never stopped looking for opportunities for Danny, even if he had.

Danny still winced every time he thought back to the talk of Giltrow's sexuality, how even he and Reed Thompson had run with the pack on the subject. Yet it was Giltrow whose efforts led to an opportunity that Danny had thought beyond his reach. Sometimes God really did work in mysterious ways.

After gathering the facts, Danny discussed the opportunity with Jerry and decided to give it a shot. He enrolled at Wright State University in Fairborn, Ohio. The campus sat next to Wright Patterson Air Force Base. Danny often thought of the Wapakoneta homecoming parades as he walked across campus and watched aircraft coming and going overhead.

He took an elective class on religious studies his sophomore year. He, quite unexpectedly, became consumed by many of the concepts covered in the class. This interest eventually led to Danny continuing his education after graduation at divinity school. He chose Cincinnati Christian University.

Danny was fascinated with the concept of resurrection. Debates in and out of the classroom served to both validate and modify some of his views. Several classmates liked to argue that to them, resurrection meant not just the literal, Biblical definition, but that even after reaching the lowest point in your life, you can find your way out.

Danny had good reason to agree.

After becoming a pastor in the Church of Christ, Danny served in several towns in Ohio and Indiana before being offered the position in his hometown. Danny, his wife Ann, who he'd met at Wright State, and their two children, Suzanne and Jack, made the move.

Jerry became a regular attendee at Sunday services, smiling at his son throughout each sermon. Danny often joked that his dad had probably turned down his hearing aids during the sermons.

Carol Roush usually sat beside Jerry. Carol had lost her husband in 1988. She and Jerry had always enjoyed each other's company. Danny smiled, remembering that his dad and Carol often went to the movies at the Wapa.

In 1998 an aneurism claimed Jerry's life. After the initial collapse, Jerry spent three days in the hospital before succumbing. He passed away, surrounded by Carol, Danny and his family, and a gold framed, enlarged photo taken at a wedding several decades earlier.

That photo now hung in Danny's home.

Jerry was buried in St. Lawrence Catholic Cemetery to the left of Jane. He was still listed as a member of that congregation, despite spending most Sundays at his son's church. Father Schwaiger, a good friend of Danny's, performed the service.

Father Schwaiger and Danny were, in fact, friendly rivals. They didn't compete professionally. Their contests took place on the golf course during their weekly match, and on the roads and trails of western Ohio. They were both avid runners, and were in the same age group. The morning after the Wink at the Moon ceremony, the two would square off at the Botkins Carousel 5K. Bragging rights were on the line.

On non-race days, the pair could be seen jogging together in and around Botkins. Locals took to calling them the "God Squad."

"So Kenny," Danny asked, "what did you think of the museum?"

Before finding a spot on the lawn, the threesome had spent two hours touring the museum. Artifacts from Armstrong's military and NASA careers were displayed, as well as items from his boyhood.

"It was cool that they had his bike. Did he really ride it to the airfield so he could take flying lessons?" Kenny inquired.

"Yep, he wasn't old enough to have a driver's license" Danny confirmed.

Kenny considered, finally asking "What would I have to do to be an astronaut?"

Danny and Al looked at each other and smiled.

An announcement was made that Wapakoneta was considering erecting a statue of Neil. Enthusiastic support was expressed by the crowd. Multiple designs were being considered. Funding was an issue, of course, but most in attendance believed it would happen.

One idea mentioned was to cast the statue in the image of Neil at the Moon Landing parade. He would be sitting, as if on top of a convertible's back seat, and waving to the crowd with a smile that showed pride in his hometown.

It was the exact memory that Danny had of the astronaut, just seconds after nearly pulling the trigger.

Danny hoped this pose would be selected.

Near the end of the ceremony, Kenny asked "Think the food will be ready when we get back?"

Reed Thompson was grilling steaks and chicken that night at his rambling property outside of Botkins for Danny's family, their guests from Virginia, and several members of the Thompson extended family. Reed and his wife April were blessed with 14 grandchildren, ten more than Danny. Several of the grandkids shared common interests with Kenny, who loved to hang out with them this one week of the year.

"Oh yeah" Danny assured him. Reed will have everything covered.

Kenny smiled, "That man is the coolest grandpa I know."

Danny and Al looked at each other with mock expressions of hurt.

Kenny saw this and said "Outside of ya'll, of course."

All three laughed. Kenny, serious, asked "Pastor Hitchens, why do you call him Mr. Fantastic?"

"Long story."

The sun set and dozens of candles were made available. A large photo of Armstrong in his Apollo spacesuit was on display at a table near the stage. A speaker invited anyone wanting to light a candle in Neil's honor to make their way up front.

Danny excused himself to hurry back to the car. He'd left his cellphone in the console and wanted to get a few pictures. Rather than following the paved walkway, he cut diagonally through the lawn toward the parking lot. Stars filled the sky. The moon was high and behind him to the east.

The walk across the grass reminded Danny again of his retreat from the barn in 1969. The world for 20-year-old Danny could not have been more bleak. The turnaround, the resurrection, seemed beyond the realm of possibility.

September 6, 1969 was the day Danny learned that shame was not the worst emotion. He remembered the assignment in Mrs. Fark's English class.

Shame, Danny thought, was often nothing more than feeling humiliation over something in your life. Sometimes it was warranted. But sometimes you felt shame over things out of your control; an older model TV, or, he remembered, picking up your prom date in a station wagon with a lumber company logo on the door.

No, the worst emotion was guilt. Guilt over having committed acts that you were forever powerless to change.

Danny had averted a lifetime of guilt on that day in 1969. Instead, he had shame.

He could live with shame.

Danny was recalling details of that day as he neared his car. Approaching it, he heard a raised voice a few spaces off to the right. Danny thought he heard a woman crying. He changed course and approached an older model minivan. The voices were coming from the other side.

"What the hell were you thinking?!" a man shouted. "We don't have that kind of money!"

The woman answered, "I thought they would be good for the kids, it was only thirty dollars."

Danny came into view of the couple as the man, enraged, began, "Dammit..."

He saw Danny approach in the darkness.

The men looked at each other. Danny realized the couple sometimes attended services at the Church of Christ. The man recognized Danny. He was mortified. He stammered, apologizing.

"I'm so sorry, Pastor Hitchens. We've been short of money the last few weeks. Angie bought some books in the museum and I... well, you saw what I did."

Danny looked from the husband to his wife, then to the van, where two frightened young children were watching the scene outside.

The rage seemed to drain out of the man. "I don't know what got into me...she was trying to do something nice for the kids..."

Danny looked at the man, turned to his right to gaze at the sky, and said, "It's alright son... full moon."

He walked away.

ACKNOWLEDGEMENTS

Thanks to the staff at the Auglaize County Library in Wapakoneta for their helpfulness. Continue to take good care of the period newspapers in your possession. They are irreplaceable.

I want to acknowledge the employees at the Armstrong Air & Space Museum. The facility, and its contents, are a national treasure.

The parades could not have been accurately recreated without the benefit of photographs posted on the ohiomemory.org website.

Thanks to Rachel Barber at the Auglaize County Historical Society in Wapak. The Jacob Zint observatory dome is displayed there, along with many other interesting pieces of Wapakoneta history. Rachel's publication, "The Book of Wapakoneta," provided me with excellent background information.

I want to recognize the Riverside Art Center in Wapak for hosting events featuring sculptor Mike Tizzano. He brought a full-scale model of the Neil Armstrong sculpture he is creating and explained why the pose was chosen. The finished version will do Wapakoneta proud.

Many thanks to the fantastic people of Botkins, Ohio. Some were named, others referred to in the abstract. Some chacters were completely made up. Thanks for being good sports. All my best.

Finally, a special thank you to "Team Van Horn;" Lauren Reneau, Sara Olding, Gary Schwaiger, Suzanne Lang, and Ann and Jack Van Horn. Some share my last name, some don't. This book would not have been possible without your talents and efforts. You were my very own Mission Control.

Look for the "Neil Down" page on Facebook and Goodreads.

Made in the USA
Middletown, DE
17 May 2024